MAN-SIZE IN MARBLE
AND OTHER HORRORS

The Best Horror & Ghost Stories of

EDITH NESBIT

Edited, Annotated, and Illustrated By
M. GRANT KELLERMEYER, M.A.

☙

— OLDSTYLE TALES PRESS —
Fort Wayne, Indiana

EXPAND YOUR SUPERNATURAL FICTION COLLECTION
By Acquiring These
— ANNOTATED AND ILLUSTRATED EDITIONS —

WWW.OLDSTYLETALES.COM

WEIRD FICTION & HORROR BY:

Algernon Blackwood
Robert W. Chambers
F. Marion Crawford
William Hope Hodgson
Arthur Machen
Guy de Maupassant
Fitz-James O'Brien
Edgar Allan Poe
Ambrose Bierce
H. G. Wells

CLASSIC GHOST STORIES BY:

Charles Dickens
Sir Arthur Conan Doyle
W. W. Jacobs
Henry James
J. Sheridan Le Fanu
E. Nesbit
Robert Louis Stevenson
Bram Stoker
Washington Irving
E. T. A. Hoffmann
M. R. James

CLASSIC GOTHIC NOVELS:

Dracula
Frankenstein
The Phantom of the Opera
Dr. Jekyll and Mr. Hyde
The Turn of the Screw
The Invisible Man
The Picture of Dorian Gray
The Hound of the Baskervilles

FIRESIDE HORROR SERIES:

Ghost Stories for Christmas Eve
Victorian Ghost Stories
Supernatural Cats
Demons and the Devil
Mummies and Curses
Pirates and Ghost Ships
Werewolves

OLDSTYLE TALES

This edition published 2016 by
OLDSTYLE TALES PRESS
2424 N. Anthony Blvd
Fort Wayne, Indiana
46805-3604

*For more information, or to request permission
to reprint selections or illustrations from
this book, write to the Editor at*
oldstyletales@gmail.com

NOTES, INTRODUCTIONS, AND ILLUSTRATIONS
COPYRIGHT © 2016 BY MICHAEL GRANT KELLERMEYER

Readers who are interested in further titles from
Oldstyle Tales Press are invited to visit our website at

— WWW.OLDSTYLETALES.COM —

—TABLE *of* CONTENTS—

Each story comes with introductory and analytical commentary.
Five of the most critically or popularly acclaimed stories also include footnotes.

Concerning What
You Are About to Read

ONE of the most psychologically fascinating horror writers of her time, Edith Nesbit, perhaps more so than any of her peers, invested herself into her fiction. The woman who is today better known as a Victorian children's book writer is often neglected as a powerful architect of the terrible and ghastly. It is tremendously fitting that Nesbit's literary reputation should be so disparate (indeed, most lovers of her children's stories are clueless about her horror oeuvre, and most fans of "Man-Size in Marble" have no idea that her fiction was inspirational to *Harry Potter, Mary Poppins, The Chronicles of Narnia*, and others). Her life was one torn between radicalism and conventionality, scandal and sobriety, defiance and compliance, and it largely orbited the actions of a cad named Hubert Bland, the man who would become her first husband.

Bland was a radical socialist and a militant misogynist. He exalted the rights of the working classes but denounced women's rights as wrong-headed fantasy. He was politically modern and radical, but socially unevolved and ultra-conservative. He resented women, but – again contradictorily – was overwhelmed with fascination for them, and was a reprehensible Casanova throughout his life – a man guilty of dozens of affairs, date rapes, and seductions. Nesbit's first biographer complained that "he could not by any effort of nature leave women alone." Even in this era of de jure sexism, Bland was a monstrous walking scandal, known for entrapping young girls in sexual mind games before abandoning them. He was charismatic, loud, and authoritative, with an upturned mustache, parted hair, and an eyebrow-arching monocle that made him the very figure of a villain from an Edwardian melodrama. In Nesbit he found a very strange partner: for all his hate of strong women, she was remarkably tall and beautiful with a distinct, Bohemian taste for fashion, and was renowned for smoking as voraciously as any man. She too was charismatic, commanding rooms, flooding her parties with personality, and yet able to sit down and write a chapter in the middle of a garden soirée without being distracted. She was a leading figure in their socialist club, the Fabian Society, and she almost single-handedly supported their family with her income as a writer when things were lean for her husband, but this did nothing to change his sexist convictions. Bland famously quipped that "Woman's metier in the world - I mean, of course, civilized woman, the woman in the world as it is - is to inspire romantic passion... Romantic passion is inspired by women who wear corsets. In other words, by the women who pretend to be what they not quite are." His wife, it would see, was one of these corset-shunning women who infringe of male-claimed stereotypes. He was, all-in-all, an egotistical conundrum. Renowned biographer Claire Tomalin dressed him down on the matter of his wishy-washy lifestyle, groaning that "Bland [was] one of the minor enigmas of literary history in that everything reported of him makes him sound repellent, yet he was admired, even adored, by many intelligent men and women... He did not aspire to be consistent. He allowed his wife to support him with her pen for some years, but was always opposed to feminism... In mid-life he joined the Catholic Church, a further cosmetic touch to his old-world image, but without modifying his behaviour or even bothering to attend more than the statutory minimum of masses." But just as Nesbit turned a blind eye to her husband's hideous behavior, so too Bland seemed oblivious to his wife's modern Bland impregnated Nesbit as he would several others – out of wedlock. While we may shake our heads today, even in our 21st Century, sexually liberated climate, an unplanned pregnancy raises eyebrows and quickens pulses, but to the Victorians it was a horror. Nesbit was seven months along when she married Bland.

Bland's lascivious lifestyle only increased with marriage, however, and while Nesbit bore him a toddling family of healthy children, he spent half of every week with his mother, even casually siring a child with her nurse, all without Nesbit's knowledge. The most brutal treachery started in 1885 when he began an affair with Nesbit's best friend, Alice Hoatson, the assistant secretary to the Fabian Society. Bland unabashedly invited Hoatson to enter their household, which immediately became a *ménage à trois*, with no objections from his obedient wife. Nesbit assumed that she was protecting her family by allowing Bland to sip from his exotic appetite for sex, but it became another matter when Hoatson became pregnant in 1886 (perhaps not coincidentally the year that she began writing horror stories). Nesbit was completely distraught, flew into a rage, and demanded that her husband's pregnant lover not be allowed to live in her house and eat at the table with her children. Bland coolly informed her that he would

10

leave her and the children if she stood by her objections. Hoatson gave birth to a girl whom Nesbit dutifully adopted. When Alice became pregnant again 13 years later, Nesbit raised no complaints, quietly adopting the little boy, and – like the victim of a cuckoo – she raised both children as if they were hers. Bland continue to be chronically adulterous, unapologetically sexist, and unrepentantly dismissive of women's rights in spite of his wife's unquestionable status as bread winner in their home. He died in 1914. What happened to Hoatson or when she died was not something I could uncover in my research.

During this time of shame, humiliation, and stifled rage, Nesbit pored herself into two very distinct genres of writing that suited two distinct parts of her already polarized life – children's literature and supernatural horror. *The Railway Children* is her most famous contribution to world literature – a series that follows a group of children and their mother who have adventures in the countryside while their father is wrongfully imprisoned. *The Story of the Treasure Seekers* and *The Wouldbegoods* also concern young families of middle-class standing who have suffered financial hardship. The theme of an absent father, money trouble, and a stiff-upper-lip mother who represses her sorrow to save face for her *children* is hopelessly autobiographical, but what these stories allowed Nesbit to do was to render a world of companionship, laughter, and quirky realism that shooed away the crushing embarrassment and alienation that she suffered with Bland. Her children's books served to nurse her dark feelings with promises of goodness, family, and emotional vulnerability. J. K. Rowling constantly refers to Nesbit in interviews as a *literary* inspiration, calling her "a groundbreaker" for featuring "very real children" rather than the well-behaved caricatures of Victorian morality stories. "I identify with the way she writes," Rowling has said, and to those who are acquainted with the Harry Potter mythos, this endorsement is telling. But there was another part of Nesbit's soul that needed voice – a submerged, tortured part that demanded license to pour out its venom and rage, to enunciate its injuries and vent its anxieties. This need was met with horror.

It is perhaps unsurprising that Nesbit found solace and voice in writing tales of terror when one accounts the various traumatizing incidents of her childhood that would later be resurrected in her imagination when faced with traumas of a more personal kind in her adulthood. For a writer of cheery children's novels, hers was a neurotic and apprehensive youth, riddled with recurring nightmares, phobias, and anxieties. One perennial phobia was a terror of being buried alive –

11

peculiarity she shared with one of her literary inspirations, Edgar Allan Poe. This was reportedly inspired by the near escape of an uncle who had been noticed twitching in his coffin during his funeral and revived just in time to avoid being laid in his grave alive. Throughout her life this event plagued her imagination, and several of her stories ("The Five Drugs" and "The Third Drug" in particular) concern persons who are either paralyzed or otherwise restrained and threatened with a slow, agonizing death by thirst or suffocation. Nesbit also claimed to have lived in no fewer than two houses which were haunted by ghosts, and suffered a peculiar terror of the revivification of corpses – so deftly handled in "John Charrington's Wedding" and "Man-Size in Marble." This specific terror seems to have been rooted in a traumatic incident from childhood where her parents took her to the burial pits at the Church of St. Michel in Bordeaux, France. The cellars had a particular atmosphere that mummified the corpses stored there, creating a macabre tourist attraction. For young Edith, however, the thrill was entirely overcome by deep terror. As an adult she described the encounter with death in stunning detail:

"[They were] skeletons with the flesh hardened on their bones, with their long dry hair hanging on each side of their brown faces, where the skin in drying had drawn itself back from their gleaming teeth and empty eye-sockets. Skeletons draped in mouldering shreds of shrouds and grave-clothes, their lean fingers still clothed with dry skin, seemed to reach out to me. I was paralysed with horror... not daring to turn my head lest one of those charnel house faces should peep out at me... On the wall near the door I saw the dried body of a little child hung up by its hair... it is to them, I think, more than to any other thing, that I owe nights and nights of anguish and horror, long years of bitterest fear and dread. "

Nesbit's horror stories are very particular and very unique for their time. They are perhaps most inspired by the stories of Rhoda Broughton (*Behold it Was a Dream!, Nothing But the Truth*), Elizabeth Gaskell (*The Old Nurse's Story, Lois the Witch*), and Margaret Oliphant (*The Open Door, The Library Window*) which regularly feature innocent people in mortal peril from wicked and merciless supernatural forces. Across the pond she was influenced by Poe's work, which she duplicated to the point of graceful homage in several of her tales, particularly indulging in themes of cursed families, live burial, decadent aristocrats, doppelgangers, and the corrupting influence of seclusion. To some degree she may also have been inspired by Charles

Dickens' few truly grim ghost stories, like "The Signal-Man" and "To Be Read at Dusk" ("John Charrington's Wedding" is partially inspired by the latter and partly by Broughton's "The Man With the Nose"). But what she did with these earlier Victorians' legacy was something unique and powerful: she invested it with a raw, white-hot emotion. Broughton and Oliphant in particular fueled their ghost stories with pathos and psychological vulnerability, but Nesbit's level of agony is truly crushing in many of these stories. David Stuart Davies aptly describes the connection between fiction and biography in Nesbit's supernatural writing, using "Man-Size in Marble" as an exemplar:

"*Stylistically she was ahead of her time, for her tales are fierce, engaging and told in a modern fashion that demands attention... One interesting aspect of these exercises in terror and in a sense one that is typical of the woman and her background and beliefs is her ability to touch upon the deeper currents of eroticism and moral ambiguity involving her characters. Man-Size in Marble is probably the best known and most anthologized of Edith Nesbit's stories... it epitomizes why she was so successful at the demanding art of telling a ghost story... The story is unremittingly savage, the prose is sharp and unfettered by overblown circumlocution and the ending is cruel and unhappy. There is an awful inevitability about the climax that one sees early on but we are held by a strange fascination to see where the narrative will take us. Nesbit never shirked from leaving the reader shocked, dismayed and abandoned. Life is cruel, she seems to be saying; you have no right to expect a happy ending. She may well have been applying that ideology to her own situation.*"

The cold brutality of fate is not limited to "Man-Size in Marble," nor the theme of a romance dashed on the rocks of a universe indifferent to love, hope, and mercy. In "From the Dead," a woman with good intentions is thrown out by her husband, and while his reaction is understandable, he is cast as a villain when she dies hours before he finally locates her. In "John Charrington's Wedding," Nesbit's second most famous work, we learn that love can overcome death, but that by the transitive property, death can overcome life, and that the heart of love may be possessive and selfish, bordering on rapacious. "The House of Silence" teaches a robber that a home lush in trappings and possessions is not worth breaking into if it happens to be a Bluebeard's castle where a beauty is wooed, bedded, and made food for the flies in short order. "The Ebony Frame" returns to the theme of love overcoming death, with a hideously disappointing and cynical conclusion interwoven with vicious irony.

"Uncle Abraham's Romance" is a soft and heartbreaking story of two misfits who find love beyond the grave, and – like so many of Nesbit's protagonists – lose it to a twist of bad timing and miscommunication. While investigating "The Mystery of the Semi-Detached," a man involved in a scandalous affair sees a vision of his lover with her throat cut, strewn across her bed in a sexually suggestive way. "The Power of Darkness" marginally addresses the inhuman lengths that two men will go to in pursuit of a pretty girl, treating the loser's insanity (driven to madness by a prank in a wax museum after hours) as a matter of life, a pattern repeated in the even more insidious plot of "The Pavilion," where a vampiric plant stars as the murder weapon. And there are more. "The Shadow," "The Violet Car," and "In the Dark" are perhaps her three greatest ghost stories other than "Man-Size in Marble," and each are beset with the specters of doomed love, bitter hearts, and inescapable fate. Failed romance seemed to be Nesbit's favorite theme, and the harder the fall, the more she appeared to invest in her writing. The weakest of her stories usually involve a successful romance, although even the strongest are haunted by her regrettable penchant for sentimentalism. "From the Dead" suffers particularly from this trend to victimize a wronged woman to the point of sappy martyrdom ("The Shadow" also lingers here), with tertiary characters being illogically brutal to the husbands and rivals of misunderstood wives and middle-aged women, though Nesbit's ire and thirst for justification is natural and easy to understand. Nonetheless, it is a blight on her otherwise excellent canon of ghost stories. The scholar Robert Hadji commented on this flaw and its ultimate redemption as a glaring weakness in an otherwise powerful oeuvre: "Nesbit's work is at times crudely sensational and even vulgar, yet it is redeemed by its emotional sensitivity, its alienated female perspective, and the lyrical clarity of her prose style which is simple and sincere." Indeed, Nesbit seems to have suffered at times to reconciled the two sets of voices crying out to be heard in her work: the optimistic desire for family and community which could sometimes veer towards the maudlin and sappy, and the cynical rejection of hope and mercy which was prone to drifting towards the brutal and heartless. More often than not, however, her stories met in the middle, resulting in an passionately rich, spiritually haunting stew of emotion: rejection, love, hate, powerlessness, and pride.

Also printed here are some science fiction tales that flirt with the legacies of Dr Frankenstein, Dr Jekyll, and Dr Moreau: blood-sucking vines, superhuman drugs, diabolical genetics, labs filled with the bodies of experimented-on victims, science-based vampirism, and even a feeble-minded lab assistant in the vein of the Universal Films' hunchbacked Igor. These are, admittedly, the weakest of Nesbit's stories – fraught with sentimental moony-ness, laughable plots, and ludicrous science – but they are fascinating studies of early science fiction, especially by a woman. Nesbit also offers us two stellar Gothic farces – ghost stories that turn out to not be ghost stories, and lighten the mood of her overall grim collection – but I won't spoil which two they are for you.

Nesbit's writing is absolutely crisp, evocative, and touching, and her legacy as both a children's writer and a master of horror is well deserved, if not far overdue. The stories in this book can best be described as raw – emotionally wringing, cruel, and richly ironic – but they are at times very tender, even in the harshest of her stories. While her worldview is largely cynical – at times even Lovecraftian – there is no doubt that at the core of her horror beats a heart – tremendously bruised, horribly misused, and shamefully denied a voice. But Nesbit's tales give voice to that heart, and its fleshy beat can be detected in the sorrow of "Man-Size," in the regret of "The Shadow," in the loss of "The Violet Car," in the twisted devotion of "John Charrington," in the vulnerability of "In the Dark," in the human revulsion of "The House of Silence," in the helplessness of "The Semi-Detached," in the heartbreak of "Uncle Abraham's Romance," "The Ebony Frame," and "From the Dead." So as you turn this page and step into Nesbit's universe, anticipate a world of painful loss, anticipate a world of emotional vulnerability, and anticipate a world of hate, jealousy, love, affection, anxiety, guilt, and fragile hope – anticipate a world of terror and dread, of sex, violence, anticipate a world of supernatural aggression, predatory spirits, and intimate horror – anticipate the world of Edith Nesbit.

M. Grant Kellermeyer
Fort Wayne, New Year's Eve 2015

MAN-SIZE IN MARBLE AND OTHERS
The Best Ghost Stories & Supernatural Tales of
E. NESBIT

E. Nesbit's grim ghost stories almost always involve a sexual tension and frustration as a major theme. They typically involve an estranged couple struggling to understand one another, a pair of possessive young spouses, or a scandalous and ill-fated affair between impulsive lovers. They are torn between desire and distrust, between fresh passion and sexual boredom. But that is not the case in her most famous story – of any genre – the brilliant, traumatic "Man-Size in Marble." While Nebit's leading couples in the *far* majority of her stories are clouded in disapproval and scandal, these spouses are cozy, charming, and romantic: they are two genuinely loving, relatable spouses, still snuggled together in a honeymooner mentality. Pet names like "wifie" and "dearest" and the petty anxieties of domestic concerns such as blacking boots and cleaning dishes make this country setting vastly different from the urbane West-Enders. But chaotic supernatural hazards menace their love-nest as surely as the vision of the ripped throat haunted the apartment in London. Failure to take heed of sincere advice – even to the slightest degree – Nesbit suggests, can rob us of all we hold dear, leaving us wiser but sadder... if we manage to survive. Nesbit constructs a universe in chaos, one deaf to entreaty and blind to love, a heartless, merciless, misanthropic cosmos that crushes hope and smothers love.

Man-Size in Marble
{1893}

ALTHOUGH every word of this story is as true as despair, I do not expect people to believe it. Nowadays a "rational explanation" is required before belief is possible. Let me then, at once, offer the "rational explanation" which finds most favour among those who have heard the tale of my life's tragedy. It is held that we were "under a delusion," Laura and I, on that 31st of October[1]; and that this supposition places the whole matter on a satisfactory and believable basis. The reader can judge, when he, too, has heard my story, how far this is an "explanation," and in what sense it is "rational." There were three who took part in this: Laura and I and another man. The other man still lives, and can speak to the truth of the least credible part of my story.

---

[1] Hallowe'en Night, of course

19

I never in my life knew what it was to have as much money as I required to supply the most ordinary needs—good colours[1], books, and cab-fares— and when we were married we knew quite well that we should only be able to live at all by "strict punctuality and attention to business[2]." I used to paint in those days, and Laura used to write, and we felt sure we could keep the pot at least simmering[3]. Living in town was out of the question, so we went to look for a cottage in the country, which should be at once sanitary and picturesque. So rarely do these two qualities meet in one cottage that our search was for some time quite fruitless. We tried advertisements, but most of the desirable rural residences which we did look at proved to be lacking in both essentials, and when a cottage chanced to have drains it always had stucco as well and was shaped like a tea-caddy[4]. And if we found a vine or rose-covered porch, corruption invariably lurked within[5]. Our minds got so befogged by the eloquence of house-agents and the rival disadvantages of the fever-traps and outrages to beauty which we had seen and scorned, that I very much doubt whether either of us, on our wedding morning, knew the difference between a house and a haystack. But when we got away from friends and house-agents, on our honeymoon, our wits grew clear again, and we knew a pretty cottage when at last we saw one. It was at Brenzett[6]—a little village set on a hill over against the southern marshes. We had gone there, from the seaside village where we were staying, to see the church, and two fields from the church we found this cottage. It stood quite by itself, about two miles from the village. It was a long, low building, with rooms sticking out in unexpected places. There was a bit of stone-work—ivy-covered and moss-grown, just two old rooms, all that was left of a big house that had once stood there—and round this stone-work the house had grown up. Stripped of its roses and jasmine it would have been

---

[1] Art supplies
[2] Our narrator aligns with the Victorian ethos of no nonsense and level-headedness -- a reliable narrator for a supernatural story
[3] That is, make a livelihood off of these little jobs – keep themselves fed
[4] A box or jar used to store tea – typically shaped like a shoe box
[5] A favorite theme of Nesbit's (and Broughton's): loveliness can conceal wickedness, and nothing is invulnerable to the ubiquitous assaults of human evil and cosmic tragedy
[6] In Kent, in southeast England – a pastoral country village, home to some 400 inhabitants

hideous[1]. As it stood it was charming, and after a brief examination we took it. It was absurdly cheap. The rest of our honeymoon we spent in grubbing about in second-hand shops in the county town, picking up bits of old oak and Chippendale[2] chairs for our furnishing. We wound up with a run up to town and a visit to Liberty's, and soon the low oak-beamed lattice-windowed rooms began to be home. There was a jolly old-fashioned garden, with grass paths, and no end of hollyhocks and sunflowers, and big lilies. From the window you could see the marsh-pastures, and beyond them the blue, thin line of the sea. We were as happy as the summer was glorious, and settled down into work sooner than we ourselves expected. I was never tired of sketching the view and the wonderful cloud effects from the open lattice, and Laura would sit at the table and write verses about them, in which I mostly played the part of foreground.

We got a tall old peasant woman to do for us. Her face and figure were good, though her cooking was of the homeliest; but she understood all about gardening, and told us all the old names of the coppices[3] and cornfields, and the stories of the smugglers and highwaymen, and, better still, of the "things that walked," and of the "sights" which met one in lonely glens of a starlight night. She was a great comfort to us, because Laura hated housekeeping as much as I loved folklore, and we soon came to leave all the domestic business to Mrs. Dorman, and to use her legends in little magazine stories which brought in the jingling guinea[4].

We had three months of married happiness, and did not have a single quarrel. One October evening I had been down to smoke a pipe with the doctor—our only neighbour—a pleasant young Irishman. Laura had stayed at home to finish a comic sketch of a village episode for the Monthly Marplot. I left her laughing over her own jokes, and came in to find her a crumpled heap of pale muslin weeping on the window seat.

"Good heavens, my darling, what's the matter?" I cried, taking her in my arms. She leaned her little dark head against my shoulder and went on crying. I had never seen her cry before—we had always been so

---

[1] External trappings dress up what is in reality a "hideous" thing. Nesbit suggests that the way something is *made* to seem can often distract us from what it in reality is

[2] Fine furniture made after the craftsmanship of the 18th century joiner, Thomas Chippendale

[3] Small glens of woodland maintained and preserved as sources of wood

[4] A gold coin worth one pound, one shilling, or £1.05

happy, you see—and I felt sure some frightful misfortune had happened.

"What is the matter? Do speak."

"It's Mrs. Dorman," she sobbed.

"What has she done?" I inquired, immensely relieved.

"She says she must go before the end of the month, and she says her niece is ill; she's gone down to see her now, but I don't believe that's the reason, because her niece is always ill. I believe someone has been setting her against us. Her manner was so queer—"

"Never mind, Pussy," I said; "whatever you do, don't cry, or I shall have to cry too, to keep you in countenance, and then you'll never respect your man again!"

She dried her eyes obediently on my handkerchief, and even smiled faintly.

"But you see," she went on, "it is really serious, because these village people are so sheepy[1], and if one won't do a thing you may be quite sure none of the others will. And I shall have to cook the dinners, and wash up the hateful greasy plates; and you'll have to carry cans of water about, and clean the boots and knives—and we shall never have any time for work, or earn any money, or anything. We shall have to work all day, and only be able to rest when we are waiting for the kettle to boil!"

I represented to her that even if we had to perform these duties, the day would still present some margin for other toils and recreations. But she refused to see the matter in any but the greyest light. She was very unreasonable, my Laura, but I could not have loved her any more if she had been as reasonable as Whately[2].

"I'll speak to Mrs. Dorman when she comes back, and see if I can't come to terms with her," I said. "Perhaps she wants a rise in her screw[3]. It will be all right. Let's walk up to the church."

The church was a large and lonely one, and we loved to go there, especially upon bright nights. The path skirted a wood, cut through it once, and ran along the crest of the hill through two meadows, and round the churchyard wall, over which the old yews loomed in black masses of shadow. This path, which was partly paved, was called "the

---

[1] Senseless, easily spooked, illogical

[2] Richard Whatley (1787 - 1863) was an English economist, logician, and theologian

[3] An increase of pay or a decrease of hours or work – literally, that she wants a torture device loosened (the same metaphor is referenced in the title of "The Turn of the Screw," wherein the implication is that the device is tightened, and with it the dramatic tension)

bier-balk[1]," for it had long been the way by which the corpses had been carried to burial. The churchyard was richly treed, and was shaded by great elms which stood just outside and stretched their majestic arms in benediction[2] over the happy dead. A large, low porch let one into the building by a Norman[3] doorway and a heavy oak door studded with iron. Inside, the arches rose into darkness, and between them the reticulated[4] windows, which stood out white in the moonlight. In the chancel[5], the windows were of rich glass, which showed in faint light their noble colouring, and made the black oak of the choir pews hardly more solid than the shadows. But on each side of the altar lay a grey marble figure of a knight in full plate armour lying upon a low slab, with hands held up in everlasting prayer, and these figures, oddly enough, were always to be seen if there was any glimmer of light in the church[6]. Their names were lost[7], but the peasants told of them that they had been fierce and wicked men, marauders by land and sea, who had been the scourge of their time, and had been guilty of deeds so foul that the house they had lived in—the big house, by the way, that had stood on the site of our cottage—had been stricken by lightning and

---

[1] A bier being a conveyance or platform for a coffin

[2] A blessing or wish for peace, literally "words of goodness"

[3] A crash course in British history: the original Britons (today the Welsh) were pushed to the west by invading Germanic tribes – the Saxons and Angles – who reigned in England for centuries. But in 1066 the French Normans invaded England in the Norman Conquest, under William the Conqueror. The Normans were depicted in English folklore and literature (e.g. *Ivanhoe* and the legends of Robin Hood) as ruthless thugs and abusers who disrespected Anglo-Saxon culture and sensibilities. Ultimately, the feudal Anglo-Saxon barons rose up against what they viewed as Norman abuses of power, and forced King John (of Robin Hood infamy) to sign the Magna Carta, assuring them of their rights, limiting the powers of the throne, and fortifying the national identity of "Englishmen"

[4] Richly decorated, made up of a network of geometric shapes

[5] Space surrounding the altar in the sanctuary

[6] Amidst all the finery and lush décor, only two things are impossible to avoid: the statues of the wicked knights. Nesbit implies that despite our attempts to fancify or glaze over the crimes of the past, they will feature prominently in our collective unconscious

[7] Names may fade, details be lost, and facts be muddled, but character and legacy are more difficult to expunge. Inhumanities have a far longer psychological shelf life than virtues

the vengeance of Heaven. But for all that, the gold of their heirs had bought them a place in the church[1]. Looking at the bad hard faces reproduced in the marble, this story was easily believed.

The church looked at its best and weirdest on that night, for the shadows of the yew trees fell through the windows upon the floor of the nave[2] and touched the pillars with tattered shade. We sat down together without speaking, and watched the solemn beauty of the old church, with some of that awe which inspired its early builders. We walked to the chancel and looked at the sleeping warriors. Then we rested some time on the stone seat in the porch, looking out over the stretch of quiet moonlit meadows, feeling in every fibre of our being the peace of the night and of our happy love; and came away at last with a sense that even scrubbing and blackleading[3] were but small troubles at their worst[4].

Mrs. Dorman had come back from the village, and I at once invited her to a tête-à-tête[5].

"Now, Mrs. Dorman," I said, when I had got her into my painting room, "what's all this about your not staying with us?"

"I should be glad to get away, sir, before the end of the month," she answered, with her usual placid dignity.

"Have you any fault to find, Mrs. Dorman?"

"None at all, sir; you and your lady have always been most kind, I'm sure—"

"Well, what is it? Are your wages not high enough?" "No, sir, I gets quite enough."

"Then why not stay?"

"I'd rather not"—with some hesitation—"my niece is ill." "But your niece has been ill ever since we came."

---

[1] Materialism, wealth, and power were enough to purchase a place for these two men in the holy sanctuary, falsifying their character and forging their legacy. And yet, the legends continue: even power cannot obstruct wickedness, and money cannot procure a reputation

[2] The main part of a church sanctuary – the central area extending from the entry to the altar

[3] To polish with black graphite (pencil lead) – typically used to clean cast iron tools like skillets

[4] At this story's most tender, this is its moral: forget the petty annoyances of life; appreciate the love and affection that you have at your disposal while you can, because there are far more menacing things in the universe than chores, and far more precious commodities than paychecks

[5] Interview or discussion – literally a mouth-to-mouth, or a face-to-face

No answer. There was a long and awkward silence. I broke it. "Can't you stay for another month?" I asked.

"No, sir. I'm bound to go by Thursday."

And this was Monday!

"Well, I must say, I think you might have let us know before. There's no time now to get any one else, and your mistress is not fit to do heavy housework. Can't you stay till next week?"

"I might be able to come back next week."

I was now convinced that all she wanted was a brief holiday, which we should have been willing enough to let her have, as soon as we could get a substitute.

"But why must you go this week?" I persisted. "Come, out with it." Mrs. Dorman drew the little shawl, which she always wore, tightly across her bosom, as though she were cold. Then she said, with a sort of effort— "They say, sir, as this was a big house in Catholic times[1], and there was a many deeds done here."

The nature of the "deeds[2]" might be vaguely inferred from the inflection of Mrs. Dorman's voice—which was enough to make one's blood run cold. I was glad that Laura was not in the room[3]. She was always nervous, as highly-strung natures are[4], and I felt that these tales about our house, told by this old peasant woman, with her impressive manner and contagious credulity, might have made our home less dear to my wife.

---

[1] Before the English reformation, circa 1530 – 1560

[2] By the end of the story it will have become apparent that many of these unspeakable "deeds" were sexual in nature, and above all violent. Rape, as in "The Semi-Detached" and several of Nesbit's other supernatural tales ("John Charrington's Wedding," etc.) is a lurking threat that – while unnamed and merely alluded to – darkens the ostensibly wholesome and happy lives of her (either sexually or – as in "Semi-Detached" – violently) repressed characters

[3] By sheltering Laura, her husband inadvertently is complicit in her own rapacious destruction. A reader might view her cripplingly neurotic nervousness as suggestive of some form of psychological repression. She might be better served by treating her with adultlike frankness. But by shielding her from the realities of the world – one in which rape and murder are realistic concerns – he only enables her squeamish disposition and jelly-like, fragile psychology

[4] Such a description can almost always be interpreted as a literary codification of psychological repression. Not necessarily sexual, it may suggest repression of the will, of the heart, of desire, of ambition, or any number of things. What is clear, however, is that Laura is an incomplete character, who for some reason is denying an element of her own nature. The conclusion implies that her anxieties surround an aversion to physical (and sexual) vulnerability

"Tell me all about it, Mrs. Dorman," I said; "you needn't mind about telling me. I'm not like the young people who make fun of such things." Which was partly true.

"Well, sir"—she sank her voice—"you may have seen in the church, beside the altar, two shapes[1]."

"You mean the effigies of the knights in armour," I said cheerfully.

"I mean them two bodies, drawed out man-size in marble[2]," she returned, and I had to admit that her description was a thousand times more graphic than mine, to say nothing of a certain weird force and uncanniness about the phrase "drawed out man-size in marble."

"They do say, as on All Saints' Eve[3] them two bodies sits up on their slabs, and gets off of them, and then walks down the aisle, in their marble"— (another good phrase, Mrs. Dorman)—"and as the church clock strikes eleven they walks out of the church door, and over the graves, and along the bier-balk, and if it's a wet night there's the marks of their feet in the morning."

"And where do they go?" I asked, rather fascinated.

"They comes back here to their home, sir, and if any one meets them—" "Well, what then?" I asked.

But no—not another word could I get from her, save that her niece was ill and she must go. After what I had heard I scorned to discuss the niece, and tried to get from Mrs. Dorman more details of the legend. I could get nothing but warnings.

"Whatever you do, sir, lock the door early on All Saints' Eve, and make the cross-sign over the doorstep and on the windows."

"But has any one ever seen these things?" I persisted.

"That's not for me to say. I know what I know, sir."

---

[1] She does not say "statues." She says "shapes." The archetypes that fill our collective unconscious are not restricted by time or place, and while the two statues are indeed physically bound by their physical nature, she suggests that they are not static statues, but fluid suggestions – symbols of something that transcends art or history, something living and mobile

[2] Implying that whatever they represent – in one sense sexual violence, in another bald human wickedness – is not restricted to the forms they occupy, but is rather transferable between human beings. Any living man can adopt their virtues, because they are not statues of dead men, but representations of a very dark and hateful component of the human condition – a man-sized evil that is neither uncommon or mythic, but a real and present danger

[3] November 1 is All Saints' Day (or All Hallows' Day, or Hallowmas) – the day set aside in Christian tradition to pray for and to all of those who are saints – known or unknown. Hallowe'en – literally All Hallows' Evening – is the evening before

"Well, who was here last year?"

"No one, sir; the lady as owned the house only stayed here in summer, and she always went to London a full month afore the night. And I'm sorry to inconvenience you and your lady, but my niece is ill and I must go on Thursday."

I could have shaken her for her absurd reiteration of that obvious fiction, after she had told me her real reasons.

She was determined to go, nor could our united entreaties move her in the least.

I did not tell Laura the legend of the shapes that "walked in their marble," partly because a legend concerning our house might perhaps trouble my wife, and partly, I think, from some more occult reason[1]. This was not quite the same to me as any other story, and I did not want to talk about it till the day was over. I had very soon ceased to think of the legend, however. I was painting a portrait of Laura[2], against the lattice window, and I could not think of much else. I had got a splendid background of yellow and grey sunset, and was working away with enthusiasm at her lace. On Thursday Mrs. Dorman went. She relented, at parting, so far as to say—

"Don't you put yourself about too much, ma'am, and if there's any little thing I can do next week, I'm sure I shan't mind."

From which I inferred that she wished to come back to us after Hallowe'en. Up to the last she adhered to the fiction of the niece with touching fidelity.

Thursday passed off pretty well. Laura showed marked ability in the matter of steak and potatoes, and I confess that my knives, and the plates, which I insisted upon washing, were better done than I had dared to expect. Friday came. It is about what happened on that Friday that this is written. I wonder if I should have believed it, if any one had

---

[1] He suggests that something supernatural may have influenced him to hold his tongue -- ostensibly because Laura's being kept in the dark on this matter is directly to blame for her ultimate fate. On another level, we might view this as an excuse on the part of a man who is all too aware of the ramifications of coddling his wife

[2] Like the relationship between the spouses in Edgar Allan Poe's "The Oval Portrait," the artist-husband may be accused of over-idealizing his wife, whom he tries to capture in art. Both men fail to appreciate the dynamic, fragile humanity of their wives. Distracted by the spiritual ideals they are drawn to, they are unavailable when to provide for their spouses' emotional and physical needs when they are necessary

told it to me. I will write the story of it as quickly and plainly as I can. Everything that happened on that day is burnt into my brain. I shall not forget anything, nor leave anything out.

I got up early, I remember, and lighted the kitchen fire, and had just achieved a smoky success, when my little wife came running down, as sunny and sweet as the clear October morning itself. We prepared breakfast together, and found it very good fun. The housework was soon done, and when brushes and brooms and pails were quiet again, the house was still indeed. It is wonderful what a difference one makes in a house. We really missed Mrs. Dorman, quite apart from considerations concerning pots and pans. We spent the day in dusting our books and putting them straight, and dined gaily on cold steak and coffee. Laura was, if possible, brighter and gayer and sweeter than usual, and I began to think that a little domestic toil was really good for her. We had never been so merry since we were married, and the walk we had that afternoon was, I think, the happiest time of all my life. When we had watched the deep scarlet clouds slowly pale into leaden grey against a pale-green sky, and saw the white mists curl up along the hedgerows in the distant marsh, we came back to the house, silently, hand in hand.

"You are sad, my darling," I said, half-jestingly, as we sat down together in our little parlour. I expected a disclaimer, for my own silence had been the silence of complete happiness. To my surprise she said—

"Yes. I think I am sad, or rather I am uneasy. I don't think I'm very well. I have shivered three or four times since we came in, and it is not cold, is it?"

"No," I said, and hoped it was not a chill caught from the treacherous mists that roll up from the marshes in the dying light. No—she said, she did not think so. Then, after a silence, she spoke suddenly—

"Do you ever have presentiments of evil?"

"No," I said, smiling, "and I shouldn't believe in them if I had."

"I do," she went on; "the night my father died I knew it, though he was right away in the north of Scotland." I did not answer in words.

She sat looking at the fire for some time in silence, gently stroking my hand. At last she sprang up, came behind me, and, drawing my head back, kissed me.

"There, it's over now," she said. "What a baby I am! Come, light the candles, and we'll have some of these new Rubinstein[1] duets."

And we spent a happy hour or two at the piano.

At about half-past ten I began to long for the good-night pipe, but Laura looked so white that I felt it would be brutal of me to fill our sitting-room with the fumes of strong cavendish[2].

"I'll take my pipe outside," I said.

"Let me come, too."

"No, sweetheart, not to-night; you're much too tired[3]. I shan't be long. Get to bed, or I shall have an invalid to nurse to-morrow as well as the boots to clean."

I kissed her and was turning to go, when she flung her arms round my neck, and held me as if she would never let me go again. I stroked her hair. "Come, Pussy, you're over-tired. The housework has been too much for you."

She loosened her clasp a little and drew a deep breath.

"No. We've been very happy to-day, Jack, haven't we? Don't stay out too long."

"I won't, my dearie."

I strolled out of the front door, leaving it unlatched[4]. What a night it was! The jagged masses of heavy dark cloud were rolling at intervals from horizon to horizon, and thin white wreaths covered the stars. Through all the rush of the cloud river, the moon swam, breasting the waves and disappearing again in the darkness. When now and again her light reached the woodlands they seemed to be slowly and noiselessly waving in time to the swing of the clouds above them. There was a strange grey light over all the earth; the fields had that shadowy bloom over them which only comes from the marriage of dew and moonshine, or frost and starlight.

I walked up and down, drinking in the beauty of the quiet earth and the changing sky. The night was absolutely silent. Nothing seemed to be abroad. There was no scurrying of rabbits, or twitter of the half-asleep birds. And though the clouds went sailing across the sky, the wind that drove them never came low enough to rustle the dead leaves in the woodland paths. Across the meadows I could see the church tower standing out black and grey against the sky. I walked there

---

[1] Anton Grigorevich Rubinstein (1829 – 1894), a Russian pianist and composer

[2] Strong pipe tobacco, specially cut and cured to produce a stronger flavor

[3] A patronizing presumption that will prove disastrous

[4] His cardinal failing is that he is too certain of his control over the forces of the universe. He fails to appreciate the fragility of life and the cruel whims of fate and the cosmos

thinking over our three months of happiness—and of my wife, her dear eyes, her loving ways. Oh, my little girl! my own little girl; what a vision came then of a long, glad life for you and me together!

I heard a bell-beat from the church. Eleven already! I turned to go in, but the night held me. I could not go back into our little warm rooms yet. I would go up to the church. I felt vaguely that it would be good to carry my love and thankfulness to the sanctuary whither so many loads of sorrow and gladness had been borne by the men and women of the dead years.

I looked in at the low window as I went by. Laura was half lying on her chair in front of the fire. I could not see her face, only her little head showed dark against the pale blue wall. She was quite still. Asleep, no doubt. My heart reached out to her, as I went on. There must be a God, I thought, and a God who was good[1]. How otherwise could anything so sweet and dear as she have ever been imagined?

I walked slowly along the edge of the wood. A sound broke the stillness of the night, it was a rustling in the wood. I stopped and listened. The sound stopped too. I went on, and now distinctly heard another step than mine answer mine like an echo. It was a poacher or a wood-stealer, most likely, for these were not unknown in our Arcadian[2] neighbourhood. But whoever it was, he was a fool not to step more lightly[3]. I turned into the wood, and now the footstep seemed to come from the path I had just left. It must be an echo, I thought. The wood looked perfect in the moonlight. The large dying ferns and the brushwood showed where through thinning foliage the pale light came down. The tree trunks stood up like Gothic columns all around me[4]. They reminded me of the church, and I turned into the bier-balk, and passed through the corpse-gate between the graves to the low porch. I paused for a moment on the stone seat where Laura and I had watched the fading landscape. Then I noticed that the door of the church was open, and I blamed myself for having left it unlatched the other night[5]. We were the only people who ever cared to come to the church except

---

[1] The conclusion conflicts with this assessment
[2] Having a charming woodland quality
[3] Bold indeed – someone who truly is not afraid to be heard or noticed, someone without fear or reservations, tramping brashly over underbrush with thuggish nonchalance
[4] Calling into question: which is the holy place, the church or the wood, and which is the protective space, the church or the wood? Is this church truly a sanctuary?
[5] Not the door he should be concerned about leaving unlatched

on Sundays, and I was vexed to think that through our carelessness the damp autumn airs had had a chance of getting in and injuring the old fabric[1]. I went in. It will seem strange, perhaps, that I should have gone half-way up the aisle before I remembered—with a sudden chill, followed by as sudden a rush of self-contempt—that this was the very day and hour when, according to tradition, the "shapes drawed out man-size in marble" began to walk. Having thus remembered the legend, and remembered it with a shiver, of which I was ashamed, I could not do otherwise than walk up towards the altar, just to look at the figures—as I said to myself; really what I wanted was to assure myself, first, that I did not believe the legend, and, secondly, that it was not true. I was rather glad that I had come. I thought now I could tell Mrs. Dorman how vain her fancies were, and how peacefully the marble figures slept on through the ghastly hour. With my hands in my pockets I passed up the aisle. In the grey dim light the eastern end of the church looked larger than usual, and the arches above the two tombs looked larger too. The moon came out and showed me the reason. I stopped short, my heart gave a leap that nearly choked me, and then sank sickeningly.

The "bodies drawed out man-size" were gone, and their marble slabs lay wide and bare in the vague moonlight that slanted through the east window.

Were they really gone? or was I mad? Clenching my nerves, I stooped and passed my hand over the smooth slabs, and felt their flat unbroken surface. Had some one taken the things away? Was it some vile practical joke? I would make sure, anyway. In an instant I had made a torch of a newspaper, which happened to be in my pocket, and lighting it held it high above my head. Its yellow glare illumined the dark arches and those slabs. The figures were gone. And I was alone in the church; or was I alone[2]?

And then a horror seized me, a horror indefinable and indescribable--an overwhelming certainty of supreme and accomplished calamity[3]. I

---

[1] Again, the most valuable treasure he has left vulnerable is at home, not in the church

[2] Suddenly reality – and security – is called into question. While he is certainly alone – there is nothing to suggest otherwise – he can longer take his security (or that of his universe, or wife) for granted

[3] The hostile universe has suddenly revealed itself in all its horrific reality: victorious and unstoppable. Nesbit calls it an "accomplished calamity." The destruction is certain – already done, already finalized and irreversible

flung down the torch and tore along the aisle and out through the porch, biting my lips as I ran to keep myself from shrieking aloud. Oh, was I mad--or what was this that possessed me? I leaped the churchyard wall and took the straight cut across the fields, led by the light from our windows. Just as I got over the first stile, a dark figure seemed to spring out of the ground. Mad still with that certainty of misfortune, I made for the thing that stood in my path, shouting, "Get out of the way, can't you!"

But my push met with a more vigorous resistance than I had expected. My arms were caught just above the elbow and held as in a vice, and the raw-boned Irish doctor actually shook me.

"Would ye?" he cried, in his own unmistakable accents—"would ye, then?"

"Let me go, you fool," I gasped. "The marble figures have gone from the church; I tell you they've gone."

He broke into a ringing laugh. "I'll have to give ye a draught to-morrow, I see. Ye've bin smoking too much and listening to old wives' tales."

"I tell you, I've seen the bare slabs."

"Well, come back with me. I'm going up to old Palmer's—his daughter's ill; we'll look in at the church and let me see the bare slabs."

"You go, if you like," I said, a little less frantic for his laughter; "I'm going home to my wife."

"Rubbish, man," said he; "d'ye think I'll permit of that? Are ye to go saying all yer life that ye've seen solid marble endowed with vitality, and me to go all me life saying ye were a coward? No, sir—ye shan't do ut."

The night air—a human voice—and I think also the physical contact with this six feet of solid common sense, brought me back a little to my ordinary self, and the word "coward" was a mental shower-bath.

"Come on, then," I said sullenly; "perhaps you're right."
He still held my arm tightly. We got over the stile and back to the church. All was still as death. The place smelt very damp and earthy[1]. We walked up the aisle. I am not ashamed to confess that I shut my eyes: I knew the figures would not be there. I heard Kelly strike a match.

"Here they are, ye see, right enough; ye've been dreaming or drinking, asking yer pardon for the imputation."

---

[1] Suggesting the domain of the grave – death is ruler in this universe

I opened my eyes. By Kelly's expiring vesta[1] I saw two shapes lying "in their marble" on their slabs. I drew a deep breath, and caught his hand.

"I'm awfully indebted to you," I said. "It must have been some trick of light, or I have been working rather hard, perhaps that's it. Do you know, I was quite convinced they were gone."

"I'm aware of that," he answered rather grimly; "ye'll have to be careful of that brain of yours, my friend, I assure ye."

He was leaning over and looking at the right-hand figure, whose stony face was the most villainous and deadly in expression.

"By Jove," he said, "something has been afoot here—this hand is broken." "That won't account for my impression," I objected.

And so it was. I was certain that it had been perfect the last time Laura and I had been there.

"Perhaps some one has tried to remove them," said the young doctor. "Too much painting and tobacco will account for that, well enough."

"Come along," I said, "or my wife will be getting anxious. You'll come in and have a drop of whisky and drink confusion to ghosts and better sense to me."

"I ought to go up to Palmer's, but it's so late now I'd best leave it till the morning," he replied. "I was kept late at the Union[2], and I've had to see a lot of people since. All right, I'll come back with ye."

I think he fancied I needed him more than did Palmer's girl, so, discussing how such an illusion could have been possible, and deducing from this experience large generalities concerning ghostly apparitions, we walked up to our cottage. We saw, as we walked up the garden-path, that bright light streamed out of the front door, and presently saw that the parlour door was open too. Had she gone out?

"Come in," I said, and Dr. Kelly followed me into the parlour. It was all ablaze with candles, not only the wax ones, but at least a dozen guttering[3], glaring tallow dips[4], stuck in vases and ornaments in unlikely places[5]. Light, I knew, was Laura's remedy for nervousness.

---

[1] Swan vestas – a brand of strike-anywhere matches, made of wooden splits dipped in wax

[2] A gentleman's club

[3] Flickering unhealthily or weakly – suggestive of an expiring life or a dying spirit

[4] An improvised candle – a strip of cloth or twine placed in a saucer of tallow grease, and lit, creating a very clean, white light

[5] Apparently a desperate, frantic attempt to stave off the darkness – or scare off an intruder. The method of lighting appears haphazard, random, and unnatural

Poor child! Why had I left her? Brute that I was[1].

We glanced round the room, and at first we did not see her. The window was open, and the draught set all the candles flaring one way. Her chair was empty and her handkerchief and book lay on the floor. I turned to the window. There, in the recess of the window, I saw her. Oh, my child, my love, had she gone to that window to watch for me? And what had come into the room behind her? To what had she turned with that look of frantic fear and horror? Oh, my little one, had she thought that it was I whose step she heard, and turned to meet— what?

She had fallen back across a table in the window, and her body lay half on it and half on the window-seat, and her head hung down over the table, the brown hair loosened and fallen to the carpet[2]. Her lips were drawn back, and her eyes wide, wide open. They saw nothing now. What had they seen last?

The doctor moved towards her, but I pushed him aside and sprang to her; caught her in my arms and cried—

"It's all right, Laura! I've got you safe, wifie."

She fell into my arms in a heap. I clasped her and kissed her, and called her by all her pet names, but I think I knew all the time that she was dead.

Her hands were tightly clenched. In one of them she held something fast. When I was quite sure that she was dead, and that nothing mattered at all any more, I let him open her hand to see what she held.

It was a grey marble finger.

---

[1] To some degree, he accepts a level of complicity in his wife's ravishing

[2] A sexually vulnerable position. The loose hair is especially suggestive, often used in 19th century literature to imply violation

REGARDLESS of its advances – of science and civility, manners and law – society remains vulnerable to the same ruthless passions which prowled boldly through it during its infancy. Nesbit used her similarly grim tale, "The Mystery of the Semi-Detached" (wherein a playboy slips into his lover's apartment at dusk only to be terrified by a gruesome sight in her bed), to expose the hidden evil that can brew in the heart of urban affluence, and sent *that* shellshocked protagonist packing for the simple domesticity of the English countryside. In this thematic foil (which, like "Semi-Detached," was likely influenced by Rhoda Broughton's gory "Behold, it was a Dream!") she tears the idyllic mask from a rural retreat, exposing a dormant misanthropic energy, ripe with thoughtless lust and bursting with psychopathic glee. The couple is sweet and careful, selecting their honeymoon cabin with precision and mindfulness. Their lives are frugal and sensible, yet still tenderly romantic. They are the very embodiment of tidy, middle-classed Englishness, which so caringly merges dutiful pragmatism with a cultivated aesthetic. Their world is purposefully manicured, and yet the sky above their caring kingdom is torn to shreds, and evil things leer through and crush them. Nesbit's universe is harsh, sudden, and sadistic, and haunted by the wickedness of mankind; though six centuries may pass, the spiritual shadows of these rapacious knights still roam. They do not represent a mythic or godlike evil, but one real, tangible, and contemporary – *man-sized* sins that beat in men's hearts and stew in their brains.

II.

There also dwells in this story, a moral sentiment prominent in the works of Poe, especially "The Oval Portrait." Both stories feature an artist who adores his wife's spirit – what she represents to him as a pure, spiritual ideal – but fails to appreciate her dynamic physicality – her rampant neuroses, psychological needs, and ever-present mortality. It isn't until the moment when the artist most needs the complex personality of his wife that he arrives to find her dead – wasted and used up during one of his reveries. Both men understand only too late that what we value most is that which is rarest and most finite: life, shared love, mutual affection and experiences – an ideal can live forever, and a portrait may outlive generations, but a life lost is a treasure destroyed. Nick Freeman appears to concur with this interpretation, viewing "Man-Size in Marble" as a feminist tragedy. The following excerpt comes from the critical anthology *Women and the*

Victorian Occult – a highly recommended read:

> '[It] remains a disturbing story more than a century after it was collected in Nesbit's bluntly titled *Grim Tales*... There is certainly no suggestion of a protecting Providence overseeing the innocent Laura as there was in many earlier Victorian ghost stories. The clergy are conspicuous by their absence, and Jack's belief that his wife's sweetness means 'there must be a God [...] and a God who was good" is the sourest of ironies. The suggestion of symbolic rape makes the story all the nastier, with Laura still clutching the phallic finger while her hair lies "loosened and fallen to the carpet." Clearly she spent her last moments in an agony of terror as the statues disregarded her protective candles and burst into the cottage. Why, then, if Nesbit can be regarded as a writer of feminist Gothic, does Laura have to die? ...

> 'In constructing a relationship in which male and female roles seem to be governed by the stereotypes of the day despite her characters' bohemian pretensions, Nesbit is exploring the consequence of a crude essentialism which configures men as rational and dynamic and women as "sensitive" and passive. Jack clearly should have paid heed to Laura's anxiety and learned from it, but he allows himself to dismiss it as "nervousness," recasting a psychic gift as a quintessentially feminine ailment of the day... Nesbit ... kills Laura not to punish her but to demonstrate the latent violence inherent in the sexual politics of the period...

> 'By injecting Gothic fantasy into what seems at first an unexceptional tale of wedded bliss, Nesbit is able to provide both the shock expected of the genre, especially in short stories, and imbue her fiction with an underlying sense of ideological dissatisfaction. Sentimental aesthetics and rationalistic doctors are just as liable to oppose or inhibit the radical woman's selfhood as the ghosts of the past, even if they balk at rape and murder.'

III.

Nesbit is not alone in her use of the trope: we see it in Bram Stoker's *Dracula* where Lucy and Mina – a self-avowed "New Woman" – are punished by every man in their lives (fiancées, husbands, friends, doctors, and relatives, not to mention the Count), and in the myriad versions of the "demon abductor" myth: J. S. Le Fanu's tragic "Schalken the Painter" where a girl is prostituted by her uncle to a living corpse, E. F. Benson's haunting "The Face" wherein a girl's recurring nightmare of abduction comes to fruition, Charles Dickens' chilling "To Be Read at Dusk" and Rhoda Broughton's "The Man With the Nose," both of which follow a respectable woman's helpless kidnapping by a possibly supernatural molester. Fitz-James O'Brien's "The Bohemian" sees a man so consumed with social climbing that he is tricked by a mesmerist into relinquishing his fiancée's soul to him. Machen's *Great God Pan* watches a simple maidservant wither into a madwoman after her master exposes her mind to another dimension. Late Victorian literature darkly mulled over the idea of systematic sexism and the vulnerability it forced on women, and "Man-Size in Marble" – savage, haunting, and poignant – remains one of the purest examples of this study.

HAUNTED portraits are a time-honored Gothic trope used for a variety of reasons: sometimes they suggest the continued ramifications of past generations' tragedies, secrets, or crimes; sometimes they symbolize the manner in which humans cling to deep-seated cycles and resist change; on other occasions, the portrait with moving eyes – or shifting positions, or changing expressions – is simply a very chilling thing to imagine. Washington Irving, Bram Stoker, J. S. Le Fanu, Arthur Conan Doyle, H. P. Lovecraft, Oscar Wilde, Edgar Allan Poe, and many others have used the motif of a haunted (or simply *haunting*) portrait which is often tied to the history of the house in which it is hanged (sometimes revealing an uncanny similarity with a living relative of the centuries-dead sitter). "The Ebony Frame" is – like so many of Nesbit's stories – one of hefty loss, romantic tragedy, and star-crossed love. Nesbit's characters are consistently punished for aspiring to happiness, and if they *manage* – against all odds – to achieve it, they are doubly punished by losing twofold what they had so briefly gained (cf. the unwitting honeymooners in "Man-Size in Marble," or the innocent but impossibly vexed sweethearts in "Uncle Abraham's Romance"). The protagonist of this tale is arguably one of the most tortured of all Nesbit's lovers, although his romance lasts just one fleeting day, because his soul has been waiting two hundred years to be reunited with the object of his passion.

The Ebony Frame
{1891}

TO be rich is a luxurious sensation—the more so when you have plumbed the depths of hard-up-ness as a Fleet Street hack, a picker-up of unconsidered pars, a reporter, an unappreciated journalist—all callings utterly inconsistent with one's family feeling and one's direct descent from the Dukes of Picardy.

When my Aunt Dorcas died and left me seven hundred a year and a furnished house in Chelsea, I felt that life had nothing left to offer except immediate possession of the legacy. Even Mildred Mayhew, whom I had hitherto regarded as my life's light, became less luminous. I was not engaged to Mildred, but I lodged with her mother, and I sang duets with Mildred, and gave her gloves when it would run to it, which was seldom. She was a dear good girl, and I meant to marry her some day. It is very nice to feel that a good little woman is thinking of you—it helps you in your work—and it is pleasant to know she will say "Yes" when you say "Will you?"

But, as I say, my legacy almost put Mildred out of my head, especially as she was staying with friends in the country just then.

Before the first gloss was off my new mourning I was seated in my aunt's own armchair in front of the fire in the dining-room of my own house. My own house! It was grand, but rather lonely. I *did* think of Mildred just then.

The room was comfortably furnished with oak and leather. On the walls hung a few fairly good oil-paintings, but the space above the mantelpiece was disfigured by an exceedingly bad print, "The Trial of Lord William Russell," framed in a dark frame. I got up to look at it. I had visited my aunt with dutiful regularity, but I never remembered seeing this frame before. It was not intended for a print, but for an oil-painting. It was of fine ebony, beautifully and curiously carved.

I looked at it with growing interest, and when my aunt's housemaid—I had retained her modest staff of servants—came in with the lamp, I asked her how long the print had been there.

"Mistress only bought it two days afore she was took ill," she said; "but the frame—she didn't want to buy a new one—so she got this out of the attic. There's lots of curious old things there, sir."

"Had my aunt had this frame long?"

"Oh yes, sir. It come long afore I did, and I've been here seven years come Christmas. There was a picture in it—that's upstairs too—but it's that black and ugly it might as well be a chimley-back."

I felt a desire to see this picture. What if it were some priceless old master in which my aunt's eyes had only seen rubbish?

Directly after breakfast next morning I paid a visit to the lumber-room.

It was crammed with old furniture enough to stock a curiosity shop. All the house was furnished solidly in the early Victorian style, and in this room everything not in keeping with the "drawing-room suite" ideal was stowed away. Tables of papier-maché and mother-of-pearl, straight-backed chairs with twisted feet and faded needlework cushions, firescreens of old-world design, oak bureaux with brass handles, a little work-table with its faded moth-eaten silk flutings hanging in disconsolate shreds: on these and the dust that covered them blazed the full daylight as I drew up the blinds. I promised myself a good time in re-enshrining these household gods in my parlour, and promoting the Victorian suite to the attic. But at present my business was to find the picture as "black as the chimley-back;" and presently, behind a heap of hideous still-life studies, I found it.

Jane the housemaid identified it at once. I took it downstairs carefully and examined it. No subject, no colour were distinguishable. There was a splodge of a darker tint in the middle, but whether it was figure or tree or house no man could have told. It seemed to be painted on a very thick panel bound with leather. I decided to send it to one of those persons who pour on rotting family portraits the water of eternal youth—mere soap and water Mr. Besant tells us it is; but even as I did so the thought occurred to me to try my own restorative hand at a corner of it.

My bath-sponge, soap, and nailbrush vigorously applied for a few seconds showed me that there was no picture to clean! Bare oak presented itself to my persevering brush. I tried the other side, Jane watching me with indulgent interest. The same result. Then the truth dawned on me. Why was the panel so thick? I tore off the leather binding, and the panel divided and fell to the ground in a cloud of dust. There were two pictures—they had been nailed face to face. I leaned them against the wall, and the next moment I was leaning against it myself.

For one of the pictures was myself—a perfect portrait—no shade of expression or turn of feature wanting. Myself—in a cavalier dress, "love-locks and all!" When had this been done? And how, without my knowledge? Was this some whim of my aunt's?

"Lor', sir!" the shrill surprise of Jane at my elbow; "what a lovely photo it is! Was it a fancy ball, sir?"

"Yes," I stammered. "I—I don't think I want anything more now. You can go."

She went; and I turned, still with my heart beating violently, to the other picture. This was a woman of the type of beauty beloved of Burne Jones and Rossetti—straight nose, low brows, full lips, thin hands, large deep luminous eyes. She wore a black velvet gown. It was a full-length portrait. Her arms rested on a table beside her, and her head on her hands; but her face was turned full forward, and her eyes met those of the spectator bewilderingly. On the table by her were compasses and instruments whose uses I did not know, books, a goblet, and a miscellaneous heap of papers and pens. I saw all this afterwards. I believe it was a quarter of an hour before I could turn my eyes away from hers. I have never seen any other eyes like hers. They appealed, as a child's or a dog's do; they commanded, as might those of an empress.

"Shall I sweep up the dust, sir?" Curiosity had brought Jane back. I acceded. I turned from her my portrait. I kept between her and the woman in the black velvet. When I was alone again I tore down "The Trial of Lord William Russell," and I put the picture of the woman in its strong ebony frame.

Then I wrote to a frame-maker for a frame for my portrait. It had so long lived face to face with this beautiful witch that I had not the heart to banish it from her presence; from which, it will be perceived that I am by nature a somewhat sentimental person.

The new frame came home, and I hung it opposite the fireplace. An exhaustive search among my aunt's papers showed no explanation of the portrait of myself, no history of the portrait of the woman with the wonderful eyes. I only learned that all the old furniture together had come to my aunt at the death of my great-uncle, the head of the family; and I should have concluded that the resemblance was only a family one, if every one who came in had not exclaimed at the "speaking likeness." I adopted Jane's "fancy ball" explanation.

And there, one might suppose, the matter of the portraits ended. One might suppose it, that is, if there were not evidently a good deal more written here about it. However, to me, then, the matter seemed ended.

I went to see Mildred; I invited her and her mother to come and stay with me. I rather avoided glancing at the picture in the ebony frame. I could not forget, nor remember without singular emotion, the look in the eyes of that woman when mine first met them. I shrank from meeting that look again.

I reorganized the house somewhat, preparing for Mildred's visit. I turned the dining-room into a drawing-room. I brought down much of the old-fashioned furniture, and, after a long day of arranging and re-arranging, I sat down before the fire, and, lying back in a pleasant languor, I idly raised my eyes to the picture. I met her dark, deep hazel eyes, and once more my gaze was held fixed as by a strong magic—the kind of fascination that keeps one sometimes staring for whole minutes into one's own eyes in the glass. I gazed into her eyes, and felt my own dilate, pricked with a smart like the smart of tears.

"I wish," I said, "oh, how I wish you were a woman, and not a picture! Come down! Ah, come down!"

I laughed at myself as I spoke; but even as I laughed I held out my arms.

I was not sleepy; I was not drunk. I was as wide awake and as sober as ever was a man in this world. And yet, as I held out my arms, I saw the eyes of the picture dilate, her lips tremble—if I were to be hanged for saying it, it is true. Her hands moved slightly, and a sort of flicker of a smile passed over her face.

I sprang to my feet. "This won't do," I said, still aloud. "Firelight does play strange tricks. I'll have the lamp."

I pulled myself together and made for the bell. My hand was on it, when I heard a sound behind me, and turned—the bell still unrung. The fire had burned low, and the corners of the room were deeply shadowed; but, surely, there—behind the tall worked chair—was something darker than a shadow.

"I must face this out," I said, "or I shall never be able to face myself again." I left the bell, I seized the poker, and battered the dull coals to a blaze. Then I stepped back resolutely, and looked up at the picture. The ebony frame was empty! From the shadow of the worked chair came a silken rustle, and out of the shadow the woman of the picture was coming—coming towards me.

I hope I shall never again know a moment of terror so blank and absolute. I could not have moved or spoken to save my life. Either all the known laws of nature were nothing, or I was mad. I stood trembling, but, I am thankful to remember, I stood still, while the black velvet gown swept across the hearthrug towards me.

Next moment a hand touched me—a hand soft, warm, and human—and a low voice said, "You called me. I am here."

At that touch and that voice the world seemed to give a sort of bewildering half-turn. I hardly know how to express it, but at once it seemed not awful—not even unusual—for portraits to become flesh—only most natural, most right, most unspeakably fortunate.

I laid my hand on hers. I looked from her to my portrait. I could not see it in the firelight.

"We are not strangers," I said.

"Oh no, not strangers." Those luminous eyes were looking up into mine—those red lips were near me. With a passionate cry—a sense of having suddenly recovered life's one great good, that had seemed wholly lost—I clasped her in my arms. She was no ghost—she was a woman—the only woman in the world.

"How long," I said, "O love—how long since I lost you?"

She leaned back, hanging her full weight on the hands that were clasped behind my head.

"How can I tell how long? There is no time in hell," she answered.

It was not a dream. Ah, no—there are no such dreams. I wish to God there could be. When in dreams do I see her eyes, hear her voice, feel

44

her lips against my cheek, hold her hands to my lips, as I did that night—the supreme night of my life? At first we hardly spoke. It seemed enough—

"... after long grief and pain, To feel the arms of my true love Round me once again."

It is very difficult to tell this story. There are no words to express the sense of glad reunion, the complete realization of every hope and dream of a life, that came upon me as I sat with my hand in hers and looked into her eyes.

How could it have been a dream, when I left her sitting in the straight-backed chair, and went down to the kitchen to tell the maids I should want nothing more—that I was busy, and did not wish to be disturbed; when I fetched wood for the fire with my own hands, and, bringing it in, found her still sitting there—saw the little brown head turn as I entered, saw the love in her dear eyes; when I threw myself at her feet and blessed the day I was born, since life had given me this?

Not a thought of Mildred: all the other things in my life were a dream—this, its one splendid reality.

"I am wondering," she said after a while, when we had made such cheer each of the other as true lovers may after long parting—"I am wondering how much you remember of our past."

"I remember nothing," I said. "Oh, my dear lady, my dear sweetheart—I remember nothing but that I love you—that I have loved you all my life."

"You remember nothing—really nothing?"

"Only that I am yours; that we have both suffered; that——Tell me, my mistress dear, all that you remember. Explain it all to me. Make me understand. And yet——No, I don't want to understand. It is enough that we are together."

If it was a dream, why have I never dreamed it again?

She leaned down towards me, her arm lay on my neck, and drew my head till it rested on my shoulder. "I am a ghost, I suppose," she said, laughing softly; and her laughter stirred memories which I just grasped at, and just missed. "But you and I know better, don't we? I will tell you everything you have forgotten. We loved each other—ah! no, you have not forgotten that—and when you came back from the war we were to be married. Our pictures were painted before you went away. You know I was more learned than women of that day. Dear one, when you were gone they said I was a witch. They tried me. They said I should be burned. Just because I had looked at the stars and had gained more knowledge than they, they must needs bind me to a stake and let me be eaten by the fire. And you far away!"

Her whole body trembled and shrank. O love, what dream would have told me that my kisses would soothe even that memory?

"The night before," she went on, "the devil did come to me. I was innocent before—you know it, don't you? And even then my sin was for you—for you—because of the exceeding love I bore you. The devil came, and I sold my soul to eternal flame. But I got a good price. I got the right to come back, through my picture (if any one looking at it wished for me), as long as my picture stayed in its ebony frame. That frame was not carved by man's hand. I got the right to come back to you. Oh, my heart's heart, and another thing I won, which you shall hear anon. They burned me for a witch, they made me suffer hell on earth. Those faces, all crowding round, the crackling wood and the smell of the smoke——"

"O love! no more—no more."

"When my mother sat that night before my picture she wept, and cried, 'Come back, my poor lost child!' And I went to her, with glad leaps of heart. Dear, she shrank from me, she fled, she shrieked and moaned of ghosts. She had our pictures covered from sight and put again in the ebony frame. She had promised me my picture should stay always there. Ah, through all these years your face was against mine."

She paused.

"But the man you loved?"

"You came home. My picture was gone. They lied to you, and you married another woman; but some day I knew you would walk the world again and that I should find you."

"The other gain?" I asked.

"The other gain," she said slowly, "I gave my soul for. It is this. If you also will give up your hopes of heaven I can remain a woman, I can move in your world—I can be your wife. Oh, my dear, after all these years, at last—at last."

"If I sacrifice my soul," I said slowly, with no thought of the imbecility of such talk in our "so-called nineteenth century"—"if I sacrifice my soul, I win you? Why, love, it's a contradiction in terms. You *are* my soul."

Her eyes looked straight into mine. Whatever might happen, whatever did happen, whatever may happen, our two souls in that moment met, and became one.

"Then you choose—you deliberately choose—to give up your hopes of heaven for me, as I gave up mine for you?"

"I decline," I said, "to give up my hope of heaven on any terms. Tell me what I must do, that you and I may make our heaven here—as now, my dear love."

"I will tell you to-morrow," she said. "Be alone here to-morrow night—twelve is ghost's time, isn't it?—and then I will come out of the picture and never go back to it. I shall live with you, and die, and be buried, and there will be an end of me. But we shall live first, my heart's heart."

I laid my head on her knee. A strange drowsiness overcame me. Holding her hand against my cheek, I lost consciousness. When I awoke the grey November dawn was glimmering, ghost-like, through the uncurtained window. My head was pillowed on my arm, which rested—I raised my head quickly—ah! not on my lady's knee, but on the needle-worked cushion of the straight-backed chair. I sprang to my feet. I was stiff with cold, and dazed with dreams, but I turned my eyes on the picture. There she sat, my lady, my dear love. I held out my arms, but the passionate cry I would have uttered died on my lips. She had said twelve o'clock. Her lightest word was my law. So I only stood in front of the picture and gazed into those grey-green eyes till tears of passionate happiness filled my own.

"Oh, my dear, my dear, how shall I pass the hours till I hold you again?"

No thought, then, of my whole life's completion and consummation being a dream.

I staggered up to my room, fell across my bed, and slept heavily and dreamlessly. When I awoke it was high noon. Mildred and her mother were coming to lunch.

I remembered, at one shock, Mildred's coming and her existence.

Now, indeed, the dream began.

With a penetrating sense of the futility of any action apart from *her*, I gave the necessary orders for the reception of my guests. When Mildred and her mother came I received them with cordiality; but my genial phrases all seemed to be some one else's. My voice sounded like an echo; my heart was other where.

Still, the situation was not intolerable until the hour when afternoon tea was served in the drawing-room. Mildred and her mother kept the conversational pot boiling with a profusion of genteel commonplaces, and I bore it, as one can bear mild purgatories when one is in sight of heaven. I looked up at my sweetheart in the ebony frame, and I felt that anything that might happen, any irresponsible imbecility, any bathos of boredom, was nothing, if, after it all, *she* came to me again.

And yet, when Mildred, too, looked at the portrait, and said, "What a fine lady! One of your flames, Mr. Devigne?" I had a sickening sense of impotent irritation, which became absolute torture when Mildred—how could I ever have admired that chocolate-box barmaid style of prettiness?—threw herself into the high-backed chair, covering the needlework with her ridiculous flounces, and added, "Silence gives consent! Who is it, Mr. Devigne? Tell us all about her: I am sure she has a story."

Poor little Mildred, sitting there smiling, serene in her confidence that her every word charmed me—sitting there with her rather pinched waist, her rather tight boots, her rather vulgar voice—sitting in the chair where my dear lady had sat when she told me her story! I could not bear it.

"Don't sit there," I said; "it's not comfortable!"

But the girl would not be warned. With a laugh that set every nerve in my body vibrating with annoyance, she said, "Oh, dear! mustn't I even sit in the same chair as your black-velvet woman?"

I looked at the chair in the picture. It *was* the same; and in her chair Mildred was sitting. Then a horrible sense of the reality of Mildred came upon me. Was all this a reality after all? But for fortunate chance might Mildred have occupied, not only her chair, but her place in my life? I rose.

"I hope you won't think me very rude," I said; "but I am obliged to go out."

I forget what appointment I alleged. The lie came readily enough.

I faced Mildred's pouts with the hope that she and her mother would not wait dinner for me. I fled. In another minute I was safe, alone, under the chill, cloudy autumn sky—free to think, think, think of my dear lady.

I walked for hours along streets and squares; I lived over again and again every look, word, and hand-touch—every kiss; I was completely, unspeakably happy.

Mildred was utterly forgotten: my lady of the ebony frame filled my heart and soul and spirit.

As I heard eleven boom through the fog, I turned, and went home.

When I got to my street, I found a crowd surging through it, a strong red light filling the air.

A house was on fire. Mine.

I elbowed my way through the crowd.

The picture of my lady—that, at least, I could save!

As I sprang up the steps, I saw, as in a dream—yes, all this was *really* dream-like—I saw Mildred leaning out of the first-floor window, wringing her hands.

"Come back, sir," cried a fireman; "we'll get the young lady out right enough."

But *my* lady? I went on up the stairs, cracking, smoking, and as hot as hell, to the room where her picture was. Strange to say, I only felt that the picture was a thing we should like to look on through the long glad wedded life that was to be ours. I never thought of it as being one with her.

As I reached the first floor I felt arms round my neck. The smoke was too thick for me to distinguish features.

"Save me!" a voice whispered. I clasped a figure in my arms, and, with a strange dis-ease, bore it down the shaking stairs and out into safety. It was Mildred. I knew *that* directly I clasped her.

"Stand back," cried the crowd.

"Every one's safe," cried a fireman.

The flames leaped from every window. The sky grew redder and redder. I sprang from the hands that would have held me. I leaped up the steps. I crawled up the stairs. Suddenly the whole horror of the situation came on me. "*As long as my picture remains in the ebony frame.*" What if picture and frame perished together?

I fought with the fire, and with my own choking inability to fight with it. I pushed on. I must save my picture. I reached the drawing-room.

As I sprang in I saw my lady—I swear it—through the smoke and the flames, hold out her arms to me—to me—who came too late to save her, and to save my own life's joy. I never saw her again.

Before I could reach her, or cry out to her, I felt the floor yield beneath my feet, and I fell into the fiery hell below.

☙

How did they save me? What does that matter? They saved me somehow—curse them. Every stick of my aunt's furniture was destroyed. My friends pointed out that, as the furniture was heavily insured, the carelessness of a nightly-studious housemaid had done me no harm.

No harm!

That was how I won and lost my only love.

I deny, with all my soul in the denial, that it was a dream. There are no such dreams. Dreams of longing and pain there are in plenty, but dreams of complete, of unspeakable happiness—ah, no—it is the rest of life that is the dream.

But if I think that, why have I married Mildred, and grown stout and dull and prosperous?

I tell you it is all *this* that is the dream; my dear lady only is the reality. And what does it matter what one does in a dream?

LIKE so many of her contemporaries, Nesbit was fascinated by the concept of reincarnation. To name just a few: E. F. Benson, Arthur Conan Doyle, Algernon Blackwood (who believed *himself* to be reincarnated), Ambrose Bierce, H. P. Lovecraft, and *especially* Robert W. Chambers and Oliver Onions (both of whose fiction is riddled with centuries-old souls walking around unawares in modern bodies) all featured stories of middle-classed plodders becoming acquainted with the fact that they were priestesses, pirates, slave girls, or sorcerers in past lives. The *Fin de Siècle* era – also called the *Belle Epoque*, or the Gay Nineties – was one noted for what the French called the "malady of the century," namely boredom, pessimism, and dissatisfaction. Intellectuals brooded over the glories of past civilizations, imagining themselves anywhere but in the stilted, affected atmosphere of conventional, pre-war Europe. Ironically, the ability to enjoy leisure – to vacation, play sports, and spend time away from work – was what seemed to draw people to fancied past lives as courtesans and cavaliers who unquestionably suffered far more from their hardships than the intelligentsia did from their boredom. As one documentary puts it "For most people, common people, things were looking up. There was time now for sports, trips to the country; even a workman could buy his own bike. But for others, the artistic, the rich, it didn't feel so good. The rabble was everywhere, standards were lower, doom was at hand." Although the socialist Nesbit was hardly a member of that class of snobs who nursed pessimism at the thought of tradesmen having time to holiday, she certainly wrote about disaffected, distracted people who longed for anything other than the society they belong to. They are frequently scandalous, adulterous, jaded, and cynical. At the end of this narrative, our lonely protagonist muses that it doesn't matter that he has married the simple Mildred, grown fat, and successful, because his waking life is a mere dream. He doesn't care a jot for reality, for it is only in his daydreams and fantasies that he can eke out a slice of genuine feeling. If any horror lurks in this otherwise mystical tale, the reader may find it there.

ASIDE from "Man-Size in Marble," none of Nesbit's short stories has received wider circulation and acclaim than "John Charrington's Wedding." A favorite amongst anthologies of classic ghost stories, it is almost as much a perennial as "The Signal-Man," "The Body Snatcher," and "The Judge's House." The appeal comes – as in "Man-Size" – from Nesbit's razor-edged taste for irony and fate. A wedding is naturally expected to be the happiest of occasions, but John Charrington's wedding is different. It had been brought about by sheer will – his will to woo and possess the prettiest girl in town, a girl whose beauty, reputation, and coquetry have resulted in her body being regarded as a highly desired local commodity. So strong is Charrington's desire to own the object of his affection that he musters the strength to do the impossible. But this is no story of "love conquers all" – indeed, the conquering hero's actual motivation is left up to debate: it might be desire, lust, pride, or sheer willpower, but love has very little to do with it. How many people, after all, have been frightened to death by love?

John Charrington's Wedding
{1891}

NO one ever thought that May Forster would marry John Charrington; but he thought differently, and things which John Charrington intended had a queer way of coming to pass[1]. He asked her to marry him before he went up to Oxford. She laughed and refused him. He asked her again next time he came home. Again she laughed, tossed her dainty blonde head, and again refused. A third time he asked her; she said it was becoming a confirmed bad habit, and laughed at him more than ever[2].

---

[1] This ghost story, like so many others, is largely concerned with the trait of willfulness. In this instance it is the power of a man's will to possess a woman, and for that reason it has many fascinating feminist subtexts

[2] May – whose name, by the way, is almost certainly meant to be suggestive of rebirth, vitality, and fresh life – seems to be a consummate tease or a coquette. She does not deal gingerly with this obviously willful man, and the lack of concern she has for his feelings and for his persistence might be a veiled warning from Nesbit to other women who don't take nonplussed suitors seriously (either as sensitive

John was not the only man who wanted to marry her: she was the belle of our village *coterie*[1], and we were all in love with her more or less; it was a sort of fashion, like heliotrope ties or Inverness capes[2]. Therefore we were as much annoyed as surprised when John Charrington walked into our little local Club[3]—we held it in a loft over the saddler's, I remember—and invited us all to his wedding.

"Your wedding?"

"You don't mean it?"

"Who's the happy fair[4]? When's it to be?"

John Charrington filled his pipe and lighted it before he replied. Then he said—

"I'm sorry to deprive you fellows of your only joke—but Miss Forster and I are to be married in September."

"You don't mean it?"

"He's got the mitten[5] again, and it's turned his head."

"No," I said, rising, "I see it's true. Lend me a pistol some one—or a first-class fare to the other end of Nowhere. Charrington has bewitched the only pretty girl in our twenty-mile radius. Was it mesmerism, or a love-potion, Jack?"

"Neither, sir, but a gift you'll never have—perseverance—and the best luck a man ever had in this world."

There was something in his voice that silenced me, and all chaff of the other fellows failed to draw him further.

The queer thing about it was that when we congratulated Miss Forster, she blushed and smiled and dimpled, for all the world as though she were in love with him, and had been in love with him all

---

humans capable of being emotionally wounded or as predators worth watching carefully). In any event, John Charrington is the sort of person that should not be underestimated, and his possessiveness of May has unpleasant sexual implications that are all too familiar to modern audiences

[1] A small group of people – a clique

[2] Heliotrope is a specific shade of lavender, and an Inverness cape – popularized by depictions of Sherlock Holmes – is a plaid cloak with slits for the arms to come through, and a short cape that covers the shoulders and upper arms – both very fashionable for men during the Gay Nineties

[3] An apartment where men would gather to smoke, drink, play cards, and do petty business, usually requiring dues to be paid to take care of operating costs

[4] Fair maiden

[5] To be "given the mitten" is a 19th century expression meaning to be rejected. Usually it refers to a romantic turn down, but could also mean to be expelled from school or fired from work

the time. Upon my word, I think she had. Women are strange creatures.

We were all asked to the wedding. In Brixham[1] every one who was anybody knew everybody else who was any one. My sisters were, I truly believe, more interested in the *trousseau*[2] than the bride herself, and I was to be best man. The coming marriage was much canvassed at afternoon tea-tables, and at our little Club over the saddler's, and the question was always asked: "Does she care for him?"

I used to ask that question myself in the early days of their engagement, but after a certain evening in August I never asked it again. I was coming home from the Club through the churchyard. Our church is on a thyme-grown hill, and the turf about it is so thick and soft that one's footsteps are noiseless.

I made no sound as I vaulted the low lichened wall, and threaded my way between the tombstones. It was at the same instant that I heard John Charrington's voice, and saw Her[3]. May was sitting on a low flat gravestone, her face turned towards the full splendour of the western sun. Its expression ended, at once and for ever, any question of love for him; it was transfigured to a beauty I should not have believed possible, even to that beautiful little face.

John lay at her feet, and it was his voice that broke the stillness of the golden August evening.

"My dear, my dear, I believe I should come back from the dead if you wanted me!"

I coughed at once to indicate my presence, and passed on into the shadow fully enlightened.

The wedding was to be early in September. Two days before I had to run up to town on business. The train was late, of course, for we are on

---

[1] There is no Brixham in Kent – the southeastern-most English county where this story is set – although there is one in Devon in the southwest
[2] Bridal garments and accoutrement: the dress, jewelry, shoes, and linens
[3] May is truly idolized, and certainly represents more than a local coquette: she is evocative of desirable womanhood and manifested Lust which inspires the narrator to capitalize her pronoun like that of a savior. And May is something of a savior, offering beauty and daydreams to an otherwise dreary town. Charrington is desperate to possess her, and with her the hope for admiration and envy of his fellows. May is treated like anything but a willful woman, and is desired by the village men as a commodity or a status symbol

the South-Eastern[1], and as I stood grumbling with my watch in my hand, whom should I see but John Charrington and May Forster. They were walking up and down the unfrequented end of the platform, arm in arm, looking into each other's eyes, careless of the sympathetic interest of the porters[2].

Of course I knew better than to hesitate a moment before burying myself in the booking-office, and it was not till the train drew up at the platform, that I obtrusively passed the pair with my Gladstone[3], and took the corner in a first-class smoking-carriage. I did this with as good an air of not seeing them as I could assume. I pride myself on my discretion, but if John were travelling alone I wanted his company. I had it.

"Hullo, old man," came his cheery voice as he swung his bag into my carriage; "here's luck; I was expecting a dull journey!"

"Where are you off to?" I asked, discretion still bidding me turn my eyes away, though I saw, without looking, that hers were red-rimmed.

"To old Branbridge's," he answered, shutting the door and leaning out for a last word with his sweetheart.

"Oh, I wish you wouldn't go, John," she was saying in a low, earnest voice. "I feel certain something will happen."

"Do you think I should let anything happen to keep me, and the day after to-morrow our wedding-day?"

"Don't go," she answered, with a pleading intensity which would have sent my Gladstone on to the platform and me after it. But she wasn't speaking to me. John Charrington was made differently; he rarely changed his opinions, never his resolutions.

He only stroked the little ungloved hands that lay on the carriage door.

"I must, May. The old boy's been awfully good to me, and now he's dying I must go and see him, but I shall come home in time for——" the rest of the parting was lost in a whisper and in the rattling lurch of the starting train.

"You're sure to come?" she spoke as the train moved.

---

[1] A rail line that passes through southeastern England. It was this rail line that Charles Dickens was riding when he was present at the Staplehurst railway crash that inspired his most famous horror story, "The Signal-Man"

[2] Railway workers

[3] Otherwise known as a doctor's bag – a leather bag that opens at the top in the middle to expose two equally sized compartments

"Nothing shall keep me," he answered; and we steamed out. After he had seen the last of the little figure on the platform he leaned back in his corner and kept silence for a minute.

When he spoke it was to explain to me that his godfather, whose heir he was, lay dying at Peasmarsh Place[1], some fifty miles away, and had sent for John, and John had felt bound to go.

"I shall be surely back to-morrow," he said, "or, if not, the day after, in heaps of time. Thank Heaven, one hasn't to get up in the middle of the night to get married nowadays!"

"And suppose Mr. Branbridge dies?"

"Alive or dead I mean to be married on Thursday!" John answered, lighting a cigar and unfolding the *Times*.

At Peasmarsh station we said "good-bye," and he got out, and I saw him ride off; I went on to London, where I stayed the night.

When I got home the next afternoon, a very wet one, by the way, my sister greeted me with—

"Where's Mr. Charrington?"

"Goodness knows," I answered testily. Every man, since Cain, has resented that kind of question[2].

"I thought you might have heard from him," she went on, "as you're to give him away to-morrow."

"Isn't he back?" I asked, for I had confidently expected to find him at home.

"No, Geoffrey,"—my sister Fanny always had a way of jumping to conclusions, especially such conclusions as were least favourable to her fellow-creatures—"he has not returned, and, what is more, you may depend upon it he won't. You mark my words, there'll be no wedding to-morrow."

My sister Fanny has a power of annoying me which no other human being possesses.

"You mark my words," I retorted with asperity, "you had better give up making such a thundering idiot of yourself. There'll be more wedding to-morrow than ever you'll take the first part in." A prophecy which, by the way, came true[3].

---

[1] A residential care home near Rye in Kent

[2] In the Bible Cain, eldest son of Adam and Eve, murdered his brother. When God confronted him about his brother's absence, asking coyly "Where is your brother Abel?" Cain snapped testily "How am I to know? Am I my brother's keeper?"

[3] This bitter comment suggests that Fanny has died before marriage, just one more shadow of tragedy which darkens the palette of this somber tale

But though I could snarl confidently to my sister, I did not feel so comfortable when, late that night, I, standing on the doorstep of John's house, heard that he had not returned. I went home gloomily through the rain. Next morning brought a brilliant blue sky, gold sun, and all such softness of air and beauty of cloud as go to make up a perfect day. I woke with a vague feeling of having gone to bed anxious, and of being rather averse to facing that anxiety in the light of full wakefulness.

But with my shaving-water came a note from John which relieved my mind and sent me up to the Forsters' with a light heart.

May was in the garden. I saw her blue gown through the hollyhocks as the lodge gates swung to behind me. So I did not go up to the house, but turned aside down the turfed path.

"He's written to you too," she said, without preliminary greeting, when I reached her side.

"Yes, I'm to meet him at the station at three, and come straight on to the church."

Her face looked pale, but there was a brightness in her eyes, and a tender quiver about the mouth that spoke of renewed happiness.

"Mr. Branbridge begged him so to stay another night that he had not the heart to refuse," she went on. "He is so kind, but I wish he hadn't stayed."

I was at the station at half-past two. I felt rather annoyed with John. It seemed a sort of slight to the beautiful girl who loved him, that he should come as it were out of breath, and with the dust of travel upon him[1], to take her hand, which some of us would have given the best years of our lives to take[2].

But when the three o'clock train glided in, and glided out again having brought no passengers to our little station, I was more than annoyed. There was no other train for thirty-five minutes; I calculated that, with much hurry, we might just get to the church in time for the ceremony; but, oh, what a fool to miss that first train! What other man could have done it?

---

[1] A very real phenomenon in a time when half of travel consisted of riding in sweaty railcars and disembarking at sooty rail stations, and the other half entailed riding down dirt roads in open carts which were infamous for throwing up dust that settled on clothing in heavy layers

[2] Once more May is depicted as a commodity the possession of which would be sure to inspire respect and envy. She is little more human to them than a high-paying job or a fine house – another mark of status and ownership

That thirty-five minutes seemed a year, as I wandered round the station reading the advertisements and the time-tables, and the company's bye-laws, and getting more and more angry with John Charrington. This confidence in his own power of getting everything he wanted the minute he wanted it was leading him too far. I hate waiting. Every one does, but I believe I hate it more than any one else. The three thirty-five was late, of course.

I ground my pipe between my teeth and stamped with impatience as I watched the signals. Click. The signal went down. Five minutes later I flung myself into the carriage that I had brought for John.

"Drive to the church!" I said, as some one shut the door. "Mr. Charrington hasn't come by this train."

Anxiety now replaced anger. What had become of the man? Could he have been taken suddenly ill? I had never known him have a day's illness in his life. And even so he might have telegraphed. Some awful accident must have happened to him. The thought that he had played her false[1] never—no, not for a moment—entered my head. Yes, something terrible had happened to him, and on me lay the task of telling his bride. I almost wished the carriage would upset and break my head[2] so that some one else might tell her, not I, who—but that's nothing to do with his story.

It was five minutes to four as we drew up at the churchyard gate. A double row of eager on-lookers lined the path from lychgate[3] to porch. I sprang from the carriage and passed up between them. Our gardener had a good front place near the door. I stopped.

"Are they waiting still, Byles?" I asked, simply to gain time, for of course I knew they were by the waiting crowd's attentive attitude.

"Waiting, sir? No, no, sir; why, it must be over by now."

"Over! Then Mr. Charrington's come?"

"To the minute, sir; must have missed you somehow, and, I say, sir," lowering his voice, "I never see Mr. John the least bit so afore, but my opinion is he's been drinking pretty free. His clothes was all dusty and his face like a sheet. I tell you I didn't like the looks of him at all, and the folks inside are saying all sorts of things. You'll see, something's gone very wrong with Mr. John, and he's tried liquor. He looked like a

---

[1] Lead her on

[2] It is perhaps cruel of me to note that this is a piece of rather precise foreshadowing

[3] In a traditional English churchyard this is an entrance in the fence which is covered by a small peaked roof, much like that of a wishing well

ghost, and in he went with his eyes straight before him[1], with never a look or a word for none of us; him that was always such a gentleman!"

I had never heard Byles make so long a speech[2]. The crowd in the churchyard were talking in whispers and getting ready rice and slippers[3] to throw at the bride and bridegroom. The ringers were ready with their hands on the ropes to ring out the merry peal as the bride and bridegroom should come out.

A murmur from the church announced them; out they came. Byles was right. John Charrington did not look himself. There was dust on his coat, his hair was disarranged. He seemed to have been in some row, for there was a black mark above his eyebrow. He was deathly pale. But his pallor was not greater than that of the bride, who might have been carved in ivory—dress, veil, orange blossoms, face and all[4].

As they passed out the ringers stooped—there were six of them—and then, on the ears expecting the gay wedding peal, came the slow tolling of the passing bell[5].

A thrill of horror at so foolish a jest from the ringers passed through us all. But the ringers themselves dropped the ropes and fled like rabbits out into the sunlight[6]. The bride shuddered, and grey shadows came about her mouth, but the bridegroom led her on[7] down the path where the people stood with the handfuls of rice; but the handfuls were never thrown, and the wedding-bells never rang. In vain the ringers were urged to remedy their mistake: they protested with many whispered expletives that they would see themselves further first[8].

---

[1] This suggests that he is looking forward with a fixed, unblinking stare

[2] Presumably Byles is very class-conscious and is soft-spoken to gentlemen like the narrator

[3] While rice is still pelted at the couple after a marriage, slippers have understandably failed to survive as a tradition

[4] This may be read either as a compliment to her beauty, or as suggesting that she is more horrified than anyone else. Both interpretations are legitimate

[5] The passing bell – or the funeral knell – was tolled as a body was taken out of a church to be buried. It's deep, mournful tone was very easy to differentiate from the cheerful clangor of the bright wedding bells

[6] The assumption is that one of the bell ringers thought it would be clever to toll the death knell (sort of a "marriage will be the death of you, old sport" type ribbing joke), but the ringers are so spooked by the independent tolling of the bell that they race out of the shadowy church for the comfort of sunlight

[7] "Like a lamb to the slaughter" is the simile that comes to my mind

[8] That is "I'll see myself in hell before I go back into that bloody bell tower"

In a hush like the hush in the chamber of death[1] the bridal pair passed into their carriage and its door slammed behind them.

Then the tongues were loosed. A babel of anger, wonder, conjecture from the guests and the spectators[2].

"If I'd seen his condition, sir," said old Forster to me as we drove off, "I would have stretched him on the floor of the church, sir, by Heaven I would, before I'd have let him marry my daughter!"

Then he put his head out of the window.

"Drive like hell," he cried to the coachman; "don't spare the horses."

He was obeyed. We passed the bride's carriage. I forebore to look at it, and old Forster turned his head away and swore. We reached home before it.

We stood in the hall doorway, in the blazing afternoon sun, and in about half a minute we heard wheels crunching the gravel. When the carriage stopped in front of the steps old Forster and I ran down.

"Great Heaven, the carriage is empty! And yet——"

I had the door open in a minute, and this is what I saw—

No sign of John Charrington; and of May, his wife, only a huddled heap of white satin lying half on the floor of the carriage and half on the seat[3].

"I drove straight here, sir," said the coachman, as the bride's father lifted her out; "and I'll swear no one got out of the carriage."

We carried her into the house in her bridal dress and drew back her veil. I saw her face. Shall I ever forget it? White, white and drawn with agony and horror, bearing such a look of terror as I have never seen since except in dreams. And her hair, her radiant blonde hair, I tell you it was white like snow[4].

As we stood, her father and I, half mad with the horror and mystery of it, a boy came up the avenue—a telegraph boy. They brought the orange envelope to me. I tore it open.

---

[1] There are some chilling implications about this phrase: the chamber of death is where the body is laid out overnight (oftentimes on its bed) before burial. When compared with a bridal chamber – where a man and wife consummate their marriage overnight – there is a very uneasy suggestion of necrophilia: May's bridal chamber will be her death chamber, and Charrington's death chamber will be his bridal chamber

[2] Most are assuming that Charrington showed up to his wedding under the influence of alcohol – even more of a taboo then than it would be today

[3] Already implying that she is dead, since nothing is left "only [the] heap of white satin" and yet she is clothed in it

[4] A medical impossibility despite wide reportage in folklore

"Mr. Charrington was thrown from the dogcart[1] on his way to the station at half-past one. Killed on the spot!"

And he was married to May Forster in our parish church at *half-past three*, in presence of half the parish.

"I shall be married, dead or alive!"

What had passed in that carriage on the homeward drive? No one knows—no one will ever know. Oh, May! oh, my dear!

Before a week was over they laid her beside her husband in our little churchyard on the thyme-covered hill—the churchyard where they had kept their love-trysts.

Thus was accomplished John Charrington's wedding.

THE problem – or *one* of the problems – with interpreting John Charrington as a *Wuthering Heights*-type love story (one where fanatical love is capable of reaching beyond the grave) is the manner of May's gruesome death. She is not found peacefully slumped over her husband's seat as if she had been laying her head in his lap, or with the blush of life lingering on her cold cheeks, with the sweetest smile on her pale lips. Her springlike personality, so aptly indicated by her name, is drained dry, leaving behind a white-haired, bloodless shell hollowed out by terror. Was it the fear of death or ghosts which killed her? Or was it the horror of how strong John's fanaticism was? That he would be so desperate to show off his conquest to the village, that he would overcome death to prove his friends wrong, and – worse of all – that he would be so obsessed with owning her that he would drag her to death with him in order to seal their promised covenant – more so than a simple fear of revenants, this moral repulsion may have been the cause of her death. And naturally Charrington must not be considered blameless here: he is not a sad ghost who dutifully keeps his promise to wed his bride, a wan phantom who is heartbroken when she faints at his misty touch. Unlike the couple in "From the Dead" there is very *little* pathos in John Charrington's abduction of his living wife to the world of the dead. It is an insidious return from the dead, one clearly

---

[1] A dogcart is a small, two-wheeled carriage pulled by one horse usually with just enough room for a driver, passenger, and the passenger's light luggage, used typically for conveying passengers from train stations over a short journey – the 19th century equivalent of taking a taxi cab from the airport

motivated by an intention to return to hell with his betrothed, and in *that* sense his resurrection might be viewed as utterly murderous.

II.

There are two very interesting literary precedents to this story which should be acknowledged: one ancient and one Victorian. The Victorian story is one of the first great tales from the pen of the century's greatest ghost story writer, J. Sheridan Le Fanu, called "Schalken the Painter." In this story, written about the eponymous, real-life 17th century Dutch portraitist, Le Fanu invents a backstory to explain Schalken's historical taste for nocturnal paintings featuring women holding candles and giving suggestive grins. In his tale, Schalken fell in love with his instructor's young ward, Rose, but thought himself too poor to propose to her. One day a grotesque gentleman appears at the art studio offering the instructor a vast sum to marry his beautiful niece. Despite her reservations (and the man's corpse-like face), the master agrees to essentially prostitute his niece. The sad bride and the ghostly groom ride off to his supposed hometown, only for the carriage to be found empty on the side of the road. Later that year, Rose bursts into Schalken's studio, raving about the unholiness of a union between the living and dead, and begging for food, wine, and a priest. They rush off to get the food, but when they return she is dragged from the room by an unseen force, never to be seen again. Years later Schalken is attending a funeral at a cathedral in the town the carriage was heading towards, and is shocked to see his lost love standing in a nightgown with a candle. She beckons him flirtatiously into the basement of the medieval church. Mesmerized, he follows her to a four-poster bed in a crypt, but is terrified when she draws the curtain to reveal the upright corpse of her "husband." She has married a ghost who came to collect her, and has spirited her irrecoverably away to the world of the dead. Like Le Fanu, whose story unquestionably influenced this one, Nesbit insinuates a sexual nature to the abduction.

III.

This violence is even more pronounced in the ancient myth which inspired *both* Victorian writers, the Greek story of the Rape of Persephone. Like May and Rose, Persephone – who is incidentally associated with springtime and flowers – attracted the attention of an unwanted suitor: Hades, king of the Underworld. He abducted her while she was picking flowers, dragged her into hell, ravaged her, and forced her to become his wife. Her mother, Demeter, was the goddess of harvest, and she blighted the world with winter until Hades allowed Persephone to return. They came to a compromise: Persephone would

62

return to the world of the living each spring (and winter would depart), and go back to her "husband" in the fall (when Demeter would send the world back into frosty mourning), thus explaining the seasons. Persephone would eternally be Hades' wife, and became the Queen of the Dead. Both of these stories – if accepted as sources – suggest the darker, violently sexual nature of Charrington's abduction, and offer a powerful and evocative commentary on male possessiveness and sexual violence, which were much easier to discuss in the disarming context of an ill-starred wedding day than an established marriage. Wife-beating, spousal rape, and zealous ownership are all possible real-world metaphors with which this story, like so many of Nesbit's, bitterly portrays the shadows that can hang so heavily upon matrimony.

PETER Yearsley, who beautifully narrated Nesbit's 1893 collection, *Grim Tales* for LibriVox, described the book's contents in the following manner: "A collection of gentle stories that draw us into that hidden world where fear is just around the next corner, and where loving hands can touch across the boundaries of death." None of those tales better matches his lovely description than "Uncle Abraham's Romance." This ghost story is the sort that one might most enjoy reading on a country porch swing as the pink light of a late summer afternoon fades into the violet of dusk. One can hear the cicadas buzzing in the shaggy elms overhead and see the white butterflies sailing in and out of the straw-colored cornfields. A beautiful, plaintive, and poetic ghost story, it smacks of a genuine family legend, and offers a complicated stew of emotions surrounding Nesbit's favorite theme: the tragic romance of love and hope dashed by death and loss.

Uncle Abraham's Romance
{1893}

"NO, my dear," my Uncle Abraham answered me, "no—nothing romantic ever happened to me—unless—but no: that wasn't romantic either——"

I was. To me, I being eighteen, romance was the world. My Uncle Abraham was old and lame. I followed the gaze of his faded eyes, and my own rested on a miniature that hung at his elbow-chair's right hand, a portrait of a woman, whose loveliness even the miniature-painter's art had been powerless to disguise—a woman with large lustrous eyes and perfect oval face.

I rose to look at it. I had looked at it a hundred times. Often enough in my baby days I had asked, "Who's that, uncle?" always receiving the same answer: "A lady who died long ago, my dear."

As I looked again at the picture, I asked, "Was she like this?"

"Who?"

"Your—your romance!"

Uncle Abraham looked hard at me. "Yes," he said at last. "Very—very like."

I sat down on the floor by him. "Won't you tell me about her?"

"There's nothing to tell," he said. "I think it was fancy, mostly, and folly; but it's the realest thing in my long life, my dear."

65

A long pause. I kept silence. "Hurry no man's cattle" is a good motto, especially with old people.

"I remember," he said in the dreamy tone always promising so well to the ear that a story delighteth—"I remember, when I was a young man, I was very lonely indeed. I never had a sweetheart. I was always lame, my dear, from quite a boy; and the girls used to laugh at me."

He sighed. Presently he went on—

"And so I got into the way of mooning off by myself in lonely places, and one of my favourite walks was up through our churchyard, which was set high on a hill in the middle of the marsh country. I liked that because I never met any one there. It's all over, years ago. I was a silly lad; but I couldn't bear of a summer evening to hear a rustle and a whisper from the other side of the hedge, or maybe a kiss as I went by.

"Well, I used to go and sit all by myself in the churchyard, which was always sweet with thyme, and quite light (on account of its being so high) long after the marshes were dark. I used to watch the bats flitting about in the red light, and wonder why God didn't make every one's legs straight and strong, and wicked follies like that. But by the time the light was gone I had always worked it off, so to speak, and could go home quietly and say my prayers without any bitterness.

"Well, one hot night in August, when I had watched the sunset fade and the crescent moon grow golden, I was just stepping over the low stone wall of the churchyard when I heard a rustle behind me. I turned round, expecting it to be a rabbit or a bird. It was a woman."

He looked at the portrait. So did I.

"Yes," he said, "that was her very face. I was a bit scared and said something—I don't know what—and she laughed and said, 'Did I think she was a ghost?' and I answered back, and I stayed talking to her over the churchyard wall till 'twas quite dark, and the glowworms were out in the wet grass all along the way home.

"Next night I saw her again; and the next night and the next. Always at twilight time; and if I passed any lovers leaning on the stiles in the marshes it was nothing to me now."

Again my uncle paused. "It's very long ago," he said slowly, "and I'm an old man; but I know what youth means, and happiness, though I was always lame, and the girls used to laugh at me. I don't know how long it went on—you don't measure time in dreams—but at last your grandfather said I looked as if I had one foot in the grave, and he would be sending me to stay with our kin at Bath and take the waters. I had to go. I could not tell my father why I would rather had died than go."

"What was her name, uncle?" I asked.

"She never would tell me her name, and why should she? I had names enough in my heart to call her by. Marriage? My dear, even then I knew marriage was not for me. But I met her night after night, always in our churchyard where the yew-trees were and the lichened gravestones. It was there we always met and always parted. The last time was the night before I went away. She was very sad, and dearer than life itself. And she said—

"'If you come back before the new moon I shall meet you here just as usual. But if the new moon shines on this grave and you are not here— you will never see me again any more.'

"She laid her hand on the yellow lichened tomb against which we had been leaning. It was an old weather-worn stone, and bore on it the inscription—

'Susannah Kingsnorth,
Ob. 1713.'

"'I shall be here.' I said.

"'I mean it,' she said, with deep and sudden seriousness, 'it is no fancy. You will be here when the new moon shines?'"

"I promised, and after a while we parted.

"I had been with my kinsfolk at Bath nearly a month. I was to go home on the next day, when, turning over a case in the parlour, I came upon that miniature. I could not speak for a minute. At last I said, with dry tongue, and heart beating to the tune of heaven and hell—

"'Who is this?'

"'That?' said my aunt. 'Oh! she was betrothed to one of our family many years ago, but she died before the wedding. They say she was a bit of a witch. A handsome one, wasn't she?'

"I looked again at the face, the lips, the eyes of my dear and lovely love, whom I was to meet to-morrow night when the new moon shone on that tomb in our churchyard.

"'Did you say she was dead?' I asked, and I hardly knew my own voice.

"'Years and years ago! Her name's on the back and her date——'

"I took the portrait from its faded red-velvet bed, and read on the back—'Susannah Kingsnorth, Ob. 1713.'

"That was in 1813." My uncle stopped short.

"What happened?" I asked breathlessly.

"I believe I had a fit," my uncle answered slowly; "at any rate, I was very ill."

"And you missed the new moon on the grave?"

"I missed the new moon on the grave."

"And you never saw her again?"

"I never saw her again——"

"But, uncle, do you really believe?—Can the dead?—was she—did you——"

My uncle took out his pipe and filled it.

"It's a long time ago," he said, "a many, many years. Old man's tales, my dear! Old man's tales! Don't you take any notice of them."

He lighted the pipe, puffed silently a moment or two, and then added: "But I know what youth means, and happiness, though I was lame, and the girls used to laugh at me."

———————————————————

FEW ghost stories – save those of Margaret Oliphant and Rhoda Broughton – effectively convey pathos with such authenticity and elegance. Nesbit conveys a rich sense of loneliness, fragile love, and tender nostalgia without evoking the gush of sentimentality that so many Victorian writers relished. Although she treaded dangerously into this territory in several horror stories (cf. the first two chapters of "From the Dead," "The Haunted Inheritance," and the unprintable "Letter in Brown Ink" – wherein a girl imprisoned in a madwoman's attic writes an SOS letter in her own blood, is rescued by her neighbor, and marries his son), her supernatural fiction was largely cynical, realistic, and genuine in tone. It is, however, refreshing to read "Uncle Abraham's Romance" as so many of Nesbit's stories end with betrayal and rejection. While this tale still closes with a rush sorrowful loss (one very much like that in "The Ebony Frame") the sense of bitter resignation is absent. Instead we are left with a wistful old man who seems to quietly relish this fleeting romance from his youth. The manner in which Nesbit paints scenery, mood, and emotion are some of the best in her oeuvre. Like "Man-Size in Marble," there is a vivid sense of setting and a delicious helping of emotionally-invigorated scenery. Despite its lack of horror, "Uncle Abraham's Romance" remains one of the best ghost stories in Nesbit's canon. Like Oliphant's "The Open Door" and Broughton's "Poor Pretty Bobby," Nesbit's tale exudes a humanity that modern horror often evades, one that makes it a vivid and elegant ghost story, unusual in its humanity and rich in its sympathy.

UNTIL its closing paragraphs this is a story of such a sentimental nature that it was a difficult decision to include it. It is among Nesbit's more perplexing tales, and the first half of the plot can be summarized thus: *after revealing that she tricked her husband into marrying her, a woman withers at his understandably negative reaction, runs away, and dies before her distraught, repentant spouse can locate her.* The story has an interesting feminist bent, and a very challenging conclusion, but at its core it *is* a schoolgirl fantasy: "don't get mad at me when I deceive you (*I always have your best interests at heart*) because I might just run away into the night, selflessly provide you with a son, and die nobly like Little Nell. Everyone will then call me angelic and tell you to go to hell. And THEN you'll be sorry!" So proceed forewarned. Now, for all my bile there are two considerations that must be made towards this story: 1. The most obnoxiously glaring fault is the idea that a woman would voluntarily exile herself for the reasons that she does. Admittedly, a Victorian audience would probably never forgive a heroine for anything stronger than forging a love letter. Had, for instance, our dear, pretty Ida committed adultery or had an abortion, this story would be far, far better (her flight would be understood, though today even those "crimes" hardly seem worth going off the grid) but unpalatable to stodgy Victorians. 2. For all of its saccharine, flagellant weepiness – and for all of its obvious warning to men about what could happen if they use harsh words with their wives ("and THEN you'll be sorry") – the last section, Chapter 3, has tremendously interesting merit in terms of the Freudian relationship between sex and death – Eros and Thanatos – the symbolic role of a mute child, and the husband's regrettable inability to accept his wife as a corruptible, fallible, mortal being.

From the Dead
{1893}

"BUT true or not true, your brother is a scoundrel. No man—no decent man—tells such things."

"He did not tell. How dare you suppose it? I found the letter in his desk; and she being my friend and you being her lover, I never thought there could be any harm in my reading her letter to my brother. Give me back the letter. I was a fool to tell you."

Ida Helmont held out her hand for the letter.

"Not yet," I said, and I went to the window. The dull red of a London sunset burned on the paper, as I read in the quaint, dainty handwriting I knew so well and had kissed so often—

"Dear, I do—I do love you; but it's impossible. I must marry Arthur. My honour is engaged. If he would only set me free—but he never will. He loves me so foolishly. But as for me, it is you I love—body, soul, and spirit. There is no one in my heart but you. I think of you all day, and dream of you all night. And we must part. And that is the way of the world. Good-bye!—Yours, yours, yours,

Elvire."

I had seen the handwriting, indeed, often enough. But the passion written there was new to me. That I had not seen.

I turned from the window wearily. My sitting-room looked strange to me. There were my books, my reading-lamp, my untasted dinner still on the table, as I had left it when I rose to dissemble my surprise at Ida Helmont's visit—Ida Helmont, who now sat in my easy-chair looking at me quietly.

"Well—do you give me no thanks?"

"You put a knife in my heart, and then ask for thanks?"

"Pardon me," she said, throwing up her chin. "I have done nothing but show you the truth. For that one should expect no gratitude—may I ask, out of mere curiosity, what you intend to do?"

"Your brother will tell you——"

She rose suddenly, pale to the lips.

"You will not tell my brother?" she began.

"That you have read his private letters? Certainly not!"

She came towards me—her gold hair flaming in the sunset light.

"Why are you so angry with me?" she said. "Be reasonable. What else could I do?"

"I don't know."

"Would it have been right not to tell you?"

"I don't know. I only know that you've put the sun out, and I haven't got used to the dark yet."

"Believe me," she said, coming still nearer to me, and laying her hands in the lightest light touch on my shoulders, "believe me, she never loved you."

There was a softness in her tone that irritated and stimulated me. I moved gently back, and her hands fell by her sides.

"I beg your pardon," I said. "I have behaved very badly. You were quite right to come, and I am not ungrateful. Will you post a letter for me?"

72

I sat down and wrote—

"I give you back your freedom. The only gift of mine that can please you now.

"Arthur."

I held the sheet out to Miss Helmont, and, when she had glanced at it, I sealed, stamped, and addressed it.

"Good-bye," I said then, and gave her the letter. As the door closed behind her I sank into my chair, and I am not ashamed to say that I cried like a child or a fool over my lost plaything—the little dark-haired woman who loved some one else with "body, soul, and spirit."

I did not hear the door open or any foot on the floor, and therefore I started when a voice behind me said—

"Are you so very unhappy? Oh, Arthur, don't think I am not sorry for you!"

"I don't want any one to be sorry for me, Miss Helmont," I said.

She was silent a moment. Then, with a quick, sudden, gentle movement she leaned down and kissed my forehead—and I heard the door softly close. Then I knew that the beautiful Miss Helmont loved me.

At first that thought only fleeted by—a light cloud against a grey sky—but the next day reason woke, and said—

"Was Miss Helmont speaking the truth? Was it possible that——?"

I determined to see Elvire, to know from her own lips whether by happy fortune this blow came, not from her, but from a woman in whom love might have killed honesty.

I walked from Hampstead to Gower Street. As I trod its long length, I saw a figure in pink come out of one of the houses. It was Elvire. She walked in front of me to the corner of Store Street. There she met Oscar Helmont. They turned and met me face to face, and I saw all I needed to see. They loved each other. Ida Helmont had spoken the truth. I bowed and passed on. Before six months were gone they were married, and before a year was over I had married Ida Helmont.

What did it I don't know. Whether it was remorse for having, even for half a day, dreamed that she could be so base as to forge a lie to gain a lover, or whether it was her beauty, or the sweet flattery of the preference of a woman who had half her acquaintances at her feet, I don't know; anyhow, my thoughts turned to her as to their natural home. My heart, too, took that road, and before very long I loved her as I had never loved Elvire. Let no one doubt that I loved her—as I shall never love again, please God!

There never was any one like her. She was brave and beautiful, witty and wise, and beyond all measure adorable. She was the only woman in the world. There was a frankness—a largeness of heart—about her that made all other women seem small and contemptible. She loved me and I worshipped her. I married her, I stayed with her for three golden weeks, and then I left her. Why?

Because she told me the truth. It was one night—late—we had sat all the evening in the verandah of our seaside lodging watching the moonlight on the water and listening to the soft sound of the sea on the sand. I have never been so happy; I never shall be happy any more, I hope.

"Heart's heart," she said, leaning her gold head against my shoulder, "how much do you love me?"

"How much?"

"Yes—how much? I want to know what place it is I hold in your heart. Am I more to you than any one else?"

"My love!"

"More than yourself?"

"More than my life!"

"I believe you," she said. Then she drew a long breath, and took my hands in hers. "It can make no difference. Nothing in heaven or earth can come between us now."

"Nothing," I said. "But, sweet, my wife, what is it?"

For she was deathly pale.

"I must tell you," she said; "I cannot hide anything now from you, because I am yours—body, soul, and spirit."

The phrase was an echo that stung me.

The moonlight shone on her gold hair, her warm, soft, gold hair, and on her pale face.

"Arthur," she said, "you remember my coming to you at Hampstead with that letter?"

"Yes, my sweet, and I remember how you——"

"Arthur!"—she spoke fast and low—"Arthur, that letter was a forgery. She never wrote it. I——"

She stopped, for I had risen and flung her hands from me, and stood looking at her. God help me! I thought it was anger at the lie I felt. I know now it was only wounded vanity that smarted in me. That *I* should have been tricked, that *I* should have been deceived, that *I* should have been led on to make a fool of myself! That *I* should have married the woman who had befooled me! At that moment she was no longer the wife I adored—she was only a woman who had forged a letter and tricked me into marrying her.

I spoke; I denounced her; I said I would never speak to her again. I felt it was rather creditable in me to be so angry. I said I would have no more to do with a liar and forger.

I don't know whether I expected her to creep to my knees and implore forgiveness. I think I had some vague idea that I could by-and-by consent with dignity to forgive and forget. I did not mean what I said. No, no; I did not mean a word of it. While I was saying it I was longing for her to weep and fall at my feet, that I might raise her and hold her in my arms again.

But she did not fall at my feet; she stood quietly looking at me.

"Arthur," she said, as I paused for breath, "let me explain—she—I——"

"There is nothing to explain," I said hotly, still with that foolish sense of there being something rather noble in my indignation, as one feels when one calls one's self a miserable sinner. "You are a liar and forger, and that is enough for me. I will never speak to you again. You have wrecked my life——"

"Do you mean that?" she said, interrupting me, and leaning forward to look at me. Tears lay on her cheeks, but she was not crying now.

I hesitated. I longed to take her in my arms and say—"Lay your head here, my darling, and cry here, and know how I love you."

But instead I kept silence.

"*Do* you mean it?" she persisted.

Then she put her hand on my arm. I longed to clasp it and draw her to me.

Instead, I shook it off, and said—

"Mean it? Yes—of course I mean it. Don't touch me, please! You have ruined my life."

She turned away without a word, went into our room, and shut the door.

I longed to follow her, to tell her that if there was anything to forgive I forgave it.

Instead, I went out on the beach, and walked away under the cliffs.

The moonlight and the solitude, however, presently brought me to a better mind. Whatever she had done had been done for love of me—I knew that. I would go home and tell her so—tell her that whatever she had done she was my dearest life, my heart's one treasure. True, my ideal of her was shattered, but, even as she was, what was the whole world of women compared to her? I hurried back, but in my resentment and evil temper I had walked far, and the way back was very long. I had been parted from her for three hours by the time I opened the door of the little house where we lodged. The house was dark and very still. I slipped off my shoes and crept up the narrow stairs, and opened the door of our room quite softly. Perhaps she would have cried herself to sleep, and I would lean over her and waken her with my kisses and beg her to forgive me. Yes, it had come to that now.

I went into the room—I went towards the bed. She was not there. She was not in the room, as one glance showed me. She was not in the house, as I knew in two minutes. When I had wasted a priceless hour in searching the town for her, I found a note on the dressing-table—

"Good-bye! Make the best of what is left of your life. I will spoil it no more."

She was gone, utterly gone. I rushed to town by the earliest morning train, only to find that her people knew nothing of her. Advertisement failed. Only a tramp said he had met a white lady on the cliff, and a fisherman brought me a handkerchief marked with her name that he had found on the beach.

I searched the country far and wide, but I had to go back to London at last, and the months went by. I won't say much about those months, because even the memory of that suffering turns me faint and sick at heart. The police and detectives and the Press failed me utterly. Her friends could not help me, and were, moreover, wildly indignant with me, especially her brother, now living very happily with my first love.

I don't know how I got through those long weeks and months. I tried to write; I tried to read; I tried to live the life of a reasonable human being. But it was impossible. I could not endure the companionship of my kind. Day and night I almost saw her face— almost heard her voice. I took long walks in the country, and her figure was always just round the next turn of the road—in the next glade of the wood. But I never quite saw her—never quite heard her. I believe I was not altogether sane at that time. At last, one morning as I was setting out for one of those long walks that had no goal but weariness, I met a telegraph boy, and took the red envelope from his hand.

On the pink paper inside was written—

"Come to me at once. I am dying. You must come.—Ida.—Apinshaw Farm, Mellor, Derbyshire."

There was a train at twelve to Marple, the nearest station. I took it. I tell you there are some things that cannot be written about. My life for those long months was one of them, that journey was another. What had her life been for those months? That question troubled me, as one is troubled in every nerve at the sight of a surgical operation or a wound inflicted on a being dear to one. But the overmastering sensation was joy—intense, unspeakable joy. She was alive! I should see her again. I took out the telegram and looked at it: "I am dying." I simply did not believe it. She could not die till she had seen me. And if she had lived all those months without me, she could live now, when I was with her again, when she knew of the hell I had endured apart from her, and the heaven of our meeting. She must live. I would not let her die.

There was a long drive over bleak hills. Dark, jolting, infinitely wearisome. At last we stopped before a long, low building, where one or two lights gleamed faintly. I sprang out.

The door opened. A blaze of light made me blink and draw back. A woman was standing in the doorway.

"Art thee Arthur Marsh?" she said.

"Yes."

"Then, th'art ower late. She's dead."

II.

I went into the house, walked to the fire, and held out my hands to it mechanically, for, though the night was May, I was cold to the bone. There were some folks standing round the fire and lights flickering. Then an old woman came forward with the northern instinct of hospitality.

"Thou'rt tired," she said, "and mazed-like. Have a sup o' tea."

I burst out laughing. It was too funny. I had travelled two hundred miles to see *her*; and she was dead, and they offered me tea. They drew back from me as if I had been a wild beast, but I could not stop laughing. Then a hand was laid on my shoulder, and some one led me into a dark room, lighted a lamp, set me in a chair, and sat down opposite me. It was a bare parlour, coldly furnished with rush chairs and much-polished tables and presses. I caught my breath, and grew suddenly grave, and looked at the woman who sat opposite me.

"I was Miss Ida's nurse," said she; "and she told me to send for you. Who are you?"

"Her husband——"

The woman looked at me with hard eyes, where intense surprise struggled with resentment. "Then, may God forgive you!" she said. "What you've done I don't know; but it'll be 'ard work forgivin' *you*— even for *Him*!"

"Tell me," I said, "my wife——"

"Tell you?" The bitter contempt in the woman's tone did not hurt me; what was it to the self-contempt that had gnawed my heart all these months? "Tell you? Yes, I'll tell you. Your wife was that ashamed of you, she never so much as told me she was married. She let me think anything I pleased sooner than that. She just come 'ere an' she said, 'Nurse, take care of me, for I am in mortal trouble. And don't let them know where I am,' says she. An' me bein' well married to an honest man, and well-to-do here, I was able to do it, by the blessing."

"Why didn't you send for me before?" It was a cry of anguish wrung from me.

"I'd *never* 'a sent for you—it was *her* doin'. Oh, to think as God A'mighty's made men able to measure out such-like pecks o' trouble for us womenfolk! Young man, I dunno what you did to 'er to make 'er leave you; but it muster bin something cruel, for she loved the ground you walked on. She useter sit day after day, a-lookin' at your picture an' talkin' to it an' kissin' of it, when she thought I wasn't takin' no notice, and cryin' till she made me cry too. She useter cry all night 'most. An' one day, when I tells 'er to pray to God to 'elp 'er through 'er trouble, she outs with *your* putty face on a card, she doez, an', says she, with her poor little smile, 'That's my god, Nursey,' she says."

"Don't!" I said feebly, putting out my hands to keep off the torture; "not any more, not now."

"*Don't?*" she repeated. She had risen and was walking up and down the room with clasped hands—"don't, indeed! No, I won't; but I shan't forget you! I tell you I've had you in my prayers time and again, when I thought you'd made a light-o'-love o' my darling. I shan't drop you outer them now I know she was your own wedded wife as you chucked away when you'd tired of her, and left 'er to eat 'er 'art out with longin' for you. Oh! I pray to God above us to pay you scot and lot for all you done to 'er! You killed my pretty. The price will be required of you, young man, even to the uttermost farthing! O God in heaven, make him suffer! Make him feel it!"

She stamped her foot as she passed me. I stood quite still; I bit my lip till I tasted the blood hot and salt on my tongue.

"She was nothing to you!" cried the woman, walking faster up and down between the rush chairs and the table; "any fool can see that with half an eye. You didn't love her, so you don't feel nothin' now; but some day you'll care for some one, and then you shall know what she felt—if there's any justice in heaven!"

I, too, rose, walked across the room, and leaned against the wall. I heard her words without understanding them.

"Can't you feel *nothin'*? Are you mader stone? Come an' look at 'er lyin' there so quiet. She don't fret arter the likes o' you no more now. She won't sit no more a-lookin' outer winder an' sayin' nothin'—only droppin' 'er tears one by one, slow, slow on her lap. Come an' see 'er; come an' see what you done to my pretty—an' then ye can go. Nobody wants you 'ere. *She* don't want you now. But p'r'aps you'd like to see 'er safe underground fust? I'll be bound you'll put a big slab on 'er—to make sure *she* don't rise again."

I turned on her. Her thin face was white with grief and impotent rage. Her claw-like hands were clenched.

"Woman," I said, "have mercy!"

She paused, and looked at me.

"Eh?" she said.

"Have mercy!" I said again.

"Mercy? You should 'a thought o' that before. You 'adn't no mercy on 'er. She loved you—she died lovin' you. An' if I wasn't a Christian woman, I'd kill you for it—like the rat you are! That I would, though I 'ad to swing for it arterwards."

I caught the woman's hands and held them fast, in spite of her resistance.

"Don't you understand?" I said savagely. "We loved each other. She died loving me. I have to live loving her. And it's *her* you pity. I tell you it was all a mistake—a stupid, stupid mistake. Take me to her, and for pity's sake let me be left alone with her."

She hesitated; then said in a voice only a shade less hard—

"Well, come along, then."

We moved towards the door. As she opened it a faint, weak cry fell on my ear. My heart stood still.

"What's that?" I asked, stopping on the threshold.

"Your child," she said shortly.

That, too! Oh, my love! oh, my poor love! All these long months!

"She allus said she'd send for you when she'd got over her trouble," the woman said as we climbed the stairs. "'I'd like him to see his little baby, nurse,' she says; 'our little baby. It'll be all right when the baby's born,' she says. 'I know he'll come to me then. You'll see.' And I never said nothin'—not thinkin' you'd come if she was your leavins, and not dreamin' as you could be 'er husband an' could stay away from 'er a hour—her bein' as she was. Hush!"

She drew a key from her pocket and fitted it to the lock. She opened the door and I followed her in. It was a large, dark room, full of old-fashioned furniture. There were wax candles in brass candlesticks and a smell of lavender.

The big four-post bed was covered with white.

"My lamb—my poor pretty lamb!" said the woman, beginning to cry for the first time as she drew back the sheet. "Don't she look beautiful?"

I stood by the bedside. I looked down on my wife's face. Just so I had seen it lie on the pillow beside me in the early morning when the wind and the dawn came up from beyond the sea. She did not look like one dead. Her lips were still red, and it seemed to me that a tinge of colour lay on her cheek. It seemed to me, too, that if I kissed her she would wake, and put her slight hand on my neck, and lay her cheek against mine—and that we should tell each other everything, and weep together, and understand and be comforted.

So I stooped and laid my lips to hers as the old nurse stole from the room.

But the red lips were like marble, and she did not wake. She will not wake now ever any more.

I tell you again there are some things that cannot be written.

III.

I lay that night in a big room filled with heavy, dark furniture, in a great four-poster hung with heavy, dark curtains—a bed the counterpart of that other bed from whose side they had dragged me at last.

They fed me, I believe, and the old nurse was kind to me. I think she saw now that it is not the dead who are to be pitied most.

I lay at last in the big, roomy bed, and heard the household noises grow fewer and die out, the little wail of my child sounding latest. They had brought the child to me, and I had held it in my arms, and bowed my head over its tiny face and frail fingers. I did not love it then. I told myself it had cost me her life. But my heart told me that it was I who had done that. The tall clock at the stairhead sounded the hours— eleven, twelve, one, and still I could not sleep. The room was dark and very still.

I had not been able to look at my life quietly. I had been full of the intoxication of grief—a real drunkenness, more merciful than the calm that comes after.

Now I lay still as the dead woman in the next room, and looked at what was left of my life. I lay still, and thought, and thought, and thought. And in those hours I tasted the bitterness of death. It must have been about two that I first became aware of a slight sound that

was not the ticking of the clock. I say I first became aware, and yet I knew perfectly that I had heard that sound more than once before, and had yet determined not to hear it, *because it came from the next room*—the room where the corpse lay.

And I did not wish to hear that sound, because I knew it meant that I was nervous—miserably nervous—a coward and a brute. It meant that I, having killed my wife as surely as though I had put a knife in her breast, had now sunk so low as to be afraid of her dead body—the dead body that lay in the room next to mine. The heads of the beds were placed against the same wall; and from that wall I had fancied I heard slight, slight, almost inaudible sounds. So when I say that I became aware of them I mean that I at last heard a sound so distinct as to leave no room for doubt or question. It brought me to a sitting position in the bed, and the drops of sweat gathered heavily on my forehead and fell on my cold hands as I held my breath and listened.

I don't know how long I sat there—there was no further sound—and at last my tense muscles relaxed, and I fell back on the pillow.

"You fool!" I said to myself; "dead or alive, is she not your darling, your heart's heart? Would you not go near to die of joy if she came to you? Pray God to let her spirit come back and tell you she forgives you!"

"I wish she would come," myself answered in words, while every fibre of my body and mind shrank and quivered in denial.

I struck a match, lighted a candle, and breathed more freely as I looked at the polished furniture—the commonplace details of an ordinary room. Then I thought of her, lying alone, so near me, so quiet under the white sheet. She was dead; she would not wake or move. But suppose she did move? Suppose she turned back the sheet and got up, and walked across the floor and turned the door-handle?

As I thought it, I heard—plainly, unmistakably heard—the door of the chamber of death open slowly—I heard slow steps in the passage, slow, heavy steps—I heard the touch of hands on my door outside, uncertain hands, that felt for the latch.

Sick with terror, I lay clenching the sheet in my hands.

I knew well enough what would come in when that door opened—that door on which my eyes were fixed. I dreaded to look, yet I dared not turn away my eyes. The door opened slowly, slowly, slowly, and the figure of my dead wife came in. It came straight towards the bed, and stood at the bed-foot in its white grave-clothes, with the white bandage under its chin. There was a scent of lavender. Its eyes were wide open and looked at me with love unspeakable.

82

I could have shrieked aloud.

My wife spoke. It was the same dear voice that I had loved so to hear, but it was very weak and faint now; and now I trembled as I listened.

"You aren't afraid of me, darling, are you, though I am dead? I heard all you said to me when you came, but I couldn't answer. But now I've come back from the dead to tell you. I wasn't really so bad as you thought me. Elvire had told me she loved Oscar. I only wrote the letter to make it easier for you. I was too proud to tell you when you were so angry, but I am not proud any more now. You'll love me again now, won't you, now I'm dead? One always forgives dead people."

The poor ghost's voice was hollow and faint. Abject terror paralyzed me. I could answer nothing.

"Say you forgive me," the thin, monotonous voice went on; "say you love me again."

I had to speak. Coward as I was, I did manage to stammer—

"Yes; I love you. I have always loved you, God help me!"

The sound of my own voice reassured me, and I ended more firmly than I began. The figure by the bed swayed a little unsteadily.

"I suppose," she said wearily, "you would be afraid, now I am dead, if I came round to you and kissed you?"

She made a movement as though she would have come to me.

Then I did shriek aloud, again and again, and covered my face with the sheet, and wound it round my head and body, and held it with all my force.

There was a moment's silence. Then I heard my door close, and then a sound of feet and of voices, and I heard something heavy fall. I disentangled my head from the sheet. My room was empty. Then reason came back to me. I leaped from the bed.

"Ida, my darling, come back! I am not afraid! I love you! Come back! Come back!"

I sprang to my door and flung it open. Some one was bringing a light along the passage. On the floor, outside the door of the death-chamber, was a huddled heap—the corpse, in its grave-clothes. Dead, dead, dead.

CR

She is buried in Mellor churchyard, and there is no stone over her.

Now, whether it was catalepsy—as the doctors said—or whether my love came back even from the dead to me who loved her, I shall never know; but this I know—that, if I had held out my arms to her as she stood at my bed-foot—if I had said, "Yes, even from the grave, my darling—from hell itself, come back, come back to me!"—if I had had room in my coward's heart for anything but the unreasoning terror that killed love in that hour, I should not now be here alone. I shrank from her—I feared her—I would not take her to my heart. And now she will not come to me any more.

Why do I go on living?

You see, there is the child. It is four years old now, and it has never spoken and never smiled.

A story which might otherwise be discarded as a literary suicide threat to the author's own polyamorous husband ends on a decidedly intriguing note. There are several reviving elements that breathe life into the final chapter: the ambiguity of the haunting which has been labelled catalepsy by doctors, the aborted second chance at reconciliation, the failed consummation of lust and death, and the motherless child who neither smiles nor speaks. Nesbit rallies in the fourth quarter to her more standard levels of complex but elegant terror. Our despairing protagonist has much to regret, but perhaps nothing so deeply as his moral failure after the apparent resurrection of his wife (although, again, it must be reiterated that anyone who has been in a long-term relationship will scoff at the idea that this little exchange of barbs would result in such a dramatic falling out; Nesbit's own husband cohabited with and twice impregnated his favorite mistress and Nesbit fully tolerated their ménage-a-trois, going so far as to adopt her husband's illegitimate children). Dear, angelic Ida (whose selfless exile is *not* to be questioned) revives with an offer to her husband: take me as I am – all of me – mortality, corruption, flaws, sins and all, and you will have the peace that you desire. Accept me as a corruptible flesh rather than an idealistic spirit, and you shall have absolution.

II.

While we may forgive her rueful spouse for not wanting to partake in necrophilia (the subtext is very clear: she is offering him the absolving baptism of sexual intercourse with her corpse), symbolically his failure to accept his wife as a flawed mortal – decay and all – is a condemnable miscarriage of love, and action which is duly represented in his mute son who – like his father – is incapable of speaking. While the boy is silent thoroughly, his father is guilty of omitting two words – two words which his marital relationship (and consequently his son) an expressionless disappointment: "I forgive." Freud would certainly find the much to mull over in the final chapter. The sexual rejection of an amorous corpse leaves much to be analyzed, naturally conjuring the age-old interplay between Eros, genius of lust, and Thanatos, genius of Death. Sex is largely interpreted as a life-affirming act – one which reinforces one's own longings for immortality, inspires the ego with feelings of being worshiped and of possessing the virtually supernatural power of another human's lust, and literally has the ability to create life – another godlike act. Other than giving birth, sex is among the most divine acts that a human can partake in, and fills the mind with chemically-charged illusions of grandeur and immortality. To unite it, therefore, with the figure of Death has been fascinating to artists and writers for centuries – from Pluto's abduction of Persephone to the marriage bed murder committed by Frankenstein's Creature, to Nesbit's own famous "John Charrington's Wedding."

III.

In "From the Dead," Nesbit appears to take potshots at the selfishness of sex, which is touted to be a moment of supreme union and acceptance, but which is truly laden with egocentric caveats: Ida's husband is flowery in his rhetoric of regret and forgiveness until he is faced with the corpse of his wife asking him to accept her as she is (and as he is as well): a mortal destined to sin and disappoint and die and rot. Union with her corpse would be a holy moment of supreme forgiveness and acceptance, but it is more than the protagonist can bear – less because of a terror of the dead, and more from horror at this macho-busting suggestion of male servitude. To bed the dead is to deny yourself the ability to reproduce, to be awash in the pungent reality of your own mortality, and to acknowledge the bestial nature of lust, and to admit the dehumanizing horror of patriarchal marriage. It is to wash the feet of your own apostles, to eat at the table of your servants, to humble yourself to inconceivable depths of self-awareness and humility. And it is more than poor Ida's macho husband can manage. He cannot forgive her – cannot accept his looming role in her failures – and as a result he is left with a mirror image of himself: an emotionally impotent child who neither emotes nor speaks.

"THE Shadow" is Nesbit's worthiest bid for the literary ghost story – that rare genre of powerful, elegant supernaturalism that squats in your imagination for days after you read it, haunts you intermittently for weeks, and disturbs some dark and quiet spot of your soul for the rest of your life. Henry James ("The Jolly Corner," "The Real, Right Thing," "The Ghostly Rental"), Edith Wharton ("The Eyes," "The Lady's Maid's Bell"), Willa Cather ("Consequences"), and Charles Dickens ("The Signal-Man," "To Be Read at Dusk") were masters of this unusual style: a ghost story that was actually not at all about supernatural mythologies, spooky sights, or Gothic atmosphere, but rather one that was deeply concerned with the condition of the human soul. In "The Real, Right Thing" a man begins to write an unsolicited biography of his dead friend – a private man burdened with secrets – until his ghost warns him away from it for what appear to be understood but unspoken reasons. In "The Eyes" a man sees a ghostly set of eyes as a youth and doesn't realize until his old age that they were his own – wrinkled and reddened by a life of negligent greed. In "The Signal-Man" a railway worker is haunted by a vision that warns him of disasters with no hope of stopping them, filling his heart with guilt and anxiety, and ultimately drawing him to his miserable demise. These smartly written stories are far more effective at *disturbing* us than *scaring* us, but they last in our memories far longer than tales of blood and vampires. "Man-Size in Marble" and "John Charrington's Wedding" are unquestionable classics – masterpieces – of supernatural fiction, but they are still more genre pieces than literary in quality. Nesbit has achieved such philosophical heights in three other stories: "The House of Silence," "The Violet Car," and "Uncle Abraham's Romance." All four of these tales evoke that same kind of realism, moral disturbance, and plot ambiguity that are the trademark of the literary ghost story, and have a very discernable kinship to the ghost stories of James, Wharton, and Dickens. An elegant and puzzling tale, Nesbit frames it at that most ghostly setting – a Christmas party in an old house – and warns us in advance: it is a mystery to be pondered. And so it is...

———————————————

The Shadow
{1905}

THIS is not an artistically rounded-off ghost story[1], and nothing is explained in it[2], and there seems to be no reason why any of it should have happened. But that is no reason why it should not be told. You must have noticed that all the real ghost stories you have ever come close to, are like this in these respects --no explanation, no logical coherence[3]. Here is the story.

There were three of us and another[4], but she had fainted suddenly at the second extra[5] of the Christmas dance[6], and had been put to bed in the dressing room next to the room which we three shared. It had been one of those jolly, old-fashioned dances where nearly everybody stays the night, and the big country house is stretched to its utmost containing --guests harbouring on sofas, couches, settles[7] and even mattresses on floors. Some of the young men actually, I believe, slept on the great dining table. We had talked of our partners, as girls will, and then the stillness of the manor house, broken only by the whisper of the wind in the cedar branches, and the scraping of their harsh fingers against our windowpanes, had pricked us to such luxurious confidence in our surroundings of bright chintz and candle-flame and firelight, that we had dared to talk of ghosts – in which, we all said, we

---

[1] Nesbit will later cite this as the tell-tale of a fake spook story. In short, this is something between a subtle hint at authenticity and a sly humble-brag

[2] Like life. As with all of her best tales (Violet Car, House of Silence, Man-Size, etc.), this story is made primarily as a philosophical vehicle, not – as with her science fiction and farces – to entertain. This story is truly grim, and the fact that "nothing is explained by it" is less an act of self-deprecation and more one of existentialism

[3] Incidentally, this actually is true of so-called "veridical" ghost stories: the ones which are said to be true have no resolution and very little narrative. For example: "My husband and I bought our house in July, and it didn't have air conditioning. One day I was home alone with the toddler, and she came in to tell me there was a man in the bathroom. I laughed but went to check. The bathroom was freezing, and just before I left I saw – in the reflection of the mirror – a man looking at me sadly, wearing a suit from what seemed like the '30s. I looked for him all over, horrified, but never saw anyone. We never learned the backstory to this man, and have never seen him since." I made that up, but it's fairly boilerplate for veridical ghost tales

[4] Pay attention to this "other" who doesn't quite fit in; right off the bat she is described as though she belongs to some different realm or order

[5] Short for "extra quick," a phase in a dance when the regular pace increased

[6] A perfect time for a ghost story – they are a traditional part of the British Christmas, and were typically recited after supper in front of the fire while everyone was drinking port or eggnog or punch

[7] A long wooden bench with arms

did not believe one bit. We had told the story of the phantom coach[1], and the horribly strange bed[2], and the lady in the sacque[3], and the house in Berkeley Square[4].

We none of us believed in ghosts, but my heart, at least, seemed to leap to my throat and choke me there when a tap came to our door --a tap faint, not to be mistaken.

'Who's there?' said the youngest of us, craning a lean neck towards the door. It opened slowly, and I give you my word the instant of suspense that followed is still reckoned among my life's least confident moments[5]. Almost at once the door opened fully, and Miss Eastwich, my aunt's housekeeper, companion and general stand-by, looked in on us.

We all said, 'Come in,' but she stood there. She was, at all normal hours, the most silent woman I have ever known. She stood and looked at us, and shivered a little. So did we --for in those days corridors were not warmed by hot-water pipes[6] and the air from the door was keen.

---

[1] Amelia B. Edwards, "The Phantom Coach." A lost traveler is directed to wait for the approaching mail carriage, but is inadvertently collected by the ghost coach containing the corpses of the men killed in it in a wreck years earlier

[2] Wilkie Collins, "The Terribly Strange Bed." Not a ghost story, but one of horror: a successful gambler is drugged and barely avoids being smothered in a bed that uses a descending canopy. A riff on Edgar Allan Poe

[3] Sir Walter Scott, "The Tapestried Chamber." An officer recuperating in a friend's manor is wakened in the night by the swish of silk. He looks up to see a woman in an old fashioned gown with an evil face. Later he recognizes her portrait, that of a wicked ancestor. A riff on the veridical Brown Lady of Raynam Hall, a similarly attired ghost with empty sockets, seen by George IV and others

[4] Rhoda Broughton, "Nothing But the Truth." A horror in a newly bought house drives a maid mad and frightens a brave soldier to death. It is never seen by the others or explained. While Broughton gives the house a different address, the legend has been attached to 50 Berkeley Square. Opinions differ as to which came first

[5] Nesbit capably summons an atmosphere of doubt and uncertainty. The girls claim to disbelieve ghosts, but we all know that this is not true. The story promises to offer no lesson, but this is also false. If anything, Nesbit hopes to create a universe where nothing is certain and human life is frail, our motives are complex, and our hearts mysterious

[6] Creating a sense of dated-ness – we don't know what period this is set in (presumably mid-Victorian), but there is an air of antiquity and decay, as if the narrator is the only surviving witness to this episode. Incidentally, water pipes became introduced into home architecture in Britain in the 1870s and 1880s as a replacement to coal fire

'I saw your light,' she said at last, 'and I thought it was late for you to be up --after all this gaiety. I thought perhaps—' her glance turned towards the door of the dressing room[1].

'No,' I said, 'she's fast asleep.' I should have added a goodnight, but the youngest of us forestalled my speech[2]. She did not know Miss Eastwich as we others did; did not know how her persistent silence had built a wall round her --a wall that no one dared to break down with the commonplaces of talk, or the littlenesses of mere human relationship. Miss Eastwich's silence had taught us to treat her as a machine; and as other than a machine we never dreamed of treating her. But the youngest of us had seen Miss Eastwich for the first time that day. She was young, crude, ill-balanced, subject to blind, calf-like impulses[3]. She was also the heiress of a rich tallow-chandler, but that has nothing to do with this part of the story. She jumped up from the hearth rug, her unsuitably rich silk lace-trimmed dressing gown falling back from her thin collarbones, and ran to the door and put an arm round Miss Eastwich's prim, lisse-encircled neck. I gasped. I should as soon have dared to embrace Cleopatra's Needle[4]. 'Come in,' said the youngest of us --'come in and get warm. There's lots of cocoa left.' She drew Miss Eastwich in and shut the door.

The vivid light of pleasure in the housekeeper's pale eyes went through my heart like a knife[5]. It would have been so easy to put an

---

[1] Note Eastwich's concern for the fainted "other" – it is important

[2] The "Youngest" seems to represent the type of woman Nesbit hated in the core of her being – blonde, perky, flirty, coquettish. This kind of woman is savaged in "The Power of Darkness," "The Pavilion," and "Mass for the Dead." In my opinion, this represents the type of woman that Nesbit's adulterous husband had a penchant for – his typical mistress. Often they were flirtatious ingénues who were unconcerned with the impact of their actions, their social standing, or their reputation. Such a girl is represented in the loud-mouthed, dense "Youngest" – the antithesis to the dark-haired, thoughtful, sad-eyed, reputation-conscious, self-giving Nesbit

[3] Like the wedding guest caught by the Ancient Mariner, this young, saucy fool will get a lesson from her encounter with the haunted sage, and will be marked for the rest of her life by it

[4] An ancient obelisk erected in London as a gift from the Egyptian Khedive in commemoration of Lord Nelson. Unrelated to Cleopatra, the monument predates her by a millennia

[5] If the Youngest is the antithesis of Nesbit, then poor Miss Eastwich is perhaps how Nesbit saw herself – a quiet, unassuming woman neglected due to her lackluster personality – and the narrator's constant lionizing of the martyr-like Eastwich can be seen, to a degree, as a scolding to all the young ladies who passed over Nesbit in her middle age

90

arm round her neck, if one had only thought she wanted an arm there. But it was not I who had thought that --and indeed, my arm might not have brought the light evoked by the thin arm of the youngest of us.

'Now,' the youngest went on eagerly, 'you shall have the very biggest, nicest chair, and the cocoa pot's here on the hob as hot as hot --and we've all been telling ghost stories, only we don't believe in them a bit; and when you get warm you ought to tell one too.'

Miss Eastwich --that model of decorum and decently done duties[1] --tell a ghost story!

'You're sure I'm not in your way,' Miss Eastwich said, stretching her hands to the blaze. I wondered whether housekeepers have fires in their rooms even at Christmas time. 'Not a bit,' I said it, and I hope I said it as warmly as I felt it. 'I --Miss Eastwich --I'd have asked you to come in other times --only I didn't think you'd care for girls' chatter.'

The third girl, who was really of no account, and that's why I have not said anything about her before, poured cocoa for our guest. I put my fleecy Madeira shawl[2] round her shoulders. I could not think of anything else to do for her and I found myself wishing desperately to do something. The smiles she gave us were quite pretty. People can smile prettily at forty or fifty, or even later, though girls don't realise this[3]. It occurred to me, and this was another knife thrust, that I had never seen Miss Eastwich smile --a real smile --before. The pale smiles of dutiful acquiescence were not of the same blood as this dimpling, happy, transfiguring look.

'This is very pleasant,' she said, and it seemed to me that I had never before heard her real voice. It did not please me to think that at the cost of cocoa, a fire, and my arm round her neck, I might have heard this new voice any time these six years.

'We've been telling ghost stories,' I said. 'The worst of it is, we don't believe in ghosts. No one we know has ever seen one.'

'It's always what somebody told somebody, who told somebody you know,' said the youngest of us, 'and you can't believe that, can you?'

---

[1] Clearly a Victorian exemplar – a model of a distant era

[2] That is, a shawl made of Madiera lace. I'm not sure how this is supposed to be warming, but at least it's a nice gesture

[3] Nesbit's wounded pride is impossible to mistake here. As her husband cavorted with pretty girls and impregnated her best friend (twice), Nesbit understandably became jaded towards unconscientious girls. At the time of this writing Nesbit was a tellingly 47 years old

'What the soldier said is not evidence[1],' said Miss Eastwich. Will it be believed that the little Dickens quotation pierced one more keenly than the new smile or the new voice?

'And all the ghost stories are so beautifully rounded off -- a murder committed on the spot --or a hidden treasure, or a warning -- I think that makes them harder to believe[2]. The most horrid ghost story I ever heard was one that was quite silly.'

'Tell it.'

'I can't --it doesn't sound anything to tell. Miss Eastwich ought to tell one.'

'Oh, do,' said the youngest of us, and her salt cellars[3] loomed dark, as she stretched her neck eagerly and laid an entreating arm on our guest's knee.

'The only thing that I ever knew of was --was hearsay,' she said slowly, 'till just the end.'

I knew she would tell her story, and I knew she had never before told it, and I knew she was only telling it now because she was proud[4], and this seemed the only way to pay for the fire and the cocoa and the laying of that arm round her neck.

'Don't tell it,' I said suddenly. 'I know you'd rather not.'

'I dare say it would bore you,' she said meekly, and the youngest of us, who, after all, did not understand everything, glared resentfully at me.

---

[1] The quote is done very loosely. It is from Pickwick Papers:

"I mean to speak up, Sir," replied Sam, "I am in the service o' that 'ere gen'l'man, and a very good service it is."

"Little to do, and plenty to get, I suppose?" said Sergeant Buzfuz, with jocularity.

"Oh, quite enough to get, Sir, as the soldier said ven they ordered him three hundred and fifty lashes," replied Sam.

"You must not tell us what the soldier, or any other man, said, Sir," interposed the Judge, " it's not evidence."

The quote is used to evoke this sentiment: a person's personal experience can often be deemed invalid if they lack social connection

[2] This argument is made in "Number 17" as well

[3] That is, her wide eyes

[4] The meaning here is a little different than ours would be. She means that Miss Eastwich has too much self-control and dignity to make a scene by refusing: she understands that the girls are being very generous by including a servant in their conversation and doesn't have the willfulness to refuse their request

'We should just *love* it,' she said. '*Do* tell us. Never mind if it isn't a real, proper, fixed-up story. I'm certain anything *you* think ghostly would be quite too beautifully horrid for anything[1].'

Miss Eastwich finished her cocoa and reached up to set the cup on the mantelpiece.

'I can't do any harm,' she said half to herself, 'they don't believe in ghosts, and it wasn't exactly a ghost either. And they're all over twenty --they're not babies.'

There was a breathing time of hush and expectancy. The fire crackled and the gas suddenly glared higher because the billiard lights had been put out[2]. We heard the steps and voices of the men going along the corridors[3].

'It is really hardly worth telling,' Miss Eastwich said doubtfully, shading her faded face from the fire with her thin hand.

We all said, 'Go on --oh, go on --do!'

'Well,' she said, 'twenty years ago[4] --and more than that --I had two friends, and I loved them more than anything in the world. And they married each other—'

She paused, and I knew just in what way she had loved each of them[5]. The youngest of us said, 'How awfully nice for you. Do go on.'

She patted the youngest's shoulder, and I was glad that I had understood, and that the youngest of all hadn't. She went on.

'Well, after they were married, I did not see much of them for a year or two; and then he wrote and asked me to come and stay, because his wife was ill[6], and I should cheer her up, and cheer him up as well; for it was a gloomy house, and he himself was growing gloomy too.'

---

[1] Miss Eastwich – stolid, sensible, and prudent – must have a wonderful story if it was good enough to catch her attention and imagination

[2] The lights in the billiard room have been turned out, sending more gas to the light in their room – not a phenomenon experienced today with electricity

[3] As the men trundle off to bed, it truly seems a lonelier, more vulnerable house

[4] Note the time and the age of the current girls

[5] If Eastwich is the Nesbit standby, this love triangle is particularly sad because she envisions herself as the other woman. In real life, her husband Hubert had an affair with her best friend Alice Hoatson. She was impregnated twice, and when Nesbit demanded her eviction (they had a ménage a trois), Bland threatened to leave Nesbit if she insisted on it. Dutifully, she adopted her husband's love child, and when Alice became pregnant again, she adopted that one as well

[6] A very vague euphemism. She is having a rough pregnancy

I knew, as she spoke, that she had every line of that letter by heart[1].

'Well, I went. The address was in Lee[2], near London; in those days there were streets and streets of new villa houses growing up round old brick mansions standing in their own grounds, with red walls round, you know, and a sort of flavour of coaching days[3], and post-chaises[4], and Blackheath highwaymen about them[5]. He had said the house was gloomy, and it was called The Firs, and I imagined my cab going through a dark, winding shrubbery, and drawing up in front of one of these sedate, old, square houses. Instead, we drew up in front of a large, smart villa, with iron railings, gay encaustic[6] tiles leading from the iron gate to the stained-glass-panelled door, and for shrubbery only a few stunted cypresses and aucubas in the tiny front garden[7]. But inside it was all warm and welcoming. He met me at the door.'

She was gazing into the fire and I knew she had forgotten us. But the youngest girl of all still thought it was to us she was telling her story[8].

'He met me at the door,' she said again, 'and thanked me for coming, and asked me to forgive the past[9].'

'What past?' said that high priestess of the *inapropos*[10], the youngest of all.

---

[1] Nesbit regrettably dips into the well of sentimentality. This reminds one of the ghastly romantic saccharine in "From the Dead"

[2] Just west of downtown, north of Waterloo Bridge, and not far from St. Paul's Cathedral

[3] That is, the days before the train but after the advent of the coaching system — namely, the Georgian 18th century

[4] A closed carriage with room for four, usually pulled by two to six horses

[5] Robbers who stalked the countryside on London's outskirts (Blackheath being a town south of London) and were the subject of simultaneous romanticism and horror

[6] Painted with wax-based pigments

[7] Far from a rambling, English ruin, this is a highly fashionable villa with a very Italian, Tuscan vibe meant to conjure the wintering homes of wealthy Britons in Northern Italy

[8] Like the Ancient Marnier, she is not speaking to anyone in particular, but ritualistically purging herself of a sin. She is confessing, not telling, and has no thought for her audience — her audience is her own conscience

[9] There is a strong suggestion that he is sorry for more than disappointing her romantic hopes — it is implied that they may have been sexual partners at one time. Further evidence points to an even more glaring crime: Miss Eastwich may have contracted syphilis from her "friend" and may now be barren. More later

[10] Awkward, rude, or indiscreet inquiries

'Oh --I suppose he meant because they hadn't invited me before, or something,' said Miss Eastwich worriedly, 'but it's a very dull story, I find, after all, and – '

'Do go on,' I said --then I kicked the youngest of us, and got up to rearrange Miss Eastwich's shawl, and said in blatant dumb show[1], over the shawled shoulder, 'Shut up, you little idiot!'

After another silence, the housekeeper's new voice went on.

'They were very glad to see me and I was very glad to be there. You girls, now, have such troops of friends, but these two were all I had --all I had ever had[2]. Mabel wasn't exactly ill, only weak and excitable[3]. I thought he seemed more ill than she did[4]. She went to bed early and before she went, she asked me to keep him company through his last pipe[5], so we went into the dining room and sat in the two armchairs on each side of the fireplace. They were covered with green leather, I remember. There were bronze groups of horses and a black marble clock on the mantelpiece[6] --all wedding presents. He poured out some whisky for himself, but he hardly touched it. He sat looking into the fire.

At last I said, "What's wrong? Mabel looks as well as you could expect."

'He said, "Yes --but I don't know from one day to another that she won't begin to notice something wrong[7]. That's why I wanted you to

---

[1] Which is to say, she mouthed the words

[2] A sentiment that the chronically lonely Nesbit seems to have shared

[3] Again, weak from the pregnancy which is implied before Nesbit confirms it

[4] With guilt, perhaps, especially if his wife's condition has been caused by his sexually transmitted infection, putting both her and their child at risk of death

[5] Men would frequently relish one long final pipe or cigar before bed

[6] Symbols of sexual vigor and lust. The cock is, of course, a rooster, but roosters are known for having dozens and dozens of mistresses which they impregnate. Roosters are useless other than as sires for chicks and eggs, and only a few are needed for procreation. Horses are famous symbols of sexual passion and vitality, as evidenced in Fuseli's "The Nightmare" where a horse thrusts its phallic head violently through a set of unmistakably vaginal bed curtains, leering with mad eyes over a woman who is being held down in a nightmare by an incubus on her breast

[7] This is a tremendously suspicious comment which could be written off as mere husbandly coddling, but strikes my ear as suggestive and sinister. There are two things which immediately crowd to my mind: poison, which I find less likely, and a sexually transmitted disease like syphilis, which could fill in several of the other mysteries of this story. Is the husband a philanderer who has contracted a vicious VD, passed it on to his wife, and gravely complicated her pregnancy? Perhaps, and

95

come. You were always so sensible and strong-minded, and Mabel's like a little bird on a flower."

'I said yes, of course, and waited for him to go on. I thought he must be in debt, or in trouble of some sort. So I just waited. Presently he said, "Margaret, this is a very peculiar house – " He always called me Margaret. You see, we'd been such old friends[1]. I told him I thought the house was very pretty, and fresh, and home-like --only a little too new --but that fault would mend with time. He said, "It *is* new: that's just it. We're the first people who've ever lived in it. If it were an old house, Margaret, I should think it was haunted[2]."

'I asked if he had seen anything. "No," he said, "not yet."

'"Heard then?" said I.

'"No --not heard either," he said, "but there's a sort of feeling: I can't describe it --I've seen nothing and I've heard nothing, but I've been so near to seeing and hearing, just near, that's all. And something follows me about --only when I turn round, there's never anything, only my shadow[3]. And I always feel that I *shall* see the thing next minute --but I never do --not quite --it's always just not visible."

'I thought he'd been working rather hard --and tried to cheer him up by making light of all this. It was just nerves, I said. Then he said he had thought I could help him, and did I think anyone he had wronged

---

if so, his candor in the presence of Miss Eastwich complicates things further by suggesting that they may share the disease from a sexual encounter prior to his marriage. Victorian innuendo throughout the story hints that Miss Eastwich has had sexual relations with her "friend" (though probably in the years before his marriage), and that she may be barren – a frequent result of syphilitic infection in women

[1] A shockingly familiar way for a married man to address a single woman. Eastwich does well to pause here and defend their intimate address – although it does little to lessen our suspicions of an illicit past

[2] This is interesting – the story of how a haunted house becomes haunted. Usually they have been haunted for years and are decades or centuries old. But here we have a fresh, new house that is steadily being overrun by a contagion. One might imagine that this makes a convenient metaphor for the husband's infidelities and their effect on his wife: a virginal body which is inhabited by an infected tenant, whose poisons spread through the unstained flesh and corrupt it gradually with each passing day – a tabula rasa on which is projected the sins of the man who possesses it

[3] The shadow – the darkness that is revealed of a man's physical character when light is cast on it. Likewise, the shadow is used to represent the darkness that is revealed of a man's moral character when truth is cast on it. The Shadow is a symbol of guilt, truth, and sin

could have laid a curse on him, and did I believe in curses. I said I didn't --and the only person anyone could have said he had wronged forgave him freely, I knew, if there was anything to forgive. So I told him this too.'

It was I, not the youngest of us, who knew the name of that person, wronged and forgiving[1].

'So then I said he ought to take Mabel away from the house and have a complete change. But he said no; Mabel had got everything in order, and he could never manage to get her away just now without explaining everything --"and, above all," he said, "she mustn't guess there's anything wrong[2]. I dare say I shan't feel quite such a lunatic now you're here."

'So we said goodnight.'

'Is that all the story!' said the third girl, striving to convey that even as it stood it was a good story.

'That's only the beginning,' said Miss Eastwich. 'Whenever I was alone with him he used to tell me the same thing over and over again, and at first when I began to notice things, I tried to think that it was his talk that had upset my nerves. The odd thing was that it wasn't only at night --but in broad daylight --and particularly on the stairs and passages. On the staircase the feeling used to be so awful that I have had to bite my lips till they bled to keep myself from running upstairs at full speed. Only I knew if I did I should go mad at the top[3]. There was always something behind me --exactly as he had said --something that one could just not see. And a sound that one could just not hear.

---

[1] Nesbit: stupid, young girls know nothing about heartache – it takes a real woman (one middle aged, probably) to understand the consequences of love

[2] Again, we have a strong suggestion that her pregnancy has been compromised. There is no talk of doctors, so we might wonder "how does he know something is wrong? ...unless another doctor some previous time has told him something about himself that eliminates the need for a professional opinion." Mabel doesn't seem to have doctors coming to check on her, otherwise she would already know that something was wrong. I again revert to the theory that the syphilitic husband has already guessed that his wife is suffering from the disease – needing no doctor's opinion – and has enlisted Miss Eastwich as a confidant because they share one another's syphilis and she can be trusted to keep mum

[3] This passage intrigues and alludes me. What is it about the stairs in particular that invites haunting? Stairs can be seen as a metaphor for literal escalation – for ascending from a lower status (friend) to a higher one (lover). The fear that she would go insane if she let down her emotional control is a common feature in Victorian literature. Madness is, of course, also a symptom of syphilis

There was a long corridor at the top of the house. I have sometimes almost seen something --you know how one sees things without looking --but if I turned round, it seemed as if the thing drooped and melted into my shadow. There was a little window at the end of the corridor.

'Downstairs there was another corridor, something like it, with a cupboard at one end and the kitchen at the other. One night I went down into the kitchen to heat some milk for Mabel[1]. The servants had gone to bed. As I stood by the fire, waiting for the milk to boil, I glanced through the open door and along the passage. I never could keep my eyes on what I was doing in that house. The cupboard door was partly open; they used to keep empty boxes and things in it. And, as I looked, I knew that now it was not going to be "almost" any more. Yet I said, "Mabel?" not because I thought it could be Mabel who was crouching down there, half in and half out of the cupboard[2]. The thing was grey at first, and then it was black. And when I whispered, "Mabel[3]", it seemed to sink down till it lay like a pool of ink on the floor, and then its edges drew in, and it seemed to flow, like ink when you tilt up the paper you have spilt it on, and it flowed into the cupboard till it was all gathered into the shadow there. I saw it go quite plainly. The gas was full on in the kitchen. I screamed aloud, but even then, I'm thankful to say, I had enough sense to upset the boiling milk, so that when he came downstairs three steps at a time[4], I had the excuse for my scream of a scalded hand. The explanation satisfied Mabel, but next night he said, "Why didn't you tell me? It was that cupboard[5]. All the horror of the house comes out of that. Tell me -- have you seen anything yet? Or is it only the nearly seeing and nearly hearing still?"

---

[1] Commonly used to battle insomnia or settle a restless mood

[2] This sizable cupboard may be more akin to a pantry, or a small closet to store kitchen goods and food

[3] There is an unstoppable urge on Miss Eastwich's part to associate the Shadow with Mabel. This is highly telling, especially since she left Mabel in bed, we assume, and the shade could not possibly be her

[4] We may not need to read into this detail, but it strikes me as indicative of his strong feelings for Miss Eastwich that he bounds heroically towards her scream – three steps at a time

[5] I might venture to point out that a cupboard or pantry is a splendid place to hide the mercury medicine needed to combat syphilis, and if this is the case, then the cupboard is the physical dwelling place of his deception

'I said, "You must tell me first what you've seen." He told me, and his eyes wandered, as he spoke, to the shadows by the curtains, and I turned up all three gas lights, and lit the candles on the mantelpiece. Then we looked at each other and said we were both mad, and thanked God that Mabel at least was sane. For what he had seen was what I had seen.

'After that I hated to be alone with a shadow, because at any moment I might see something that would crouch, and sink, and lie like a black pool, and then slowly draw itself into the shadow that was nearest. Often that shadow was my own[1]. The thing came first at night, but afterwards there was no hour safe from it. I saw it at dawn and at noon, in the dusk and in the firelight, and always it crouched and sank, and was a pool that flowed into some shadow and became part of it. And always I saw it with a straining of the eyes --a pricking and aching. It seemed as though I could only just see it, as if my sight, to see it, had to be strained to the uttermost. And still the sound was in the house -- the sound that I could just not hear. At last, one morning early, I did hear it. It was close behind me, and it was only a sigh[2]. It was worse than the thing that crept into the shadows.

'I don't know how I bore it. I couldn't have borne it, if I hadn't been so fond of them both. But I knew in my heart that, if he had no one to whom he could speak openly, he would go mad, or tell Mabel[3]. His was not a very strong character; very sweet, and kind, and gentle, but not strong[4]. He was always easily led. So I stayed on and bore up, and we were very cheerful, and made little jokes, and tried to be amusing when

---

[1] She feels that she shares the guilt – that the Shadow is both his and hers: their joint deception (and potentially infection) of Mabel

[2] A sound made during human experiences of deep satisfaction, sorrow, or misery: all of which Miss Eastwich has felt through her relationship with Mabel's husband, and which is fittingly projected onto the Shadow

[3] So fascinating. There is definitely something that they aren't talking about, some secret. I still feel inclined to diagnose an STD, but the possibilities are many. It would truly be interesting to know what anyone else senses behind this subterfuge and nervousness

[4] To the Victorian, this unquestionably – UNQUESTIONABLY – was a code: kind, attentive, and sensitive, but not strong, not manly. This means that he is prone to give into his impulses, that he is led by his heart and his lusts, and that he is vulnerable to misguided immorality. His kindness rules out the character of a Don Juan or some corrupt, wicked tempter, but suggests a man who, like Othello, "loved not wisely but too well." This is not a Don Juan, but a Romeo – foolish, romantic, easily consumed by his romantic feelings – prone to love affairs

Mabel was with us. But when we were alone, we did not try to be amusing. And sometimes a day or two would go by without our seeing or hearing anything, and we should perhaps have fancied that we had fancied what we had seen and heard --only there was always the feeling of there being something about the house, that one could just not hear and not see. Sometimes we used to try not to talk about it, but generally we talked of nothing else at all. And the weeks went by, and Mabel's baby was born. The nurse and the doctor said that both mother and child were doing well. He and I sat late in the dining room that night. We had neither of us seen or heard anything for three days; our anxiety about Mabel was lessened. We talked of the future --it seemed then so much brighter than the past. We arranged that, the moment she was fit to be moved, he should take her away to the sea, and I should superintend the moving of their furniture into the new house he had already chosen. He was gayer than I had seen him since his marriage --almost like his old self. When I said goodnight to him, he said a lot of things about my having been a comfort to them both. I hadn't done anything much, of course, but still I am glad he said them.

'Then I went upstairs, almost for the first time without that feeling of something following me. I listened at Mabel's door. Everything was quiet. I went on towards my own room, and in an instant I felt that there *was* something behind me. I turned. It was crouching there; it sank, and the black fluidness of it seemed to be sucked under the door of Mabel's room.

'I went back. I opened the door a listening inch. All was still. And then I heard a sigh close behind me. I opened the door and went in. The nurse and the baby were asleep. Mabel was asleep too --she looked so pretty --like a tired child[1] --the baby was cuddled up into one of her arms with its tiny head against her side. I prayed then that Mabel might never know the terrors that he and I had known. That those little ears might never hear any but pretty sounds, those clear eyes never see any but pretty sights. I did not dare to pray for a long time after that. Because my prayer was answered[2]. She never saw, never

---

[1] Note the continued element of childlike innocence that Mabel is sanctified with – that her husband and best friend lack

[2] Freud would stand up, point a finger at this line, and shout "Aha!" He would be happy because this is an almost textbook case of wish fulfilment, and any poor person who experienced a similar situation would be burdened with a lifetime of misery. She loves the husband and prays an ambiguous prayer over his sleeping

heard anything more in this world. And now I could do nothing more for him or for her.

'When they had put her in her coffin, I lighted wax candles round her, and laid the horrible white flowers that people will send near her, and then I saw he had followed me. I took his hand to lead him away[1].

'At the door we both turned. It seemed to us that we heard a sigh[2]. He would have sprung to her side in I don't know what mad, glad hope. But at that instant we both saw it. Between us and the coffin, first grey, then black, it crouched an instant, then sank and liquefied --and was gathered together and drawn till it ran into the nearest shadow. And the nearest shadow was the shadow of Mabel's coffin[3]. I left the next day. His mother came. She had never liked me[4].'

Miss Eastwich paused. I think she had quite forgotten us[5].

---

wife that – "Monkey's Paw"-style – gets answered in a way that satisfies her selfish desire: to have the husband alone to herself. Surely she must imagine that it was her repressed (if we can even call it that) love for the husband that killed Mabel

[1] Here is the continued theme of inappropriate intimacy and the man who is in need of female leadership – a man who is servile to his feelings and fancies. They depart Mabel's coffin like a bride and groom departing an altar – hand in hand, one leading the other into a new future. But it is, of course, a mockery of a wedding, and the result is misery manifest

[2] They were unquestionably on their way to begin a new life together, but their union is kept apart by the manifestation of the Shadow: whatever it represents – guilt, shame, anger, jealousy, physical infection – it will not allow these two to become one

[3] The Shadow cleaves to the meaning of Mabel's death – whatever it means to the two characters. This might be an indictment against them, a retreat to their memory of her, or something else. I personally suspect that the Shadow is a great finger pointing to the coffin with an air of incrimination and accusation. It now leaves its former abode in the cupboard (where mercury medicine may have been hidden) to the coffin where the fruits of their indiscretions and deceptions has been harvested: Mabel's fooled, coddled corpse

[4] The husband may unsurprisingly be nursing a Freudian attachment to his mother. At any rate, this opinionated woman has a strong dislike for Miss Eastwich – a sure sign of unwholesomeness in a Victorian novel. During this era more than any before it the idea of "mother" and of a son's dutiful devotion to his mother (rather than his father, his family, or his country) was being espoused. His mother's disapproval casts its own shadow on Eastwich, reinforcing the idea that she may be aware of a shocking scandal between her son and his little friend

[5] Again, this story-telling process appears to be a cathartic, almost therapeutic act of confession for the emotionally-burdened Miss Eastwich -- it has virtually nothing to do with the listeners and is largely a form of psychological introspection

'Didn't you see him again?' asked the youngest of us all.

'Only once,' Miss Eastwich answered, 'and something black crouched then between him and me. But it was only his second wife, crying beside his coffin[1]. It's not a cheerful story, is it? And it doesn't lead anywhere. I've never told anyone else[2]. I think it was seeing his daughter that brought it all back[3].'

She looked towards the dressing-room door.

'Mabel's baby?'

'Yes --and exactly like Mabel, only with his eyes[4].'

The youngest of all had Miss Eastwich's hands and was petting them[5].

Suddenly the woman wrenched her hands away and stood at her gaunt height, her hands clenched, eyes straining. She was looking at something that we could not see[6], and I know what the man in the Bible meant when he said, 'The hair of my flesh stood up.'[7]

What she saw seemed not quite to reach the height of the dressing-room door handle. Her eyes followed it down, down --widening and widening. Mine followed them --all the nerves of them seemed strained to the uttermost --and I almost saw --or did I quite see? I can't be

---

[1] The Shadow is now linked with the image of a widow hunched in mourning. Has the Shadow been a premonition of his death, possibly from symptoms of a venereal disease – the same which took his wife and – potentially – his daughter in the future? In any case, it is clear: the Shadow is a harbinger of death

[2] This confession seems to absolve Eastwich of her sins, and although it is at a cost, it also leads up to her complete release from this tragic narrative through the death of the daughter

[3] The girl who fainted in the beginning ties this story all together and this revelation immediately ramps up the tension and intensity of this heretofore plaintive plot: now there is some skin in the game, something at stake to be lost or better understood

[4] The eyes being the windows to the soul, we can assume that his daughter has inherited his spirit, kind but weak-willed, and perhaps his guilt

[5] The telling of the tale has had a transformative effect on the young brat. Like the wedding guest who hears the tale of the Ancient Mariner, she leaves the encounter with this personification of remorse and sad wisdom "a sadder and a wiser" girl – matured and developed by the cathartic experience of hearing the melancholy tale of warning

[6] Nesbit uses remarkable control and avoids telling us outright that she has seen the long absent Shadow – harbinger of death – allowing the reader to make the grim connection

[7] Job 4:15 "A spirit glided past my face, and the hair of my flesh stood up"

certain. But we all heard the long-drawn, quivering sigh. And to each of us it seemed to be breathed just behind us.

It was I who caught up the candle --it dripped all over my trembling hand --and was dragged by Miss Eastwich to the girl who had fainted during the second extra. But it was the youngest of all whose lean arms were round the housekeeper when we turned away, and that have been round her many a time since, in the new home where she keeps house for the youngest of us[1].

The doctor who came in the morning said that Mabel's daughter had died of heart disease --which she had inherited from her mother[2]. It was that that had made her faint during the second extra. But I have sometimes wondered whether she may not have inherited something from her father[3]. I had never been able to forget the look on her dead face[4].

---

[1] The experience has been so emotionally traumatizing that the youngest girl has taken it upon herself to house and nourish the childless, loveless Miss Eastwich. If we are correct in reading Eastwich as barren from syphilis, and in viewing the couple's daughter as her vicarious child, then the youngest girl rewards her years of silent remorse by becoming her adoptive daughter – a reward that might be little comfort to poor Miss Eastwich

[2] Heart diseases in literature are traditionally seen as symbolic of a crushed spirit or a guilty conscience – one's heart is literally and figuratively afflicted. Such might be the case if a woman were to know that her husband had been sexually or emotionally involved with a close friend

[3] This is such a loaded comment! What does she mean? In the literal sense she may have congenital syphilis transferred from her father to her mother, which may have weakened her body, some of the symptoms of which include enlarged organs which would be prone to failure. On a more spiritual tack, the one trait that we are assured of on his part is a kind but weak nature – a Romeo-esque predilection for feeling over prudence and emotion over sense. Perhaps his daughter is also of this kind – a passionate but naïve girl driven to emotional weakness and acts of indiscretion. She may have had a tumultuous affair with one of the men in the dining room, or she may be afflicted with a venereal disease of her own from a past relationship. In any case, the narrator seems to suggest that the girl carries her father's weaknesses in her spirit, and suggests that they are to blame for her death. We are left to connect the dots

[4] What emotion could it possibly have expressed? This is tremendously cryptic and tremendously alluring. There can be no question now that Nesbit is writing in code, and that this code – if unraveled – will reveal that emotion: fear? Rage? Meekness? What emotion could she possibly have been projecting that would have drawn a line to the man in Miss Eastwich's short tale?

As my notes will reveal, I have a strong opinion about the meaning of this story, but my interpretation is certainly not gospel, so feel free to dissent. I have read the story many times, and it wasn't until the second-to-last time before I began to write my notes that a meaning emerged from the shadows. In my opinion, this is a deeply personal story about the consequences of a free-living lifestyle, the moral damages of guilt, and the brutal pain of a love triangle. Nesbit writes herself into the story repeatedly: she (47 at the time, and constantly aware of Hubert Bland's taste for silly, young girls) warns young women from dismissing homely, middle aged ladies ("People can smile prettily at forty or fifty, or even later, though girls don't realise this"); she creates a character – the youngest girl, pretty, vain, obtuse – who is then eviscerated by the narrator as a pompous and self-involved coquette; she writes of a ménage-a-trois between a married couple and a single female friend, and of a pregnancy overshadowed by unhappiness and shame (like those of her one-time best friend Alice Hoatson, who became Bland's live-in mistress and bore him two children, whom Nesbit raised as her own). Throughout the story we see imagery and hear innuendo that suggest that the relationship between Miss Eastwich and "*him*" is not one of innocent unrequited love. Her "friend" – who brazenly calls her by her first name in spite of all codes of propriety between married and single persons of the opposite gender – has one explicit character flaw: "His was not a very strong character; very sweet, and kind, and gentle, but not strong. He was easily led." Led by his emotions. Led by his lusts. Led by his desires and the women in his life. Led from the coffin by Miss Eastwich. Led from Miss Eastwich by his disapproving mother. He is a man who is generous but lacks self-control, and an affair between the two conspirators is easy to imagine. On the page that's what it sounds like, but between the lines I sense something far more sinister: there is a strong suggestion that "he" is sorry for more than disappointing her romantic hopes – it is implied that they may have been sexual partners at one time. Further evidence points to an even more glaring crime: Miss Eastwich may have contracted syphilis from her "friend" and may now be barren. And there is more – if so, is the husband a philanderer who has contracted a vicious VD, passed it on to his wife, and gravely complicated her pregnancy? Perhaps, and if that is indeed so, his candor in the presence of Miss Eastwich complicates things further by suggesting that they may share the disease from a sexual encounter prior to his marriage. Victorian innuendo throughout the story hints that Miss Eastwich has had sexual relations with her "friend" (though probably in the years before his marriage), and that she may be barren – a frequent result of syphilitic infection in women. Certainly our two characters are tremendously suspicious to behold: they anxiously play doctor to his wife without ever telling her about her affliction – whatever its nature may be – and try their hardest to keep her in the dark. No doctors seem to visit until the birth, and they are very clear that there is something specifically wrong – not just a pregnancy. "I don't know [whether she] will begin to notice something wrong," he says conspiratorially. They work feverishly to distract Mabel, but it is no good: Mabel dies the night that Miss Eastwich breathes an ambiguous prayer that she should hear, see, and know no evil ever again. Freud would call this cut and dry wish fulfilment – she prays vaguely for Mabel to be at peace, and we are left to wonder what her emotional response was to the response to this prayer which she herself calls an affirmative response. But then comes the Shadow.

II.

What this entity represents is certainly up to interpretation, but it can clearly be seen as a response to the relationship between the three friends: it may be a manifestation of "his" guilt, shame, desire, embarrassment, and fear; it may be Miss Eastwich's jealousy, anger, resentment, repression, lust, and hate; it may be Mabel's jealousy, repression, suspicion, and unspoken knowledge of the affair. Perhaps it is a combination or selection of these, or something entirely different, but one thing it is *not* is a conventional ghost. They live in a new house, fresh and without history, yet it festers with the infection passed to it from the first couple to live there. Nesbit defies Gothic conventions by avoiding an old home, making the unconventional haunting all the more chilling. We hear one particularly telling detail from Miss Eastwich: "[It would] draw itself into the shadow that was nearest. Often that shadow was my own." Freud, Jung, and Lacan are now all on high alert. The Shadow appears to be a projection of the two friends' own guilty consciences. Afterall, a shadow is the darkness that is revealed of a man's physical character when light is cast on it. Likewise, the Shadow is used to represent the darkness that is revealed of these two friends' *moral* character when the truth is cast over them. The

Shadow is a symbol of guilt, truth, and sin. That is dwells in a cupboard where one might be expected to secretly store the mercury required to combat the effects of syphilis might be my reading too much into things, *but* it is certainly meaningful to Nesbit that the Shadow lives in that particular spot. Perhaps it is the hiding place of a poison, instead – an alternative to my theory – with which the couple (for such they are) dose Mabel's nightly milk. The most terrifying moment in the story is when Eastwich sees the Shadow brooding in the cupboard and weakly imagines it to be her sick friend crouched in its darkness like a toad: Mabel is what they fear – her hate, her knowledge of their past, her impediment to their future. And in the end, Mabel comes between them for good when the Shadow of her coffin parts them forever. This is one of Nesbit's most complex stories – one unquestionably worthy of Henry James of Edith Wharton – and genuinely one of the most powerful literary ghost stories ever written. It follows the model of Coleridge's "Rime of the Ancient Mariner" wherein a busy man is stopped by a spiritually-scarred, wandering outcast who forces him to hear the tale of his greatest sin, and then leaves the encounter fundamentally changed. The same happens between the "youngest girl" and Miss Eastwich – she begins the story vain, petty, and dense, and ends it traumatized, solemn, and responsible, even taking in Miss Eastwich as her own maid, as if they are now sharing a moral burden together. The same is true of its readers: we put the tale down. Our brows are furrowed, our minds confused, our hearts disturbed. We walk away different than we came.

NESBIT mastered the late Victorian clairvoyant tale, and this very short sketch – almost flash fiction – is an underappreciated jewel of her work. Her stories featured calamity reaching out of the invisible world, afflicting completely innocent persons. Most Victorian tales of this genre – the clairvoyant dream – result in prevention and avoidance (Riddell's "Forewarned, Forearmed" is a fine example). While the vision is partially avoided, it proves fateful, challenging Victorians' optimism and trust in the power of will and industry. Apparently based on Rhoda Broughton's dreary, pessimistic (and horrendously gory) clairvoyant story, "Behold, it was a Dream!," this tale offers a glimpse into a misanthropic and incomprehensible cosmos – hostile and cruelly indifferent to the efforts of human diligence. This report is called "The Mystery of the Semi-Detached," and it is no misnomer because unanswered questions and unoffered explanation fuel the heat of the revulsion this sketch engenders. Grim, cynical, and inexplicable, the vision of the semi-detached is perhaps more atrocious to the unwitting, helpless seer than to its slaughtered victim.

The Mystery of the Semi-Detached
{1893}

HE was waiting for her, he had been waiting an hour and a half in a dusty suburban lane, with a row of big elms on one side and some eligible building sites on the other – and far away to the south-west the twinkling yellow lights of the Crystal Palace[1]. It was not quite like a country lane, for it had a pavement and lamp-posts, but it was not a bad place for a meeting[2] all the same: and farther up, towards the cemetery, it was really quite rural, and almost pretty, especially in twilight. But twilight had long deepened into the night, and still he waited. He loved her, and he was engaged to be married to her, with the complete disapproval of every reasonable person who had been

---

[1] Massive cast iron and plate glass structure built in Hyde Park, London, to house the Great Exhibition of 1851. It was (appropriately) 1,851 feet long and 128 feet high

[2] By "meeting" he means a tryst. The nature of this meeting – combined with the family's disapproval, and with his later familiarity with her bedroom – suggest a sexual encounter

consulted[1]. And this half-clandestine meeting was tonight to take the place of the grudgingly sanctioned weekly interview[2] –because a certain rich uncle was visiting at her house, and her mother was not the woman to acknowledge to a moneyed uncle, who might "go off" any day, a match so deeply ineligible as hers with him[3].

So he waited for her, and the chill of an unusually severe May evening entered into his bones[4].

The policeman passed him with a surly response to his "Good night". The bicyclists went by him like grey ghosts with foghorns; and it was nearly ten o'clock, and she had not come[5].

He shrugged his shoulders and turned towards his lodgings. His road led him by her house—desirable, commodious, semi-detached[6]—and he walked slowly as he neared it. She might, even now, be coming out. But she was not There was no sign of movement about the house, no sign of life, no lights even in the windows. And her people were not early people. He paused by the gate, wondering.

Then he noticed that the front door was open-wide open-and the street lamp shone a little way into the dark hail. There was something about all this that did not please him—that scared him a little, indeed. The house had a gloomy and deserted air. It was obviously impossible that it harboured a rich uncle. The old man must have left early. In which case—

He walked up the path of patent glazed tiles, and listened. No sign of life. He passed into the hall. There was no light anywhere. Where was everybody, and why was the front door open? There was no one in the drawing room, the dining room and the study (nine feet by seven) were

---

[1] Stubborn, proud, and resistant to external advice, the couple who feature in this tale are universally disapproved of. This might be due to a difference in social rank or in personality, character, or disposition, but subtle clues throughout the piece imply that the libertine nature of their "meetings" have caused a moral scandal

[2] The couple pay court to each other only once a week due to the disapproval of the families

[3] The concern here is that the wealthy uncle who may die at any moment would disinherit his niece if he was made aware of the pairing

[4] It is important to note the emotional backdrop that Nesbit has woven: before encountering the horror, the protagonist's personal life is fraught with uncertainty, whisperings, and danger

[5] Once again, ten o'clock is a very late hour for a respectable, unmarried couple to be rendezvousing – the meeting is almost certainly not of a reputable nature

[6] That is to say, a duplex; two identical houses built alongside one another sharing a party wall and a floor plan Chic, modern, and fashionable for a young woman of society

equally blank. Everyone was out, evidently. But the unpleasant sense that he was, perhaps, not the first casual visitor to walk through that open door impelled him to look through the house before he went away and closed it after him. So he went upstairs, and at the door of the first bedroom he came to he struck a wax match, as he had done in the sitting rooms[1]. Even as he did so he felt that he was not alone. And he was prepared to see something but for what he saw he was not prepared. For what he saw lay on the bed, in a white loose gown—and it was his sweetheart, and its[2] throat was cut from ear to ear[3]. He doesn't know what happened then, nor how he got downstairs and into the street; but he got out somehow, and the policeman found him in a fit, under the lamp-post at the corner of the street. He couldn't speak when they picked him up, and he passed the night in the police cells, because the policeman had seen plenty of drunken men before, but never one in a fit[4].

The next morning he was better, though still very white and shaky. But the tale he told the magistrate[5] was convincing, and they sent a couple of constables with him to her house.

There was no crowd about it as he had fancied there would be, and

---

[1] The scandalous nature of the protagonist and his fiancée's relationship is apparent in their friends' responses, but it is heavily implied by his intrusion into the bedroom – an act of familiarity that would have been perceived as indecent and crass. The Freudian implications of his disquieting sense that he was "not the first casual visitor to walk through [the] open door" of her apartment and his subsequent suspicious intrusion into the bedroom may speak to the loose sexual nature of their relationship, and the anxieties of a man who is undaunted by entering into an erotic relationship with a woman, but desperately resents any previous dalliances with past lovers. Has anyone else entered this room?

[2] Laid suggestively across a bed, dressed in what appears to be a revealing, negligee-like garment, with her throat viciously mangled, the figure is comfortably codified as a victim of rape. Considering the suspected nature of his relationship with his fiancée, the protagonist almost certainly feels a soup of emotions on seeing her sexually-receptive body violated: outrage, sorrow, and agony, yes, but also jealousy, suspicion, and lust

[3] The rapacious imagery is self-incriminating. The protagonist will be the first suspect, will have no alibi, and will have had excellent opportunity, but beyond these simply logistical issues, psychologically he must question his ability to perform such an act

[4] Agitated to the point of wild spasms and convulsions

[5] He has been taken to jail as a suspected drunk, but successfully appeals his case

the blinds were not down[1].

He held on to the door-post for support...

"She's all right, you see," said the constable, who had found him under the lamp. "I told you you was drunk, but you would know best—"

When he was alone with her he told her—not all—for that would not bear telling—but how he had come into the commodious[2] semi-detached, and how he had found the door open and the lights out, and that he had been into that long back room facing the stairs, and had seen something—in even trying to hint at which he turned sick and broke down and had to have brandy given him.

"But, my dearest," she said, "I dare say the house was dark, for we were all at the Crystal Palace with my uncle, and no doubt the door was open, for the maids will run out if they're left. But you could not have been in that room, because I locked it when I came away, and the key was in my pocket. I dressed in a hurry and I left all my odds and ends lying about."

"I know," he said; "I saw a green scarf on a chair, and some long brown gloves, and a lot of hairpins and ribbons, and a prayerbook, and a lace handkerchief on the dressing table. Why, I even noticed the almanack on the mantelpiece—21 October. At least it couldn't be that, because this is May. And yet it was. Your almanack is at 21 October, isn't it?"

"No, of course it isn't," she said, smiling rather anxiously; "but all the other things were just as you say. You must have had a dream, or a vision, or something[3]."

He was a very ordinary, commonplace, City young man, and he didn't believe in visions, but he never rested day or night till he got his sweetheart and her mother away from that commodious semi-detached, and settled them in a quiet distant suburb[4]. In the course of the removal

---

[1] A traditional practice during mourning done to keep the family's trauma private

[2] Comfortable, inviting

[3] Considering that the articles on the dressing table were all hers, the vision certainly suggests that the disaster would have befallen her had not her fiancée been supernaturally alerted. The mangled woman on the bed was not meant to be anyone other than her – without the interference of fate – and the implications suggest that the future killer may indeed have been our protagonist (inspired by who knows what – jealousy, anxiety, lust) had he continued courting her in that place

[4] The theme of the corrupting influence of the city versus the purifying spirit of the country runs throughout this brief piece – in the beginning he is comforted by the

he incidentally married her, and the mother went on living with them[1].

His nerves must have been a good bit shaken, because he was very queer for a long time, and was always enquiring if anyone had taken the desirable semi-detached; and when an old stockbroker with a family took it, he went the length of calling on the old gentleman and imploring him by all that he held dear, not to live in that fatal house.

"Why?" said the stockbroker, not unnaturally.

And then he got so vague and confused, between trying to tell why and trying not to tell why, that the stockbroker showed him out, and thanked his God he was not such a fool as to allow a lunatic to stand in the way of his taking that really remarkably cheap[2] and desirable semi-detached residence.

Now the curious and quite inexplicable part of this story is that when she came down to breakfast on the morning of the 22 October she found him looking like death, with the morning paper in his hand. He caught hers—he couldn't speak, and pointed to the paper. And there she read that on the night of the 21st a young lady, the stockbroker's daughter, had been found, with her throat cut from ear to ear, on the bed in the long back bedroom facing the stairs of that desirable semi-detached[3].

---

almost "rural" scenery of Hyde Park while the Crystal Palace gleams coldly in the background

[1] A life of "semi-clandestine" courtship – including, I suspect, sexual exploration – has been traded for a settled, domestic life with a respectable marriage and a settled mother-in-law

[2] Recall "Nothing But the Truth" – could the low price of the Semi-Detached be due to the fact that some influence inhabits it, which causes tragedies to occur there?

[3] With no report of a burglary or of stolen items (as may explain a person's murder in their sleep), with no suggestion of a family-wide massacre (as may befall a rich and important man), and no mention of a loud brawl between lovers (as may befall a young woman whose throat is cut), the implication is that the girl was slain while sleeping in bed, and that the crime extends beyond murder to rape. By whom is unimportant to Nesbit – the antagonist is the spirit that inhabits the house, and it may be possessing any of a variety of faceless, motiveless agents

A brief sketch in raw horror (elegant terror takes the back seat in this nightmarish episode), Nesbit's story begins with an emotional atmosphere in an unlikely setting. Bourgeois, posh, and refined, the neighborhood is nonetheless crawling with unease. The policeman's brusque salute, the fog-polluted avenues, and the protagonist's brooding mind introduce us to an impressionistic landscape of doom. Little time passes before the young man casually enters the gaping door and stumbles on the gore-drenched vision. The mechanics of the vision are never explained: who was the murderer, why did the vision appear to the young fellow, and why was the butchery and inevitability? Nesbit is not concerned with explaining the supernatural engineering to her story, but with the emotional trauma of the young man and the cruel unflappability of fate. Powerless to prevent the murder – one with definite overtones of sexual violence – he is deflated from a reckless playboy to a shaken phantom of his former self. Formerly engaged in a sexually scandalous relationship (familiar with his lover's bedroom and resistant to the "complete disapproval of every reasonable person who had been consulted") the protagonist is shocked into adopting a safe and settled lifestyle of cautious marriage. The power of a single episode of horror to utterly transform a man's spirit is the heart of Nesbit's cynical meditation.

NOT all of Nesbit's marriage pieces follow the same pattern (though of course, most of them do), and while this story begins with a predicatble plot, the twist is genuinely clever, and filled with an unsettling stew of emotions. It begins with a man who is infatuated with a woman who says she loves him but is content to marry a relative stranger for the money that he has promised to pay her destitute father. On the eve of her wedding the wilted suitor hears a gloomy funeral mass drifting from some unseen place. Shaken by what he takes to be a sign of impending disaster, he finds that the bride has heard the same music, and writes it off as a coincidence. But there is a reason for funerary music looming in the future, and until you arrive at the last page the subject of the mass for the dead will likely surprise you.

The Mass for the Dead
{1892}

I was awake—widely, cruelly awake. I had been awake all night; what sleep could there be for me when the woman I loved was to be married next morning—married, and not to me?

I went to my room early; the family party in the drawing-room maddened me. Grouped about the round table with the stamped plush cover, each was busy with work, or book, or newspaper, but not too busy to stab my heart through and through with their talk of the wedding.

Her people were near neighbours of mine, so why should her marriage not be canvassed in my home circle?

They did not mean to be cruel; they did not know that I loved her; but she knew it. I told her, but she knew it before that. She knew it from the moment when I came back from three years of musical study in Germany—came back and met her in the wood where we used to go nutting when we were children.

I looked into her eyes, and my whole soul trembled with thankfulness that I was living in a world that held her also. I turned and walked by her side, through the tangled green wood, and we talked of the long-ago days, and it was, "Have you forgotten?" and "Do you remember?" till we reached her garden gate. Then I said—

"Good-bye; no, *auf wiedersehn*, and in a very little time, I hope."

And she answered—

117

"Good-bye. By the way, you haven't congratulated me yet."

"Congratulated you?"

"Yes, did I not tell you I am to marry Mr. Benoliel next month?"

And she turned away, and went up the garden slowly.

I asked my people, and they said it was true. Kate, my dear playfellow, was to marry this Spaniard, rich, wilful, accustomed to win, polished in manners and base in life. Why was she to marry him?

"No one knows," said my father, "but her father is talked about in the city, and Benoliel, the Spaniard, is rich. Perhaps that's it."

That was it. She told me so when, after two weeks spent with her and near her, I implored her to break so vile a chain and to come to me, who loved her—whom she loved.

"You are quite right," she said calmly. We were sitting in the window-seat of the oak parlour in her father's desolate old house. "I do love you, and I shall marry Mr. Benoliel."

"Why?"

"Look around you and ask me why, if you can."

I looked around—on the shabby, bare room, with its faded hangings of sage-green moreen, its threadbare carpet, its patched, washed-out chintz chair-covers. I looked out through the square, latticed window at the ragged, unkempt lawn, at her own gown—of poor material, though she wore it as queens might desire to wear ermine—and I understood.

Kate is obstinate; it is her one fault; I knew how vain would be my entreaties, yet I offered them; how unavailing my arguments, yet they were set forth; how useless my love and my sorrow, yet I showed them to her.

"No," she answered, but she flung her arms round my neck as she spoke, and held me as one may hold one's best treasure. "No, no; you are poor, and he is rich. You wouldn't have me break my father's heart: he's so proud, and if he doesn't get some money next month, he will be ruined. I'm not deceiving any one. Mr. Benoliel knows I don't care for him; and if I marry him, he is going to advance my father a large sum of money. Oh, I assure you that everything has been talked over and settled. There is no going from it."

"Child! child!" I cried, "how calmly you speak of it! Don't you see that you are selling your soul and throwing mine away?"

"Father Fabian says I am doing right," she answered, unclasping her hands, but holding mine in them, and looking at me with those clear, grey eyes of hers. "Are we to be unselfish in everything else, and in love to think only of our own happiness? I love you, and I shall marry him. Would you rather the positions were reversed?"

"Yes," I said, "for then I would make you love me."

"Perhaps *he* will," she said bitterly. Even in that moment her mouth trembled with the ghost of a smile. She always loved to tease. She goes through more moods in a day than most other women in a year. Drowning the smile came tears, but she controlled them, and she said—

"Good-bye; you see I am right, don't you? Oh, Jasper, I wish I hadn't told you I loved you. It will only make you more unhappy."

"It makes my one happiness," I answered; "nothing can take that from me. And that happiness *he* will never have. Say again that you love me!"

"I love you! I love you! I love you!"

With further folly of tears and mad loving words we parted, and I bore my heartache away, leaving her to bear hers into her new life.

And now she was to be married to-morrow, and I could not sleep.

When the darkness became unbearable I lighted a candle, and then lay staring vacantly at the roses on the wall-paper, or following with my eyes the lines and curves of the heavy mahogany furniture.

The solidity of my surroundings oppressed me. In the dull light the wardrobe loomed like a hearse, and my violin case looked like a child's coffin.

I reached a book and read till my eyes ached and the letters danced a *pas fantastique* up and down the page.

I got up and had ten minutes with the dumbbells. I sponged my face and hands with cold water and tried again to sleep—vainly. I lay there, miserably wide awake.

I tried to say poetry, the half-forgotten tasks of my school days even, but through everything ran the refrain—

"Kate is to be married to-morrow, and not to me, not to me!"

I tried counting up to a thousand. I tried to imagine sheep in a lane, and to count them as they jumped through a gap in an imaginary hedge—all the time-honoured spells with which sleep is wooed—vainly.

Then the Waits came, and a torture to the nerves was superadded to the torture of the heart. After fifteen minutes of carols every fibre of me seemed vibrating in an agony of physical misery.

To banish the echo of "The Mistletoe Bough," I hummed softly to myself a melody of Palestrina's, and felt more awake than ever.

Then the thing happened which nothing will ever explain. As I lay there I heard, breaking through and gradually overpowering the air I was suggesting, a harmony which I had never heard before, beautiful beyond description, and as distinct and definite as any song man's ears have ever listened to.

My first half-formed thought was, "more Waits," but the music was choral music, true and sweet; with it mingled an organ's notes, and with every note the music grew in volume. It is absurd to suggest that I dreamed it, for, still hearing the music, I leaped out of bed and opened the window. The music grew fainter. There was no one to be seen in the snowy garden below. Shivering, I shut the window. The music grew more distinct, and I became aware that I was listening to a mass—a funeral mass, and one which I had never heard before. I lay in my bed and followed the whole course of the office.

The music ceased.

I was sitting up in bed, my candle alight, and myself as wide awake as ever, and more than ever possessed by the thought of *her*.

But with a difference. Before, I had only mourned the loss of her: now, my thoughts of her were mingled with an indescribable dread. The sense of death and decay that had come to me with that strange, beautiful music, coloured all my thoughts. I was filled with fancies of hushed houses, black garments, rooms where white flowers and white linen lay in a deathly stillness. I heard echoes of tears, and of dim-voiced bells tolling monotonously. I shivered, as it were on the brink of irreparable woe, and in its contemplation I watched the dull dawn slowly overcome the pale flame of my candle, now burnt down into its socket.

I felt that I must see Kate once again before she gave herself away. Before ten o'clock I was in the oak parlour. She came to me. As she entered the room, her pallor, her swollen eyelids and the misery in her eyes wrung my heart as even that night of agony had not done. I literally could not speak. I held out my hands.

Would she reproach me for coming to her again, for forcing upon her a second time the anguish of parting?

She did not. She laid her hands in mine, and said—

"I am thankful you have come; do you know, I think I am going mad? Don't let me go mad, Jasper."

The look in her eyes underlined her words.

I stammered something and kissed her hands. I was with her again, and joy fought again with grief.

"I must tell some one. If I am mad, don't lock me up. Take care of me, won't you?"

Would I not?

"Understand," she went on, "it was not a dream. I was wide awake, thinking of you. The Waits had not long gone, and I—I was looking at your likeness. I was not asleep."

I shivered as I held her fast.

"As Heaven sees us, I did not dream it. I heard a mass sung, and, Jasper, it was a mass for the dead. I followed the office. You are not a Catholic, but I thought—I feared—oh, I don't know what I thought. I am thankful there is nothing wrong with you."

I felt a sudden certainty, and complete sense of power possess me. Now, in this her moment of weakness, while she was so completely under the influence of a strong emotion, I could and would save her from Benoliel, and myself from life-long pain.

"Kate," I said, "I believe it is a warning. You shall not marry this man. You shall marry me, and none other."

She leaned her head against my shoulder; she seemed to have forgotten her father and all the reasons for her marriage with Benoliel.

"You don't think I'm mad? No? Then take care of me; take me away; I feel safe with you."

Thus all obstacles vanished in less time than the length of a lover's kiss. I dared not stop to consider the coincidence of supernatural warning—nor what it might mean. Face to face with crowned hope, I am proud to remember that common sense held her own. The room in which we were had a French window. I fetched her garden hat and a shawl from the hall, and we went out through the still, white garden. We did not meet a soul. When we reached my father's garden I took her in by the back way, to the summer-house, and left her, though I was half afraid to leave her, while I went into the house. I snatched my violin and cheque book, took all my spare money, scrawled a line to my father and rejoined her.

Still no one had seen us.

We walked to a station five miles away; and by the time Benoliel would reach the church, I was leaving Doctors' Commons with a special licence in my pocket. Two hours later Kate was my wife, and we were quietly and prosaically eating our wedding-breakfast in the dining-room of the Grand Hotel.

"And where shall we go?" I said.

"I don't know," she answered, smiling; "you have not much money, have you?"

122

"Oh dear me, yes. I'm not rich, but I'm not absolutely a church mouse."

"Could we go to Devonshire?" she asked, twisting her new ring round and round.

"Devonshire! Why, that is where——"

"Yes, I know: Benoliel arranged to go there. Jasper, I am afraid of Benoliel."

"Then why——"

"Foolish person," she answered. "Do you think that Benoliel will be likely to go to Devonshire *now*?"

We went to Devonshire—I had had a small legacy a few months earlier, and I did not permit money cares to trouble my new and beautiful happiness. My only fear was that she would be saddened by thoughts of her father; but I am thankful to remember that in those first days she, too, was happy—so happy that there seemed to be hardly room in her mind for any thought but of me. And every hour of every day I said to my soul—

"But for that portent, whatever it boded, she might have been not my wife but his."

The first four or five days of our marriage are flowers that memory keeps always fresh. Kate's face had recovered its wild-rose bloom, and she laughed and sang and jested and enjoyed all our little daily adventures with the fullest, freest-hearted gaiety. Then I committed the supreme imbecility of my life—one of those acts of folly on which one looks back all one's life with a half stamp of the foot, and the unanswerable question, "How on earth could I have been such a fool?"

We were sitting in a little sitting-room, hideous in intention, but redeemed by blazing fire and the fact that two were there, sitting hand-in-hand, gazing into the fire and talking of their future and of their love. There was nothing to trouble us; no one had discovered our whereabouts, and my wife's fear of Benoliel's revenge seemed to have dissolved before the flame of our happiness.

And as we sat there, peaceful and untroubled, the Imp of the Perverse jogged my elbow, as, alas! he does so often, and I was moved to tell my wife that I, too, had heard that unearthly midnight music—that her hearing of it was not, as she had grown to think, a mere nightmare—a strange dream—but something more strange, more significant. I told her how I had heard the mass for the dead, and all the tale of that night. She listened silently, and I thought her strangely indifferent. When I had finished, she took her hand from mine and covered her face.

"I believe it was a warning to us to flee temptation. We ought never to have married. Oh, my poor father!"

Her tone was one that I had never heard before. Its hopeless misery appalled me. And justly. For no arguments, no entreaties, no caresses, could win my wife back to the mood of an hour before.

She tried to be cheerful, but her gaiety was forced, and her laughter stung my heart.

She spoke no more about the music, and when I tried to reason with her about it she smiled a gloomy little smile, and said—

"I cannot be happy. I will not be happy. It is wrong. I have been very selfish and wicked. You think me very idiotic, I know, but I believe there is a curse on us. We shall never be happy again."

"Don't you love me any more?" I asked like a fool.

"Love you?" She only repeated my words, but I was satisfied on that score. But those were miserable days. We loved each other passionately, yet our hours were spent like those of lovers on the eve of parting. Long, long silences took the place of foolish little jokes and childish talk which happy lovers know. And more than once, waking in the night, I heard my wife sobbing, and feigned sleep, with the bitter knowledge that I had no power to comfort her. I knew that the thought of her father was with her always, and that her anxiety about him grew, day by day. I wore myself out in trying to think of some way to divert her thoughts from him. I could not, indeed, pay his debts, but I could have him to live with us, a much greater sacrifice; and having a good connection, both as a musician and composer, I did not doubt that I could support her and him in comfort.

But Kate had made up her mind that the disgrace of bankruptcy would break her father's heart; and my Kate is not easy to convince or persuade.

At Torquay it occurred to me that perhaps it would be well for her to see a priest. True, Father Fabian had counselled her to marry Benoliel, but I could hardly believe that most priests would advise a girl to marry a bad man, whom she did not love, for the sake of any worldly gain whatsoever.

She received the suggestion with favour, but without enthusiasm, and we sought out a Catholic church to make inquiries. As we opened the outer door of the church we heard music, and as we stood in the entrance and I laid my hand on the heavy inner door, my other hand was caught by Kate.

"Jasper," she whispered, "it is the same!"

Some person opening the door behind us compelled us to move forward. In another moment we stood in the dusky church—stood hand-in-hand in dim daylight, listening to the same music that each had heard in the lonely night on the eve of our wedding.

I put my arm round my wife and drew her back.

"Come away, my darling," I whispered; "it is a funeral service."

She turned her eyes on me. "I *must* understand, I must see who it is. I shall go mad if you take me away now. I cannot bear any more."

We walked up the aisle, and placed ourselves as near as possible to the spot where the coffin lay, covered with flowers and with tapers burning about it. And we heard that music again, every note of it the same that each had heard before. And when the service was over I whispered to the sacristan—

"Whose music was that?"

"Our organist's," he answered; "it is the first time they've had it. Fine, wasn't it?"

"Who is the—who was—who is being buried?"

"A foreign gentleman, sir; they do say as his lady as was to be gave him the slip on his wedding day, and he'd given her father thousands they say, if the truth was known."

"But what was he doing here?"

"Well, that's the curious part, sir. To show his independence, what does he do but go the same tour he'd planned for his wedding trip. And there was a railway accident, and him and every one in his carriage killed in a twinkling, so to speak. Lucky for the young lady she was off with somebody else."

The sacristan laughed softly to himself.

Kate's fingers gripped my arm.

"What was his name?" she asked.

I would not have asked: I did not wish to hear it.

"Benoliel," said the sacristan. "Curious name and curious tale. Every one's talking of it."

Every one had something else to talk of when it was found that Benoliel's pride, which had permitted him to buy a wife, had shrunk from reclaiming the purchase money when the purchase was lost to him. And to the man who had been willing to sell his daughter, the retention of her price seemed perfectly natural.

From the moment when she heard Benoliel's name on the sacristan's lips, all Kate's gaiety and happiness returned. She loved me, and she hated Benoliel. She was married to me, and he was dead; and his death was far more of a shock to me than to her. Women are curiously kind and curiously cruel. And she never could see why her father should not have kept the money. It is noteworthy that women, even the cleverest and the best of them, have no perception of what men mean by honour.

How do I account for the music? My good critic, my business is to tell my story—not to account for it.

And do I not pity Benoliel? Yes. I can afford, now, to pity most men, alive or dead.

THIS is, of course, one of Nesbit's few happy endings, which is quite nice for variety, though the story suffers as a result. It is a quirky romance that takes its reader for several turns before depositing them in an unexpectedly cushy conclusion. It resembles the premonition tales of Rhoda Broughton, whose supernatural fiction chiefly consisted of unattached young women, pitied by relatives and disregarded by society, who foresee future disasters and are met with disbelief and skepticism. The result is typically grisly: in "Behold, It Was a Dream!" a spinster is the overnight guest of her recently married friend when she has a nightmare – vividly and chillingly described – where the newlyweds are graphically slaughtered by a workman wielding a scythe, who then marches down the hall after making eye contact with the terrified dreamer. The wife is disturbed by the dream, but her pride is pricked, and she accuses her friend of jealousy (until recently she, too, had been excepted to be an old maid), and they part on bad terms. Soon after the dreamer's escape, of course, a farmhand butchers the couple in their beds. Broughton had one tale in which the advice was duly taken: in "Mrs Smith of Longmains" a very similar setup occurs, where the eponymous Mrs Smith is dreamed of by a female friend. In her vision the girl sees her friend being assaulted and murdered by her butler. Mrs Smith takes heed of the warning, firing the butler, and in a move that presages Nesbit's "Mystery of the Semi-Detached" a newspaper relays news that although Mrs Smith averted tragedy, another wealthy widow hired the man and suffered the averted fate of her predecessor. This story, although it shares the near-escape of "Mass for the Dead," is much more interesting than Nesbit's, which lacks the bite and social commentary of her regular fare.

TAKING its cue from Amelia B. Edward's supernatural masterpiece "The Phantom Coach," Nesbit's "The Head" is a landmark in horror camp. The villain of the piece is theatrical, eccentric, and fey – a perfect prototype to the mannered acting of Vincent Price, Basil Rathbone, or Bela Lugosi. In fact, I find it difficult not to picture Price as the tall, wan antagonist, effeminate yet charismatic, and – like so many of Price's characters – fixated on the death of a lover. Like "The Power of Darkness," "The Head" explores the Valley of the Uncanny in the form of wax sculptures posed in *tableaux vivants*. In this case, the eccentric rogue has obsessively recreated the scene of his crush's fiery death. Left to die by his drunken rival, she and her child perish despite our anti-hero's attempts to reach her. Like a super-villain he has aged prematurely, obsessively pondering the event, and recreating it as a model in his basement. However, there is one alteration – in his eyes a correction: his rival lays in the street, bleeding from a throat wound. When an equally campy playboy arrives at his home in the middle of a storm, he sees the painstaking model as an opportunity to make money. While his newfound patron sees this as a chance to manipulate his emotional trauma for quick cash, he considers it an opportunity of another sort: one for revenge.

The Head
{1907}

IF your personal appearance is best described by the enumeration of your clothes, your character by the trade mark on the gilt waistband of your cigar, and your profession as "just anything that comes along, don't you know," you are not exactly the right man in the right place, up to your knees in mud, your carriage with a wheel off lying prone in a ditch several fields off, and your chance of getting to the house where a capricious music hall star has given you an inconvenient rendezvous less than the least crumb of the biscuit you wish you had put in your pocket before starting.

Morris Diehl cursed his luck in the grey of a winter's dusk. His driver had left the carriage and gone back with the horses to the inn where he had lunched. His boots were full of water, his high hat seamed and scratched by the lean-fingered trees that stooped here and there over the stone walls. His cigar, long since cold, its end wet and flattened and gnawed, lay foul between his lips. He threw it away. He was lost, be yond a doubt —lost on these confounded Derbyshire hills, where every field is just the same as every other field, and the stone walls have no more of individual distinction than the faint blue-grey lines of a copy-book.

If he had only had the sense to stay where the coachman had left him, or, better still, at the inn —the inn down in the valley, where the station was — where there were lights and voices and things to drink! Tottie de Vere, the star on whom hung all the hopes of his newest venture — a company for promoting *café chantants* in Manchester, Liverpool, and Bolton — had declined to give him any appointment save this; he might call on her between six and seven at Sir Alexander Brisbane's, the grey house with acres of glass, ten miles from anywhere. And he had tried to keep the appointment — tried with unreasonable determination, and -there he was.

Lights and voices— and things to drink. To eat also; for Mr. Diehl was not only thirsty, he was hungry as well, and cold and lonely. He thought of the Strand and the lights of the Strand, lights from restaurants and theatres, where one smelt the French cooking, and the patchouli, and the Regalias. These were to him what, to some of us, the home pastures and the scent of stocks and wood-smoke are. He had waited by the carriage till he had grown certain that all men were alike, and that his driver would, warmed and comforted in the ale-house, not be such. a fool as to keep his promise and come back " with a trap." He had walked up and down the road for a while, the bleak wind nuzzling in between his neck and the fur collar of his big coat ; and then he hail started to reach Sir Alexander's on foot, had seen a light, and been beguiled by it to what he esteemed a short cut. Even if it were not Sir Alexander's light, yet any light meant a possible fire— shelter, at any rate, from that too intimate north-easter.

He was going now, difficultly, towards the light; across fields and over the eternal sameness of grey walls — black they seemed in that sombre twilight of cold stars. Beyond the last wall was a little hill-brook. 1 le was in it almost knee-deep before he guessed at anything worse than the cold, muddy grass of the pastures. The next wall had a gate; he saw the blacker blank and made for it. His fur-lined coat caught on its hasp and ripped, loudly. And his hat was struck by some silly arch or other above the gate, and fell, rolling hollowly on the flags.

Mr. Diehl exploded passionately. He groped for the hat in the dark dampness, found it, and then he was at the door of the cottage whose windows, all alight, had beckoned him from afar. "There must be a wedding or a wake," said he. "Copy, either way." He was, casually, a journalist, when financial enterprises were cold to him. He knocked. He had not been conscious of any movement in the house, but now he was conscious of a cessation of movement, and of a silence as though something inside the house were holding its breath. " Who's there ? " The voice came from behind the door — low down, as though the speaker had been trying to look out into the dark through the keyhole.

"I've lost my way," said Mr. Diehl.

"You'll find it, some way or other," said the voice.

"I'm very wet — and tired. I should be very grateful for a night's lodging, sir."

He added the "sir " because the note of the voice was distinctly feminine, and he saw that the door would open more readily to one whose honesty of purpose was so clear and fine that it could persist even in the fact of the conviction that there was "a man in the house." Mr. Diehl's mind — it was not the mind of a fool —pictured a faded woman, her terror at this late visit soothed and charmed by the solid compliments it was part of his trade to sow broadcast, with both hands, on any soil. The harvest, he knew, rarely failed.

"Ah, have pity," he said, all the pathos of a hundred melodramas reinforcing the earnest pleading of gross physical discomfort. "I am lost on these wild moors —I shall die if you do not assist me. Have pity on me and Heaven will reward you."

"You can go back the way you came," said the voice.

"I shall die," he said, piteously, but very distinctly, as his elocution master had taught him in the days when he meant to be an actor. "I shall die if you turn me away. My death will be at your door. Ah, save me, for the love of Heaven."

" For the love of Heaven," the voice repeated, slowly. " For the love— "

The rest was lost in the rusty withdrawal of bolts. The door creaked open a brilliant inch.

"No one's crossed this door this ten years past," said the voice : "but I can't let a human creature perish by fire or by cold. For the love of Heaven —come in."

The door was flung back. Within was a little square hall or lobby ; narrow stairs led up in front of Mr. Diehl. To the right a closed door; to the left the outer door held open.

"Go and stand on the stairs," said the thin treble voice, "till I get the door shut."

129

From the stairs Morris watched to see the door closed by that spare, fluttering woman's form. But it was a man who shut the door and barred it, and then turned to the visitor the cold, calm face of one" wholly self-possessed.

"Come in," he said. "Since you arc here I'll do what I can for you. Get outer your wet things. I'll go fetch you a change."

Diehl, alone in a fire-lit kitchen, threw the wet fur coat across a brown wood settle, loosened his squelching patent leather boots, and heard above him the muffled sound of footsteps on old, worm-eaten boards, the creak of old beams, the opening and shutting of drawers and presses.

He had got to bare feet and a costume like that of a Corsican brother in reduced and muddy circumstances when his host returned, an armful of clothing over his arm.

"Here," he said, in his thin treble, "get into these. It'll be easy. I was a bigger man than ever you'll be."

He was now a smaller man — smaller by the stooping shoulders, the narrow chest, the yellow leanness of wrists and neck — by, in a word, age. He was an old man, whitehaired and pale. Nothing was young in face or figure, save only the eyes — and they would not have shone amiss in the face of an adventurer of twenty.

Hot gin and water, the generous half of a Yorkshire pie, one's feet in borrowed large shoes among the grey ashes, to whose centre fire had been forced to life by big bellows...

Morris Diehl expanded — and, expanded, he looked better than in his fur coat. He was resolved to stay the night. He pledged his host again and again in the hot, sugary drink, furtively adding strength to the other's glass from the brown demijohn whenever the old man left the fire for more wood, or to fill the kettle, or to bring out his tobacco-jar from the disused oven where he stored it— " to keep it moist," he said. He grew more cordial, and Diehl, who was by nature an actor anywhere but on the boards, which paralyzed him, set so gay a tune of good fellowship that the other's mind soon danced to it.

"I'm glad I let you in. Yes, I'm very glad I broke my vow. You're a good fellow, sir, pardoning the liberty, and this night's the whitest I've known for ten years. How old would you take me to be now?"

The question was awkward. As a woman of thirty is said to sub tract passionately to make a total of twenty- seven, so men who are far gone in their seventies will add to their years, and claim your amazed admiration as gaffers of eighty-six.

Diehl looked hard at the old man.

He would have liked to rest his decision on the spinning of a coin.

"Not much past sixty," struck him as a tactful com promise.

The old man laughed, well pleased, as it seemed.

"I'm forty-three come Lady Day and seven days beyond," he said. "I was born on All Fools' Day three-and-forty years ago and christened April, by the same token, like the fool I am. April Vane's my name. ' Vane by name and vain by nature,' they used to say when I was a young man— though you wouldn't think it to look at me now."

"I beg your pardon." Diehl had no other counter ready.

"Not at all, sir, not at all," the old man rejoined. "It 'ud be a wonder if you could guess my age. Why, my hair went white, like you see it, in three days."

"You had some shock, I suppose?" said Morris, and he sipped the hot gin. "It's a sad world, Heaven help us."

"I don't tell my story to strangers," said the other, with shrill, sudden dignity. "I trust," said Diehl, in his best manner, "that I can sympathize with another man's sorrows without seeking to thrust myself into his confidence."

Even as he spoke he saw how well the old man, the remote house, the air of mystery would serve him in an article for the *Daily Bellower,* could he but learn the secret of this hermit's grief. He saw the headlines :—

AN ENGLISH HERMIT.
TRAGIC STORY.
A BROKEN LIFE.

"No," said the other, "no, of course not. You're a gentleman. Anyone could see that — let alone your fur coat."

"I've known trouble myself," said the guest, and told a tale, a long tale full of pathetic incidents, a tale whose denouement may have been suggested by the prostrate stump of a cigar against the leg of the table — by " that, or by something more subtle. I saw my angel girl," he ended, "at the window of that burning house. How could I save her? I rushed forward. 'Darling !' I cried,'I am coming to rescue you!' I plunged among the burning debris, and knew no more till I woke in hospital with a broken heart — and this." He pulled up' the sleeve and showed a scar —got in a drunken fight with a Jew in Johannesburg — the weapons whisky bottles.

"They cured my face-burns," he added, smoothing his heavy moustache; "these hardly show, even by daylight, but that scar I shall carry to my grave."

There was a silence. Then "Why did you go on living?" asked the other man, his voice tense as the string of a violin.

"I —oh — my poor old mother,' said Diehl, whose mother had died in giving birth to him, her only child ; " for her sake, don't you know, and my little sister." went on living," said the other man, and now his voice was no longer like stretched wire, but like the sharp, unyielding blade of a steel poniard.

"*I* went on living because -"

There was a silence. Diehl could almost hear his heart beat, so sure he was that there was here material for head-lines, so keen was he to secure it.

He sighed elaborately. "Ah," he said, "it is a relief to tell your troubles to someone who understands."

He was quite right to say it. He really sometimes had a wonderful flair for the things to be said and not to say.

"Does it really?" asked the man with the young eyes — "relief, I mean? I've lived here ten years, and never a word except when I bought the things I needed. Does talking help? Are you sure? Doesn't it open the old wounds wide till the blood squirts out of them? Don't you wish after wards that you'd held your silly tongue? Aren't you ashamed and afraid and sick "with yourself for every word that's passed your lips about *her*?"

"No," said Diehl, slowly, stretching his feet towards the ash's red centre;" no. But then I've never told my story to anyone but you. There's something about you —I don't know what it is —that makes me feel I can trust you. So I'm glad I've told you my story. If it's not bored you? "The last five words were a misdeal, but the other man did not notice it.

"I don't know," he said; "you may be right, and perhaps, if told someone I could trust, my brain and heart would leave off feeling as though they were going to burst and make my clean floor all in a mess. You don't think I'm mad, do you?"

It was just what he was thinking. So, suddenly, very anxious to be alone, with a locked door between him and his host, he said, hastily: "Not at all. But I see I've awakened painful memories with my talk. Will you let me sleep here —on the settle on the floor — anywhere? I don't want a bed. I won't give an ounce of trouble. May I?"

"May you what? "

"Spend the night," said Diehl, and, laboriously explaining, added: "Sleep here, you know."

"In this house? "

"Of course."

"Yes." The answer was very strong, very definite. " You shall sleep here, in this house— if you can. But first I should like to show you the reason why I never sleep in this house. I sleep in the croft when it's warm, and when it's winter in the shippen. But I keep the lights burning all night in every room."

"I don't half like this," Morris Diehl told himself, and perceived that attractive headlines may be bought too dearly. Aloud he said: "I'm so tired I could sleep anywhere. I believe I'm almost asleep now. Won't you show me whatever it is to-morrow?"

"To-morrow may never come," said the host, cheerfully. "I'll go first—just to turn up the lights and that. Then you shall see."

He went out, quite quietly and soberly, and Mr. Diehl shivered. Now that he was warm and gin-filled, the bleak, windy hillside, the chess-board of those confounded stone walls, seemed a security lightly thrown away.

"Alone with a lunatic," he mused, "in a house a hundred miles from anywhere." He fingered a short, broad knife whose sheath fitted closely against his hip. If worst comes to the worst— in self defence," he assured himself. "But all the same I jolly well wish I was jolly well out of it. Silly lunatic! "

" Come, now! " said the voice of the silly lunatic, and said it so trustfully, yet so compellingly, that Mr. Diehl rose and followed it, half reassured, half curious, and wholly over mastered.

"It's in the cellar," said the voice; "people do pry so."

Mr. Diehl drew back; he could not help it.

"You're not afraid of a *cellar*?" said the voice; "besides, it's what we used to call a basement in London."

Morris Diehl felt his knife's comforting weight and followed the voice.

The stairs were of stone, broad and shallow — there were many of them. The wavering yellow light of the lamp the other man carried showed the stairs neatly yellowed, as the North Country lovingly yellows the stones which make the floors to its homes. The stairs ended in a flagged passage, with doors. Outside the right-hand door the lamp-bearer paused.

"You told me your story with words," said he, and his language as well as his very intonation had changed. Before he had spoken in colourless accents. Now he spoke in the very key of uneducated London.

"I never heard so many words all different in all my born days. I haven't got no power of jaw like that there. You told me your story, and it's the same as my story. That's why I'm a-going to show you my story. 'Cause I can't use my tongue worth tuppence — but my hands I can. Now don't you be frightened; it ain't real."

Mr. Diehl reassured himself with a laugh. "I'm not so easily frightened," he said.

"Nor don't you laugh neither," said the other man, with sudden breathless intensity. "I couldn't answer for myself what I should do if you was to laugh in there. It's the work of my hands. And I love the work of my hands same as Almighty God did. Don't you go to laugh in there, sir, or it'll be the worse for both of us. But you wouldn't.-" His voice grew suddenly tender. "Ain't you showed me your 'art — put it into my 'and to look at? Don't I know you?"

The dramatic instinct taught Mr. Diehl to hold out his hand in the dim lamplight and press the other man's, with a fine show of manly emotion.

"I was a stonemason by trade," said the host;" apprenticed in the King's Road, Chelsea, I was. That's how I got the hang of it."

Mr. Diehl had a sudden, swift Vision of an elaborate monument erected in the cellar over the body of the victim of homicidal mania.

"Now!" said the other, and flung open the door.

Mr. Diehl was pre pared for a shock of some kind, but he was not prepared for the shock he got.

The opened door disclosed a village street, lit warm and red —a village street at night. It was the village where the inn was that he wished he had stayed at— where the lights were, and the voices, and the drinks. There, by the same token, was the inn, its sign emblazoned with the arms of the local landowner, lit redly by the flames of conflagration. There was the square church tower, flushed against a dark sky; the tombstones in the raised churchyard gleaming rosy beneath the yew shadows. There was a crowd in the street —men with pails and cans of water. This side of the inn half the street was in flames ; from the window of a burning house a girl leaned out ; below, a man holding a ladder was in the act of planting it against the window. At his feet lay a body — a dead man, as it seemed, but not dead by burning. Blood showed at mouth and nose. The whole thing was worked out,

134

with wax and wood and paint and paper and a dozen odd yet adequate materials, at much less than half life, but so perfect were the perspective and the proportion that that scene would have appeared to a spectator half-way up the village street just as, and not otherwise than, it now appeared to the spectator at the cellar door. The peculiar and desperate terror— the mad, splendid heroism that fire engenders —these were here, visible to the onlooker.

" Splendid. Ripping. A1." The words sprang to Mr. Diehl's lips — and stayed there. The other man was speaking, and in a low, thin, untroubled voice.

"That's me," he said, " with the ladder. And that dog in the gutter — that's him she threw me over for. He was my mate, too, one time. She was Mrs. Dog, her that was to have been Mrs. April Vane. But I loved her. That's her, leanin' out of their bedroom window. And when the fire broke out, where was he? In heaven, where he'd got the right to be by the marriage-lines? Not him! He was in the public, silly drunk. When I come along he was crying — crying there in front of the house where she was a-burning, crying and shivering and saying, ' Oh, I shall be burnt; I know I shall.' And she was screaming, 'For God's sake, save the child!'"

"What did you do?" Mr. Diehl's voice was tact fully attuned.

"Knocked him down, of course. Thought I'd "killed him; wish I had. Then, when I'd got the ladder and set it up against the window, I was three - quarters up it when the window-frame went smash — burnt from underneath. I never seed him again. He went to London, I've heard say. But I've made his face ; you go in an' look, and you'll see the man I wish I'd swung for. If he'd bin where he ought to 'a' bin — but he left her all alone, her and the kid that wasn't three days old."

Again Morris wrung his hand. The vision of attractive head - lines had faded, grown dim, vanished in the red glow of the burning village.

He walked gingerly into the picture and looked closely at the wax puppets. Perfect in every detail, each little effigy was in itself a finer work of art even than the tableau which included them all.

"It's — it's beautiful," said Morris Diehl. "I never saw anything like it."

"It's taken me my life to make," said its maker.

"But why did you make it so small — why not life-size? There'd have been room —for part of it, "anyway."

"Money," came sharply the reply. "I've only got the house and the croft, and thirty pound a year that come too late for me to marry her."

"The whole thing's a marvel. You ought to have been a sculptor with a proper studio and all that," said the guest.

"I ought to have been a married with kids of my own," said the host.

"Wouldn't you like to make them size?" Morris Diehl asked, gently.

"I'm putting by every week for that very thing."

"I could advance you the money," said the man who took his living where he found it.

"No; I won't be beholden to nobody." The tone was decisive.

"You needn't be beholden. Come to London. I'll find you a fine big room, twice the size of this; you shall make the things life-size — the best materials money can buy. We'll charge a shilling a head to come in and see it. You'll pay me back in no time, and make your fortune besides."

"I don't want to make my fortune," said the old man, staring with his young eyes at the blazing village street. "I want to get alongside of him."

"Well," said Mr. Diehl, "you're much more likely to do that in London than here, you know. Suppose he saw the outside of our show, having been in a fire himself it's a million to one he'd turn in to have a look, and then you could tell him what you thought of him".

"Do you think he would? Do you?"

"Certain of it," said Mr. Diehl, who thought nothing less likely.

"Then I'll do it. All life-size —life-size."

"You could have men to help you."

"Not with the faces. The houses and that I don't say. Not the faces."

"Of course not the faces," Mr. Diehl assented, cordially. "Let's come back to the fire and talk it over. And tomorrow we'll get the agreement signed— and Tottie de Vere can go to the deuce. This is a big thing we're in now."

"Eh ?" the other party to the agreement queried. He had not heard. All his senses scream and roar. And it will go," This said Vere can This is a big thing we're were deep plunged in the joy of his master piece. He sighed at last and spoke.

"There ought to be *noise*" he said ; "that's the worst thing about a fire ; when it's taking hold it's as quiet as a mouse. When it's got hold it roars like a lion and screams —like a woman."

"We'll make it scream and roar. This thing's got to go, said" Morris Diehl.

II.

It did go. The whole picture — the graduated houses, the little figures of wood and wax and paper, the ingenious lanterns that lighted, the tinsel flames that gleamed —all was taken to London, and set up in a big attic in Fitzroy Street. Mr. Diehl brought men to see it. Men with shiny hats and fur coats, and cigars like his own. And when they had seen they went away and drank brandy and soda at marble-topped tables while Morris Diehl talked. And they "came into it "with him, as he had known they would. April Vane was shy and moody at first; would have no help; but when he saw the life-sized body produced by a trained workman from one of his own little models, he drew a long breath. "You may go ahead," he said. "I'll have more time for the faces."

It cost the enterprising Mr. Diehl a great deal of patience, and his enterprising friends a great deal of money. The big fight was over the subject of the tableau. Vane wanted to reproduce the village scene exactly as it had been burnt into his mind. Diehl wanted the Great Fire of Lon don, with old London Bridge and the heads of the traitors above the gate. But though Vane had been the other man's slave since the night he had thought that he had seen the other man's heart, he was obstinate till Diehl said: " More people will come to the Great Fire of London than just to a village fire ; you've got more chance of seeing him."

Then Vane yielded.

No expense was spared. The best scene painters and carpenters that the syndicate could buy for money were bought. An eminent archaeologist was feed to advise, an expert in acoustics solved the problem of the roar of fire triumphant. The thing was boomed a month in advance by all the venal Press. A big room in the West-end that had failed as an art gallery was hired for this that should not fail. Vane was often wearied, often disheartened.

"I liked the other best," he said;" that was" mine. This will be everybody's."

"Wait till you see the real thing all put together," Diehl urged, continually. He was very gentle and patient. It was important to him to keep the old man's adoration alive. "That will be yours, and you'll never be able to leave it. You mark my words."

The old man marked them, and they came true.

The thing caught on. "Have you seen the Great Fire of London?" people asked each other between dances and during dinners, in the train and on the tops of omnibuses. "Like Mme. Tussaud's? Oh, no—

not in the least. It's absolutely thrilling! Just for the first moment you can hardly believe it's not real. You must go ! "

And everybody went.

And it was not like Mme. Tussaud's or like any waxwork show that ever was before. To the making of Mme. Tussaud's goes, perhaps, talent. To the making of the Musée Grévin, certainly, genius. But to the making of this went the heart and soul of a man.

And from the first moment when he saw the completed picture, perfect from the life-size figures in the foreground to the little paper figures in the far distance, he gave himself up to it, as to his real life. The interludes when he showed it to visitors, mechanically warned them not to pass its low barrier, explained it in a monologue learned by heart—these were dull dreams. The real moments were those when he was alone— could overstep the barriers, clap the hurrying soldier on the back, whisper encouragement to the old woman hastening away on her son's strong arm, calling shrilly by name these images of dead citizens who had been alive and furious in flight under the horror of that great blaze. For to him they were not strangers out of the time of the Second Charles; each wore the face of some man or woman in the Derbyshire village. But to his own effigy he never spoke, nor to the woman whose face looked out of the burning window, nor to the corpse that lay at the feet of the ladder-bearer. For now there was no room for doubt that it was the figure of a corpse. That change he had made without consulting Mr. Diehl and the syndicate. Its mouth was bloody, as had been the mouth of the little effigy in the Derbyshire cellar, and the mouth of the man whom he had struck down long ago under the eyes of the deserted wife. Only now the throat too was bloody.

"Oh, let him alone," said Mr. Diehl, when one of the syndicate remarked that, by Jove, it was just a bit too ghastly ; " it pleases him, and you can't lay the horror on too thick for the B.P."

April Vane slept at his lodgings, but he did nothing else there — and not that every night. Sometimes he slept in the gallery on one of the red velvet seats, and always he ate and drank there, talking to the figures whenever he was alone with them. " They're company for me," he said, when Diehl tried remonstrance. And Diehl noted curiously that the life-sized figures did not hold for their maker the horror that, in the first little models, had driven him to sleep in barn or croft — anywhere but in the house where they were.

It was in August, when the crowd had worn thin, that Vane stayed away for one day. I've seen Aim," he told Diehl, standing by his bedside

very early, for he had told the hotel people that it was a matter of life and death. " I must have a day off ; I must try to find him."

"But who's to run the show ? " asked Diehl, in his blue silk pyjamas and blue jowl. "I must have my day off," said Vane. "I don't want to worry you, but I must have one day off. Shut the show up or run it yourself."

The show was that day run by Mr. Diehl. The takings were two bags of silver only that day—and that day the head was stolen. It was the head of the corpse broken off sharp at the neck, where the blood began. It was stolen, and the careless silk-hatted custodian knew no more than you and I who had done it.

Vane had not found the man he sought, but when he found out that theft he forgot the fruitless search. His grief was like that of a mother who loses her child —a woman who loses her lover. "

But it's all right," Diehl told him again and again. " Throw the comer of the mantle up —so, and it'll never show. Or leave it as it is ; it's pretty average ghastly like that." It was. But- I want his face," Vane said again and again. Well, then, for goodness' sake make his face." Diehl was losing patience a little at last. " Make his face again and have done with it ! " he said, and lit one of his eternal cigars ; " you can do it at home in the evenings." can't do it," said Vane, very low. "I've been trying — I can't see his face." "You sleep on it," said Mr. Diehl, cheer fully. " It'll come back to you all right in the morning. Besides, you've got the little model."

" I cut the face off of that," said Vane, gently. " I cut it off a little bit at a time to see if it would bleed. I can't remember his face."

" That head must have been stolen for a lark," said Diehl. "Look here —I'll advertise for it, and we'll get it back all right."

"Yes," said Vane, with trembling eager ness. " Get it back. I must see his face."

He saw it next day, on the shoulders of a living man—a tall, thick set man with dirty hands and a ready-made suit, who knocked at the gallery door just as it was being closed. The same face, but not the same expression.

"You were advertising for a head,'; said the man.

"Yes," said Vane. "Come in," and shut the door on the two of them.

"Well, I ain't goin' to name no names, but a pal of mine come in here day before yesterday, and one of your blessed dolls had got my pal's face. So he pinched it."

" Why ? " Vane softly asked.

"Well, if a man ain't got a right to his own chump, what has he got a right to ? But he'll let you have it back, but not for the fiver you offers. I take it if you offers five you'll give twenty. Say the word, and put it down in writing to prevent mistakes, and I'll guarantee you shall have the head."

"Yes," said Vane, "I shall have the head."

He advanced on the other man, and now, for the first time, his own face showed plainly.

"Heavens !" The man retreated, his hands held out to keep off—something ; and now he looked like the head that he had stolen.

" Great heavens, it's April Vane !"

" Yes, you'd better say your prayers. It *is* April Vane," April Vane said, and came at him.

❧

It must have been a couple of days later that Diehl strolled in at closing-time with that member of the syndicate who had felt so squeamish about the cut throat. The lights were low. There was no blaze to illumine the picture, and the machine was silent that in the day roared and screamed in the very voice of lire.

"So you've got the head all right? You remembered ? I told you you would," said Mr. Diehl , glancing at the corpse.

"Yes," said old April. " I've got the head—I remembered."

Mr. Diehl went into the enclosure, and the cinders crunched under his boots.

"By Jove !" he said, "you're an artist, Vane. I say, Montague, look at this corpse, the thing you didn't like— why, it's the best of the lot. You've improved it, Vane old chap. It's just the old expression, but by George! It's more life-like than ever. What is it? Something in the lie of the body, I suppose. It's just like life – isn't it, now Monty?"

"It's more like death," said Montague. "I don't like it. And it's stuffy in here, and the place is as quiet as a churchyard. Come along out."

"You're a schoolgirl, Montague— a silly schoolgirl ! I believe you're frightened of the thing."

Mr. Diehl kicked it contemptuously and without violence.

" Good night, Vane. Why don't you go to one of the halls and have a gay evening? I'll stand treat."

"You're always kind," said Vane, grate fully, "but all the evenings will be gay now. I have got the head. I have remembered."

The two members of the Great Fire Syndicate went out into the light of Regent Street.

"Ugh!" said Montague; "that place gives me the horrors."

"It's jolly well meant to," said Diehl, handing out his cigar case. "That corpse— "

"It's not canny," said Montague, and he laughed, not quite easily. "Why, it makes me fancy I say, what's that on your boot ? Heavens ! man, it's blood, as the chap says in "the story."

"Don't talk rot," said Diehl. He did not see that his right foot had stained the pavement.

Montague stooped.

"But — it *is* blood," he said.

PERFECTLY Price-esque, April Vane is a woefully underappreciated prototype of camp and queer horror. The story even combines plots with another of Nesbit's stories ("The Power of Darkness") to form the overall plot of one of Vincent Price's most notable films, *House of Wax*, which features an eccentric wax artist who wreaks vengeance on his enemies and puts their corpses in the place of statues. Complete with his female name, an effeminate surname, his campy mannerisms, girlish voice, and theatrical diabolism, Vane's kitschy style is a predecessor to *The Rocky Horror Picture Show*, *The Invisible Man*, *Theatre of Blood*, *The Abominable Dr Phibes*, *The Bride of Frankenstein*, and the films of Ed Wood. Although Nesbit likely didn't mean for Vane to be read as a homosexual, his unquestionably queer characterization is a landmark in literature – one which merits far more attention than it has so far attracted from critics. Vane's flamboyant mannerisms and theatrical eccentricity is reminiscent of Fitz-James O'Brien's kitschy, queered villains ("The Diamond Lens," "Jubal the Ringer," and "The Wondersmith" in particular, which features an affected man who plays with toys and possesses them with evil spirits in a vengeful plot), and the equally remote eccentric recluse in Edwards' "Phantom Coach." In Edwards' story, a man gets lost on the northern moors during a storm and begs to be admitted into a solitary house at the peril of his life. He is rebuffed several times before appealing to the man's humanity, at which he begrudgingly relents. The eccentric inhabitant (picture *Bride of Frankenstein's* Dr Pretorious – a campy scientist rejected by his mainstream colleagues for his lavish embrace of metaphysics) hasn't stepped outside of his home – or seen another human – for an entire decade. As such, the earlier "Phantom Coach" nearly shares an identical first act as this later story. Nesbit clearly launched off of Edwards' beginnings, fascinated by the charisma of her reclusive maverick, but while Edwards' protagonist trudges away from the home of his rescuer only to run into the ghostly mail-coach roaming the highway where, years earlier, it had been destroyed in a fatal accident, Nesbit decides to stay put at the gloomy crank's hermitage. While Edwards used her queer little man as a tool for exposition – a philosophical sage who prepares the hero for his encounter with the eponymous coach – Nesbit saw the use of such a personality for non-conformist villainy. April Vane's unconventional taste for revenge, peculiar hobbies, and kitschy personality may have been lost on most critics of queer studies, but a quick viewing of *House of Wax, Dr Phibes, Bride, Theatre of Blood,* or *Rocky Horror* assures us that his legacy was fruitful.

AN elegant, poetic, and dreamlike haunted house story, "The House of Silence" evokes the best works of Lord Dunsany, Edgar Allan Poe, and W. W. Jacobs with its emphasis on atmosphere and muscular self-discipline. As such, it remains one of the most beautifully written of Nesbit's entire oeuvre, an impressionistic prose poem of suggestion and mood. And like Poe's "House of Usher" or Jacobs' "The Well," this horror story is rich with subtle complexities, supernatural suggestion, and natural explanations. When the horror does come, it is actually rather Aickman-esque – bizarre, unexplained, and disturbing, with suggestions of some hideous moral crime. "Unlucky" homes are among the first ghost stories that we have in writing. Pliny the Younger recorded a story about a spirit who haunted a house with clanking chains; the Tower of London is so famous for its ghosts that they are virtually part of the furnishings; "The Fall of the House of Usher," *The House of Seven Gables, The Turn of the Screw,* "The Yellow Wallpaper," *The Haunting of Hill House,* and *The Shining* are all considered classics of world literature, even outside of the genre. Bad places are symbols of the institutions in life which convey the wickedness of previous generations forward into the future: patriarchies, prejudices, inequalities, unspoken segregations. Houses symbolize the heart of man, and for a house to be haunted, its previous owner must be symbolically guilty of some unresolved sin which society has agreed to ignore. For this reason – like the crimes of a civilization – the house propagates its evil with each generation until someone resists it. Such is the case with the House of Silence – a house where treasures lure and horrors reside.

The House of Silence
{1906}

THE thief stood close under the high wall, and looked to right and left. To the right the road wound white and sinuous, lying like a twisted ribbon over the broad grey shoulder of the hill; to the left the road turned sharply down towards the river; beyond the ford the road went away slowly in a curve, prolonged for miles through the green marshes.

No least black fly of a figure stirred on it. There were no travellers at such an hour on such a road.

The thief looked across the valley, at the top of the mountain flushed with sunset, and at the grey-green of the olives about its base. The terraces of olives were already dusk with twilight, but his keen eyes could not have missed the smallest variance or shifting of their lights and shadows. Nothing stirred there. He was alone.

Then, turning, he looked again at the wall behind him. The face of it was grey and sombre, but all along the top of it, in the crannies of the coping stones, orange wallflowers and sulphur-coloured snapdragons shone among the haze of feathery-flowered grasses. He looked again at the place where some of the stones had fallen from the coping—had fallen within the wall, for none lay in the road without. The bough of a mighty tree covered the gap with its green mantle from the eyes of any chance wayfarer; but the thief was no chance wayfarer, and he had surprised the only infidelity of the great wall to its trust.

To the chance wayfarer, too, the wall's denial had seemed absolute, unanswerable. Its solid stone, close knit by mortar hardly less solid, showed not only a defence, it offered a defiance—a menace. But the thief had learnt his trade; he saw that the mortar might be loosened a little here, broken a little there, and now the crumbs of it fell rustling on to the dry, dusty grass of the roadside. He drew back, took two quick steps forward, and, with a spring, sudden and agile as a cat's, grasped the wall where the gap showed, and drew himself up. Then he rubbed his hands on his knees, because his hands were bloody from the sudden grasping of the rough stones, and sat astride on the wall.

He parted the leafy boughs and looked down; below him lay the stones that had fallen from the wall—already grass was growing upon the mound they made. As he ventured his head beyond the green leafage, the level light of the sinking sun struck him in the eyes. It was like a blow. He dropped softly from the wall and stood in the shadow of the tree—looking, listening.

Before him stretched the park—wide and still; dotted here and there with trees, and overlaid with gold poured from the west. He held his breath and listened. There was no wind to stir the leaves to those rustlings which may deceive and disconcert the keenest and the boldest; only the sleepy twitter of birds, and the little sudden soft movements of them in the dusky privacy of the thick-leaved branches. There was in all the broad park no sign of any other living thing.

The thief trod softly along under the wall where the trees were thickest, and at every step he paused to look and listen.

It was quite suddenly that he came upon the little lodge near the great gates of wrought iron with the marble gate-posts bearing upon them the two gaunt griffins, the cognisance of the noble house whose lands these were. The thief drew back into the shadow and stood still, only his heart beat thickly. He stood still as the tree trunk beside him, looking, listening. He told himself that he heard nothing—saw nothing—yet he became aware of things. That the door of the lodge was not closed, that some of its windows were broken, and that into its little garden straw and litter had drifted from the open door: and that between the stone step and the threshold grass was growing inches high. When he was aware of this he stepped forward and entered the lodge. All the sordid sadness of a little deserted home met him here—broken crocks and bent pans, straw, old rags, and a brooding, dusty stillness.

"There has been no one here since the old keeper died. They told the truth," said the thief; and he made haste to leave the lodge, for there was nothing in it now that any man need covet—only desolation and the memory of death.

So he went slowly among the trees, and by devious ways drew a little nearer to the great house that stood in its walled garden in the middle of the park. From very far off, above the green wave of trees that broke round it, he could see the towers of it rising black against the sunset; and between the trees came glimpses of its marble white where the faint grey light touched it from the east.

Moving slowly—vigilant, alert, with eyes turning always to right and to left, with ears which felt the intense silence more acutely than they could have felt any tumult—the thief reached the low wall of the garden, at the western side. The last redness of the sunset's reflection had lighted all the many windows, and the vast place blazed at him for an instant before the light dipped behind the black bar of the trees, and left him face to face with a pale house, whose windows now were black and hollow, and seemed like eyes that watched him. Every window was closed; the lower ones were guarded by jalousies; through the glass of the ones above he could see the set painted faces of the shutters.

From far off he had heard, and known, the plash-plash of fountains, and now he saw their white changing columns rise and fall against the background of the terrace. The garden was full of rose bushes trailing and unpruned; and the heavy, happy scent of the roses, still warm from the sun, breathed through the place, exaggerating the sadness of its tangled desolation. Strange figures gleamed in the deepening dusk, but they were too white to be feared. He crept into a corner where Psyche

147

drooped in marble, and, behind her pedestal, crouched. He took food from his pockets and ate and drank. And between the mouthfuls he listened and watched.

The moon rose, and struck a pale fire from the face of the house and from the marble limbs of the statues, and the gleaming water of the fountains drew the moonbeams into the unchanging change of its rise and fall.

Something rustled and stirred among the roses. The thief grew rigid: his heart seemed suddenly hollow; he held his breath. Through the deepening shadows something gleamed white; and not marble, for it moved, it came towards him. Then the silence of the night was shattered by a scream, as the white shape glided into the moonlight. The thief resumed his munching, and another shape glimmered after the first. "Curse the beasts!" he said, and took another draught from his bottle, as the white peacocks were blotted out by the shadows of the trees, and the stillness of the night grew more intense.

In the moonlight the thief went round and about the house, pushing through the trailing briers that clung to him—and now grown bolder he looked closely at doors and windows. But all were fast barred as the doors of a tomb. And the silence deepened as the moonlight waxed.

There was one little window, high up, that showed no shutter. He looked at it; measured its distance from the ground and from the nearest of the great chestnut trees. Then he walked along under the avenue of chestnuts with head thrown back and eyes fixed on the mystery of their interlacing branches.

At the fifth tree he stopped; leaped to the lowest bough, missed it; leaped again, caught it, and drew up his body. Then climbing, creeping, swinging, while the leaves, agitated by his progress, rustled to the bending of the boughs, he passed to that tree, to the next—swift, assured, unhesitating. And so from tree to tree, till he was at the last tree—and on the bough that stretched to touch the little window with its leaves.

He swung from this. The bough bent and cracked, and would have broken, but that at the only possible instant the thief swung forward, felt the edge of the window with his feet, loosed the bough, sprang, and stood, flattened against the mouldings, clutching the carved drip-stone with his hands. He thrust his knee through the window, waiting for the tinkle of the falling glass to settle into quietness, opened the window, and crept in. He found himself in a corridor: he could see the long line of its white windows, and the bars of moonlight falling across the inlaid wood of its floor.

148

He took out his thief's lantern—high and slender like a tall cup—lighted it, and crept softly along the corridor, listening between his steps till the silence grew to be like a humming in his ears.

And slowly, stealthily, he opened door after door; the rooms were spacious and empty—his lantern's yellow light flashing into their corners told him this. Some poor, plain furniture he discerned, a curtain or a bench here and there, but not what he sought. So large was the house, that presently it seemed to the thief that for many hours he had been wandering along its galleries, creeping down its wide stairs, opening the grudging doors of the dark, empty rooms, whose silence spoke ever more insistently in his ears.

"But it is as he told me," he said inwardly: "no living soul in all the place. The old man—a servant of this great house—he told me; he knew, and I have found all even as he said."

Then the thief turned away from the arched emptiness of the grand staircase, and in a far corner of the hall he found himself speaking in a whisper because now it seemed to him that nothing would serve but that this clamorous silence should be stilled by a human voice.

"The old man said it would be thus—all emptiness, and not profit to a man; and he died, and I tended him. Dear Jesus! how our good deeds come home to us! And he told me how the last of the great family had gone away none knew whither. And the tales I heard in the town—how the great man had not gone, but lived here in hiding—— It is not possible. There is the silence of death in this house."

He moistened his lips with his tongue. The stillness of the place seemed to press upon him like a solid thing. "It is like a dead man on one's shoulders," thought the thief, and he straightened himself up and whispered again: "The old man said, 'The door with the carved griffin, and the roses enwreathed, and the seventh rose holds the secret in its heart.'"

With that the thief set forth again, creeping softly across the bars of moonlight down the corridor.

And after much seeking he found at last, under the angle of the great stone staircase behind a mouldering tapestry wrought with peacocks and pines, a door, and on it carved a griffin, wreathed about with roses. He pressed his finger into the deep heart of each carven rose, and when he pressed the rose that was seventh in number from the griffin, he felt the inmost part of it move beneath his finger as though it sought to escape. So he pressed more strongly, leaning against the door till it swung open, and he passed through it, looking behind him to see that nothing followed. The door he closed as he entered.

And now he was, as it seemed, in some other house. The chambers were large and lofty as those whose hushed emptiness he had explored—but these rooms seemed warm with life, yet held no threat, no terror. To the dim yellow flicker from the lantern came out of the darkness hints of a crowded magnificence, a lavish profusion of beautiful objects such as he had never in his life dreamed of, though all that life had been one dream of the lovely treasures which rich men hoard, and which, by the thief's skill and craft, may come to be his.

He passed through the rooms, turning the light of his lantern this way and that, and ever the darkness withheld more than the light revealed. He knew that thick tapestries hung from the walls, velvet curtains masked the windows; his hand, exploring eagerly, felt the rich carving of chairs and presses; the great beds were hung with silken cloth wrought in gold thread with glimmering strange starry devices. Broad sideboards flashed back to his lantern's questionings the faint white laugh of silver; the tall cabinets could not, with all their reserve, suppress the confession of wrought gold, and, from the caskets into whose depths he flashed the light, came the trembling avowal of rich jewels. And now, at last, that carved door closed between him and the poignant silence of the deserted corridors, the thief felt a sudden gaiety of heart, a sense of escape, of security. He was alone, yet warmed and companioned. The silence here was no longer a horror, but a consoler, a friend.

And, indeed, now he was not alone. The ample splendours about him, the spoils which long centuries had yielded to the grasp of a noble family—these were companions after his own heart.

He flung open the shade of his lantern and held it high above his head. The room still kept half its secrets. The discretion of the darkness should be broken down. He must see more of this splendour—not in unsatisfying dim detail, but in the lit gorgeous mass of it. The narrow bar of the lantern's light chafed him. He sprang on to the dining-table, and began to light the half-burnt chandelier. There were a hundred candles, and he lighted all, so that the chandelier swung like a vast living jewel in the centre of the hall. Then, as he turned, all the colour in the room leapt out at him. The purple of the couches, the green gleam of the delicate glass, the blue of the tapestries, and the vivid scarlet of the velvet hangings, and with the colour sprang the gleams of white from the silver, of yellow from the gold, of many-coloured fire from strange inlaid work and jewelled caskets, till the thief stood

150

aghast with rapture in the strange, sudden revelation of this concentrated splendour.

He went along the walls with a lighted candle in his hand—the wax dripped warm over his fingers as he went—lighting one after another, the tapers in the sconces of the silver-framed glasses. In the state bedchamber he drew back suddenly, face to face with a death-white countenance in which black eyes blazed at him with triumph and delight. Then he laughed aloud. He had not known his own face in the strange depths of

this mirror. It had no sconces like the others, or he would have known it for what it was. It was framed in Venice glass—wonderful, gleaming, iridescent.

The thief dropped the candle and threw his arms wide with a gesture of supreme longing.

"If I could carry it all away! All, all! Every beautiful thing! To sell some—the less beautiful, and to live with the others all my days!"

And now a madness came over the thief. So little a part of all these things could he bear away with him; yet all were his—his for the taking—even the huge carved presses and the enormous vases of solid silver, too heavy for him to lift—even these were his: had he not found them—he, by his own skill and cunning? He went about in the rooms, touching one after the other the beautiful, rare things. He caressed the gold and the jewels. He threw his arms round the great silver vases; he wound round himself the heavy red velvet of the curtain where the griffins gleamed in embossed gold, and shivered with pleasure at the soft clinging of its embrace. He found, in a tall cupboard, curiously-shaped flasks of wine, such wine as he had never tasted, and he drank of it slowly—in little sips—from a silver goblet and from a green Venice glass, and from a cup of rare pink china, knowing that any one of his drinking vessels was worth enough to keep him in idleness for a long year. For the thief had learnt his trade, and it is a part of a thief's trade to know the value of things.

He threw himself on the rich couches, sat in the stately carved chairs, leaned his elbows on the ebony tables. He buried his hot face in the chill, smooth linen of the great bed, and wondered to find it still scented delicately as though some sweet woman had lain there but last night. He went hither and thither laughing with pure pleasure, and making to himself an unbridled carnival of the joys of possession.

In this wise the night wore on, and with the night his madness wore away. So presently he went about among the treasures—no more with the eyes of a lover, but with the eyes of a Jew—and he chose those precious stones which he knew for the most precious, and put them in the bag he had brought, and with them some fine-wrought goldsmith's work and the goblet out of which he had drunk the wine. Though it was but of silver, he would not leave it. The green Venice glass he broke and the cup, for he said: "No man less fortunate than I, to-night, shall ever again drink from them." But he harmed nothing else of all the beautiful things, because he loved them.

Then, leaving the low, uneven ends of the candles still alight, he turned to the door by which he had come in. There were two doors, side by side, carved with straight lilies, and between them a panel wrought with the griffin and the seven roses enwreathed. He pressed his finger in the heart of the seventh rose, hardly hoping that the panel would move, and indeed it did not; and he was about to seek for a secret spring among the lilies, when he perceived that one of the doors wrought with these had opened itself a little. So he passed through it and closed it after him.

"I must guard my treasures," he said. But when he had passed through the door and closed it, and put out his hand to raise the tattered tapestry that covered it from without, his hand met the empty air, and he knew that he had not come out by the door through which he had entered.

When the lantern was lighted, it showed him a vaulted passage, whose floor and whose walls were stone, and there was a damp air and a mouldering scent in it, as of a cellar long unopened. He was cold now, and the room with the wine and the treasures seemed long ago and far away, though but a door and a moment divided him from it, and though some of the wine was in his body, and some of the treasure in his hands. He set about to find the way to the quiet night outside, for this seemed to him a haven and a safeguard since, with the closing of that door, he had shut away warmth, and light, and companionship. He was enclosed in walls once more, and once more menaced by the invading silence that was almost a presence. Once more it seemed to him that he must creep softly, must hold his breath before he ventured to turn a corner—for always he felt that he was not alone, that near him was something, and that its breath, too, was held.

So he went by many passages and stairways, and could find no way out; and after a long time of searching he crept by another way back to come unawares on the door which shut him off from the room where the many lights were, and the wine and the treasure. Then terror leaped out upon him from the dark hush of the place, and he beat on the door with his hands and cried aloud, till the echo of his cry in the groined roof cowed him back into silence.

Again he crept stealthily by strange passages, and again could find no way except, after much wandering, back to the door where he had begun.

And now the fear of death beat in his brain with blows like a hammer. To die here like a rat in a trap, never to see the sun alight again, never to climb in at a window, or see brave jewels shine under his lantern, but to wander, and wander, and wander between these inexorable walls till he died, and the rats, admitting him to their brotherhood, swarmed round the dead body of him.

"I had better have been born a fool," said the thief.

Then once more he went through the damp and the blackness of the vaulted passages, tremulously searching for some outlet, but in vain.

Only at last, in a corner behind a pillar, he found a very little door and a stair that led down. So he followed it, to wander among other corridors and cellars, with the silence heavy about him, and despair growing thick and cold like a fungus about his heart, and in his brain the fear of death beating like a hammer.

It was quite suddenly in his wanderings, which had grown into an aimless frenzy, having now less of search in it than of flight from the insistent silence, that he saw at last a light—and it was the light of day coming through an open door. He stood at the door and breathed the air of the morning. The sun had risen and touched the tops of the towers of the house with white radiance; the birds were singing loudly. It was morning, then, and he was a free man.

He looked about him for a way to come at the park, and thence to the broken wall and the white road, which he had come by a very long time before. For this door opened on an inner enclosed courtyard, still in damp shadow, though the sun above struck level across it—a courtyard where tall weeds grew thick and dank. The dew of the night was heavy on them.

As he stood and looked, he was aware of a low, buzzing sound that came from the other side of the courtyard. He pushed through the weeds towards it; and the sense of a presence in the silence came upon him more than ever it had done in the darkened house, though now it was day, and the birds sang all gaily, and the good sun shone so bravely overhead.

As he thrust aside the weeds which grew waist-high, he trod on something that seemed to writhe under his feet like a snake. He started back and looked down. It was the long, firm, heavy plait of a woman's hair. And just beyond lay the green gown of a woman, and a woman's hands, and her golden head, and her eyes; all about the place where she lay was the thick buzzing of flies, and the black swarming of them.

The thief saw, and he turned and he fled back to his doorway, and down the steps and through the maze of vaulted passages—fled in the dark, and empty-handed, because when he had come into the presence that informed that house with silence, he had dropped lantern and treasure, and fled wildly, the horror in his soul driving him before it. Now fear is more wise than cunning, so, whereas he had sought for hours with his lantern and with all his thief's craft to find the way out, and had sought in vain, he now, in the dark and blindly, without thought or will, without pause or let, found the one way that led to a door, shot back the bolts, and fled through the awakened rose garden and across the dewy park.

He dropped from the wall into the road, and stood there looking eagerly to right and left. To the right the road wound white and sinuous, like a twisted ribbon over the great, grey shoulder of the hill; to the left the road curved down towards the river. No least black fly of a figure stirred on it. There are no travellers on such a road at such an hour.

THE House of Silence is a House of Sin – one which shelters wickedness and ordains death. There are two ways of interpreting this story: one based on the literal plot and one founded in the suggestive atmosphere. To first time readers, the former is the most pressing one ("who was the corpse and why was it there?"), and while this interpretation is ultimately far less important than examining the emotional impressions given, we can begin there. Nesbit – as in "The Mystery of the Semi-Detached" – exerts a great deal of commendable self-control in this story, and offers no definitive solution to the riddle of the body consumed by flies, but we have some clues. The family of the house has disappeared for unknown reasons, although it is rumored that "the great man" still lives on the estate like a fugitive. This implies that some horrible crime or crimes may have been committed (either by the family itself or by the "great man" specifically). When the thief presses his face against the sheets, he is surprised to find them fresh and fragrant – "*scented delicately as*

155

though some sweet woman had lain there but last night." This is a particularly telling phrase since it implies that a woman of flesh and blood was bedding in the sheets less than twenty-four hours ago. As with so many of Nesbit's stories, there is a subtle eroticism about the detail, particularly in the word "lain." There is both a suggestiveness about the term (a euphemism for sex) and a voyeuristic quality to the thief's fantasy of "some sweet woman" whom he pictures in the bed that he is currently pressing his skin against. When the thief finds the body, it is still fresh, which is to say it still has skin and eyes and hair, but it has been dead long enough to attract hordes of carrion flies – roughly a day or two, or long enough for the woman to have been bedded the night before. The fact that she wears a braid implies one of two things – either she is very young (braids were worn by younger women, especially single women) or that she was ready for bed (many women braided their hair before bed to keep their long hair controlled during sleep). Either option has a suggestive nature. What we are left with are a few possibilities: if the corpse is real – that is, not a ghostly vision or a (M. R.) Jamesian revenant (cf. "Martin's Close") – then we might suspect that the family fled their home due to the scandals of its patriarch (scandals which may have been sexual, violent, or both), and that he has indeed remained behind in his palace of evil, that he had only the night before seduced or raped the dead girl, and that shortly after he killed her. The fact that she is found in the courtyard which the thief finds in his attempt to leave the building might imply that she was *also* trying to escape – running for her life. If the corpse is a ghost, then we might assume that the fragrance on the bed was also ghostly, and that the corpse is that of a woman whose death was the cause of the family's flight (again, probably at the hands of "the great man," who may not have stayed behind, although his spirit seems to have). As a final word to this interpretation, I cannot be wholly confident in this analysis, but my *instinct* is that Nesbit is showing us the body of a *recent* victim of a brutal date rape, and implying that the wicked patriarch of a shamed family still uses the old home as his base of operations.

II.

This leads us into the more nuanced analysis of mood and theme. The thief is himself lured to the home by promises of riches and wealth, and he is at first dazzled by what he finds. It *is* a fine home, and he wishes that he could own it or at least the possessions therein. He lusts over the opulence and admires it approvingly, only to be traumatized when he realizes what its elegance has allowed to be concealed. The

156

mood goes from trepid curiosity, to awestruck delight, to lusty greed, to anxious concern, to horror. As I mentioned in the opening notes, haunted houses are emblematic of a society or a person with a secret sin. This house (read society) has gone unquestioned because of its grandeur and affluence, and yet – behind the curtains – great sins are left unseen and unnoticed, or otherwise knowingly unreported. It seems to me that Nesbit may be critiquing the patriarchy of Edwardian Britain where the dodgy behavior of "great" men were often left unchallenged and unquestioned simply because of their status. The thief is drawn to the opulence of the great house and pictures himself as master of it; he envies the man who could claim such extravagant wealth up until he realizes what that wealth has been used to justify. At the heart of this story, I can't help but sense a feminist message that cries out accusatorily against the "great men" of Nesbit's society and powerful patriarchies that ravage colonies, industries, slums, and economies but are themselves left gently unmolested about their wrong doings. While the literal plot of the story may follow – like "The Semi-Detached" and "Man-Size in Marble" among others – the problem of sexually-motivated murder, the larger picture appears to be an indictment of the broader British machismo, capitalism, cronyism, and classism.

III.

The House of Silence is silent because no one talks about it. No one questions it. No one resists it. It is a society gone silent – a nation at odds with its conscience, muted by awe and gagged by vain respect for status and privilege. Nesbit's thief is at first enamored by the status of his unseen guest, but at the heart of the estate (literally – and with symbolic import – at the very center of the mansion) he realizes that it has all been a Bluebeard's castle. And such might be said of Edwardian England: magisterial and majestic, powerful, and princely, yet behind the regal façade lurk unnoticed crimes of power. In the end, the thief refuses to be a "fly": the final lines compare human beings with flies – mindless sycophants that feed off of misery and tragedy – and it is fitting to think of the thief as a fly himself: an amoral renegade who hopes to nurse himself on the luxury of the well-off. But seeing the corpse blackened with flies is an indictment of his own complicity in this societal sin, and he leaves both his loot and his burglar's tools behind. No longer wishing to be a fly on the carcass of the oppressed, he leaves it all behind – the stinking cadaver in the tall grass, and the House of Silence, a house not haunted by bangings and moanings and rage, but by collective denial, passive allowance, and silent permission.

WAX museums have been objects of horror and attraction for centuries. Although Madame Tussaud's (which opened in Baker Street in 1835) is popularly considered the first of its kind, wax sculpture has been a popular medium of art for hundreds of years. And yet, Tussaud certainly did bring an element of popular horror to the practice with its "Chamber of Horrors" and the legends that she sifted through the recently cloven heads of aristocrats to make their busts. The "Chamber of Horrors" – like the one depicted in this story – became a staple of wax museums during the Victorian period: a safe, managed way to satisfy the British taste for gore and sex. Repressed, emotionally stifled, and socially segregated, the British middle class had removed itself from the drama of its feudal past of livestock being butchered in backyards, gibbeted highwaymen rotting overhead, and traitors being drawn and quartered on the scaffold, with their legs, arms, and heads displayed in the open air until the flesh dripped away and the sun faded the bone. Death and decay had been tucked tidily away from the middle classes – made neat and polite with the rise of professional morticians – and yet just three generations earlier it had teemed relentlessly around the rural villages and market towns. Indeed, underneath the tidy polish of the middle-class, the radical evolution from peasantry to gentry had not tidied up their taste for the macabre. Wax museums wisely merged tasteless melodrama with respectable art, making lower class amusements palatable to the gentry: upright gentlewomen could browse through a Chamber of Horrors and watch nude slaves squirming under lions, satin-bosomed aristocrats cringing under guillotines, muscular traitors being wrenched apart on the rack, or nubile beauties lashed provocatively to the executioner's stake without feeling *déclassé*. By setting her story in the dark halls of a wax museum, Nesbit taps into what Freud called the Valley of the Uncanny – that point where an artistic representation of a human being is so realistic, but not quite natural, that it causes deep revulsion and fear.

The Power of Darkness
{1905}

IT was an enthusiastic send-off. Half the students from her Atelier were there, and twice as many more from other studios. She had been the belle of the Artists' Quarter in Montparnasse for three golden months. Now she was off to the Riviera to meet her people, and every one she knew was at the Gare de Lyons to catch the pretty last glimpse of her. And, as had been more than once said late of an evening, "to see her was to love her." She was one of those agitating blondes, with the naturally rippled hair, the rounded rose-leaf cheeks, the large violet-blue eyes that look all things and mean Heaven alone knows how little. She held her court like a queen, leaning out of the carriage window and receiving bouquets, books, journals, long last words, and last longing looks. All eyes were on her, and her eyes were for all—and her smile. For all but one, that is. Not a single glance went Edward's way, and Edward, tall, lean, gaunt, with big eyes, straight nose, and mouth somewhat too small, too beautiful, seemed to grow thinner and paler before one's eyes. One pair of eyes at least saw the miracle worked, the paling of what had seemed absolute pallor, the revelation of the bones of a face that seemed already covered but by the thinnest possible veil of flesh.

And the man whose eyes saw this rejoiced, for he loved her, like the rest, or not like the rest; and he had had Edward's face before him for the last month, in that secret shrine where we set the loved and the hated, the shrine that is lighted by a million lamps kindled at the soul's flame, the shrine that leaps into dazzling glow when the candles are out and one lies alone on hot pillows to outface the night and the light as best one may.

"Oh, good-bye, good-bye, all of you," said Rose. "I shall miss you— oh, you don't know how I shall miss you all!"

She gathered the glances of her friends and her worshippers on her own glance, as one gathers jewels on a silken string. The eyes of Edward alone seemed to escape her.

"Em voiture, messieurs et dames."

Folk drew back from the train. There was a whistle. And then at the very last little moment of all, as the train pulled itself together for the start, her eyes met Edward's eyes. And the other man saw the meeting, and he knew—which was more than Edward did.

So, when the light of life having been borne away in the retreating train, the broken-hearted group dispersed, the other man, whose name by the way was Vincent, linked his arm in Edward's and asked cheerily: "Whither away, sweet nymph?"

"I'm off home," said Edward. "The 7.20 to Calais."

"Sick of Paris?"

"One has to see one's people sometimes, don't you know, hang it all!" was Edward's way of expressing the longing that tore him for the old house among the brown woods of Kent.

"No attraction here now, eh?"

"The chief attraction has gone, certainly," Edward made himself say.

"But there are as good fish in the sea——?"

"Fishing isn't my trade," said Edward.

"The beautiful Rose!——" said Vincent.

Edward raised hurriedly the only shield he could find. It happened to be the truth as he saw it.

"Oh," he said, "of course, we're all in love with her—and all hopelessly."

Vincent perceived that this was truth, as Edward saw it.

"What are you going to do till your train goes?" he asked.

"I don't know. Café, I suppose, and a vilely early dinner."

"Let's look in at the Musée Grévin," said Vincent.

The two were friends. They had been school-fellows, and this is a link that survives many a strain too strong to be resisted by more intimate and vital bonds. And they were fellow-students, though that counts for little or much—as you take it. Besides, Vincent knew something about Edward that no one else of their age and standing even guessed. He knew that Edward was afraid of the dark, and why. He had found it out that Christmas that the two had spent at an English country house. The house was full: there was a dance. There were to be theatricals. Early in the new year the hostess meant to "move house" to an old convent, built in Tudor times, a beautiful place with terraces and clipped yew trees, castellated battlements, a moat, swans, and a ghost story.

"You boys," she said, "must put up with a shake-down in the new house. I hope the ghost won't worry you. She's a nun with a bunch of keys and no eyes. Comes and breathes softly on the back of your neck when you're shaving. Then you see her in the glass, and, as often as not, you cut your throat." She laughed. So did Edward and Vincent, and the other young men; there were seven or eight of them.

But that night, when sparse candles had lighted "the boys" to their rooms, when the last pipe had been smoked, the last good-night said, there came a fumbling with the handle of Vincent's door. Edward entered an unwieldy figure clasping pillows, trailing blankets.

"What the deuce?" queried Vincent in natural amazement.

"I'll turn in here on the floor, if you don't mind," said Edward. "I know it's beastly rot, but I can't stand it. The room they've put me into, it's an attic as big as a barn—and there's a great door at the end, eight feet high—raw oak it is—and it leads into a sort of horror-hole—bare beams and rafters, and black as Hell. I know I'm an abject duffer, but there it is—I can't face it."

Vincent was sympathetic, though he had never known a night-terror that could not be exorcised by pipe, book, and candle.

"I know, old chap. There's no reasoning about these things," said he, and so on.

"You can't despise me more than I despise myself," Edward said. "I feel a crawling hound. But it is so. I had a scare when I was a kid, and it seems to have left a sort of brand on me. I'm branded 'coward,' old man, and the feel of it's not nice."

Again Vincent was sympathetic, and the poor little tale came out. How Edward, eight years old, and greedy as became his little years, had sneaked down, night-clad, to pick among the outcomings of a dinner-party, and how, in the hall, dark with the light of an "artistic" coloured glass lantern, a white figure had suddenly faced him—leaned towards him it seemed, pointed lead-white hands at his heart. That next day, finding him weak from his fainting fit, had shown the horror to be but a statue, a new purchase of his father's, had mattered not one whit.

Edward had shared Vincent's room, and Vincent, alone of all men, shared Edward's secret.

And now, in Paris, Rose speeding away towards Cannes, Vincent said: "Let's look in at the Musée Grévin."

The Musée Grévin is a wax-work show. Your mind, at the word, flies instantly to the excellent exhibition founded by the worthy Madame Tussaud, and you think you know what wax-works mean. But you are wrong. The exhibition of Madame Tussaud—in these days, at any rate—is the work of bourgeois for a bourgeois class. The Musée Grévin contains the work of artists for a nation of artists. Wax, modelled and retouched till it seems as near life as death is: this is what one sees at the Musée Grévin.

"Let's look in at the Musée Grévin," said Vincent. He remembered the pleasant thrill the Musée had given him, and wondered what sort of a thrill it would give his friend.

"I hate museums," said Edward.

"This isn't a museum," Vincent said, and truly; "it's just wax-works."

"All right," said Edward indifferently. And they went. They reached the doors of the Musée in the grey-brown dusk of a February evening.

One walks along a bare, narrow corridor, much like the entrance to the stalls of the Standard Theatre, and such daylight as there may be fades away behind one, and one finds oneself in a square hall, heavily decorated, and displaying with its electric lights Loie Fuller in her

162

accordion-pleated skirts, and one or two other figures not designed to quicken the pulse.

"It's very like Madame Tussaud's," said Edward.

"Yes," Vincent said; "isn't it?"

Then they passed through an arch, and behold, a long room with waxen groups life-like behind glass—the coulisses of the Opéra, Kitchener at Fashoda—this last with a desert background lit by something convincingly like desert sunlight.

"By Jove!" said Edward, "that's jolly good."

"Yes," said Vincent again; "isn't it?"

Edward's interest grew. The things were so convincing, so very nearly alive. Given the right angle, their glass eyes met one's own, and seemed to exchange with one meaning glances.

Vincent led the way to an arched door labelled: "Gallerie de la Revolution."

There one saw, almost in the living, suffering body, poor Marie Antoinette in prison in the Temple, her little son on his couch of rags, the rats eating from his platter, the brutal Simon calling to him from the grated window; one almost heard the words, "Ho la, little Capet—are you asleep?"

One saw Marat bleeding in his bath—the brave Charlotte eyeing him—the very tiles of the bath-room, the glass of the windows with, outside, the very sunlight, as it seemed, of 1793 on that "yellow July evening, the thirteenth of the month."

The spectators did not move in a public place among wax-work figures. They peeped through open doors into rooms where history seemed to be re-lived. The rooms were lighted each by its own sun, or lamp, or candle. The spectators walked among shadows that might have oppressed a nervous person.

"Fine, eh?" said Vincent.

"Yes," said Edward; "it's wonderful."

A turn of a corner brought them to a room. Marie Antoinette fainting, supported by her ladies; poor fat Louis by the window looking literally sick.

"What's the matter with them all?" said Edward.

"Look at the window," said Vincent.

There was a window to the room. Outside was sunshine—the sunshine of 1792—and, gleaming in it, blonde hair flowing, red mouth half open, what seemed the just-severed head of a beautiful woman. It was raised on a pike, so that it seemed to be looking in at the window.

"I say!" said Edward, and the head on the pike seemed to sway before his eyes.

"Madame de Lamballe. Good thing, isn't it?" said Vincent.

"It's altogether too much of a good thing," said Edward. "Look here—I've had enough of this."

"Oh, you must just see the Catacombs," said Vincent; "nothing bloody, you know. Only Early Christians being married and baptized, and all that."

He led the way, down some clumsy steps to the cellars which the genius of a great artist has transformed into the exact semblance of the old Catacombs at Rome. The same rough hewing of rock, the same sacred tokens engraved strongly and simply; and among the arches of these subterranean burrowings the life of the Early Christians, their sacraments, their joys, their sorrows—all expressed in groups of wax-work as like life as Death is.

"But this is very fine, you know," said Edward, getting his breath again after Madame de Lamballe, and his imagination loved the thought of the noble sufferings and refrainings of these first lovers of the Crucified Christ.

"Yes," said Vincent for the third time; "isn't it?"

They passed the baptism and the burying and the marriage. The tableaux were sufficiently lighted, but little light strayed to the narrow passage where the two men walked, and the darkness seemed to press, tangible as a bodily presence, against Edward's shoulder. He glanced backward.

"Come," he said, "I've had enough."

"Come on, then," said Vincent.

They turned the corner—and a blaze of Italian sunlight struck at their eyes with positive dazzlement. There lay the Coliseum—tier on tier of eager faces under the blue sky of Italy. They were level with the arena. In the arena were crosses; from them drooped bleeding figures. On the sand beasts prowled, bodies lay. They saw it all through bars. They seemed to be in the place where the chosen victims waited their turn, waited for the lions and the crosses, the palm and the crown. Close by Edward was a group—an old man, a woman—children. He could have touched them with his hand. The woman and the man stared in an agony of terror straight in the eyes of a snarling tiger, ten feet long, that stood up on its hind feet and clawed through the bars at them. The youngest child, only, unconscious of the horror, laughed in the very face of it. Roman soldiers, unmoved in military vigilance, guarded the group of martyrs. In a low cage to the left more wild beasts cringed and seemed to growl, unfed. Within the grating on the wide circle of yellow sand lions and tigers drank the blood of Christians. Close against the bars a great lion sucked the chest of a corpse on whose blood-stained face the horror of the death-agony was printed plain.

"Good God!" said Edward. Vincent took his arm suddenly, and he started with what was almost a shriek.

"What a nervous chap you are!" said Vincent complacently, as they regained the street where the lights were, and the sound of voices and the movement of live human beings—all that warms and awakens nerves almost paralysed by the life in death of waxen immobility.

"I don't know," said Edward. "Let's have a vermouth, shall we? There's something uncanny about those wax things. They're like life—but they're much more like death. Suppose they moved? I don't feel at all sure that they don't move, when the lights are all out, and there's no one there." He laughed. "I suppose you were never frightened, Vincent?"

"Yes, I was once," said Vincent, sipping his absinthe. "Three other men and I were taking turns by twos to watch a dead man. It was a fancy of his mother's. Our time was up, and the other watch hadn't come. So my chap—the one who was watching with me, I mean—went to fetch them. I didn't think I should mind. But it was just like you say."

"How?"

"Why, I kept thinking: suppose it should move—it was so like life. And if it did move, of course it would have been because it was alive, and I ought to have been glad, because the man was my friend. But all the same, if it had moved I should have gone mad."

"Yes," said Edward; "that's just exactly it."

Vincent called for a second absinthe.

"But a dead body's different to wax-works," he said. "I can't understand any one being frightened of them."

"Oh, can't you?" The contempt in the other's tone stung him. "I bet you wouldn't spend a night alone in that place."

"I bet you five pounds I do!"

"Done!" said Edward briskly. "At least, I would if you'd got five pounds."

"But I have. I'm simply rolling. I've sold my Dejanira, didn't you know? I shall win your money, though, anyway. But you couldn't do it, old man. I suppose you'll never outgrow that childish scare."

"You might shut up about that," said Edward shortly.

"Oh, it's nothing to be ashamed of; some women are afraid of mice or spiders. I say, does Rose know you're a coward?"

"Vincent!"

"No offence, old boy. One may as well call a spade a spade. Of course, you've got tons of moral courage, and all that. But you are afraid of the dark—and wax-works!"

"Are you trying to quarrel with me?"

"Heaven in its mercy forbid; but I bet you wouldn't spend a night in the Musée Grévin and keep your senses."

"What's the stake?"

"Anything you like."

"Make it, that if I do, you'll never speak to Rose again—and what's more, that you'll never speak to me," said Edward, white-hot, knocking down a chair as he rose.

"Done!" said Vincent; "but you'll never do it. Keep your hair on. Besides, you're off home."

"I shall be back in ten days. I'll do it then," said Edward, and was off before the other could answer.

Then Vincent, left alone, sat still, and over his third absinthe remembered how, before she had known Edward, Rose had smiled on him; more than on the others, he had thought. He thought of her wide, lovely eyes, her wild-rose cheeks, the scented curves of her hair, and then and there the devil entered into him.

In ten days Edward would undoubtedly try to win his wager. He would try to spend the night in the Musée Grévin. Perhaps something could be arranged before that. If one knew the place thoroughly! A little scare would serve Edward right for being the man to whom that last glance of Rose's had been given.

Vincent dined lightly, but with conscientious care—and as he dined, he thought. Something might be done by tying a string to one of the figures, and making it move, when Edward was going through that impossible night among the effigies that are so like life—so like death. Something that was not the devil said: "You may frighten him out of his wits." And the devil answered: "Nonsense! do him good. He oughtn't to be such a schoolgirl."

Anyway, the five pounds might as well be won to-night as any other night. He would take a great coat, sleep sound in the place of horrors, and the people who opened it in the morning to sweep and dust would bear witness that he had passed the night there. He thought he might trust to the French love of a sporting wager to keep him from any bother with the authorities.

166

So he went in among the crowd, and looked about among the wax-works for a place to hide in. He was not in the least afraid of these lifeless images. He had always been able to control his nervous tremors. He was not even afraid of being frightened, which, by the way, is the worst fear of all. As one looks at the room of the poor little Dauphin, one sees a door to the left. It opens out of the room on to blackness. There were few people in the gallery. Vincent watched, and in a moment when he was alone he stepped over the barrier and through this door. A narrow passage ran round behind the wall of the room. Here he hid, and when the gallery was deserted he looked out across the body of little Capet to the gaolers at the window. There was a soldier at the window, too. Vincent amused himself with the fancy that this soldier might walk round the passage at the back of the room and tap him on the shoulder in the darkness. Only the head and shoulders of the soldier and the gaoler showed, so, of course, they could not walk, even if they were something that was not wax-work.

Presently he himself went along the passage and round to the window where they were. He found that they had legs. They were full-sized figures dressed completely in the costume of the period.

"Thorough the beggars are, even the parts that don't show—artists, upon my word," said Vincent, and went back to his doorway, thinking of the hidden carving behind the capitols of Gothic cathedrals.

But the idea of the soldier who might come behind him in the dark stuck in his mind. Though still a few visitors strolled through the gallery, the closing hour was near. He supposed it would be quite dark then. And now he had allowed himself to be amused by the thought of something that should creep up behind him in the dark, he might possibly be nervous in that passage round which, if wax-works could move, the soldier might have come.

"By Jove!" he said, "one might easily frighten oneself by just fancying things. Suppose there were a back way from Marat's bath-room, and instead of the soldier Marat came out of his bath, with his wet towels stained with blood, and dabbed them against your neck."

When next the gallery was empty he crept out. Not because he was nervous, he told himself, but because one might be, and because the passage was draughty, and he meant to sleep.

He went down the steps into the Catacombs, and here he spoke the truth to himself.

"Hang it all!" he said, "I was nervous. That fool Edward must have infected me. Mesmeric influences, or something."

"Chuck it and go home," said Commonsense.

"I'm damned if I do!" said Vincent.

There were a good many people in the Catacombs at the moment—live people. He sucked confidence from their nearness, and went up and down looking for a hiding-place.

Through rock-hewn arches he saw a burial scene—a corpse on a bier surrounded by mourners; a great pillar cut off half the still, lying figure. It was all still and unemotional as a Sunday School oleograph. He waited till no one was near, then slipped quickly through the mourning group and hid behind the pillar. Surprising—heartening too—to find a plain rushed chair there, doubtless set for the resting of tired officials. He sat down in it, comforted his hand with the commonplace lines of its rungs and back. A shrouded waxen figure just behind him to the left of his pillar worried him a little, but the corpse left him unmoved as itself. A far better place this than that draughty passage where the soldier with legs kept intruding on the darkness that is always behind one.

Custodians went along the passages issuing orders. A stillness fell. Then suddenly all the lights went out.

"That's all right," said Vincent, and composed himself to sleep.

But he seemed to have forgotten what sleep was like. He firmly fixed his thoughts on pleasant things—the sale of his picture, dances with Rose, merry evenings with Edward and the others. But the thoughts rushed by him like motes in sunbeams—he could not hold a single one of them, and presently it seemed that he had thought of every pleasant thing that had ever happened to him, and that now, if he thought at all, he must think of the things one wants most to forget. And there would be time in this long night to think much of many things. But now he found that he could no longer think.

The draped effigy just behind him worried him again. He had been trying, at the back of his mind, behind the other thoughts, to strangle the thought of it. But it was there—very close to him. Suppose it put out its hand, its wax hand, and touched him. But it was of wax: it could not move. No, of course not. But suppose it did?

He laughed aloud, a short, dry laugh that echoed through the vaults. The cheering effect of laughter has been over-estimated, perhaps. Anyhow, he did not laugh again.

The silence was intense, but it was a silence thick with rustlings and breathings, and movements that his ear, strained to the uttermost, could just not hear. Suppose, as Edward had said, when all the lights were out, these things did move. A corpse was a thing that had moved—given a certain condition—Life. What if there were a

168

condition, given which these things could move? What if such conditions were present now? What if all of them—Napoleon, yellow-white from his death sleep—the beasts from the Amphitheatre, gore dribbling from their jaws—that soldier with the legs—all were drawing near to him in this full silence? Those death masks of Robespierre and Mirabeau, they might float down through the darkness till they touched his face. That head of Madame de Lamballe on the pike might be thrust at him from behind the pillar. The silence throbbed with sounds that could not quite be heard.

"You fool," he said to himself, "your dinner has disagreed with you, with a vengeance. Don't be an ass. The whole lot are only a set of big dolls."

He felt for his matches, and lighted a cigarette. The gleam of the match fell on the face of the corpse in front of him. The light was brief, and it seemed, somehow, impossible to look, by that light, in every corner where one would have wished to look. The match burnt his fingers as it went out; and there were only three more matches in the box.

It was dark again, and the image left on the darkness was that of the corpse in front of him. He thought of his dead friend. When the cigarette was smoked out, he thought of him more and more, till it seemed that what lay on the bier was not wax. His hand reached forward, and drew back more than once. But at last he made it touch the bier, and through the blackness travel up along a lean, rigid arm to the wax face that lay there so still. The touch was not reassuring. Just so, and not otherwise, had his dead friend's face felt, to the last touch of his lips: cold, firm, waxen. People always said the dead were "waxen." How true that was! He had never thought of it before. He thought of it now.

He sat still, so still that every muscle ached, because if you wish to hear the sounds that infest silence, you must be very still indeed. He thought of Edward, and of the string he had meant to tie to one of the figures.

"That wouldn't be needed," he told himself. And his ears ached with listening—listening for the sound that, it seemed, must break at last from that crowded silence.

He never knew how long he sat there. To move, to go up, to batter at the door and clamour to be let out—that one could have done if one had had a lantern, or even a full matchbox. But in the dark, not knowing the turnings, to feel one's way among these things that were so like life and yet were not alive—to touch, perhaps, these faces that were not dead, and yet felt like death. His heart beat heavily in his throat at the thought.

No, he must sit still till morning. He had been hypnotised into this state, he told himself, by Edward, no doubt; it was not natural to him.

Then suddenly the silence was shattered. In the dark something moved. And, after those sounds that the silence teemed with, the noise seemed to him thunder-loud. Yet it was only a very, very little sound, just the rustling of drapery, as though something had turned in its sleep. And there was a sigh—not far off.

Vincent's muscles and tendons tightened like fine-drawn wire. He listened. There was nothing more: only the silence, the thick silence.

The sound had seemed to come from a part of the vault where, long ago, when there was light, he had seen a grave being dug for the body of a young girl martyr.

"I will get up and go out," said Vincent. "I have three matches. I am off my head. I shall really be nervous presently if I don't look out."

He got up and struck a match, refused his eyes the sight of the corpse whose waxen face he had felt in the blackness, and made his way through the crowd of figures. By the match's flicker they seemed to make way for him, to turn their heads to look after him. The match lasted till he got to a turn of the rock-hewn passage. His next match showed him the burial scene: the little, thin body of the martyr, palm in hand, lying on the rock floor in patient waiting, the grave-digger, the mourners. Some standing, some kneeling, one crouched on the ground.

This was where that sound had come from, that rustle, that sigh. He had thought he was going away from it: instead, he had come straight to the spot where, if anywhere, his nerves might be expected to play him false.

"Bah!" he said, and he said it aloud, "the silly things are only wax. Who's afraid?" His voice sounded loud in the silence that lives with the wax people. "They're only wax," he said again, and touched with his foot, contemptuously, the crouching figure in the mantle.

And, as he touched it, it raised its head and looked vacantly at him, and its eyes were mobile and alive. He staggered back against another figure, and dropped the match. In the new darkness he heard the crouching figure move towards him. Then the darkness fitted in round him very closely.

"What was it exactly that sent poor Vincent mad: you've never told me?" Rose asked the question. She and Edward were looking out over the pines and tamarisks, across the blue Mediterranean. They were very happy, because it was their honeymoon.

He told her about the Musée Grévin and the wager, but he did not state the terms of it.

"But why did he think you would be afraid?"

He told her why.

"And then what happened?"

"Why, I suppose he thought there was no time like the present—for his five pounds, you know—and he hid among the wax-works. And I missed my train, and I thought there was no time like the present. In fact, dear, I thought if I waited I should have time to make certain of funking it, so I hid there, too. And I put on my big black capuchon, and sat down right in one of the wax-work groups—they couldn't see me from the passage where you walk. And after they put the lights out I simply went to sleep; and I woke up—and there was a light, and I heard some one say: 'They're only wax,' and it was Vincent. He thought I was one of the wax people, till I looked at him; and I expect he thought I was one of them even then, poor chap. And his match went out, and while I was trying to find my railway reading-lamp that I'd got near me, he began to scream, and the night watchman came running. And now he thinks every one in the asylum is made of wax, and he screams if they come near him. They have to put his food beside him while he's asleep. It's horrible. I can't help feeling as if it were my fault, somehow."

"Of course it's not," said Rose. "Poor Vincent! Do you know I never really liked him." There was a pause. Then she said: "But how was it you weren't frightened?"

"I was," he said, "horribly frightened. I—I—it sounds idiotic, but I thought I should go mad at first—I did really: and yet I had to go through with it. And then I got among the figures of the people in the Catacombs, the people who died for—for things, don't you know, died in such horrible ways. And there they were, so calm—and believing it was all all right. And I thought about what they'd gone through. It sounds awful rot I know, dear—but I expect I was sleepy. Those wax people, they sort of seemed as if they were alive, and were telling me there wasn't anything to be frightened about. I felt as if I were one of them, and they were all my friends, and they'd wake me if anything went wrong, so I just went to sleep."

"I think I understand," she said. But she didn't.

"And the odd thing is," he went on, "I've never been afraid of the dark since. Perhaps his calling me a coward had something to do with it."

"I don't think so," said she. And she was right. But she would never have understood how, nor why.

NESBIT'S ending is admittedly flat – she seems to have been unable to resist the temptation to insert one of her more conventional romantic endings – but the psychological complexity of the second act is truly eloquent. Fear looms in the background like dark, rolling vapor piling on the horizon and gradually drinking up the light. Nesbit deftly captures the psychological impressions of terror. Although Nesbit ultimately fails to maintain the dramatic tension by including a full third act instead of a tidy epilogue, and by shifting the mood from psychological to romantic, the legacy of "The Power of Darkness" continues in the legacy of wax museums in horror films and the collective imagination. The uncanny dreadfulness of wax statuary have been used in cinema multiple times since Nesbit's story became a sensation: the 1933 murder thriller, *Mystery of the Wax Museum*, its 1953 remake starring Vincent Price, *House of Wax*, and the unrelated Paris Hilton slasher flick of the same name.

A psychological, "haunted conscience" ghost story written in the vein of W. W. Jacobs, Algernon Blackwood, J. S. Le Fanu, E. F. Benson, and Ambrose Bierce, "In the Dark" is one of Nesbit's very best. The story is a vivid, genuine portrayal of a guilty conscience which pulls no punches, and ends with a hideous absolution of sin worthy of the Old Testament (or M. R. James for that matter). Instilled with brilliant Freudian implications, and rich in its emotional intensity, it is a truly excellent story. The title effectively conveys the essence of the plot, as it explores the hidden corners of one man's unconscious, where – when left alone with himself, stripped of all other points of reference, naked before one's conscience – he is as vulnerable to danger as a child lost in the dark: the unyielding pit of his own loathsome thoughts and fears. Darkness is a motif which Nesbit frequently employs ("Dark," or words relating to darkness occur in the titles of no fewer than four of her short stories), and one which helps her to convey the sense of existential terror which occurs without the reference points of society to distract us. Blackwood held this opinion as well, often deriving horror from the lack of civilization by marooning his witless victims in the wildernesses of the Canadian taiga, the Egyptian deserts, the Danube willow-marshes, or even the lonely fens and spinneys of the English countryside. But Nesbit has no need to go quite so far afield to isolate her victim from his surroundings, friends, and petty distractions: she need only turn out the light.

In The Dark
{1910}

IT may have been a form of madness. Or it may be that he really was what is called haunted. Or it may-though I don't pretend to understand how-have been the development, through intense suffering, of a sixth sense in a very nervous, highly strung nature. Something certainly led him where They were. And to him They were all one.

He told me the first part of the story, and the last part of it I saw with my own eyes.

Chapter I
Haldane and I were friends even in our school-days. What first brought us together was our common hatred of Visger, who came from

our part of the country. His people knew our people at home, so he was put on to us when he came. He was the most intolerable person, boy and man, that I have ever known. He would not tell a lie. And that was all right. But he didn't stop at that. If he were asked whether any other chap had done anything-been out of bounds, or up to any sort of lark-he would always say, 'I don't know, sir, but I believe so. He never did know-we took care of that. But what he believed was always right. I remember Haldane twisting his arm to say how he knew about that cherry-tree business, and he only said, 'I don't know-I just feel sure. And I was right, you see.' What can you do with a boy like that?

We grew up to be men. At least Haldane and I did. Visger grew up to be a prig. He was a vegetarian and a teetotaller, and an all-wooler and Christian Scientist, and all the things that prigs are-but he wasn't a common prig. He knew all sorts of things that he oughtn't to have known, that he couldn't have known in any ordinary decent way. It wasn't that he found things out. He just knew them. Once, when I was very unhappy, he came into my rooms-we were all in our last year at Oxford-and talked about things I hardly knew myself. That was really why I went to India that winter. It was bad enough to be unhappy, without having that beast knowing all about it.

I was away over a year. Coming back, I thought a lot about how jolly it would be to see old Haldane again. If I thought about Visger at all, I wished he was dead. But I didn't think about him much.

I did want to see Haldane. He was always such a jolly chap-gay, and kindly, and simple, honourable, uptight, and full of practical sympathies. I longed to see him, to see the smile in his jolly blue eyes, looking out from the net of wrinkles that laughing had made round them, to hear his jolly laugh, and feel the good grip of his big hand. I went straight from the docks to his chambers in Gray's Inn, and I found him cold, pale, anaemic, with dull eyes and a limp hand, and pale lips that smiled without mirth, and uttered a welcome without gladness.

He was surrounded by a litter of disordered furniture and personal effects half packed. Some big boxes stood corded, and there were cases of books, filled and waiting for the enclosing boards to be nailed on.

'Yes, I'm moving,' he said. 'I can't stand these rooms. There's something rum about them--something devilish rum. I clear our tomorrow.'

The autumn dusk was filling the corners with shadows. 'You got the furs,' I said, just for something to say, for I saw the big case that held them lying corded among the others.

'Furs?' he said. 'Oh yes. Thanks awfully. Yes. I forgot about the furs.' He laughed, out of politeness, I suppose, for there was no joke about the furs. They were many and fine-the best I could get for money, and I had seen them packed and sent off when my heart was very sore. He stood looking at me, and saying nothing.

'Come out and have a bit of dinner,' I said as cheerfully as I could.

'Too busy,' he answered, after the slightest possible pause, and a glance round the room--'look here-I'm awfully glad to see you-If you'd just slip over and order in dinner-I'd go myself-only-Well, you see how it is.'

I went. And when I came back, he had cleared a space near the fire, and moved his big gate-table into it. We dined there by candle light. I tried to be amusing. He, I am sure, tried to be amused. We did not succeed, either of us. And his haggard eyes watched me all the time, save in those fleeting moments when, without turning his head, he glanced back over his shoulder into the shadows that crowded round the little lighted place where we sat.

When we had dined and the man had come and taken away the dishes, I looked at Haldane very steadily, so that he stopped in a pointless anecdote, and looked interrogatively at me. 'Well?' I said.

'You're not listening,' he said petulantly. 'What's the matter?'

'That's what you'd better tell me,' I said.

He was silent, gave one of those furtive glances at the shadows, and stooped to stir the fire to--I knew it-a blaze that must light every corner of the room.

'You're all to pieces,' I said cheerfully. 'What have you been up to? Wine? Cards? Speculation? A woman? If you won't tell me, you'll have to tell your doctor. Why, my dear chap, you're a wreck.'

'You're a comfortable friend to have about the place,' he said, and smiled a mechanical smile not at all pleasant to see.

'I'm the friend you want, I think,' said I. 'Do you suppose I'm blind? Something's gone wrong and you've taken to something. Morphia, perhaps? And you've brooded over the thing till you've lost all sense of proportion. Out with it, old chap. I bet you a dollar it's not so bad as you think it.'

'If I could tell you-or tell anyone,' he said slowly, 'it wouldn't be so bad as it is. If I could tell anyone, I'd tell you. And even as it is, I've told you more than I've told anyone else.'

I could get nothing more out of him. But he pressed me to stay-would have given me his bed and made himself a shake-down, he said. But I had engaged my room at the Victoria, and I was expecting letters.

So I left him, quite late-and he stood on the stairs, holding a candle over the bannisters to light me down.

When I went back next morning, he was gone. Men were moving his furniture into a big van with somebody's Pantechnicon painted on it in big letters.

He had left no address with the porter, and had driven off in a hansom with two portmanteaux-to Waterloo, the porter thought.

Well, a man has a right to the monopoly of his own troubles, if he chooses to have it. And I had troubles of my own that kept me busy.

Chapter II

It was more than a year later that I saw Haldane again. I had got rooms in the Albany by this time, and he turned up there one morning, very early indeed-before breakfast in fact. And if he looked ghastly before, he now looked almost ghostly. His face looked as though it had worn thin, like an oyster shell that has for years been cast up twice a day by the sea on a shore all pebbly. His hands were thin as bird's claws, and they trembled like caught butterflies.

I welcomed him with enthusiastic cordiality and pressed breakfast on him. This time, I decided, I would ask no questions. For I saw that none were needed. He would tell me. He intended to tell me. He had come here to tell me, and for nothing else.

I lit the spirit lamp-I made coffee and small talk for him, and I ate and drank, and waited for him to begin. And it was like this that he began:

'I am going,' he said, 'to kill myself-oh, don't be alarmed,'-I suppose I had said or looked something-'I shan't do it here, or now. I shall do it when I have to-when I can't bear it any longer. And I want someone to know why. I don't want to feel that I'm the only living creature who does know. And I can trust you, can't I?'

I murmured something reassuring.

'I should like you, if you don't mind, to give me your word, that you won't tell a soul what I'm going to tell you, as long as I'm alive. Afterwards. . . you can tell whom you please.' I gave him my word.

He sat silent looking at the fire. Then he shrugged his shoulders.

'It's extraordinary how difficult it is to say it,' he said, and smiled. 'The fact is-you know that beast, George Visger.'

'Yes,' I said. 'I haven't seen him since I came back. Some one told me he'd gone to some island or other to preach vegetarianism to the cannibals. Anyhow, he's out of the way, bad luck to him.'

'Yes,' said Haldane, 'he's out of the way. But he's not preaching anything. In point of fact, he's dead.'

'Dead?' was all I could think of to say.

'Yes,' said he; 'it's not generally known, but he is.'

'What did he die of?' I asked, not that I cared. The bare fact was good enough for me.

'You know what an interfering chap he always was. Always knew everything. Heart to heart talks-and have everything open and above board. Well, he interfered between me and some one else-told her a pack of lies.'

'Lies?'

'Well, the things were true, but he made lies of them the way he told them-you know.' I did. I nodded. 'And she threw me over. And she died. And we weren't even friends. And I couldn't see her-before-I couldn't even. . . Oh, my God. . . But I went to the funeral. He was there. They'd asked him. And then I came back to my rooms. And I was sitting there, thinking. And he came up.'He would do. It's just what he would do. The beast! I hope you kicked him out.'

'No, I didn't. I listened to what he'd got to say. He came to say, No doubt it was all for the best. And he hadn't known the things he told her. He'd only guessed. He'd guessed right, damn him. What right had he to guess right? And he said it was all for the best, because, besides that, there was madness in my family. He'd found that out too-'

'And is there?'

'If there is, I didn't know it. And that was why it was all for the best. So then I said, "There wasn't any madness in my family before, but there is now," and I got hold of his throat. I am not sure whether I meant to kill him; I ought to have meant to kill him. Anyhow, I did kill him. What did you say?'

I had said nothing. It is not easy to think at once of the tactful and suitable thing to say, when your oldest friend tells you that he is a murderer.

'When I could get my hands out of his throat-it was as difficult as it is to drop the handles of a galvanic battery-he fell in a lump on the hearth-rug. And I saw what I'd done. How is it that murderers ever get found out?'

'They're careless, I suppose,' I found myself saying, 'they lose their nerve.'

'I didn't,' he said. 'I never was calmer, I sat down in the big chair and looked at him, and thought it all out. He was just off to that island--I knew that. He'd said goodbye to everyone. He'd told me that. There

179

was no blood to get rid of-or only a touch at the corner of his slack mouth. He wasn't going to travel in his own name because of interviewers. Mr Somebody Something's luggage would be unclaimed and his cabin empty. No one would guess that Mr Somebody Something was Sir George Visger, FRS. It was all as plain as plain. There was nothing to get rid of, but the man. No weapon, no blood-and I got rid of him all right.'

'How?'

He smiled cunningly.

'No, no,' he said; 'that's where I draw the line. It's not that I doubt your word, but if you talked in your sleep, or had a fever or anything. No, no. As long as you don't know where the body is, don't you see, I'm all right. Even if you could prove that I've said all this-which you can't-- it's only the wanderings of my poor unhinged brain. See?'

I saw. And I was sorry for him. And I did not believe that he had killed Visger. He was not the sort of man who kills people. So I said:

'Yes, old chap, I see. Now look here. Let's go away together, you and I-travel a bit and see the world, and forget all about that beastly chap.'

His eyes lighted up at that.

'Why,' he said, 'you understand. You don't hate me and shrink from me. I wish I'd told you before-you know-when you came and I was packing all my sticks. But it's too late now.

'Too late? Not a bit of it,' I said. 'Come, we'll pack our traps and be off tonight-out into the unknown, don't you know.

'That's where I'm going,' he said. 'You wait. When you've heard what's been happening to me, you won't be so keen to go travelling about with me.'

'But you've told me what's been happening co you,' I said, and the more I thought about what he had told me, the less I believed it.

'No,' he said, slowly, 'no-I've told you what happened to him. What happened to me is quite different. Did I tell you what his last words were? Just when I was coming at him. Before I'd got his throat, you know. He said, "Look out. You'll never to able to get rid of the body-Besides, anger's sinful." You know that way he had, like a tract on its hind legs. So afterwards I got thinking of that. But I didn't think of it for a year. Because I did get rid of his body all right. And then I was sitting in that comfortable chair, and I thought, "Hullo, it must be about a year now, since that-" and I pulled out my pocket-book and went to the window to look at a little almanac I carry about-it was getting dusk-and sure enough it was a year, to the day. And then I remembered what he'd said. And I said to myself, "Not much trouble

180

about getting rid of your body, you brute." And then I looked at the hearth-rug and-Ah!' he screamed suddenly and very loud-'I can't tell you-no, I can't.'

My man opened the door-he wore a smooth face over his wriggling curiosity. 'Did you call, sir?'

'Yes,' I lied. 'I want you to take a note to the bank, and wait for an answer.'

When he was got rid of, Haldane said: 'Where was I?-'

'You were just telling me what happened after you looked at the almanac. What was it?'

'Nothing much,' he said, laughing softly, 'oh, nothing much-only that I glanced at the hearthrug-and there he was-the man I'd killed a year before. Don't try to explain, or I shall lose my temper. The door was shut. The windows were shut. He hadn't been there a minute before. And he was there then. That's all.'

Hallucination was one of the words I stumbled among.

'Exactly what I thought,' he said triumphantly, 'but-I touched it. It was quite real. Heavy, you know, and harder than live people are somehow, to the touch-more like a stone thing covered with kid the hands were, and the arms like a marble statue in a blue serge suit. Don't you hate men who wear blue serge suits?' 'There are halllucinations of touch too,' I found myself saying..

'Exactly what I thought,' said Haldane more triumphant than ever, 'but there are limits, you know-limits. So then I thought someone had got him out-the real him-and stuck him there to frighten me-while my back was turned, and I went to the place where I'd hidden him, and he was there-ah!-jusr as I'd left him. Only. . . it was a year ago. There are two of him there now.'

'My dear chap,' I said 'this is simply comic.'

'Yes,' he said, 'It is amusing. I find it so myself. Especially in the night when I wake up and think of it. I hope I shan't die in the dark, Winston: That's one of the reasons why I think I shall have to kill myself. I could be sure then of not dying in the dark.'

'Is that all?' I asked, feeling sure that it must be.

'No,' said Haldane at once. 'That's not all. He's come back to rue again. In a railway carriage it was. I'd been asleep. When I woke up, there he was lying on the seat opposite me. Looked just the same. I pitched him out on the line in Red Hill Tunnel. And if I see him again, I'm going out myself. I can't stand it. It's too much. I'd sooner go. Whatever the next world's like, there aren't things in it like that. We leave them here, in graves and boxes and . . You think I'm mad. But I'm

182

not. You can't help me-no one can help me. He knew, you see. He said I shouldn't be able to get rid of the body. And I can't get rid of it. I can't. I can't. He knew. He always did know things that he couldn 't know. But I'll cut his game short. After all, I've got the ace of trumps, and I'll play it on his next trick. I give you my word of honour, Winston, that I'm not mad.'

'My dear old man,' I said, 'I don't think you're mad. But I do think your nerves are very much upset. Mine are a bit, too. Do you know why I went to India? It was because of you and her. I couldn't stay and see it, though I wished for your happiness and all that; you know I did. And when I came back, she . . . and you . . . Let's see it out together,' I said. 'You won't keep fancying things if you've got me to talk to. And I always said you weren't half a bad old duffer.'

'She liked you,' he said.

'Oh, yes,' I said, 'she liked me.

Chapter III

That was how we came to go abroad together. I was full of hope for him. He'd always been such a splendid chap-so sane and strong. I couldn't believe that he was gone mad, gone for ever, I mean, so that he'd never come right again. Perhaps may own trouble made it easy for me to see things not quite straight. Anyway, I took him away to recover his mind's health, exactly as I should have taken him away to get strong after a fever. And the madness seemed to pass away, and in a month or two we were perfectly jolly, and I thought I had cured him. And I was very glad because of that old friendship of ours, and because she had loved him and liked me.

We never spoke of Visger. I thought he had forgotten all about him. I thought I understood how his mind, over-strained by sorrow and anger, had fixed on the man he hated, and woven a nightmare web of horror round that detestable personality. And I had got the whip hand of my own trouble. And we were as jolly as sandboys together all those months.

And we came to Bruges at last in our travels, and Bruges was very full, because of the Exhibition. We could only get one room and one bed. So we tossed for the bed, and the one who lost the toss was to make the best of the night in the armchair. And the bedclothes we were to share equitably.

We spent the evening at a café chantant and finished at a beer hall, and it was late and sleepy when we got back to the Grande Vigne. I took our key from its nail in the concierge's room, and we went up. We talked awhile, I remember, of the town, and the belfry, and the Venetian aspect of the canals by moonlight, and then Haldane got into bed, and I made a chrysalis of myself with my share of the blankets and fitted the tight roll into the armchair. I was not at all comfortable, but I was compensatingly tired, and I was nearly asleep when Haldane roused me up to tell me about his will.

'I've left everything to you, old man,' he said. 'I know I can trust you to see to everything.' 'Quite so,' said I, 'and if you don't mind, we'll talk about it in the morning.'

He tried to go on about it, and about what a friend I'd been, and all that, but I shut him up and told him to go to sleep. But no. He wasn't comfortable, he said. And he'd got a thirst like a lime kiln. And he'd noticed that there was no water-bottle in the room. 'And the water in the jug's like pale soup,' he said.

'Oh, all right,' said I. 'Light your candle and go and get some water, then, in Heaven's name, and let me get to sleep.'

But he said, 'No-you light it. I don't want to get out of bed in the dark. I might-I might step on something, mightn't I-or walk into something that wasn't there when I got into bed.'

'Rot,' I said, 'walk into your grandmother.' But I lit the candle all the same. He sat up in bed and looked at me-very pale-with his hair all tumbled from the pillow, and his eyes blinking and shining/ 'That's better,' he said. And then, 'I say-look here. Oh-yes-I see. It's all right. Queer how they mark the sheets here. Blest if I didn't think it was blood, just for the minute.' The sheet was marked, not at the corner, as sheets are marked at home, but right in the middle where it turns down, with big, red, cross-stitching.

'Yes, I see,' I said, 'it is a queer place to mark it.'

'It's queer letters to have on it,' he said. 'G.V.'

'Grande Vigne,' I said. 'What letters do you expect them to mark things with? Hurry up.

'You come too,' he said. 'Yes, it does stand for Grande Vigne, of course. I wish you'd come down too, Winston.'

'I'll go down,' I said and turned with the candle in my hand.

He was out of bed and close to me in a flash.

'No,' said he, 'I don't want to stay alone in the dark.'

He said it just as a frightened child might have done.

'All right then, come along,' I said. And we went. I tried to make some joke, I remember, about the length of his hair, and the cut of his pajamas-but I was sick with disappointment. For it was almost quite plain to me, even then, that all my time and trouble had been thrown

184

away, and that he wasn't cured after all. We went down as quietly as we could, and got a carafe of water from the long bare dining table in the sale à manger. He got hold of my arm at first, and then he got the candle away from me, and went very slowly, shading the light with his hand, and looking very carefully all about, as though he expected to see something that he wanted very desperately nor to see. And of course, I knew what that something was. I didn't like the way he was going on. I can't at all express how deeply I didn't like it. And he looked over his shoulder every now and then, just as he did that first evening after I came back from India.

The thing got on my nerves so that I could hardly find the way back to our room. And when we got there, I give you my word, I more than half expected to see what he had expected to see--that, or something like that, on the hearth-rug. But of course there was nothing.

I blew out the light and tightened my blankets round me-I'd been trailing them after me in our expedition. And I was settled in my chair when Haldane spoke.

'You've got all the blankets,' he said.

'No, I haven't,' said I, 'only what I've always had.' 'I can't find mine then,' he said and I could hear his teeth chattering. 'And I'm cold. I'm. . .

For God's sake, light the candle. Light it. Light it. Something horrible. . .'

And I couldn't find the matches.

'Light the candle, light the candle,' he said, and his voice broke, as a boy's does sometimes in chapel. 'If you don't he'll come to me. It is so easy to come at any one in the dark. Oh Winston, light the candle, for the love of God! I can't die in the dark.'

'I am lighting it,' I said savagely, and I was feeling for the matches on the marble-topped chest of drawers, on the mantelpiece-everywhere but on the round centre table where I'd put them. 'You're not going to die. Don't be a fool,' I said. 'It's all right. I'll get a light in a second.'

He said, 'It's cold. It's cold. It's cold,' like that, three times. And then he screamed aloud, like a woman-like a child-like a hare when the dogs have got it. I had heard him scream like that once before.

'What is it?' I cried, hardly less loud. 'For God's sake, hold your noise. What is it?' There was an empty silence. Then, very slowly:

'It's Visger,' he said. And he spoke thickly, as through some stifling veil.

'Nonsense. Where?' I asked, and my hand closed on the matches as he spoke.

'Here,' he screamed sharply, as though he had torn the veil away, 'here, beside me. In the bed.' I got the candle alight. I got across to him.

He was crushed in a heap at the edge of the bed. Stretched on the bed beyond him was a dead man, white and very cold.

Haldane had died in the dark.

It was all so simple.

We had come to the wrong room. The man the room belonged to was there, on the bed he had engaged and paid for before he died of heart disease, earlier in the day. A French commis-voyageur representing soap and perfumery; his name, Felix Leblanc.

Later, in England, I made cautious enquiries. The body of a man had been found in the Red Hill tunnel-a haberdasher man named Simmons, who had drunk spirits of salts, owing to the depression of trade. The bottle was clutched in his dead hand.

For reasons that I had, I took care to have a police inspector with me when I opened the boxes that came to me by Haldane's will. One of them was the big box, metal lined, in which I had sent him the skins from India-for a wedding present, God help us all!

It was closely soldered.

Inside were the skins of beasts? No. The bodies of two men. One was identified, after some trouble, as that of a hawker of pens in city offices-subject to fits. He had died in one, it seemed. The other body was Visger's, right enough.

Explain it as you like. I offered you, if you remember, a choice of explanations before I began the story. I have not yet found the explanation that can satisfy me.

THE story is genuinely of the first water of ghost stories – one tremendously underrated and horribly under-anthologized. There stirs within it the spirts of many classic, ambiguous tales of ghostly revenge: Jacobs' "The Well," Bierce's "Death of Halpin Frayser," M. R. James' "Stalls of Barchester Cathedral," and M. E. Braddon's "The Cold Embrace." It stands alongside these masterworks of the genre as an exemplar of psychological horror. Like the stories mentioned, there is every reason (in fact, so *many* that it is admirable on Nesbit's behalf that she even *suggests* that there could be a supernatural explanation) to believe that the horrors wrought on poor Haldane are entirely psychological. There is almost no reason to suspect preternatural agency. But the narrator strongly implies that although he has seen with his own eyes and heard with his own ears the rational explanations for each haunting, he is inclined (though he may demur gently) towards a paranormal understanding of Haldane's last years on earth. He suggests that while the bodies were all those of strangers, the sheer coincidence of so many encounters with corpses, with the significant "G.V.," and with the sense of predatory doom is unsettling to a rational worldview. The story, like so many of Nesbit's, is redolent with Freudian imagery and meaning: one could easily view the death of Visger – the truthful, all-knowing tattle-tale – as a man's attempt to squelch his overactive conscience, or Super-Ego. In a scene that resembles Edgar Allan Poe's "William Wilson," (wherein a man murders his bothersome Doppelganger, who represents conscience), Haldane can no longer stand the accusations that Visger levels at him, especially those that cost him the love of his life. If any supernaturalism is present in this story, it is unquestionably Visger's preternatural sensitivity to secret sins: he knows Haldane's indiscretions, and gently reminds him of their reality. He is both literally and figuratively Haldane's conscience, and it is more out of bitter self-hatred (he did, after all, trigger his lover's death through his own sexual recklessness), than hatred of Visger that chokes the life out of his peculiar Jiminy Cricket. Without the Super-Ego – the judiciary branch of the human consciousness – there is nothing left to guide the Ego through the inferno of the unconscious. Visger continues on, nonetheless, performing his regulating office as a ghost, but he is no longer the emissary of guilt and remorse: killing his conscience was a *capital* crime against his own self, and Haldane will now suffer the ultimate consequence for trying to silence it.

MUCH like "In the Dark," "The Violet Car" has become a classic of the English ghost story, and is an exemplar of the form – one which stands admirably alongside the best supernatural tales of Amelia B. Edwards, Mrs Oliphant, Elizabeth Gaskell, and Charles Dickens. It is – I should say – very similar in mood and timbre to these practitioners of the Victorian ghost story, and unlike her more brutal masterpieces – "Man-Size," "Charrington's Wedding," "Semi-Detached," etc. – it has the graceful elegance and haunting, Old Testament morality of the Victorians' best speculative fiction. In particular it owes a debt to Kipling's "The Phantom Rickshaw" (which in turn owes a debt to Edwards' "Phantom Coach"), Dickens' "The Signal-Man," Le Fanu's "The Familiar," and Gaskell's "The Old Nurse's Story," all of which concern characters hounded by a relentless supernatural agent whose demands for justice are impossible to silence, and whose unalterable momentum ultimately crushes their hapless victims. The Victorian ghost story was largely a moral parable of karmic justice and a deaf universe bent on restoring order regardless of intentions or justice: an eye for an eye, a misery for a misery. Although this may seem moralistic, the effect is truly chilling, and can at times even be Lovecraftian: no benevolent forces are here to arbiter justice – a man who kills his true love's wicked murderer may be haunted to death by the evil man's ghost; a woman who unintentionally caused the heartbreak of a dear friend can expect no mercy or understanding, only destruction; a hapless railroad worker is warned about impending tragedies, but only just enough to be distraught when they happen – never enough to prevent them – and his reward for his attentiveness is death. "In the Dark" and "The Violet Car" each contain the Old Testament vitriol that made Le Fanu and M. R. James such feared nighttime reading, but none of Nesbit's tales (other than "Man-Size," of course) contain the level of merciless vindication that "The Violet Car" delivers. It is a savage tale of guilt, punishment, and loss, and it is among Nesbit's very best.

The Violet Car
{1910}

DO you know the downs-the wide, windy spaces, the rounded shoulders of hills leaned against the sky, the hollows where farms and homesteads nestle sheltered, with trees round them pressed close and tight as a carnation in a button- hole?

On long summer days it is good to lie on the downs, between short turf and pale, clear sky, to smell the wild thyme, and hear the tiny tinkle of the sheep-bells and the song of the skylark. But on winter evenings when the wind is waking up to its work, spitting rain in your eyes, beating the poor, naked trees and shaking the dusk across the hills like a grey pall, then it is better to be by a warm fireside, in one of the farms that lie lonely where shelter is, and oppose their windows glowing with candle light and firelight to the deepening darkness, as faith holds up its love-lamp in the night of sin and sorrow that is life.

I'm unaccustomed to literary effort - and I feel that I shall not say what I have to say, or that it will convince you, unless I say it very plainly. I thought I could adorn my story with pleasant words, prettily arranged. But as I pause to think of what really happened, I see that the plainest words will be the best. I do not know how to weave a plot, nor how to embroider it. It is best not to try. These things happened. I have no skill to add to what happened, nor is any adding of mine needed.

I'm a nurse - and I was sent for to go to Charlestown - a mental case. It was November - and the fog was thick in London, so that my cab went at a foot's pace, so I missed the train by which I should have gone. I sent a telegram to Charlestown, and waited in the dismal waiting room at London Bridge. The time was passed for me by a little child. Its mother, a widow, seemed too crushed to be able to respond to its quick questionings. She answered briefly, and not, as it seemed, to the child's satisfaction. The child itself presently seemed to perceive that its mother was not, so to speak, available. It leaned back on the wide, dusty seat and yawned. I caught its eye, and smiled. It would not smile, but it looked, I took out of my bag a silk purse, bright with beads and steel tassels and turned it over and over. Presently, the child slid along the seat and said, "Let me" - After that all was easy. The mother sat with eyes closed. When I rose to go, she opened them and thanked me. The child, clinging, kissed me. Later I saw them get into a first -class carriage in my train. My ticket was a third-class one.

I expected, of course, that there would be a conveyance of some sort to meet me at the station - but there was nothing. Nor was there a cab or a fly to be seen. It was by the time nearly dark, and the wind was driving, the rain almost horizontally along the unfrequented road that lay beyond the door of the station. I looked out, forlorn and perplexed.

"Haven't you engaged a carriage?" It was the window lady who spoke. I explained.

"My motor will be here directly," she said, "you'll let me drive you? Where is it you are going?

"Charlestown," I said, and as I said it, I was aware of a very odd change in her face. A faint change, but quite unmistakable.

"Why do you look like that? I asked her bluntly. And, of course, she said, "Like what?"

"There is nothing wrong with the house?" I said, for that, I found, was what I had taken that faint change to signify; and I was very young, and one has heard tales. "No reason, why I shouldn't go there, I mean?"

"No - oh no - " she glanced out through the rain, and I knew as well as though she had told me that there was a reason why she should not wish to go there.

"Don't trouble," I said, "Its "its very kind of you - but it's probably out of your way and..."

"Oh- but I 'll take you - of course I'll take you", she said and the child said "Mother, here comes the car."

And come it did, though neither of us heard it till the child had spoken. I know nothing of motor cars, and I don't know the names of any of the parts of them. This was like a brougham - only you got in at the back, as you do in a waggonette, the seats were in the corners, and when the door was shut there was a little seat that pulled up, and the child sat on it between us. And it moved like magic- or like a dream of a train.

We drove quickly through the dark - I could hear the wind screaming, and the wild dashing of the rain against the windows, even through the whirring of the machinery. One could see nothing of the country -only the black night, and the shafts of light from the lamps in front.

After, as it seemed, a very long time, the chauffeur got down and opened a gate. We went through it, and after that the road was very much rougher. We were quite silent in the car, and the child had fallen asleep.

We stopped, and the car stood pulsating as though it were out of breath, while the chauffeur hauled down my box. It was so dark that I could not see the shape of the house, only the lights in the downstairs windows, and the low-walled front garden faintly revealed by their light and the light of the motor lamps. Yet I felt that it was a fair-sized house, that it was surrounded by big trees, and that there was a pond or river close by. In daylight next day I found that all this was so. I have never been able to tell us how I knew it that first night, in the dark, but I did know it. Perhaps there was something in the way the rain fell on the trees and on the water, I don't know.

The chauffeur took my box up a stone path, whereon I got out, and said my good byes and thanks.

"Don't wait, please don't " I said "I am all right now. Thank you a thousand times."

The car however stood pulsating till I had reached the doorstep, then it caught its breath, as it were, throbbed more loudly, turned, and went.

And still the door had not opened. I felt for the knocker, and rapped smartly. Inside the door I was sure I heard whispering. The car light was fast diminishing to a little distant star, and it panting sounded now hardly at all. When it ceased to sound at all, the place was quiet as death. The lights glowed redly from curtained windows, but there was no other sign of life. I wished I had not been in such a hurry to part from my escort, from my human companionship, and from the great, solid, competent presence of the moto car, I knocked again, and this time I followed the knock by a shout.

"Hello!" I cried. "Let me in. I'm the nurse!"
There was a pause, such a pause as would allow time for whisperers to exchange glances on the other side of a door.
Then a bolt ground back, a key turned, and the doorway framed no longer cold, wet wood, but light and welcoming warmth- and faces.

"Come in, oh, come in" said a voice, a woman's voice and the voice of a man said: "We didn't know there was anyone there."
And I had shaken the very door with my knockings!
I went in, blinking at the light, and the man called a servant, and between them they carried my box upstairs.

The woman took my arm and led me into a low, square room, pleasant, homely and comfortable, with solid mid-Victorian comfort - the kind that expressed iself in rep and mahogany. In the lamplight I turned to look at her. She was small and thin, her hair, her face, and her hands were of the same tint of greyish yellow.

"Mrs Eldridge?" I asked.

"Yes" said he, very softly."Oh! I am so glad you've come. I hope you won't be dull here. I hope you'll stay. I hope I shall be able to make you comfortable.

She had a gentle, urgent way of speaking that was very winning.
I'm sure I shall be very comfortable," I said;"but it's I that am to take care of you. Have you been ill long?

It's not me that's ill, really," she said , "its him."

Now it was Mr Robert Eldridge who had written to engage me to

192

attend on his wife, who was, he said, slightly deranged.

"I see", said I. One must never contradict them, it only aggravates their disorder.

"The reason..." she was beginning, when his foot sounded on the stairs,and she fluttered off to get candles and hot water.

He came in and shut the door. A fair, bearded, elderly man, quite ordinary.

"You will take care of her" he said, "I don't want her to get talking to people. She fancies things."

"What form do the illusions take?" I asked prosaically.

"She thinks I am mad," he said with a short laugh.

"It is a very usual form. Is that all?

"Its about enough. And she can't hear things that I can hear, see things that I can see, and she can't smell things. By the way, you didn't see or hear anything of a motor car as you came up, did you?"

"I came up in a motor car," I said shortly. "You never sent to meet me, and a lady gave me a lift." I was going to explain about my missing the earlier train, when I found that he was not listening to me. He was watching the door. When his wife came in, with a steaming jug in one hand and a flat candlestick in the other, he went towards her, and whispered eagerly. The only words I caught were: "She came in a real motor."

Apparently, to these simple people a motor was a great a novelty as to me.   My telegram, by the way, was delivered next morning.

They were very kind to me, they treated me as an honoured guest. When the rain stopped, as it did late the next day, and I was able to go out, I found that Charlestown was a farm, a large farm, but even to my inexperienced eyes, it seemed neglected and unprosperous. There was absolutely nothing for me to do but to follow Mrs Eldridge, helping her where I could in her household duties, and to sit with her while she sewed in the homely parlour. When I had been in the house a few days, I began to put together the little things that I had noticed singly, and the life at the farm seemed suddenly to come into focus, as strange surroundings do after a while.

I found that I had noticed that Mr and Mrs Eldridge were very fond of each other, and that it was a fondness, and their way of shewing it was a way that told that they had known sorrow, and had borne it together. That she shewed no sign of mental derangement, save in the persistent belief of hers that he was deranged. That the morning found them fairly cheerful, that after the early dinner they seemed to grow more and more depressed, that after the early cup of tea -that is just as dusk was falling - they always went for a walk together. That they never ask me to join them in this walk, and that it always took the same direction - across the downs towards the sea. That they always returned from this walk pale and dejected, that she sometimes cried afterwards alone in their bedroom, while he was shut up in the little room they called the office, where he did his account, and paid his men's wages, and where his hunting-crops and guns were kept. After supper, which was early, they always made an effort to be cheerful. I knew that this effort was for my sake, and I knew that each of them thought it was good for the other to make it.

Just as I had known before they shewed it to me that Charlestown was surrounded by big trees and had a great pond beside it, so I knew, and in as inexplicable a way, that with these two fear lived. It looked at me out of their eyes. And I knew too , that this fear was not her fear. I had not been two days in the place before I found that I was beginning to be fond of them both. They were so kind, so gentle, so ordinary, so homely - the kind of people who ought not to have known the name of fear - the kind of people to whom all honest, simple joys should have come by right, and no sorrows but such as come to us all, the death of old friends, and the slow changes of advancing years.

They seemed to belong to the land - to the downs, and the copses, and the old pastures, and the lessening cornfields. I found myself wishing that I, too, belonged to these, that I had been born a farmer's daughter. All the stress and struggle of cram and exam, of school, and college and hospital, seemed so loud and futile, compared with these open secrets of the down life. And I felt this the more, as more and more I felt that I must leave it all - that there was, honestly, no work for me here such as for good or ill I had been trained to do.

"I ought not to stay" I said to her one afternoon, as we stood at the open door. It was February now, and the snowdrops were thick in tufts beside the flagged path. "You are quite well."

"I am" she said.

"You are quite well, both of you," I said. "I oughtn't to be taking your money and doing nothing for it"

"You are doing everything" she said, "you don't know how much you are doing."

"We had a daughter of our own once," she added vaguely, and then, after a very long pause, she said very quietly and distinctly: "He has never been the same since."

"How not the same?" I asked, turning my face up to the thin February sunshine.

194

She tapped her wrinkled, yellow-grey forehead, as country people do. "Not right here," she said.

"How?" I asked, "Dear Mrs Eldridge, tell me; perhaps I could help somehow."

Her voice was so sane, so sweet. It had come to this with me, that I did not know which of those two was the one who needed my help.

"He sees things that no one else sees, and hear things no one else hears, and smells things that you can't smell if you are standing there beside him."

I remember with a sudden smile his words to me on the morning of my arrival: "She can't see, or hear, or smell."

And once more I wondered to which of the two I owed my service.

Have you any idea why? I asked. She caught at my arm.

"It was after our Bessie died," she said - the very day she was buried. The motor that killed her - they said it was an accident- it was on the Brighton Road. It was a violet colour. They go into mourning for Queens with violet, don't they? she added; "and my Bessie, she was a Queen. So the motor was violet: That was all right, wasn't it?

I told myself now that I saw the woman was not normal, and I saw why. It was grief that had turned her brain. There must have been some change in my look, though I ought to have known better, for she said suddenly, "No, I'll not tell you any more."

And then he came out. He never left me alone with her for very long. Nor did she ever leave him for very long alone with me.

I did not intend to spy upon them, though I am not sure that my position as nurse to one mentally afflicted would not have justified such spying. But I did not spy. It was chance. I had been to village to get some blue sewing silk for a blouse I was making, and there was a royal sunset which tempted me to prolong my walk. That was how I found myself on the high downs where they slope to the broken edge of England - the sheer, white cliffs against which the English Channel beats for ever. The furze was in flower, and the skylarks were singing, and my thoughts were with my own life, my own hopes and dreams. So I found that I had struck a road, without knowing when I had struck it. I followed it towards the sea, and quite soon it ceased to be a road, and merged in the pathless turf as a tream sometimes disappears in sand. There was nothing but turf and furze bushes, the song of the skylarks, and beyond the slope that ended at the cliff's edge, the booming of the sea. I turned back, following the road, which defined itself again a few yards back and presently sank to a lane, deep-banked and bordered with brown hedge stuff . It was there that I came upon them in the dusk. And I heard their voices before I saw them, and before it was possible for them to see me. It was her voice that I heard first.

"No,no,no,no,no" it said.

"I tell you yes," that was his voice; there -can't you hear it, that panting sound - right away -away? It must be at the very edge of the cliff."

"There is nothing dearie," she said, "indeed there's nothing"

"You are deaf - and blind - stand back I tell you, it's close upon us." I came round the corner of the lane then, and as I came, I saw him catch her arm and throw her against the hedge - violently, as though the danger be feared were indeed close upon them. I stopped behind the turn of the hedge and stepped back. They had not seen me. Her eyes were on his face, and they held a world of pity, love, agony - his face was set in a mask of terror, and his eyes moved quickly as though they followed down the lane the swift passage of something -something that neither she nor I could see. Next moment he was cowering, pressing his body into the hedge - his face hidden in his hands, and his whole body tembling so that I could see it, even from where I was a dozen yards away, through the light screen of the overgrown hedge.

"And the smell of it" he said, "Do you mean to tell me you can't smell it?"

She had her arms round him.

"Come home, dearie," she said."Come home! It's all your fancy -come home with your old wife that loves you."

They went home

Next day I asked her to come to my room to look at the new blue blouse. When I had shown it to her I told her, what I had seen and heard yesterday in the lane.

"And now I know," I said, "which of you it is that wants care." To my amazement she said very eagerly, "Which?"

"Why, he - of course" - I told her, "there was nothing there." She sat down in the chintz covered armchair by the window, and broke into wild weeping. I stood by her and soothed her as well as I could.

"It's a comfort to know," she said at last, "I haven't known what to believe. Many a time, lately, I've wondered whether after all it could be me that was mad, like he said. And there was nothing there? There always was nothing there- and it's on him the judgement, not on me. On him. Well, that's something to be thankful for."

So her tears, I told myself, had been more of relief at her own escape, I looked at her with distate, and forgot that I had been fond of her. So that her next words cut me like little knives.

196

"It's bad enough for him as it is," she said, "but it's nothing to what it would be for him, if I was really to go off my head and him left to think he'd brought it on me. You see, now I can look after him the same as I've always done. It's only once in the day it come over him. He couldn't bear it, if it was all the time - like it'll be for me now. It's much better it should be him - I'm better able to bear it than he is."

I kissed her then and put my arms round her, and said, "Tell me what it is that frightens him so - and it's every day, you say?"

"Yes,- ever since...I 'll tell you. It's a sort of comfort to speak out. It was a violet-coloured car that killed our Bessie. You know, our girl that I have told you about. And it's a violet -coloured car that he thinks he sees - every day up there in the lane. And he says he hears it, and that he smells the smell of the machinery - the stuff they put in it - you know."

"Petrol?"

"Yes, and you can see he hears it, and you can see he sees it. It haunts him, as if it was a ghost. You see, it was he that picked her up after the violet car went over her, It was that that turned him. I only saw her as he carried her in, in his arms - and then he'd covered her face. But he saw her just as they 'd left her, lying in the dust...you could see the place on the road where it happened for days and days."

"Didn't they come back?"

"Oh yes...they came back. But Bessie didn't come back. But there was a judgement on them. The very night of the funeral, that violetcar went over the cliff -dashed to pieces - every soul in it. That was that man's widow that drove you home the first night."

"I wonder she uses a car after that," I said - I wanted something commonplace to say.

"Oh," said Mrs Eldridge, "it's all what you're used to. We don't stop walking because our girl was killed on the road. Motoring comes as natural to them as walking to us. There's my old man calling - poor old dear. He wants me to go out with him

She went, all in hurry, and in her hurry slipped on the stairs and twisted her ankle. It all happened in a minute and it was a bad sprain. When I had bound it up, and she was on the sofa, she looked at him, standing as if he were undecided, staring out of the window, with his cap in his hand. And she looked at me.

"Mr Eldridge musn't miss his walk," she said. "You go with him my dear,. A breath of air will do you good,"

So I went, understanding as well as though he had told me, that he did not want me with him, and that he was afraid to go alone, and that he yet had to go.

We went up the lane in silence. At that corner he stopped suddenly, caught my arm, dragged me back. His eyes followed something that I could not see. Then he exhaled a held breath, and said, "I thought I heard a motor coming." He had found it hard to control his terror, and I saw beads of sweat on his forehead and temples. Then we went back to the house.

The sprain was a bad one. Mrs Eldridge had to rest, and again next day it was I who went with him to the corner of the lane.
This time he could not, or did not try to, conceal what he felt. "There - listen!" he said. "Surely you can hear it?"

I heard nothing.

"Stand back," he cried shrilly, suddenly, and we stood back close against the hedge.

Again the eyes followed something invisible to me, and again the held breath exhaled.

"It will kill me one of these days," he said, "and I don't know that I care how soon - if it wasn't for her."

"Tell me," I said, full of that importance, that conscious competence, that one feels in the presence of other people's troubles. He looked at me.

"I will tell you, by God." he said. "I couldn't tell her. Young lady, I've gone so far as wishing myself a Roman for the sake of a priest to tell it to. But I can tell you, without losing my soul more than it's lost already. Did you ever hear tell of a violet car that got smashed up - went over the cliff?

"Yes" I said "Yes"

The man that killed my girl was new to the place. And he hadn't any eyes - or ears - or he'd have known me, seeing we'd been face to face at the inquest. And you'd have thought he had have stayed at home that one day, with the blinds drawn down. But not he. He was swirling and swiveling all about the country in his cursed violet car, the very time we were burying her. And at dusk - there was a mist coming up- he come up behind me in this very lane, and I stood back, and he pulls up, and he calls out, with his damned lights full in my face: "Can you tell me the way to Hexham, my man?" says he.

"I'd have liked to shew him the way to hell. And that was the way for me, not him. I don't know how I came to do it. I didn't mean to do it. I didn't think I was going to - and before I knew anything, I'd said it "Straight ahead," I said "Keep straight ahead." Then the motor-thing panted, chuckled and he was off. I ran after him to try to stop him - but

198

what's the use of running after these motor-devils? And he kept straight on. And every day since then, every dear day, the car comes by, the violet car that nobody see but me and it keeps straight on."

"You ought to go away," I said, speaking as I trained to speak. "You fancy these things. You probably fancied the whole thing. I don't suppose you ever did tell the violet car to go straight ahead. I expect it was all imagination, and the shock of your poor daughter's death. You ought to go right away."

"I can't, he said earnestly. "If I did, some one else would see the car. You see, somebody has to see it everyday as long as I live. If it wasn't me, it would be someone else. And I'm the only person who deserves to see it. I wouldn't like anyone else to see it - it's too horrible. It's much more horrible than you think," he added slowly.

I asked him, walking beside him down the quiet lane, what it was that was so horrible about the violet car. I think I quite expected him to say that it was splashed with his daughter's blood...What he did say was, "It's too horrible to tell you," and he shuddered.

I was young then, and youth always thinks it can move moutains. I persuaded myself that I could cure him of his delusion by attacking - not the main fort - that is always, to begin with, impregnable, but one, so to speak, of the outworks. I set myself to persuade him not to go to that corner in the lane, at that hour in the afternoon.

"But if I don't, someone else will see it."

"There'll be nobody there to see it," I said briskly.

"Someone will be there. Mark my words, someone will be there - and then they'll know."

"Then I'll be the someone," I said. "Come - you stay at home with your wife, and I'll go - and if I see it I'll promise to tell you and if I don't - well, then I will be able to go away with a clear conscience."

"A clear conscience," he repeated.

I argued with him in every moment when it was possible to catch him alone. I put all my will and all my energy in to my persuasions. Suddenly, like a door that you've been trying to open, and that has resisted every key till the last one, he gave way. Yes - I should go to the lane. And he would not go.

I went.

Being, as I said before, a novice in the writing of stories, I perhaps haven't made you understand that it was quite hard for me to go - that I felt myself at once a coward and a heroine. This business of an imaginary motor that only one poor old farmer could see, probably appears to you quite commonplace and ordinary. It was not so with

me. You see, the idea of this thing had dominated my life for weeks and months, had dominated even before I knew the nature of the domination. It was this that was the fear that I had known to walk with these two people, the fear that shared their bed and board, that lay down and rose up with them. The old man's fear of this and his fear of his fear. And the old man was terribly convincing. When one talked with him, it was quite difficult to believe that he was mad, and that there wasn't, and coudn't be, a mysteriously horrible motor that was visible to him, and invisible to other poeple. And when he said that, if he were not in lane, someone else would see it - it was easy to say "Nonsense", but to think "Nonsense" was not so easy and to feel "Nonsense" quite oddly difficult.

I walked up and down the lane in the dusk, wishing not to wonder what might be the hidden horror in the violet car. I would not let blood into my thoughts. I was not going to be fooled by thought transference, or any of those transcendental follies. I was not going to be hypnotized into seeing things.

I walked up the lane -- I had promised him to stand near that corner for five minutes, and I stood there in the deepening dusk, looking up towards the downs and the sea. There were pale stars. Everything was very still. Five minutes is a long time. I held my watch in my hand. Four -- four and a quarter --four and a half. Five. I turned instantly. And then I saw that he had followed me -- he was standing a dozen yards away -- and his face was turned from me. It was turned towards a motor car that shot up the lane.   It came very swiftly, and before it came to where he was, I knew that it was very horrible. I crushed myself back in to the crackling bare hedge, as I should have done to leave room for the passage of a real car -though I knew that this one was not real. It looked real - but I knew it was not.

As it neared him. he started back, then suddenly he cried out. I heard him,"No,no,no,no - no more, no more," was what he cried, with that he flung himself down on the road in front of the car, and its great tyres passed over him. Then the car shot past me and I saw what the full horror of it was. There was no blood - that was not the horror. The colour of it was, as she had said, violet.

I got to him and got his head up. He was dead. I was quite calm and collected now, and felt that to be so was extremely creditable to me. I went to a cottage where a labourer was having tea -he got some men and a hurdle.

When I told his wife, the first intelligible thing she said was:"It's better for him. Whatever he did he's paid for now -So it's looks as though she had known - or guessed - more than he thought.

I stayed with her till her death. She did not live long.

You think perhaps that the old man was knocked down and killed by a real motor, which happened to come that way of all ways, at that hour of all hours, and happened to be, of all colours, violet. Well, a real motor leaves its mark on you where it kills you, doesn't it? But when I lifted up that old man's head from the road, there was no mark on him, no blood - no broken bones - his hair was not disordered, nor his dress.I tell you there was not even a speck of mud on him, except where he had touched the road in falling. There were no tyre - marks in the mud.

The motor car that killed him came and went like a shadow. As he threw himself down, it swerved a little so that both its wheels should go over him

He died, the doctor said, of heart failure. I am the only person to know that he was killed by a violet car, which, having killed him, went noiselessly away towards the sea. And that car was empty - there was no one in it. It was just a violet car that moved along the lanes swiftly and silently, and was empty.

NESBIT'S nuanced artistry in this story is brilliant: her sweeping, desolate landscapes (described in a paragraph before the narrator coyly downplay's her literary merits – *pshaw*!), the unsettling personification of the first automobile (it breaths, shivers, lurches, and coughs – it has an animal stench, a beastly voice, and a savage personality), the cold way she refers to the widow's un-fathered, faceless child as "it," the ambiguous madness of the heartbroken couple, the lonely journey of the narrator from practical psychiatric nurse to eye-widened seer, and the vicious, karmic brutality of the universe that they inhabit is truly inspired. The story is among the first water of ghost tales from this era, although it has sadly been neglected by most critics. Nesbit effortlessly intermingles the practical realism of the Edwardians with the windswept Romanticism of the Victorians (don't you sense elements of *Jane Eyre, Wuthering Heights,* and *Carmilla* in those shaggy downs that hunker under the broad, unblinking sky?), and ignites her luscious prose with a moral heartbeat. While modern horror fiction is typically consumed with purposelessness, the sentience of the Victorian

202

universe strikes me as far more terrifying, for as much as atheist apologists delight in shooing theism away as a child's comfort blanket, *nothing* would be more horrible to me than to learn that a brutal, merciless force existed in the world, relentlessly doling out justice regardless of intent or grounds. This is a universe whose god is a law book, not a human heart or a celestial spirit – a cosmos whose divinity is a hangman. "The Violet Car" features a man who is hounded to his death for luring his daughter's remorseless murderer to a justified destruction. In one sense, the old man should be seen as his own karmic agent, but this martinet-god only recognizes its own authority, and punishes heartbroken vigilantes as well as callous evil doers. In another, more terrifying sense, we get the impression that his fatal advice may have been given in an unconscious daze of grief and loss – not the malicious act of a conniving mind, but the sorrow-muted mistake of a brain fogged by despair. This universe will have none of it, though, and the poor couple who were traumatized by their daughter's loss – which never would have been rectified by any court in the land – are doubly cursed by the ghost of her killer and driven to early graves.

II.

Nesbit's work here is profoundly skilled – she sets up a cosmic morality, paints a sweeping landscape with her powerful prose, invests it with raw emotion, sublime awe, and the pathos of a Greek tragedy. Also noteworthy is her treatment of automobiles as agents of the supernatural. Like Arthur Conan Doyle's "Horror of the Heights" – wherein sky monsters are discovered at a middling altitude which jet planes have since made into well-traveled highways – this story should have aged badly, but somehow has not. Doyle's tale of early aviation somehow – for all of its debunking – elicits wonder and terror in the 21st century. Likewise, Nesbit uses the car – still a novelty, though hardly a rarity – because to her audience nothing could seem less haunted than a car. It would be like having a haunted iPhone or Netflix account: while the idea might sound like a good story, it isn't scary because they are new and fresh things. A haunted mail coach, yes. A haunted rickshaw, even, yes. But a car? And yet, she uses the car to terrifying effect, and the image of the driverless motorcar careening soullessly down the highway is the perfect metaphor for the heartless, faceless moral authority that rules over her universe dolling out karmic punishments without considering just cause or human weakness. It is a universe driven by pure logic without a drop of blood – or gasoline – to warm its vacant heart.

PERMIT me, if you will, to immediately dispel any pretensions about this story: it is not a tale of terror, though it is certainly Gothic – part of one of the most underrated subgenre's in speculative fiction, the supernatural burlesque. Dry, ironic, and gently mocking, this genre has been a favorite of Charles Dickens, Washington Irving, and Oscar Wilde, and although it was popular during the *Fin de Siècle*, it has been unjustly neglected for the past century. This particular farce is a rare gem in this collection, and to speak much more of it is to give much away. I recommend – especially after reading so many of Nesbit's justly titled *Grim Tales* – that you not pass over this clever campfire story. Like many of the best of its kind it equally intermingles fear, humor, romance, irony, and atmosphere to create a piece of writing that offers the best of what Nesbit is most known for. It isn't exactly a comedy, but more of a farce, and a rather clever one, too. So especially after "Man-Size in Marble," "The Ebony Frame," and "From the Dead," kick back to a very different couple who take it upon themselves to investigate the haunted inheritance.

The Haunted Inheritance
{1900}

THE most extraordinary thing that ever happened to me was my going back to town on that day. I am a reasonable being; I do not do such things. I was on a bicycling tour with another man. We were far from the mean cares of an unremunerative profession; we were men not fettered by any given address, any pledged date, any preconcerted route. I went to bed weary and cheerful, fell asleep a mere animal—a tired dog after a day's hunting—and awoke at four in the morning that creature of nerves and fancies which is my other self, and which has driven me to all the follies I have ever kept company with. But even that second self of mine, whining beast and traitor as it is, has never played me such a trick as it played then. Indeed, something in the result of that day's rash act sets me wondering whether after all it could have been I, or even my other self, who moved in the adventure; whether it was not rather some power outside both of us ... but this is a speculation as idle in me as uninteresting to you, and so enough of it.

From four to seven I lay awake, the prey of a growing detestation of bicycling tours, friends, scenery, physical exertion, holidays. By seven o'clock I felt that I would rather perish than spend another day in the society of the other man—an excellent fellow, by the way, and the best of company.

At half-past seven the post came. I saw the postman through my window as I shaved. I went down to get my letters—there were none, naturally.

At breakfast I said: "Edmundson, my dear fellow, I am extremely sorry; but my letters this morning compel me to return to town at once."

"But I thought," said Edmundson—then he stopped, and I saw that he had perceived in time that this was no moment for reminding me that, having left no address, I could have had no letters.

He looked sympathetic, and gave me what there was left of the bacon. I suppose he thought that it was a love affair or some such folly. I let him think so; after all, no love affair but would have seemed wise compared with the blank idiocy of this sudden determination to cut short a delightful holiday and go back to those dusty, stuffy rooms in Gray's Inn.

After that first and almost pardonable lapse, Edmundson behaved beautifully. I caught the 9.17 train, and by half-past eleven I was climbing my dirty staircase.

I let myself in and waded through a heap of envelopes and wrappered circulars that had drifted in through the letter-box, as dead leaves drift into the areas of houses in squares. All the windows were shut. Dust lay thick on everything. My laundress had evidently chosen this as a good time for her holiday. I wondered idly where she spent it. And now the close, musty smell of the rooms caught at my senses, and I remembered with a positive pang the sweet scent of the earth and the dead leaves in that wood through which, at this very moment, the sensible and fortunate Edmundson would be riding.

The thought of dead leaves reminded me of the heap of correspondence. I glanced through it. Only one of all those letters interested me in the least. It was from my mother:—

"Elliot's Bay, Norfolk,
17th August.

"Dear Lawrence,—I have wonderful news for you. Your great-uncle Sefton has died, and left you half his immense property. The other half is left to your second cousin Selwyn. You must come home at once. There are heaps of letters here for you, but I dare not send them on, as goodness only knows where you may be. I do wish you would remember to leave an address. I send this to your rooms, in case you have had the forethought to instruct your charwoman to send your letters on to you. It is a most handsome fortune, and I am too happy about your accession to it to scold you as you deserve, but I hope this will be a lesson to you to leave an address when next you go away. Come home at once.—Your loving Mother,

"Margaret Sefton.

"*P.S.*—It is the maddest will; everything divided evenly between you two except the house and estate. The will says you and your cousin Selwyn are to meet there on the 1st September following his death, in presence of the family, and decide which of you is to have the house. If you can't agree, it's to be presented to the county for a lunatic asylum. I should think so! He was always so eccentric. The one who doesn't have the house, etc., gets £20,000 extra. Of course you will choose *that*.

"*P.P.S.*—Be sure to bring your under-shirts with you—the air here is very keen of an evening."

I opened both the windows and lit a pipe. Sefton Manor, that gorgeous old place,—I knew its picture in Hasted, cradle of our race, and so on—and a big fortune. I hoped my cousin Selwyn would want the £20,000 more than he wanted the house. If he didn't—well, perhaps my fortune might be large enough to increase that £20,000 to a sum that he *would* want.

And then, suddenly, I became aware that this was the 31st of August, and that to-morrow was the day on which I was to meet my cousin Selwyn and "the family," and come to a decision about the house. I had never, to my knowledge, heard of my cousin Selwyn. We were a family rich in collateral branches. I hoped he would be a reasonable young man. Also, I had never seen Sefton Manor House, except in a print. It occurred to me that I would rather see the house before I saw the cousin.

I caught the next train to Sefton.

"It's but a mile by the field way," said the railway porter. "You take the stile—the first on the left—and follow the path till you come to the wood. Then skirt along the left of it, cater across the meadow at the end, and you'll see the place right below you in the vale."

"It's a fine old place, I hear," said I.

"All to pieces, though," said he. "I shouldn't wonder if it cost a couple o' hundred to put it to rights. Water coming through the roof and all."

"But surely the owner——"

"Oh, he never lived there; not since his son was taken. He lived in the lodge; it's on the brow of the hill looking down on the Manor House."

"Is the house empty?"

"As empty as a rotten nutshell, except for the old sticks o' furniture. Any one who likes," added the porter, "can lie there o' nights. But it wouldn't be me!"

"Do you mean there's a ghost?" I hope I kept any note of undue elation out of my voice.

"I don't hold with ghosts," said the porter firmly, "but my aunt was in service at the lodge, and there's no doubt but *something* walks there."

"Come," I said, "this is very interesting. Can't you leave the station, and come across to where beer is?"

"I don't mind if I do," said he. "That is so far as your standing a drop goes. But I can't leave the station, so if you pour my beer you must pour it dry, sir, as the saying is."

So I gave the man a shilling, and he told me about the ghost at Sefton Manor House. Indeed, about the ghosts, for there were, it seemed, two; a lady in white, and a gentleman in a slouch hat and black riding cloak.

"They do say," said my porter, "as how one of the young ladies once on a time was wishful to elope, and started so to do—not getting further than the hall door; her father, thinking it to be burglars, fired out of the window, and the happy pair fell on the doorstep, corpses."

"Is it true, do you think?"

The porter did not know. At any rate there was a tablet in the church to Maria Sefton and George Ballard—"and something about in their death them not being divided."

I took the stile, I skirted the wood, I "catered" across the meadow—and so I came out on a chalky ridge held in a net of pine roots, where dog violets grew. Below stretched the green park, dotted with trees. The lodge, stuccoed but solid, lay below me. Smoke came from its chimneys. Lower still lay the Manor House—red brick with grey lichened mullions, a house in a thousand, Elizabethan—and from its twisted beautiful chimneys no smoke arose. I hurried across the short turf towards the Manor House.

I had no difficulty in getting into the great garden. The bricks of the wall were everywhere displaced or crumbling. The ivy had forced the coping stones away; each red buttress offered a dozen spots for foothold. I climbed the wall and found myself in a garden—oh! but

208

such a garden. There are not half a dozen such in England—ancient box hedges, rosaries, fountains, yew tree avenues, bowers of clematis (now feathery in its seeding time), great trees, grey-grown marble balustrades and steps, terraces, green lawns, one green lawn, in especial, girt round with a sweet briar hedge, and in the middle of this lawn a sundial. All this was mine, or, to be more exact, might be mine, should my cousin Selwyn prove to be a person of sense. How I prayed that he might not be a person of taste! That he might be a person who liked yachts or racehorses or diamonds, or motor-cars, or anything that money can buy, not a person who liked beautiful Elizabethan houses, and gardens old beyond belief.

The sundial stood on a mass of masonry, too low and wide to be called a pillar. I mounted the two brick steps and leaned over to read the date and the motto:

"Tempus fugit manet amor."

The date was 1617, the initials S. S. surmounted it. The face of the dial was unusually ornate—a wreath of stiffly drawn roses was traced outside the circle of the numbers. As I leaned there a sudden movement on the other side of the pedestal compelled my attention. I leaned over a little further to see what had rustled—a rat—a rabbit? A flash of pink struck at my eyes. A lady in a pink dress was sitting on the step at the other side of the sundial.

I suppose some exclamation escaped me—the lady looked up. Her hair was dark, and her eyes; her face was pink and white, with a few little gold-coloured freckles on nose and on cheek bones. Her dress was of pink cotton stuff, thin and soft. She looked like a beautiful pink rose.

Our eyes met.

"I beg your pardon," said I, "I had no idea——" there I stopped and tried to crawl back to firm ground. Graceful explanations are not best given by one sprawling on his stomach across a sundial.

By the time I was once more on my feet she too was standing.

"It is a beautiful old place," she said gently, and, as it seemed, with a kindly wish to relieve my embarrassment. She made a movement as if to turn away.

"Quite a show place," said I stupidly enough, but I was still a little embarrassed, and I wanted to say something—anything—to arrest her departure. You have no idea how pretty she was. She had a straw hat in her hand, dangling by soft black ribbons. Her hair was all fluffy-soft— like a child's. "I suppose you have seen the house?" I asked.

She paused, one foot still on the lower step of the sundial, and her face seemed to brighten at the touch of some idea as sudden as welcome.

"Well—no," she said. "The fact is—I wanted frightfully to see the house; in fact, I've come miles and miles on purpose, but there's no one to let me in."

"The people at the lodge?" I suggested.

"Oh no," she said. "I—the fact is I—I don't want to be shown round. I want to explore!"

She looked at me critically. Her eyes dwelt on my right hand, which lay on the sundial. I have always taken reasonable care of my hands, and I wore a good ring, a sapphire, cut with the Sefton arms: an heirloom, by the way. Her glance at my hand preluded a longer glance at my face. Then she shrugged her pretty shoulders.

"Oh well," she said, and it was as if she had said plainly, "I see that you are a gentleman and a decent fellow. Why should I not look over the house in your company? Introductions? Bah!"

All this her shrug said without ambiguity as without words.

"Perhaps," I hazarded, "I could get the keys."

"Do you really care very much for old houses?"

"I do," said I; "and you?"

"I care so much that I nearly broke into this one. I should have done it quite if the windows had been an inch or two lower."

"I am an inch or two higher," said I, standing squarely so as to make the most of my six-feet beside her five-feet-five or thereabouts.

"Oh—if you only would!" said she.

"Why not?" said I.

She led the way past the marble basin of the fountain, and along the historic yew avenue, planted, like all old yew avenues, by that industrious gardener our Eighth Henry. Then across a lawn, through a winding, grassy, shrubbery path, that ended at a green door in the garden wall.

"You can lift this latch with a hairpin," said she, and therewith lifted it.

We walked into a courtyard. Young grass grew green between the grey flags on which our steps echoed.

"This is the window," said she. "You see there's a pane broken. If you could get on to the window-sill, you could get your hand in and undo the hasp, and——"

"And you?"

"Oh, you'll let me in by the kitchen door."

I did it. My conscience called me a burglar—in vain. Was it not my own, or as good as my own house?

I let her in at the back door. We walked through the big dark kitchen where the old three-legged pot towered large on the hearth, and the old spits and firedogs still kept their ancient place. Then through another kitchen where red rust was making its full meal of a comparatively modern range.

Then into the great hall, where the old armour and the buff-coats and round-caps hang on the walls, and where the carved stone staircases run at each side up to the gallery above.
The long tables in the middle of the hall were scored by the knives of the many who had eaten meat there—initials and dates were cut into them. The roof was groined, the windows low-arched.

"Oh, but what a place!" said she; "this must be much older than the rest of it——"

"Evidently. About 1300, I should say."

"Oh, let us explore the rest," she cried; "it is really a comfort not to have a guide, but only a person like you who just guesses comfortably at dates. I should hate to be told *exactly* when this hall was built."

We explored ball-room and picture gallery, white parlour and library. Most of the rooms were furnished—all heavily, some magnificently—but everything was dusty and faded.

It was in the white parlour, a spacious panelled room on the first floor, that she told me the ghost story, substantially the same as my porter's tale, only in one respect different.

"And so, just as she was leaving this very room—yes, I'm sure it's this room, because the woman at the inn pointed out this double window and told me so—just as the poor lovers were creeping out of the door, the cruel father came quickly out of some dark place and killed them both. So now they haunt it."

"It is a terrible thought," said I gravely. "How would you like to live in a haunted house?"

"I couldn't," she said quickly.

"Nor I; it would be too——" my speech would have ended flippantly, but for the grave set of her features.

"I wonder who *will* live here?" she said. "The owner is just dead. They say it is an awful house, full of ghosts. Of course one is not afraid now"—the sunlight lay golden and soft on the dusty parquet of the floor—"but at night, when the wind wails, and the doors creak, and the things rustle, oh, it must be awful!"

"I hear the house has been left to two people, or rather one is to have the house, and the other a sum of money," said I. "It's a beautiful house, full of beautiful things, but I should think at least one of the heirs would rather have the money."

"Oh yes, I should think so. I wonder whether the heirs know about the ghost? The lights can be seen from the inn, you know, at twelve o'clock, and they see the ghost in white at the window."

"Never the black one?"

"Oh yes, I suppose so."

"The ghosts don't appear together?"

"No."

"I suppose," said I, "whoever it is that manages such things knows that the poor ghosts would like to be together, so it won't let them."

She shivered.

"Come," she said, "we have seen all over the house; let us get back into the sunshine. Now I will go out, and you shall bolt the door after me, and then you can come out by the window. Thank you so much for all the trouble you have taken. It has really been quite an adventure...."

I rather liked that expression, and she hastened to spoil it.

"... Quite an adventure going all over this glorious old place, and looking at everything one wanted to see, and not just at what the housekeeper didn't mind one's looking at."

She passed through the door, but when I had closed it and prepared to lock it, I found that the key was no longer in the lock. I looked on the floor—I felt in my pockets, and at last, wandering back into the kitchen, discovered it on the table, where I swear I never put it.

When I had fitted that key into the lock and turned it, and got out of the window and made that fast, I dropped into the yard. No one shared its solitude with me. I searched garden and pleasure grounds, but never a glimpse of pink rewarded my anxious eyes. I found the sundial again, and stretched myself along the warm brick of the wide step where she had sat: and called myself a fool.

I had let her go. I did not know her name; I did not know where she lived; she had been at the inn, but probably only for lunch. I should never see her again, and certainly in that event I should never see again such dark, soft eyes, such hair, such a contour of cheek and chin, such a frank smile—in a word, a girl with whom it would be so delightfully natural for me to fall in love. For all the time she had been talking to me of architecture and archæology, of dates and periods, of carvings and mouldings, I had been recklessly falling in love with the idea of falling in love with her. I had cherished and adored this delightful

213

possibility, and now my chance was over. Even I could not definitely fall in love after one interview with a girl I was never to see again! And falling in love is so pleasant! I cursed my lost chance, and went back to the inn. I talked to the waiter.

"Yes, a lady in pink had lunched there with a party. Had gone on to the Castle. A party from Tonbridge it was."

Barnhurst Castle is close to Sefton Manor. The inn lays itself out to entertain persons who come in brakes and carve their names on the walls of the Castle keep. The inn has a visitors' book. I examined it. Some twenty feminine names. Any one might be hers. The waiter looked over my shoulder. I turned the pages.

"Only parties staying in the house in this part of the book," said the waiter.

My eye caught one name. "Selwyn Sefton," in a clear, round, black hand-writing.

"Staying here?" I pointed to the name.

"Yes, sir; came to-day, sir."

"Can I have a private sitting-room?"

I had one. I ordered my dinner to be served in it, and I sat down and considered my course of action. Should I invite my cousin Selwyn to dinner, ply him with wine, and exact promises? Honour forbade. Should I seek him out and try to establish friendly relations? To what end?

Then I saw from my window a young man in a light-checked suit, with a face at once pallid and coarse. He strolled along the gravel path, and a woman's voice in the garden called "Selwyn."

He disappeared in the direction of the voice. I don't think I ever disliked a man so much at first sight.

"Brute," said I, "why should he have the house? He'd stucco it all over as likely as not; perhaps let it! He'd never stand the ghosts, either——"

Then the inexcusable, daring idea of my life came to me, striking me rigid—a blow from my other self. It must have been a minute or two before my muscles relaxed and my arms fell at my sides.

"I'll do it," I said.

I dined. I told the people of the house not to sit up for me. I was going to see friends in the neighbourhood, and might stay the night with them. I took my Inverness cape with me on my arm and my soft felt hat in my pocket. I wore a light suit and a straw hat.

Before I started I leaned cautiously from my window. The lamp at the bow window next to mine showed me the pallid young man, smoking a fat, reeking cigar. I hoped he would continue to sit there smoking. His window looked the right way; and if he didn't see what I wanted him to see some one else in the inn would. The landlady had assured me that I should disturb no one if I came in at half-past twelve.

"We hardly keep country hours here, sir," she said, "on account of so much excursionist business."

I bought candles in the village, and, as I went down across the park in the soft darkness, I turned again and again to be sure that the light and the pallid young man were still at that window. It was now past eleven.

I got into the house and lighted a candle, and crept through the dark kitchens, whose windows, I knew, did not look towards the inn. When I came to the hall I blew out my candle. I dared not show light prematurely, and in the unhaunted part of the house.

I gave myself a nasty knock against one of the long tables, but it helped me to get my bearings, and presently I laid my hand on the stone balustrade of the great staircase. You would hardly believe me if I were to tell you truly of my sensations as I began to go up these stairs. I am not a coward—at least, I had never thought so till then—but the absolute darkness unnerved me. I had to go slowly, or I should have lost my head and blundered up the stairs three at a time, so strong was the feeling of something—something uncanny—just behind me.

I set my teeth. I reached the top of the stairs, felt along the walls, and after a false start, which landed me in the great picture gallery, I found the white parlour, entered it, closed the door, and felt my way to a little room without a window, which we had decided must have been a powdering-room.

Here I ventured to re-light my candle.

The white parlour, I remembered, was fully furnished. Returning to it I struck one match, and by its flash determined the way to the mantelpiece.

Then I closed the powdering-room door behind me. I felt my way to the mantelpiece and took down the two brass twenty-lighted candelabra. I placed these on a table a yard or two from the window, and in them set up my candles. It is astonishingly difficult in the dark to do anything, even a thing so simple as the setting up of a candle.

Then I went back into my little room, put on the Inverness cape and the slouch hat, and looked at my watch. Eleven-thirty. I must wait. I sat down and waited. I thought how rich I was—the thought fell flat; I wanted this house. I thought of my beautiful pink lady; but I put that thought aside; I had an inward consciousness that my conduct, more heroic than enough in one sense, would seem mean and crafty in her eyes. Only ten minutes had passed. I could not wait till twelve. The chill of the night and of the damp, unused house, and, perhaps, some less material influence, made me shiver.

I opened the door, crept on hands and knees to the table, and, carefully keeping myself below the level of the window, I reached up a trembling arm, and lighted, one by one, my forty candles. The room was a blaze of light. My courage came back to me with the retreat of the darkness. I was far too excited to know what a fool I was making of myself. I rose boldly, and struck an attitude over against the window, where the candle-light shone upon as well as behind me. My Inverness was flung jauntily over my shoulder, my soft, black felt twisted and slouched over my eyes.

There I stood for the world, and particularly for my cousin Selwyn, to see, the very image of the ghost that haunted that chamber. And from my window I could see the light in that other window, and indistinctly the lounging figure there. Oh, my cousin Selwyn, I wished many things to your address in that moment! For it was only a moment that I had to feel brave and daring in. Then I heard, deep down in the house, a sound, very slight, very faint. Then came silence. I drew a deep breath. The silence endured. And I stood by my lighted window.

After a very long time, as it seemed, I heard a board crack, and then a soft rustling sound that drew near and seemed to pause outside the very door of my parlour.

Again I held my breath, and now I thought of the most horrible story Poe ever wrote—"The Fall of the House of Usher"—and I fancied I saw the handle of that door move. I fixed my eyes on it. The fancy passed: and returned.

Then again there was silence. And then the door opened with a soft, silent suddenness, and I saw in the doorway a figure in trailing white. Its eyes blazed in a death-white face. It made two ghostly, gliding steps forward, and my heart stood still. I had not thought it possible for a man to experience so sharp a pang of sheer terror. I had masqueraded as one of the ghosts in this accursed house. Well, the other ghost—the real one—had come to meet me. I do not like to dwell on that moment. The only thing which it pleases me to remember is that I did not scream or go mad. I think I stood on the verge of both.

The ghost, I say, took two steps forward; then it threw up its arms, the lighted taper it carried fell on the floor, and it reeled back against the door with its arms across its face.

216

The fall of the candle woke me as from a nightmare. It fell solidly, and rolled away under the table.

I perceived that my ghost was human. I cried incoherently: "Don't, for Heaven's sake—it's all right."

The ghost dropped its hands and turned agonised eyes on me. I tore off my cloak and hat.

"I—didn't—scream," she said, and with that I sprang forward and caught her in my arms—my poor, pink lady—white now as a white rose.

I carried her into the powdering-room, and left one candle with her, extinguishing the others hastily, for now I saw what in my] extravagant folly had escaped me before, that my ghost exhibition might bring the whole village down on the house. I tore down the long corridor and double locked the doors leading from it to the staircase, then back to the powdering-room and the prone white rose. How, in the madness of that night's folly, I had thought to bring a brandy-flask passes my understanding. But I had done it. Now I rubbed her hands with the spirit. I rubbed her temples, I tried to force it between her lips, and at last she sighed and opened her eyes.

"Oh—thank God—thank God!" I cried, for indeed I had almost feared that my mad trick had killed her. "Are you better? oh, poor little lady, are you better?"

She moved her head a little on my arm.

Again she sighed, and her eyes closed. I gave her more brandy. She took it, choked, raised herself against my shoulder.

"I'm all right now," she said faintly. "It served me right. How silly it all is!" Then she began to laugh, and then she began to cry.

It was at this moment that we heard voices on the terrace below. She clutched at my arm in a frenzy of terror, the bright tears glistening on her cheeks.

"Oh! not any more, not any more," she cried. "I can't bear it."

"Hush," I said, taking her hands strongly in mine. "I've played the fool; so have you. We must play the man now. The people in the village have seen the lights—that's all. They think we're burglars. They can't get in. Keep quiet, and they'll go away."

But when they did go away they left the local constable on guard. He kept guard like a man till daylight began to creep over the hill, and then he crawled into the hayloft and fell asleep, small blame to him.

But through those long hours I sat beside her and held her hand. At first she clung to me as a frightened child clings, and her tears were the prettiest, saddest things to see. As we grew calmer we talked.

"I did it to frighten my cousin," I owned. "I meant to have told you to-day, I mean yesterday, only you went away. I am Lawrence Sefton, and the place is to go either to me or to my cousin Selwyn. And I wanted to frighten him off it. But you, why did you——?"

Even then I couldn't see. She looked at me.

"I don't know how I ever could have thought I was brave enough to do it, but I did want the house so, and I wanted to frighten you——"

"To frighten *me*. Why?"

"Because I am your cousin Selwyn," she said, hiding her face in her hands.

"And you knew me?" I asked.

"By your ring," she said. "I saw your father wear it when I was a little girl. Can't we get back to the inn now?"

"Not unless you want every one to know how silly we have been."

"I wish you'd forgive me," she said when we had talked awhile, and she had even laughed at the description of the pallid young man on whom I had bestowed, in my mind, her name.

"The wrong is mutual," I said; "we will exchange forgivenesses."

"Oh, but it isn't," she said eagerly. "Because I knew it was you, and you didn't know it was me: you wouldn't have tried to frighten *me*."

"You know I wouldn't." My voice was tenderer than I meant it to be. She was silent.

"And who is to have the house?" she said.

"Why you, of course."

"I never will."

"Why?"

"Oh, because!"

"Can't we put off the decision?" I asked.

"Impossible. We must decide to-morrow—to-day I mean."

"Well, when we meet to-morrow—I mean to-day—with lawyers and chaperones and mothers and relations, give me one word alone with you."

"Yes," she answered, with docility.

☙

"Do you know," she said presently, "I can never respect myself again? To undertake a thing like that, and then be so horribly frightened. Oh! I thought you really *were* the other ghost."

"I will tell you a secret," said I. "I thought *you* were, and I was much more frightened than you."

"Oh well," she said, leaning against my shoulder as a tired child might have done, "if you were frightened too, Cousin Lawrence, I don't mind so very, very much."

It was soon afterwards that, cautiously looking out of the parlour window for the twentieth time, I had the happiness of seeing the local policeman disappear into the stable rubbing his eyes.

We got out of the window on the other side of the house, and went back to the inn across the dewy park. The French window of the sitting-room which had let her out let us both in. No one was stirring, so no one save she and I were any the wiser as to that night's work.

℞

It was like a garden party next day, when lawyers and executors and aunts and relations met on the terrace in front of Sefton Manor House.

Her eyes were downcast. She followed her Aunt demurely over the house and the grounds.

"Your decision," said my great-uncle's solicitor, "has to be given within the hour."

"My cousin and I will announce it within that time," I said and I at once gave her my arm.

Arrived at the sundial we stopped.

"This is my proposal," I said: "we will say that we decide that the house is yours—we will spend the £20,000 in restoring it and the grounds. By the time that's done we can decide who is to have it."

"But how?"

"Oh, we'll draw lots, or toss a halfpenny, or anything you like."

"I'd rather decide now," she said; "*you* take it."

"No, *you* shall."

"I'd rather you had it. I—I don't feel so greedy as I did yesterday," she said.

"Neither do I. Or at any rate not in the same way."

"Do—do take the house," she said very earnestly.

Then I said: "My cousin Selwyn, unless you take the house, I shall make you an offer of marriage."

"*Oh!*" she breathed.

"And when you have declined it, on the very proper ground of our too slight acquaintance, I will take my turn at declining. I will decline the house. Then, if you are obdurate, it will become an asylum. Don't be obdurate. Pretend to take the house and——"

219

She looked at me rather piteously.

"Very well," she said, "I will pretend to take the house, and when it is restored——"

"We'll spin the penny."

So before the waiting relations the house was adjudged to my cousin Selwyn. When the restoration was complete I met Selwyn at the sundial. We had met there often in the course of the restoration, in which business we both took an extravagant interest.

"Now," I said, "we'll spin the penny. Heads you take the house, tails it comes to me."

I spun the coin—it fell on the brick steps of the sundial, and stuck upright there, wedged between two bricks. She laughed; I laughed.

"It's not *my* house," I said.

"It's not *my* house," said she.

"Dear," said I, and we were neither of us laughing then, "can't it be *our* house?"

And, thank God, our house it is.

BY this point in your life, I suppose you have had several teachers explain – when discussing history or literature – that a marriage between cousins – especially distant cousins – was a fairly common and simple arrangement before the 1960s when understandable taboos began to form around the practice. So I shall leave that subject alone and tend to the content of this story. I hope that you are not utterly disappointed by the romantic nature of this little tale: considering the rest of Nesbit's grisly oeuvre, I regard it a refreshing infusion of quaint cheer. The farcical ghost story is a staple of the genre, one which is accepted by critics and readers alike as an self-conscious deconstruction of the Poe-esque/Lovecraftian terrors and miseries that make up that vast majority of the tradition. W. W. Jacobs' "In Mid-Atlantic," Stephen Crane's "The Ghoul's Accountant", Saki's "The Open Window," Oscar Wilde's "The Canterville Ghost," Dicken's "Baron Koeldwethout's Apparition," Washington Irving's "The Spectre Bridegroom," and Poe's "Some Words With a Mummy" are all exemplars of farcical horror. There are several things that an excellent supernatural farce does, three which are necessary to be very good: it manipulates tropes and expectations to highlight our cultural biases, emotional desires, and socio-political investments by setting up a predictable scenario and delivering something entirely different (our response to the twist informs us more about *ourselves* than anything); it uses fear unapologetically for entertainment rather than philosophical or literary value; and it pokes fun at the reader either for hoping for a supernatural plot (in this case the reader is hooked and *wants* to see ghosts!), or for being cynical (in this case the reader groans – oh boy, here's another predictable ghost story). In either case the reader either must confess to either being a sensationalist, or to having underestimated the writer's ability to entertain. This tale is just such a ghost story: it highlights Victorian gender prejudices and expectations, unabashedly indulges in Gothic and romantic excess, and teases sensationalists (who are excited) and cynics (who are underwhelmed) with the false assumption that the pink lady is a ghost. In spite of falling prey to sentimentalism – and falling short of Nesbit's acerbic standards – the resultant tale – like the protagonist's harmless "adventure" – is a good piece of indulgent, spooky fun.

THE following story is one of the most time-honored tropes of British supernatural fiction: a ghost story told over the fire of an inn about a spirit that roams its very halls. The conventional story goes thus: a group of travelers – strangers to one another – seek shelter from a winter storm at a wayside inn. Bored and tired, they begin talking about metaphysics after they have wasted small talk, politics, and gossip. The conversation turns to the existence of ghosts, and one or more of those present explain that the very house they have taken refuge in hosts a supernatural tradition. The ghost is frequently a victim of violent death – suicide or murder – and typically its appearance heralds the death of its witness. The story is common in both literary and veridic ghost stories (that is, urban legends). One such veridic folk story is that of the Radiant Boy – the ghost of a young boy who has been killed by his mother, who haunts the rooms they were smothered in. Radiant Boys appear to unwitting guests at the darkest hours of night in the form of a blazing, yellow specter, awakening their victims who typically suspect a house fire, only to see a beautiful, blond lad motioning sinisterly to their throats. These unhappy men are destined to commit suicide within the year. Robert Stewart, Viscount Castlereagh (1769 - 1822) is one such historical person who is said to have cut his throat after witnessing a Radiant Boy at a manor house. The trope is also very popular in literary stories: W. W. Jacobs' masterful Christmas tragedy "Jerry Bundler" tells the story of a ghostly highwayman who lingers at an inn after hanging himself in an upstairs room. H. G. Wells' "The Inexperienced Ghost" – like "Jerry Bundler" – goes from humorous to tragic after a man at a country lodge recounts his conversation with a ghost the night before and jokingly performs the spirit's invisibility ritual. Washington Irving depicts a group of overnight guests pondering the subject of a transfixing portrait in "The Haunted Painting," only to have the sitter appear to them in the night, and J. S. Le Fanu's "Dickon the Devil" features an inn where a mad ghost roams the countryside, peering in the windows and pleading for divine mercy. Nesbit enters into this tradition in fine form, but be warned: like "Jerry Bundler" and "The Inexperienced Ghost," this story takes you down a long, predictable hallway, only to jerk you around with a twist at the end. It is not un-pleasant.

Number 17
{1910}

I yawned. I could not help it. But the flat, inexorable voice went on.

"Speaking from the journalistic point of view—I may tell you, gentlemen, that I once occupied the position of advertisement editor to the *Bradford Woollen Goods Journal*[1]—and speaking from that point of view, I hold the opinion that all the best ghost stories have been written over and over again[2]; and if I were to leave the road[3] and return to a literary career[4] I should never be led away by ghosts. Realism's[5] what's wanted nowadays, if you want to be up-to-date."

The large commercial[6] paused for breath.

"You never can tell with the public," said the lean, elderly traveller; "it's like in the fancy[7] business. You never know how it's going to be. Whether it's a clockwork ostrich or Sometite silk or a particular shape of shaded glass novelty or a tobacco-box got up to look like a raw chop, you never know your luck."

"That depends on who you are," said the dapper man in the corner by the fire. "If you've got the right push about you, you can make a thing go, whether it's a clockwork kitten or imitation meat, and with stories, I take it, it's just the same—realism or ghost stories. But the best ghost story would be the realest one[8], *I* think."

The large commercial had got his breath.

"I don't believe in ghost stories, myself," he was saying with earnest dullness; "but there was a rather a queer thing happened to a second

---

[1] This would essentially be a department store catalog of wool clothing. Humorously, the speaker imagines that this editorship entitles him to a respectable literary opinion

[2] A popular sentiment in the literary world at the time – one still prevalent today

[3] As a travelling salesman

[4] Still humorous – he considers his stint as catalog editor to have been the beginning of a literary career

[5] The highly fashionable school of writing that dominated literature after the American Civil War, dominated by Henry James, Mark Twain, Stephen Crane, Jack London, Thomas Hardy, and others. This school of thought encouraged writing that was set in everyday locales and situations, concerned with regular people doing regular things (no Pits or Pendulums, Headless Horsemen, Treasure Islands, or knights of the Round Table need apply). Before this Romanticism (Byron, Poe, Hawthorne, Wordsworth, Tennyson) was the prevailing school

[6] A salesman

[7] Novelties

[8] The entire purpose of this story is to illustrate this point – what's best is not what is most realistic, but most *Real* – most felt

cousin of an aunt of mine by marriage—a very sensible woman with no nonsense about her. And the soul of truth and honour. I shouldn't have believed it if she had been one of your flighty, fanciful sort."

"Don't tell us the story," said the melancholy man who travelled in hardware; "you'll make us afraid to go to bed."

The well-meant effort failed. The large commercial went on, as I had known he would; his words overflowed his mouth, as his person overflowed his chair. I turned my mind to my own affairs, coming back to the commercial room in time to hear the summing up.

"The doors were all locked, and she was quite certain she saw a tall, white figure glide past her and vanish. I wouldn't have believed it if——" And so on *da capo*[1], from "if she hadn't been the second cousin" to the "soul of truth and honour."

I yawned again.

"Very good story," said the smart little man by the fire. He was a traveller, as the rest of us were; his presence in the room told us that much. He had been rather silent during dinner, and afterwards, while the red curtains were being drawn and the red and black cloth laid between the glasses and the decanters and the mahogany, he had quietly taken the best chair in the warmest corner. We had got our letters written and the large traveller had been boring for some time before I even noticed that there was a best chair and that this silent, bright-eyed, dapper, fair man had secured it[2].

"Very good story," he said; "but it's not what I call realism. You don't tell us half enough, sir. You don't say when it happened or where, or the time of year, or what colour your aunt's second cousin's hair was. Nor yet you don't tell us what it was she saw, nor what the room was like where she saw it, nor why she saw it, nor what happened afterwards. And I shouldn't like to breathe a word against anybody's aunt by marriage's cousin, first or second, but I must say I like a story about what a man's seen *himself*."

"So do I," the large commercial snorted, "when I hear it."

He blew his nose like a trumpet of defiance.

"But," said the rabbit-faced man, "we know nowadays, what with the advance of science and all that sort of thing, we know there aren't any

---

[1] An Italian term meaning "from the top" – used in music meaning "go back to the beginning and play until a certain point." Its use here is a comical insult deriding the fat man's circular story

[2] This telegraphs the fair man's character: observant, quick-witted, intelligent, and resourceful. In a very literal way it foreshadows the conclusion

such things as ghosts. They're hallucinations[1]; that's what they are—hallucinations."

"Don't seem to matter what you call them," the dapper one urged. "If you see a thing that looks as real as you do yourself, a thing that makes your blood run cold and turns you sick and silly with fear—well, call it ghost, or call it hallucination, or call it Tommy Dodd; it isn't the *name* that matters[2]."

The elderly commercial coughed and said, "You might call it another name. You might call it[3]——"

"No, you mightn't," said the little man, briskly; "not when the man it happened to had been a teetotal Bond of Joy[4] for five years and is to this day."

"Why don't you tell us the story?" I asked.

"I might be willing," he said, "if the rest of the company were agreeable. Only I warn you it's not that sort-of-a-kind-of-a-somebody-fancied-they-saw-a-sort-of-a-kind-of-a-something-sort of story. No, sir. Everything I'm going to tell you is plain and straightforward and as clear as a time-table—clearer than some. But I don't much like telling it, especially to people who don't believe in ghosts."

Several of us said we did believe in ghosts. The heavy man snorted and looked at his watch. And the man in the best chair began.

"Turn the gas down a bit, will you[5]? Thanks. Did any of you know Herbert Hatteras? He was on this road a good many years. No? well, never mind. He was a good chap, I believe, with good teeth[6] and a black whisker[7]. But I didn't know him myself. He was before my time. Well, this that I'm going to tell you about happened at a certain commercial hotel[8]. I'm not going to give it a name, because that sort of

---

[1] A reference to the then-new theory that ghosts were hallucinations caused by carbon monoxide poisoning – a common occurrence in old houses with inferior venting

[2] Nesbit argues this point by the very act of writing this story: it doesn't matter what a thing IS so much as what it DOES. This is rather like the "if a tree falls and no one hears it does it really fall?" argument, and Nesbit argues the point rather effectively (see conclusion)

[3] "drunkenness"

[4] A teetotaler's pledge to never drink alcohol

[5] This is the light, not the heat: a clever man and a good story teller, he knows to set the mood

[6] Suggestive of good hygiene habits, which in turn suggest good mental health

[7] Moustache

[8] We might call it a motel or a truck stop inn in America

226

thing gets about, and in every other respect it's a good house and reasonable, and we all have our living to get[1]. It was just a good ordinary old-fashioned commercial hotel, as it might be this. And I've often used it since, though they've never put me in that room again. Perhaps they shut it up after what happened.

"Well, the beginning of it was, I came across an old schoolfellow; in Boulter's Lock[2] one Sunday it was, I remember. Jones was his name, Ted Jones. We both had canoes. We had tea at Marlow, and we got talking about this and that and old times and old mates; and do you remember Jim, and what's become of Tom, and so on. Oh, you know. And I happened to ask after his brother, Fred by name. And Ted turned pale and almost dropped his cup, and he said, 'You don't mean to say you haven't heard?' 'No,' says I, mopping up the tea he'd slopped over with my handkerchief[3]. 'No, what?' I said.

"'It was horrible,' he said. 'They wired for me, and I saw him afterwards. Whether he'd done it himself or not, nobody knows; but they'd found him lying on the floor with his throat cut.' No cause could be assigned for the rash act, Ted told me. I asked him where it had happened, and he told me the name of this hotel—I'm not going to name it. And when I'd sympathised with him and drawn him out about old times and poor old Fred being such a good old sort and all that, I asked him what the room was like. I always like to know what the places look like where things happen[4].

"No, there wasn't anything specially rum about the room, only that it had a French bed with red curtains in a sort of alcove; and a large mahogany wardrobe as big as a hearse, with a glass door; and, instead of a swing-glass[5], a carved, black-framed glass screwed up against the wall between the windows[6], and a picture of 'Belshazzar's Feast'[7] over

---

[1] A rumor of a sinister haunting could (and often did) hurt business for innkeepers

[2] A canal lock on the River Thames in Maidenhead, Berkshire

[3] At this point it should be noted that the man in the best chair is enlisting Realism as his style of storytelling – describing commonplace details and events rather than focusing on dramatics

[4] Another tip of the hat to Realism

[5] A mirror that can be tilted on pivots for shaving

[6] Important to note because it cannot be moved – it must stay where it is

[7] Likely a reference to the painting by Rembrandt. Belshazzar was a Babylonian king who desecrated the holy Jewish gold by using it at a debauched feast. The feast was interrupted by a giant hand (presumably God's) which wrote a message of doom on the wall in fiery letters. Shortly thereafter Belshazzar was assassinated. The painting

227

the mantelpiece. I beg your pardon?" He stopped, for the heavy commercial had opened his mouth and shut it again.

"I thought you were going to say something," the dapper man went on. "Well, we talked about other things and parted, and I thought no more about it till business brought me to—but I'd better not name the town either—and I found my firm had marked this very hotel—where poor Fred had met his death, you know—for me to put up at. And I had to put up there too, because of their addressing everything to me there. And, anyhow, I expect I should have gone there out of curiosity.

"No. I didn't believe in ghosts in those days. I was like you, sir." He nodded amiably to the large commercial.

"The house was very full, and we were quite a large party in the room—very pleasant company, as it might be to-night; and we got talking of ghosts—just as it might be us. And there was a chap in glasses, sitting just over there, I remember—an old hand on the road[1], he was; and he said, just as it might be any of you, 'I don't believe in ghosts, but I wouldn't care to sleep in Number Seventeen, for all that'; and, of course, we asked him why. 'Because,' said he, very short, 'that's why.'

"But when we'd persuaded him a bit, he told us.

"'Because that's the room where chaps cut their throats[2],' he said. "There was a chap called Bert Hatteras began it. They found him weltering in his gore. And since that every man that's slept there's been found with his throat cut.'

"I asked him how many had slept there. 'Well, only two beside the first,' he said; 'they shut it up then.' 'Oh, did they?' said I. 'Well, they've opened it again. Number Seventeen's my room!'

"I tell you those chaps looked at me.

"'But you aren't going to *sleep* in it?' one of them said. And I explained that I didn't pay half a dollar[3] for a bedroom to keep awake in.

---

is a fitting one for a room with such a dire reputation, and such paintings (sometimes Judas' betrayal, Isaac's sacrifice, or the plagues of Egypt) are typical in ghost stories about haunted rooms

[1] That is, a seasoned salesman used to the ways of travelling for a living

[2] A common superstition – for a manor, inn, or castle to have a cursed room known for inducing suicide either during the night or at some point in the near future after sleeping there

[3] This is a joke. At the time, the dollar was worth about five pounds, and a pound was worth $140 in 2015 – half a dollar would have been about $15. "Half a dollar" just meant a beggarly sum

"'I suppose it's press of business has made them open it up again,' the chap in spectacles said. 'It's a very mysterious affair. There's some secret horror about that room that we don't understand,' he said, 'and I'll tell you another queer thing. Every one of those poor chaps was a commercial gentleman. That's what I don't like about it. There was Bert Hatteras—he was the first, and a chap called Jones—Frederick Jones, and then Donald Overshaw—a Scotchman he was, and travelled in children's underclothing.'

"Well, we sat there and talked a bit, and if I hadn't been a Bond of Joy, I don't know that I mightn't have exceeded[1], gentlemen—yes, positively exceeded; for the more I thought about it the less I liked the thought of Number Seventeen. I hadn't noticed the room particularly, except to see that the furniture had been changed since poor Fred's time. So I just slipped out, by and by, and I went out to the little glass case under the arch where the booking-clerk sits—just like here, that hotel was—and I said:—

"'Look here, miss; haven't you got another room empty except seventeen?'

"'No,' she said; 'I don't think so.'"

"'Then what's that?' I said, and pointed to a key hanging on the board, the only one left.

"'Oh,' she said, 'that's sixteen.'

"'Anyone in sixteen?' I said. 'Is it a comfortable room?'

"'No,' said she. 'Yes; quite comfortable. It's next door to yours— much the same class of room.'

"'Then I'll have sixteen, if you've no objection,' I said, and went back to the others, feeling very clever.

"When I went up to bed I locked my door, and, though I didn't believe in ghosts, I wished seventeen wasn't next door to me, and I wished there wasn't a door between the two rooms, though the door was locked right enough and the key on my side. I'd only got the one candle besides the two on the dressing-table, which I hadn't lighted; and I got my collar and tie off before I noticed that the furniture in my new room was the furniture out of Number Seventeen; French bed with red curtains, mahogany wardrobe as big as a hearse, and the carved mirror over the dressing-table between the two windows, and 'Belshazzar's Feast' over the mantelpiece. So that, though I'd not got the *room* where the commercial gentlemen had cut their throats, I'd got the *furniture* out of it. And for a moment I thought that was worse

---

[1] A euphemism for getting drunk

than the other. When I thought of what that furniture could tell, if it could speak——

"It was a silly thing to do—but we're all friends here and I don't mind owning up—I looked under the bed and I looked inside the hearse-wardrobe and I looked in a sort of narrow cupboard there was, where a body could have stood upright——"

"A body?" I repeated.

"A man, I mean. You see, it seemed to me that either these poor chaps had been murdered by someone who hid himself in Number Seventeen to do it, or else there was something there that frightened them into cutting their throats; and upon my soul, I can't tell you which idea I liked least!"

He paused, and filled his pipe very deliberately. "Go, on," someone said. And he went on.

"Now, you'll observe," he said, "that all I've told you up to the time of my going to bed that night's just hearsay. So I don't ask you to believe it—though the three coroners' inquests would be enough to stagger most chaps, I should say[1]. Still, what I'm going to tell you now's *my* part of the story—what happened to me myself in that room."

He paused again, holding the pipe in his hand, unlighted.

There was a silence, which I broke.

"Well, what *did* happen?" I asked.

"I had a bit of a struggle with myself," he said. "I reminded myself it was not *that* room, but the next one that it had happened in. I smoked a pipe or two and read the morning paper[2], advertisements and all. And at last I went to bed. I left the candle burning, though, I own that."

"Did you sleep?" I asked.

"Yes. I slept. Sound as a top. I was awakened by a soft tapping on my door. I sat up. I don't think I've ever been so frightened in my life. But I made myself say, 'Who's there?' in a whisper. Heaven knows I never expected any one to answer. The candle had gone out and it was pitch-dark. There was a quiet murmur and a shuffling sound outside. And no

---

[1] The story-teller's version of a humble brag: "I'm not asking you to believe me – I mean, it's just hearsay, right? But boy howdy! You should see those coroner's reports; they'd put the fear of God into you"

[2] The morning paper is the larger edition of a daily newspaper (the evening edition is largely a supplement to the morning edition). This is a pertinent fact because the story-teller is trying to emphasize how he has been desperately trying to occupy himself and kill time until morning: reading the entire morning edition, ads and all, a feat which would have probably taken an hour or more even for a quick reader

231

one answered. I tell you I hadn't expected any one to. But I cleared my throat and cried out, 'Who's there?' in a real out-loud voice. And 'Me, sir,' said a voice. 'Shaving-water, sir; six o'clock, sir.'

"It was the chambermaid."

A movement of relief ran round our circle.

"I don't think much of your story," said the large commercial.

"You haven't heard it yet," said the story-teller, dryly. "It was six o'clock on a winter's morning, and pitch-dark. My train went at seven. I got up and began to dress. My one candle wasn't much use. I lighted the two on the dressing-table to see to shave by. There wasn't any shaving-water outside my door, after all. And the passage was as black as a coal-hole[1]. So I started to shave with cold water; one has to sometimes, you know. I'd gone over my face and I was just going lightly round under my chin, when I saw something move in the looking-glass. I mean something that moved was reflected in the looking-glass. The big door of the wardrobe had swung open, and by a sort of double reflection I could see the French bed with the red curtains. On the edge of it sat a man in his shirt and trousers[2]—a man with black hair and whiskers, with the most awful look of despair and fear on his face that I've ever seen or dreamt of. I stood paralyzed, watching him in the mirror. I could not have turned round to save my life. Suddenly he laughed. It was a horrid, silent laugh, and showed all his teeth. They were very white and even[3]. And the next moment he had cut his throat from ear to ear, there before my eyes. Did you ever see a man cut his throat? The bed was all white before[4]."

The story-teller had laid down his pipe, and he passed his hand over his face before he went on.

---

[1] An underground coal bunker

[2] The modern equivalent of seeing a man sitting on your bed in his boxers and an undershirt: gentlemen never wore bare shirtsleeves except in the intimacy of the bedroom; even after taking off his coat or jacket he would then don a smoking jacket or dressing gown in order to be presentable

[3] A detail that – along with the black mustache – matches this to Hatteras' physical description

[4] I love this detail – using characteristic discipline Nesbit suggests much by showing little. There is also the unlikely question "have you ever seen a man cut his own throat?" Surely no one else in the room (or in the whole inn) could relate to his macabre experience, but he mentions it like it's a simple and common event. He then implies the sudden torrent of blood gushing from the wound by commenting on the color of the sheets. A masterful touch

"When I could look around I did. There was no one in the room. The bed was as white as ever. Well, that's all," he said, abruptly, "except that now, of course, I understood how these poor chaps had come by their deaths. They'd all seen this horror—the ghost of the first poor chap, I suppose—Bert Hatteras, you know; and with the shock their hands must have slipped and their throats got cut before they could stop themselves. Oh! by the way, when I looked at my watch it was two o'clock; there hadn't been any chambermaid at all[1]. I must have dreamed that. But I didn't dream the other. Oh! And one thing more. It was the same room. They hadn't changed the room, they'd only changed the number. *It was the same room!*"

"Look here," said the heavy man; "the room you've been talking about. *My* room's sixteen. And it's got that same furniture in it as what you describe, and the same picture and all."

"Oh, has it?" said the story-teller, a little uncomfortable, it seemed. "I'm sorry. But the cat's out of the bag now, and it can't be helped. Yes, it *was* this house I was speaking of. I suppose they've opened the room again. But you don't believe in ghosts; *you'll* be all right."

"Yes," said the heavy man, and presently got up and left the room.

"He's gone to see if he can get his room changed. You see if he hasn't," said the rabbit-faced man; "and I don't wonder."

The heavy man came back and settled into his chair.

"I could do with a drink," he said, reaching to the bell.

"I'll stand[2] some punch, gentlemen, if you'll allow me," said our dapper story-teller. "I rather pride myself on my punch[3]. I'll step out to the bar and get what I need for[4]."

---

[1] Insidiously implying that this is a sinister trick designed by the ghost to lure victims into shaving in the lonely dark

[2] Concoct, to make

[3] In the United States, punch is a dry, fizzy dessert beverage (typically ice cream, fruit juice, frozen fruits, and a clear soda like Sprite or ginger ale, served from a bowl with a ladle). In the UK, however, punch is almost always a giant cocktail: fruit juice, sugar water, fruit slices, and lots of liquor – typically brandy, rum, or whiskey. To make a good punch was a quality associated with a seasoned drinker, similar to making a great old fashioned or a fantastic Manhattan

[4] A turn of the century recipe for "cardinal punch" – a Christmas drink – calls for half a pound of powdered sugar dissolved in a quart of ice water, the rind of a large lemon, the juice of three lemons (beat together for five minutes), four ounces of red liquer, four ounces of maraschino, half a pint of Jamaica rum, and rock salt

"I thought he said he was a teetotaller[1]," said the heavy traveller when he had gone. And then our voices buzzed like a hive of bees. When our story-teller came in again we turned on him—half-a-dozen of us at once—and spoke.

"One at a time," he said, gently. "I didn't quite catch what you said."

"We want to know," I said, "how it was—if seeing that ghost made all those chaps cut their throats by startling them when they were shaving—how was it *you* didn't cut *your* throat when you saw it?"

"I should have," he answered, gravely, "without the slightest doubt—I should have cut my throat, only," he glanced at our heavy friend, "I always shave with a safety razor[2]. I travel in them[3]," he added, slowly, and bisected a lemon.

"But—but," said the large man, when he could speak through our uproar, "I've gone and given up my room."

"Yes," said the dapper man, squeezing the lemon; "I've just had my things moved into it. It's the best room in the house. I always think it worth while to take a little pains to secure it[4]."

---

[1] Of course he isn't; he is a clever trickster who knows how to get what he wants, whether it be a comfortable chair, a deal on a sale, or the best room in the house

[2] Straight razors – or cutthroat razors (think Sweeney Todd) – are long blades that fold out of a sheath and are controlled and angled by the shaver's hand. If his grip is lose or his hand unsteady, butchery can result. The safety razor (I shave with both incidentally, and can authoritatively describe the mechanics of both instruments) locks a double-edged razor blade between two plates and is moved by a handle in its base. The hairline edges of the blades are all that is exposed, so even if a cut is made, it will go no deeper than a graze. The handle also offers more stable control and leverage since the handle and blade are fixed at a 90 degree angle. They were largely popularized due to their safety (hence the name) which prevented accidental (or purposeful) throat cuts. Invented in 1880, they became popular

[3] Brilliant salesmanship! The entire story has essentially been a coy commercial for the product that he totes

[4] Leading us to conclude that the whole story was a tall tale, and proving the story teller's earlier point that the best story isn't the most realistic, but the most real-seeming – the most impacting, visceral tale. Nesbit herself makes this point by tricking the reader into believing her narrator before revealing that the story isn't a tale of horror at all, but a tale of humor. Notwithstanding, the ghost-story-in-a-story is genuinely chilling – as horrific as "The Mystery of the Semi-Detached"

"One at a time," he said, gently. "I didn't quite catch what you said."
"We want to know," I said, "how it was—if seeing that ghost made all those chaps cut their throats by startling them when they were shaving—how was it *you* didn't cut *your* throat when you saw it?"
"I should have," he answered, gravely, "without the slightest doubt—I should have cut my throat, only," he glanced at our heavy friend, "I always shave with a safety razor[1]. I travel in them[2]," he added, slowly, and bisected a lemon[3].
"But—but," said the large man, when he could speak through our uproar, "I've gone and given up my room."

   "Yes," said the dapper man, squeezing the lemon; "I've just had my things moved into it. It's the best room in the house. I always think it worth while to take a little pains to secure it[4]."

———————————————————————

WHILE "Jerry Bundler" begins with a false haunting that leads ends in an accidental murder, and the "Inexperienced Ghost" begins with a satirical ghost but ends with a traumatic death – both of which play with the expectations of the fireside ghost story – Nesbit does the same amount of impish defiance to the cliché, but ends on a light rather than tragic note. The story also doubles as an interesting treatise on literary aesthetics. At the time of its writing, realism was *de rigueur*, and romanticism was a thing of the past – of grandmothers and doe-eyed ingénues. Realism – stories told in everyday settings, with everyday people, and everyday details, about everyday events – was championed by Jack London, Mark Twain, Henry James, Stephen Crane, and Thomas Hardy (all of whom, by the way, wrote ghost stories, notwithstanding), and the movement had steamrolled over the romanticism of the previous generations (e.g., Poe, Scott, Stevenson, Hawthorne, and the Brontës). Their fantastical tales of treasure, ghosts, mountain vistas, white whales, and haunted houses peopled by decadent aristocrats were replaced by stories of middle classed clerks courting plain-faced stenographers, tidy tea rooms, fishing boats, whitewashed fences, unplanned pregnancies, farmers covered in pig shit, and foul-mouthed prospectors. The fat man – who thinks that an editorship at a wool catalog is sufficient experience to make him a literary critic – is a parody of the style-loathing realists: a man who looks down on purple prose, who would probably prefer to read a journalist's cold account of a factory workers' strike to the lush indulgence of *Kidnapped, The Scarlet Letter,* or *Walden.*

II.

Nesbit's writing was heavily influenced by both the romantics and the realists (not unlike Crane, James, and London whose blend of the two came to be called "naturalism"), reveling in regionalism, folklore, and natural dynamism. In "Number 17" we are handed a romantic realist's ghost story (compare to James' ambiguous "Turn of the Screw" or Hardy's plain-spoken "The Superstitious Man's Story") – a philosophical attempt to reconcile the sincerity of realism with the indulgences of romanticism. "Number 17" is a delicious Gothic farce (far better than her fun but overly sentimental "Haunted Inheritance") with wry humor lurking impishly behind the unpretentious prose. The storyteller is an archetypal trickster – an impish but lovable character who uses wit, intelligence, and reverse psychology to secure an advantage over pompous, imperceptive people who typically mock or condescend the trickster. In this way our winsome rogue is a spirit of flesh and blood – like Shakespeare's Puck, Ireland's fairy folk, Africa's Anansi, airmen's gremlins, Southerners' Br'er Rabbit, Native Americans' Coyote, the Grimms' wolves, or Aesop's foxes, the man who found the comfortable chair that no one else noticed is a figure of admirable mischief and brilliant tomfoolery. He manages to turn the tables on the skeptical fat man – a condescending prig who writes off the supernatural and resents romanticism – by frightening him with a romantic ghost story told in a realistic way.

LATE nineteenth century Paris' working class neighborhoods have been romanticized by the artwork of Lautrec, Renoir, and Caillebotte. By daytime Montmartre and Montparnasse were realms of sunny imagination, by evening they were kingdoms of sensuality and decadence, but by night they were labyrinths of terror. Underworld gangs referred to collectively as "Apaches" stalked the streets: muggers, garrotters, and savage criminals. "The Third Drug" takes place in this world and follows a refugee whose flight from these gang members sends him to the home of a kindly scientist. But what begins as a crime story – one that could easily be transported to the streets of Chicago in the 1920s or Los Angeles in the 1940s – quickly transitions to a wild fantasy of science fiction. The tale shares its spirit with *Dr Jekyll and Mr Hyde, Frankenstein,* and *The Invisible Man,* among others.

The Third Drug
{1908}

ROGER Wroxham looked round his studio before he blew out the candle, and wondered whether, perhaps, he looked for the last time. It was large and empty, yet his trouble had filled it and, pressing against him in the* prison of those four walls, forced him out into the- world, where lights and voices and the presence of other men should give him room to draw back, to set a space between it and him, to decide whether he would ever face it again — he and it alone together. The nature of his trouble is not germane to this story. There was a woman in it, of course, and money, and a friend, and regrets and embarrassments —and all of these reached out tendrils that wove and interwove till they made a puzzle problem of which heart and brain were now weary.

He blew out the candle and went quietly downstairs. It was nine at night, a soft night of May in Paris. Where should he go? He thought of the Seine, and took — an omnibus. When at last it stopped he got off, and so strange was the place to him that it almost seemed as though the trouble itself had been left behind. He did not feel it in the length of three or four streets that he traversed slowly. But in the open space, very light and lively, where he recognised the *Taverne de Paris* and knew himself in Montmartre, the trouble set its teeth in his heart again, and he broke away from the lamps and the talk to struggle with it in the dark, quiet streets beyond.

A man braced for such a fight has little thought to spare for the details of his surroundings. The next thing that Wroxham knew of the outside world was the fact which he had known for some time that he was not alone in the street. There was someone on the other side of the road keeping pace with him -— yes, certainly keeping pace, for, as he slackened his own, the feet on the other pavement also went more slowly. And now they were four feet, not two. Where had the other man sprung from? He had not been there a moment ago. And now, from an archway a little ahead of him, a third man came.

Wroxham stopped. Then three men converged upon him, and, like a sudden magic-lantern picture on a sheet prepared, there came to him all that he had heard and read of Montmartre — dark archways, knives, Apaches, and men who went away from homes where they were beloved and never again returned. He, too —well, if he never returned again, it would be quicker than the Seine, and, in the event of ultra mundane possibilities, safer.

He stood still and laughed in the face of the man who first reached him.

"Well, my friend?" said he; and at that the other two drew close.

"Monsieur walks late," said the first, a little confused, as it seemed, by that laugh.

"And will walk still later if it pleases him," said Roger. "Good night, my friends."

"Ah!" said the second, "friends do not say adieu so quickly. Monsieur will tell us the hour."

"I have not a watch," said Roger, quite truthfully.

"I will assist you to search for it," said the third man, and laid a hand on his arm.

Roger threw it off. The man with the hand staggered back.

"The knife searches more surely," said the second.

"No, no," said the third, quickly; "he is too heavy. I for one will not carry him afterwards."

They closed round him, hustling him between them. Their pale, degenerate faces spun and swung round him in the struggle. For there was a struggle. He had not meant that there should be a struggle. Someone would hear — someone would come.

But if any heard none came. The street retained its empty silence; the houses, masked in close shutters, kept their reserve. The four were wrestling, all pressed close together in a writhing bunch, drawing breath hardly through set teeth, their feet slipping and not slipping on the rounded cobble-stones.

The contact with these creatures, the smell of them, and the warm, greasy texture of their flesh as, in the conflict, his face or neck met neck or face of theirs – Roger felt a cold rage possess him. He wrung two clammy hands apart and threw something off – something that staggered back clattering, fell in the gutter, and lay there.

It was then that Roger felt the knife. Its point glanced off the cigarette-case in his breast pocket and bit sharply at his inner arm. And at the sting of it Roger knew, suddenly and quite surely, that he did not desire to die. He feigned a reeling weakness, relaxed his grip, swayed sideways, and then suddenly caught the other two in a new grip, crushed their faces together, flung them off, and ran. It was but for an instant that his feet were the only ones that echoed in the street. Then he knew that the others too were running.

It was like one of those nightmares wherein one runs for ever, leaden-footed, through a city of the dead. Roger turned sharply to the right. The sound of the other footsteps told that the pursuers also had turned that corner. Here was another street – a steep ascent. He ran more swiftly – he was running now for his life – the life that he held so cheap three minutes before. And all the streets were empty – empty like dream-streets, with all their windows dark and unhelpful, their doors fast closed against his need. Only now and again he glanced to right or left, if perchance some window might show light to justify a cry for help, some door advance the welcome of an open inch.

There was at last such a door. He did not see it till it was almost behind him. Then there was the drag of the sudden stop — the eternal instant of indecision. Was there time? There must be. He dashed his fingers through the inch-crack, grazing the backs of them, leapt within, drew the door outside; there was the sound of feet that went away.

He found himself listening, listening, and there was nothing to hear but the silence, and once, before he thought to twist his handkerchief round it, the drip of blood from his hand.

By and by he knew that he was not alone in this house, for from far away there came the faint sound of a footstep, and, quite near, the faint answering echo of it. And at a window high up on the other side of the courtyard a light showed. Light and sound and echo intensified, the light passing window after window, till at last it moved across the courtyard and the little trees threw black shifting shadows as it came towards him — a lamp in the hand of a man.

It was a short, bald man, with pointed beard and bright, friendly eyes. He held the lamp high as he came, and when he saw Roger he drew his breath in an inspiration that spoke of surprise, sympathy, pity.

"Hold! Hold!" He said, in a singularly pleasant voice; "there has been a misfortune? You are wounded, monsieur?"

"Apaches," said Roger, and was surprised at the weakness of his own voice.

"Your hand?"

"My arm," said Roger.

"Fortunately," said the other, "I am a surgeon. Allow me."

He set the lamp on the step of a closed door, took off Roger's coat, and quickly tied his own handkerchief round the wounded arm.

"Now," he said, "courage! I am alone in the house. No one comes here but me. If you can walk up to my rooms you will save us both much trouble. If you cannot, sit here and I will (etch you a cordial. But I advise you to try to walk. That pork cohere is, unfortunately, not very strong, and the lock is a common spring lock, and your friends may return with their friends; whereas the door across the courtyard is heavy, and the bolts are new."

Roger moved towards the heavy door whose bolts were new. The stairs seemed to go on forever. The doctor lent his arm, but the carved banisters and their lively shadows whirled before Roger's eyes. Also he seemed to be shod with lead, and to have in his legs bones that were red hot. Then the stairs ceased, and there was light, and a cessation of the dragging of those leaden feet. He was on a couch, and his eyes might close.

When next he saw and heard he was lying at ease, the close intimacy of a bandage clasping his arm, and in his mouth the vivid taste of some cordial.

The doctor was sitting in an arm chair near a table, looking benevolent through gold-rimmed pince-nez.

"Better?" He said. "No; lie still, you'll be a new man soon."

"I am desolated," said Roger, "to have occasioned you all this trouble."

"Not at all," said the doctor. "We live to heal, and it is a nasty cut, that in your arm. If you are wise, you will rest at present. I shall be honoured if you will be my guest for the night."

Roger again murmured something about trouble.

"In a big house like this," said the doctor, 'the doctor was sitting in an arm-chair near a table as it seemed a little sadly, "there are many empty rooms, and some rooms which are not empty. There is a bed altogether at your service, monsieur, and I counsel you not to delay in seeking it. You can walk?"

240

Wroxham stood up." Why, yes," he said, stretching himself. "I feel, as you say, a new man."

A narrow bed and rush-bottomed chair showed like doll's - house furniture in the large, high, gaunt room to which the doctor led him.

"You are too tired to undress yourself," said the doctor; "rest — only rest," and covered him with a rug, snugly tucked him up, and left him.

"I leave the door open," he said," in case you should have any fever. Good night. Do not torment yourself. All goes well."

Then he took away the lamp, and Wroxham lay on his back and saw the shadows of the window-frames cast by the street lamps on the high ceiling. His eyes, growing accustomed to the darkness, perceived the carving of the white paneled walls and mantelpiece. There was a door in the room, another door than the one which the doctor had left open. Roger did not like open doors. The other door, however, was closed. He wondered where it led, and whether it were locked. Presently he got up to see. It was locked. He lay down again.

His arm gave him no pain, and the night's adventure did not seem to have over set his nerves. He felt, on the contrary, calm, confident, extraordinarily at ease, and master of himself. The trouble — how could that ever have seemed important? This calmness — it felt like the calmness that precedes sleep. Yet sleep was far from him. What was it that kept sleep away? The bed was comfortable — the pillows soft. What was it? It came to him presently that it was the scent which distracted him, worrying him with a memory that he could not define. A faint scent of — what was it? Perfumery? Yes —and camphor— and something else — something vaguely disquieting. He had not noticed it before he had risen and tried the handle of that other door. But now He covered his face with the sheet, but through the sheet he smelt it still. He rose and threw back one of the long French windows. It opened with a click and a jar, and he looked across the dark well of the courtyard. He leaned out, breathing the chill pure air of the May night, but when he withdrew his head the scent was there again. Camphor - perfume —and something else. What was it that it reminded him of? He had his knee on the bed-edge when the answer came to that question. It was the scent that had struck at him from the darkened room when, a child, clutching at a grown-up hand, he had been led to the bed where, amid flowers, something white lay under a sheet – his mother they had told him. It was the scent of death, disguised with drugs and perfumes.

He stood up and went, with carefully controlled swiftness, towards the open door. He wanted light and a human voice.

The doctor was in the room upstairs; he the doctor was face to face with him on the landing, not a yard away, moving towards him quietly in shoeless feet.

"I can't sleep," said Wroxham, a little wildly; "it's too dark -- "

"Come upstairs," said the doctor, and Wroxham went.

There was comfort in the large, lighted room. A green shaded lamp stood on the table.

"What's behind that door," said Wroxham, abruptly — "that door downstairs?"

"Specimens," the doctor answered; "preserved specimens. My line is physiological research. You understand?"

So that was it.

"I feel quite well, you know," said Wroxham, laboriously explaining — "fit as any man — only I can't sleep."

"I see," said the doctor.

"It's the scent from your specimens, I think," Wroxham went on; "there's something about that scent."

"Yes," said the doctor.

"It's very odd." Wroxham was leaning his elbow on his knee and his chin on his hand. "I feel so frightfully well— and yet there's a strange feeling -- "

" Yes," said the doctor. "Yes, tell me exactly how you feel."

"I feel," said Wroxham, slowly, "like a man on the crest of a wave."

The doctor stood up.

"You feel well, happy, full of life and energy — as though you could walk to the world's end, and yet-- "

"And yet," said Roger, "as though my next step might be my last — as though I might step into a grave."

He shuddered.

"Do you," asked the doctor, anxiously — " do you feel thrills of pleasure —something like the first waves of chloroform — thrills running from your hair to your feet ? "

"I felt all that," said Roger, slowly, downstairs before I opened the window."

The doctor looked at his watch, frowned, and got up quickly. "There is very little time," he said.

Suddenly Roger felt an unexplained thrill of pain.

The doctor went to a long laboratory bench with bottle-filled shelves above it, and on it crucibles and retorts, test tubes, beakers—all a chemist's apparatus — reached a bottle from a shelf, and measured out certain drops into a graduated glass, added water, and stirred it with a glass rod.

"Drink that," he said.

"No," said Roger, and he spoke a thrill like the first thrill of the first chloroform wave swept through him, and it was a thrill, not of pleasure, but of pain. "No," he said, and "Ah!" for the pain was sharp.

"If you don't drink," said the doctor carefully, "you are a dead man."

"You may be giving me poison," Roger gasped, his hands at his heart.

"I may," said the doctor. "What do you suppose poison makes you feel like? What do you feel like now? "

"I feel," said Roger, "like death."

Every nerve, every muscle thrilled to a pain not too intense to be underlined by a shuddering nausea. "Like death," he said again.

"Then drink," cried the doctor, in tones of such cordial entreaty, such evident anxiety, that Wroxham half held his hand out for the glass. Drink! Believe me, it is your only chance."

Again the pain swept through him like an electric current. The beads of sweat sprang out on his forehead.

"That wound," the doctor pleaded, standing over him with the glass held "For Heaven's sake, drink! Don't you understand, man? You are poisoned. Your wound "

"The knife?" Wroxham murmured, and as he spoke his eyes seemed to swell in his head, and his head itself to grow enormous. "Do you know the poison — and its antidote?"

"I know all." The doctor soothed him. "Drink, then, my friend."

As the pain caught him again in a clasp more close than any lover's he clutched at the glass and drank. The drug met the pain and mastered it. Roger, in the ecstasy of pain's cessation, saw the world fade and go out in a haze of vivid violet.

II.

Faint films of lassitude shot with contentment wrapped him round. He lay passive as a man lies in the convalescence that follows a long fight with Death.

"I'm better now," he said, in a voice that was a whisper — tried to raise his hand from where it lay help less in his sight, failed, and lay looking at it in confident repose — " much better."

"Yes," said the doctor, and his pleasant, soft voice had grown softer, pleasanter. "You are now in the second stage. An interval is necessary before you can pass to the third. I will enliven the interval by conversation. Is there anything you would like to know?"

"Nothing," said Roger; "I am quite happy — quite contented."

"This is very interesting," said the doctor. "Tell me exactly how you feel."

Roger faintly and slowly told him.

"Ah!" the doctor said, "I have not before heard this. You are the only one of them all who ever passed the first stage. The others--"

"The others?" said Roger, but he did not care much about the others."

"The others," said the doctor, frowning," were unsound. Decadent students, de generate Apaches. You are highly trained — in fine physical condition. And your brain! The Lord be good to the Apaches who so delicately excited it to just the degree of activity needed for my purpose."

"The others?" Wroxham insisted.

"The others? They are in the room whose door was locked. Look — you should be able to see them. The second drug should lay your consciousness before me like a sheet of white paper on which I can write what I choose. If I choose that you should see my specimens. *Allons donc.* I have no secrets from you now. Look —look — strain your eyes. In theory I know all that you can do and feel and see in this second stage. But practically enlighten me — look —shut your eyes and look!"

Roger closed his eyes and looked. He saw the gaunt, uncarpeted staircase, the open doors of the big rooms, passed to the locked door, and it opened at his touch. The room inside was, like the other, spacious and paneled. A lighted lamp with a blue shade hung from the ceiling, and below it an effect of spread whiteness. Roger looked. There were things to be seen.

With a shudder he opened his eyes on the doctor's delightful room, the doctor's intent face.

"What did you see?" the doctor asked. "Tell me!"

"Did you kill them all?" Roger asked back.

"They died — of their own inherent weakness," the doctor said. "And you saw them?"

"I saw," said Roger, " the quiet people lying all along the floor in their death clothes — the people who have come in at that door of yours that is a trap— for robbery, or curiosity, or shelter — and never gone out any more." "Right," said the doctor.

"Right. My theory is proved at every point. You can see what 1 choose you to see. Yes; decadents all. It was in embalming that I was a specialist before I began these other investigations."

"What," Roger whispered — "what is it all for?"

"To make the superman," said the doctor. "I will tell you."

He told. It was a long story— the story of a man's life, a man's work, a man's dreams, hopes, ambitions.

"The secret of life," the doctor ended. "That is what all the alchemists sought. They sought it where Fate pleased. I sought it where I have found it — in death."

Roger thought of the room behind the locked door.

"And the secret is?" asked Roger.

"I have told you," said the doctor, impatiently; "it is in the third drug that life — splendid, superhuman life— is found. I have tried it on animals. 'Always they became perfect, all that an animal should be. And more, too — much more. They were too perfect, too near humanity. They looked at me with human eyes. I could not let them live. Such animals it is not necessary to embalm. I had a laboratory in those days — and assistants. They called me the Prince of Vivisectors."

The man on the sofa shuddered.

"I am naturally" the doctor went on, "a tender-hearted man. You see it in my face; my voice proclaims it. Thing what I have suffered in the sufferings of these poor beasts who never injured me. My God! Bear witness that I have not buried my talent. I have been faithful. I have laid it down all – love, and joy, and pity, and the little beautiful things of life – all, all, on the altar of science, and seen them consume away. I deserve my heaven, if ever man did. And now by all the saints in heaven I am near it!"

"What is the third drug?" Roger asked, lying limp and flat on his couch.

"It is the Elixir of Life," said the doctor. "I am not its discoverer; the old alchemists knew it well, but they failed because they sought to apply the elixir to a normal — that is, a diseased and faulty — body. I knew better. One must have first a body abnormally healthy, abnormally strong. Then, not the elixir, but the two drugs that pre pare. The first excites prematurely the natural conflict between the principles of life and death, and then, just at the point where Death is about to win his victory, the second drug intensifies life so that it conquers — intensifies, and yet chastens. Then the whole life of the subject, risen to an ecstasy, falls prone in an almost voluntary submission to the coming super-life. Submission — submission! The garrison must surrender before the splendid conqueror can enter and make the citadel his own. Do you understand? Do you submit? "

"I submit," said Roger, for, indeed, he did. "But — soon — quite soon— I will not submit."

He was too weak to be wise, or those words had remained unspoken.

The doctor sprang to his feet.

"It works too quickly!" he cried. "Everything works too quickly with you. Your condition is too perfect. So now I bind you."

From a drawer beneath the bench where the bottles gleamed the doctor drew rolls of bandages — violet, like the haze that had drowned, at the urgence of the second drug, the consciousness of Roger. He moved, faintly resistant, on his couch. The doctor's hands, most gently, most irresistibly, controlled his movement.

"Lie still," said the gentle, charming voice. "Lie still; all is well." The clever, soft hands were unrolling the bandages — passing them round arms and throat — under and over the soft narrow couch. "I cannot risk your life, my poor boy. The least movement of yours might ruin everything. The third drug, like the first, must be offered directly to the blood which absorbs it. I bound the first drug as an unguent upon your knife-wound."

The swift hands passed the soft bandages back and forth, over and under— flashes of violet passed to and fro in the air like the shuttle of a weaver through his warp. As the" bandage clasped his knees Roger moved.

"For God's sake, no!" the doctor cried; "the time is so near. If you cease to submit it is death."

With an incredible accelerated swiftness he swept the bandages round and round knees and ankles, drew a deep breath —stood upright.

"I must make an incision," he said -"in the head this time it will not hurt. See! I spray it with the Constantia Nepenthe; that also I discovered. My boy. In a moment you know all things —you are as a god. Be patient. Preserve your submission."

And Roger, with life and will resurgent hammering at his heart, preserved it.

He did not feel the knife that made the cross cut on his temple, but he felt the hot spurt of blood that followed the cut, he felt the cool flap of a plaster spread with some sweet, clean smelling unguent that met the blood and stanched it. There was a moment – or was it hours? – of nothingness. Then from that cut on his forehead there seemed to radiate threads of infinite length, and of a strength that one could trust to – threads that linked one to all knowledge past and present. He felt that he controlled all wisdom, as a driver controls his four-in-hand. Knowledge he perceived, belonged to him, as the air belongs to the eagle. He swam in it, as great fish in a limitless ocean.

He opened his eyes and met those of the doctor, who sighed as one to whom breath has grown difficult.

"Ah, all goes well. Oh, my boy, was it not worth it? What do you feel?"

"I. Know. Everything," said Roger, with full stops between the words.

"Everything? The future? "

"No. I know all that man has ever known."

"Look back — into the past. See someone. See Pharaoh. You see him— on his throne?"

"Not on his throne. He is whispering in a corner of his great gardens to a girl who is the daughter of a water-carrier."

"Bah! Any poet of my dozen decadents who lie so still could have told me that. Tell me secrets — the *Masque de Fer*."

The other told a tale, wild and incredible, but it satisfied the listener.

"That too — it might be imagination. Tell me the name of the woman I loved and—"

The echo of the name of the anesthetic came to Roger; "Constantia," said he, in an even voice.

"Ah," the doctor cried, "now I see you know all things. It was not murder. I hoped to dower her with all the splendors of the superlife."

"Her bones lie under the lilacs, where you used to kiss her in the spring," said Roger, quite without knowing what it was that he was going to say.

"It is enough," the doctor cried. He sprang up, ranged certain bottles and glasses on a table convenient to his chair. "You know all things. It was not a dream, this, the dream of my life. It is true. It is a fact accomplished. Now I, too, will know all things. I will be as the gods."

He sought among leather cases on a far table and came back swiftly into the circle of light that lay below the green-shaded lamp.

Roger, floating contentedly on the new sea of knowledge that seemed to support him, turned eyes on the trouble that had driven him

248

out of that large, empty studio so long ago, so far away. His new-found wisdom laughed at that problem, laughed and solved it. "To end that trouble I must do so-and-so, say such-and-such," Roger told himself again and again.

And now the doctor, standing by the table, laid on it his pale, plump hand outspread He drew a knife from a case —a long, shiny knife —and scored his hand across and across its back, as a cook scores pork for cooking. The slow blood followed the cuts in beads and lines.

Into the cuts he dropped a green liquid from a little bottle, replaced its stopper, bound up his hand, and sat down.

"The beginning of the first stage," he said; "almost at once I shall begin to be a new man. It will work quickly. My body, like yours, is sane and healthy."

There was a long silence.

"Oh, but this is good," the doctor broke it to say. "I feel the hand of Life sweeping my nerves like harp-strings."

Roger had been thinking, the old common sense that guides an ordinary man breaking through this consciousness of illimitable wisdom. "You had better," he said, "unbind me; when the hand of Death sweeps your nerves you may need help."

"No," the doctor said, and no, and no, and no many times. "I am afraid of you. You know all things, and even in your body you are stronger than I."

And then suddenly and irresistibly the pain caught him. Roger saw his face contorted with agony, his hands clench on the arm of his chair; and it seemed that either this man was less able to bear pain than he, or that the pain was much more violent than had been his own. And the plump, pale hand, writhing and distorted by anguish, again and again drew near to take the glass that stood ready on the table, and with convulsive self-restraint again and again drew back without it.

The short May night was waning — the shiver of dawn rustled the leaves of the plant whose leaves were like red misshaped hearts.

"Now!" The doctor screamed the word, grasped the glass, drained it, and sank back in his chair. His hand struck the table beside him. Looking at his limp body and head thrown back one could almost see the cessation of pain, the coming of kind oblivion.

III.

The dawn had grown to daylight, a poor, grey, rain-stained daylight, not strong enough to pierce the curtains and *persiennes*, and yet not so weak but that it could mock the lamp, now burnt low and smelling vilely.

Roger lay very still on his couch, a man wounded, anxious, and extravagantly tired. In those hours of long, slow dawning, face to face with the unconscious figure in the chair, he had felt, slowly and little by little, the recession of that sea of knowledge on which he had felt himself float in such large content. The sea had withdrawn itself, leaving him high and dry on the shore of the normal. The only relic that he had clung to and that he still grasped was the answer to the problem of the trouble — the only wisdom that he had put into words. These words remained to him, and he knew that they held wisdom — very simple wisdom, too.

"To end the trouble I must do so-and-so and say such-and-such."

Slowly a dampness spread itself over Wroxham's forehead and tingled among the roots of his hair. He writhed in his bonds. They held fast. He could not move hand or foot. Only his head could turn a little, so that he could at will see the doctor or not see him. A shaft of desolate light pierced the *persienne* at its hinge and rested on the table, where an overturned glass lay.

Wroxham thrilled from head to foot. The body in the chair stirred — hardly stirred — shivered, rather— and a very faint, far-away voice said :—

"Now the third — give me the third."

"What?" said Roger, stupidly; and he had to clear his throat twice before he could say even that.

"The moment is now," said the doctor. "I remember all. I made you a god. Give me the third drug."

"Where is it?" Roger asked.

"It is at my elbow," the doctor murmured. "I submit — I submit. Give me the third drug, and let me be as you are."

"As *I* am? " said Roger. "You forget. *I* am bound."

"Break your bonds," the doctor urged, in a quick, small voice. "I trust you now. You are stronger than all men, as you are wiser. Stretch your muscles, and the bandages will fall asunder like snow-wreaths."

"It is too late," Wroxham said, and laughed; "all that is over. I am not wise any more, and I have only the strength of a man. I am tired and wounded. I cannot break my bonds — I cannot help you! "

"But if you cannot help me — it is death," said the doctor.

"It is death," said Roger. "Do you feel it coming on you?"

"I feel life returning," said the doctor, "it is now the moment —the one possible moment. And I cannot reach it. Oh, give it me —give it me!"

Then Roger cried out suddenly, in a loud voice: "Now, by all that's sacred, you infernal decadent, I am glad that I cannot give it. Yes, if it costs me my life, it's worth it, you madman, so that your life ends too. Now be silent, and die like a man if you have it in you."

Roger lay and watched him, and presently he writhed from the chair to the floor, tearing feebly at it with his fingers, moaned, shuddered, and lay very still.

Of all that befell Roger in that house the worst was now. For now he knew that he was alone with the dead, and between him and death stretched certain hours and days For the *parte cochere* was locked; the doors of the house itself were locked — heavy doors and the locks new.

"I am alone in the house," the doctor had said. "No one comes here but me."

No one would come. He would die there —he, Roger Wroxham — "poor old Roger Wroxham, who was no one's enemy but his own." Tears pricked his eyes. He shook his head impatiently and they fell from his lashes.

"You fool," he said," can't you die like a man either?"

Then he set his teeth and made himself lie still. It seemed to him that now Despair laid her hand on his heart. But, to speak truth, it was Hope whose hand lay there. This was so much more than a man should be called on to bear — it could not be true. It was an evil dream. He would awake presently. Or if it were, indeed, real — then someone would come, someone must come. God could not let nobody come to save him.

And late at night, when heart and brain had been stretched almost to the point where both break and let in the sea of madness, someone came.

The interminable day had worn itself out. Roger had screamed, yelled, shouted till his throat was dried up, his lips baked and cracked. No one heard. How should they? The twilight had thickened and thickened till at last it made a shroud for the dead man on the floor by the chair. And there were other dead men in that house ; and as Roger ceased to see the one he saw the others —the quiet, awful faces, the lean hands, the straight, stiff limbs laid out one beyond another in the room of death. They at least were not bound. If they should rise in their white wrappings and, crossing that empty sleeping chamber very softly, come slowly up the stairs--

A stair creaked.

His ears, strained with hours of listening, thought themselves befooled. But his cowering heart knew better.

Again a stair creaked. There was a hand on the door.

"Then it is all over," said Roger in the darkness, "and I am mad."

The door opened very slowly, very cautiously. There was no light. Only the sound of soft feet and draperies that rustled. Then suddenly a match spurted— light struck at his eyes; a flicker of lit candlewick steadying to flame. And the things that had come were not those quiet people creeping up to match their death with his death in life, but human creatures, alive, breathing, with eyes that moved and glittered, lips that breathed and spoke.

"He must be here," one said. "Lisette watched all day; he never came out. He must be here — there is nowhere else."

Then they set up the candle-end on the table, and he saw their faces. They were the Apaches who had set on him in that lonely street, and who had sought him here — to set on him again.

He sucked his dry tongue, licked his dry lips, and cried aloud: —

"Here I am! Oh, kill me! For the love of Heaven, brothers, kill me *now!*"

And even before he spoke had seen and seen lay on the they him, what floor.

"He died this morning. I am bound. Kill me, brothers; I cannot die slowly here alone. Oh, kill me, for pity's sake!"

But already the three were pressing on each other at a doorway suddenly grown too narrow. They could kill a living man, but they could not face death, quiet, enthroned.

"For the love of Heaven," Roger screamed, " have pity! Kill me outright! Come back — come back!"

And then, since even Apaches are human, they did come back. One of them caught up the candle and bent over Roger, knife in hand.

"Make sure!" said Roger, through set teeth.

"*Nom d'un nom*," said the Apache, with worse words, and cut the bandages here, and here, and here again, and there, and lower, to the very feet.

Then this good Samaritan helped Roger to rise, and when he could not stand, the Samaritan half pulled, half carried him down those many steps, till they came upon the others putting on their boots at the stair-foot.

Then between them the three men carried the other out and slammed the outer door, and presently set him against a gate-post in another street, and went their wicked ways.

And after a time a girl with furtive eyes brought brandy and hoarse muttered kind nesses, and slid away in the shadows.

Against that gate-post the police came upon him. They took him to the address they found on him. When they came to question him he said, "Apaches," and his variations on that theme were deemed sufficient, though not one of them touched truth or spoke of the third drug.

There has never been anything in the papers about that house. I think it is still closed, and inside it still lie in the locked room the very quiet people ; and above, there is the room with the narrow couch and the scattered, cut, violet bandages, and the Thing on the floor by the chair, under the lamp that burned itself out in that May dawning.

THE Third Drug, like many of Nesbit's science fiction stories, is not particularly strong, but it benefits from a uniquely female authorial hand. Where most sci-fi, mad scientist narratives are driven by ambition, the desire for control, or the thirst for godlike power, this one is undergirded by emotions of loss, vulnerability, and fear. Make no mistake – the wretched armchair chemist/taxidermist who uncovers the three drugs is wholly motivated by a lust for omnipotence, but his victim is the focus, and the villain's shenanigans are merely a catalyst to shake him from his suicidal reverie, and to reprioritize his life. At its heart, this science fiction story is more like *Frankenstein* than *The Island of Dr Moreau:* a tale of pathos, emotional exposure, and pity. It also includes a clue to Nesbit's own personal phobias: live burial. Like Edgar Allan Poe, she was obsessed with the fear of being trapped underground – or otherwise restrained – and slowly starved of food, water, and oxygen while her mind wriggled and spasmed under the strain of horror. There is a report that during her childhood one of her uncles had appeared to die and was laid in his coffin. As the mourners passed by, one godsend noticed some animation in his face, and he was revived and spared a live burial. In another childhood incident, she was taken to the crypts at St. Michel in Bordeaux, where mummified bodies were exposed in their tombs for a fascinated public to view. But Nesbit was not fascinated. She was terrified:

"[They were] skeletons with the flesh hardened on their bones, with their long dry hair hanging on each side of their brown faces, where the skin in drying had drawn itself back from their gleaming teeth and empty eye-sockets. Skeletons draped in mouldering shreds of shrouds and grave-clothes, their lean fingers still clothed with dry skin... it is to them, I think, more than to any other thing, that I owe nights and nights of anguish and horror, long years of bitterest fear and dread..."

I can only imagine that *this* sort of vision is "the Thing on the floor by that chair" that she pictures in her mind at the story's close.

THE following story can be easily classified as science fiction. It features a scientist who may be rhetorically termed mad, whose experiments on live animals enrage the humanitarian sensibilities of his fiancée – a member of the Anti-vivisection League (precursor to the Society for the Prevention of Cruelty to Animals). Chided for torturing animals, he is driven to experiment on *himself* – drugs which enhance the senses, giving stereophonic powers to the ears, microscopic detection to the eyes, and acuteness of touch to rival Roderick Usher. This is not the only Poe-like quality to this story, in fact an immoderate dose of his potion shuttles the scientist into a mind-melting enhancement of all five senses at once, knocking him into a passive state of motionless hypersensitivity which puts him in danger of a predictable peril: live burial.

The Five Senses
{1909}

PROFESSOR Boyd Thompson's services to the cause of science are usually spoken of as inestimable, and so indeed they probably are, since in science, as in the rest of life, one thing leads to another, and you never know where anything is going to stop. At any rate, inestimable or not, they are world-renowned, and he with them. The discoveries which he gave to his time are a matter of common knowledge among biological experts, and the sudden ending of his experimental activities caused a few days' wonder in even lay circles. Quite unintelligent people told each other that it seemed a pity, and persons on omnibuses exchanged commonplaces starred with his name.

But the real meaning and cause of that ending have been studiously hidden, as well as the events which immediately preceded it. A veil has been drawn over all the things that people would have liked to know, and it is only now that circumstances so arrange themselves as to make it possible to tell the whole story. I propose to avail myself of this possibility.

It will serve no purpose for me to explain how the necessary knowledge came into my possession; but I will say that the story was only in part pieced together by me. Another hand is responsible for much of the detail and for a certain occasional emotionalism which is, I believe, wholly foreign to my own style. In my original statement of the following facts I dealt fully, as I am, I may say without immodesty,

255

qualified to do, with all the scientific points of the narrative. But these details were judged, unwisely as I think, to be needless to the expert, and unintelligible to the ordinary reader, and have therefore been struck out; the merest hints have been left as necessary links in the story. This appears to me to destroy most of its interest, but I admit that the elisions are perhaps justified. I have no desire to assist or encourage callow students in such experiments as those by which Professor Boyd Thompson brought his scientific career to an end.

Incredible as it may appear, Professor Boyd Thompson was once a little boy who wore white embroidered frocks and blue sashes; in that state he caught flies and pulled off their wings to find out how they flew. He did not find out, and Lucilla, his little girl-cousin, also in white frocks, cried over the dead, dismembered flies, and buried them in little paper coffins. Later, he wore a holland blouse with a belt of leather, and watched the development of tadpoles in a tin bath in the stable yard. A microscope was, on his eighth birthday, presented to him by an affluent uncle. The uncle showed him how to surprise the secrets of a drop of pond water, which, limpid to the eye, confessed under the microscope to a whole cosmogony of strenuous and undesirable careers. At the age of ten, Arthur Boyd Thompson was sent to a private school, its Headmaster an acolyte of Science, who esteemed himself to be a high priest of Huxley and Tyndal, a devotee of Darwin. Thence to the choice of medicine as a profession was, when the choice was insisted on by the elder Boyd Thompson, a short, plain step. Inorganic chemistry failed to charm, and under the cloak of Medicine and Surgery the growing fever of scientific curiosity could be sated on bodies other than the cloak-wearer's. He became a medical student and an enthusiast for vivisection.

The bow of Apollo was not always bent. In a rest-interval, the summer vacation, to be exact, he met again the cousin – second, once removed – Lucilla, and loved her. They were betrothed. It was a long, bright summer full of sunshine, garden-parties, picnics, archery – a decaying amusement – and croquet, then coming to its own. He exulted in the distinction already crescent in his career, but some half-formed wholly unconscious desire to shine with increased lustre in the eyes of the beloved caused him to invite, for the holiday's ultimate week, a fellow student, one who knew and could testify to the quality of the laurels already encircling the head of the young scientist. The friend came, testified, and in a vibrating interview under the lime-trees of Lucilla's people's garden, Mr Boyd Thompson learned that Lucilla never could, never would, love or marry a vivisectionist.

The moon hung low and yellow in the spacious calm of the sky; the hour was propitious, the lovers fond. Mr Boyd Thompson vowed that his scientific research should henceforth deal wholly with departments into which the emotions of the non-scientific cannot enter. He went back to London, and within the week bought four dozen frogs, twelve guinea-pigs, five cats, and a spaniel. His scientific aspirations met his love-longings, and did not fight them. You cannot fight beings of another world. He took part in a debate on 'Blood Pressure', which created some little stir in medical circles, spoke eloquently, and distinction surrounded him with a halo.

He wrote to Lucilla three times a week, took his degree, and published that celebrated paper of his which set the whole scientific world by the ears; 'The Action of Choline on the Nervous System' I think its name was.

Lucilla surreptitiously subscribed to a press-cutting agency for all snippets of print relating to her lover. Three weeks after the publication of that paper, which really was the beginning of Professor Boyd Thompson's fame, she wrote to him from her home in Kent.

ARTHUR, you have been doing it again. You know how I love you, and I believe you love me; but you must choose between loving me and torturing dumb animals. If you don't choose right, then it's goodbye, and God forgive you.

Your poor Lucilla, who loved you very dearly.

He read the letter, and the human heart in him winced and whined. Yet not so deeply now, nor so loudly, but that he bethought himself to seek out a friend and pupil, who would watch certain experiments, attend to the cutting of certain sections, before he started for Tenterden, where she lived. There was no station at Tenterden in those days, but a twelve-mile walk did not dismay him.

Lucilla's home was one of those houses of brave proportions and an inalienable bourgeois stateliness, which stand back a little from the noble High Street of that most beautiful of Kentish towns. He came there, pleasantly exercised, his boots dusty, and his throat dry, and stood on the snowy doorstep, beneath the Jacobean lintel. He looked down the wide, beautiful street, raised eyebrows, and shrugged uneasy shoulders within his professional frock-coat.

'It's all so difficult,' he said to himself.

Lucilla received him in a drawing-room scented with last year's rose leaves, and fresh with chintz that had been washed a dozen times. She stood, very pale and frail; her blonde hair was not teased into fluffiness, and rounded over the chignon of the period but banded Madonnawise, crowning her with heavy burnished plaits. Her gown was of white muslin, and round her neck black velvet passed, supporting a gold locket. He knew whose picture it held. The loose bell sleeves fell away from the slender arms with little black velvet bracelets, and she leaned one hand on a chiffonier of carved rosewood, on whose marble top stood, under a glass case, a Chinese pagoda, carved in ivory, and two Bohemian glass vases with medallions representing young women nursing pigeons. There were white curtains of darned net, in the fireplace white ravelled muslin spread a cascade brightened with threads of tinsel. A canary sang in a green cage, wainscoted with yellow tarlatan, and two red rosebuds stood in lank specimen glasses on the mantelpiece.

Every article of furniture in the room spoke eloquently of the sheltered life, the iron obstinacy of the well-brought-up.

It was a scene that invaded his mental vision many a time, in the laboratory, in the lecture-room. It symbolized many things, all dear, and all impossible.

They talked awkwardly, miserably. And always it came round to this same thing.

'But you don't mean it,' he said, and at last came close to her.

'I do mean it,' she said, very white, very trembling, very determined.

'But it's my life,' he pleaded; 'it's the life of thousands. You don't understand.'

'I understand that dogs are tortured. I can't bear it.'

He caught at her hand.

'Don't,' she said. 'When I think what that hand does!'

'Dearest,' he said very earnestly, 'which is the more important, a dog or a human being?'

'They're all God's creatures,' she flashed, unorthodoxly unorthodox. 'They're all God's creatures.' With much more that he heard and pitied and smiled at miserably in his heart.

'You don't understand,' he kept saying, stemming the flood of her rhetorical pleadings. 'Spencer Wells alone has found out wonderful things, just with experiments on rabbits.'

'Don't tell me,' she said. 'I don't want to hear.'

The conventions of their day forbade that he should tell her anything plainly. He took refuge in generalities. 'Spencer Wells, that operation he perfected, it's restored thousands of women to their husbands – saved thousands of women for their children.'

'I don't care what he's done – it's wrong if it's done in that way.'

It was on that day that they parted, after more than an hour of mutual misunderstood reiteration. He, she said, was brutal. And, besides, it was plain that he did not love her. To him she seemed unreasonable, narrow, prejudiced, blind to the high ideals of the new science.

'Then it's goodbye,' he said at last. 'If I gave way, you'd only despise me, because I should despise myself. It's no good. Goodbye, dear.'

'Goodbye,' she said. 'I know I'm right. You'll know I am, some day.'

'Never,' he answered, more moved and in a more diffused sense than he had ever believed he could be. 'I can't set my pleasure in you against the good of the whole world.'

'If that's all you think of me,' she said, and her silk and her muslin whirled from the room.

He walked back to Staplehurst, thrilled with the conflict. The thrill died down, went out, and left as ashes a cold resolve.

That was the end of Mr Boyd Thompson's engagement.

It was quite by accident that he made his greatest discovery. There are those who hold that all great discoveries are accident – or Providence. The terms are, in this connection, interchangeable. He plunged into work to wash away the traces of his soul's wounds, as a man plunges into water to wash off red blood. And he swam there, perhaps, a little blindly. The injection with which he treated that white rabbit was not compounded of the drugs he had intended to use. He could not lay his hand on the thing he wanted, and in that sort of frenzy of experiment, to which no scientific investigator is wholly a stranger, he cast about for a new idea. The thing that came to his hand was a drug that he had never in his normal mind intended to use – an unaccredited, wild, magic medicine obtained by a missionary from some savage South Sea tribe and brought home as an example of the ignorance of the heathen.

And it worked a miracle.

He had been fighting his way through the unbending opposition of known facts, he had been struggling in the shadows, and this discovery was like the blinding light that meets a man's eyes when his pick-axe knocks a hole in a dark cave and he finds himself face to face with the sun. The effect was undoubted. Now it behoved him to make sure of the cause, to eliminate all those other factors to which that effect might have been due. He experimented cautiously, slowly. These things take years, and the years he did not grudge. He was never tired, never impatient; the slightest variations, the least indications, were eagerly observed, faithfully recorded.

259

His whole soul was in his work. Lucilla was the one beautiful memory of his life. But she was a memory. The reality was this discovery, the accident, the Providence.

Day followed day, all alike, and yet each taking almost unperceived, one little step forward; or stumbling into sudden sloughs, those losses and lapses that take days and weeks to retrieve. He was Professor, and his hair was grey at the temples before his achievement rose before him, beautiful, inevitable, austere in its completed splendour, as before the triumphant artist rises the finished work of his art.

He had found out one of the secrets with which Nature has crammed her dark hiding-places. He had discovered the hidden possibilities of sensation. In plain English, his researches had led him thus far; he had found – by accident or Providence – the way to intensify sensation. Vaguely, incredulously, he had perceived his discovery; the rabbits and guinea-pigs had demonstrated it plainly enough. Then there was a night when he became aware that those results must be checked by something else. He must work out in marble the form he had worked out in clay. He knew that by this drug, which had, so to speak, thrust itself upon him, he could intensify the five senses of any of the inferior animals. Could he intensify those senses in man? If so, worlds beyond the grasp of his tired mind opened themselves before him. If so, he would have achieved a discovery, made a contribution to the science he had loved so well and followed at such a cost, a discovery equal to any that any man had ever made.

Ferrier, and Leo, and Horsley; those he would outshine. Galileo, Newton, Harvey; he would rank with these.

Could he find a human rabbit to submit to the test?

The soul of the man Lucilla had loved, turned and revolted. No: he had experimented on guinea-pigs and rabbits, but when it came to experimenting on men, there was only one man on whom he chose to use his new-found powers. Himself.

At least she would not have it to say that he was a coward, or unfair, when it came to the point of what a man could do and dare, could suffer and endure.

His big laboratory was silent and deserted. His assistants were gone, his private pupils dispersed. He was alone with the tools of his trade. Shelf on shelf of smooth stoppered bottles, drugs and stains, the long bench gleaming with beakers, test tubes, and the glass mansions of costly apparatus. In the shadows at the far end of the room, where the last going assistant had turned off the electric lights, strange shapes lurked: wicker-covered carboys, kinographs, galvanometers, the faintly

261

threatening aspect of delicate complex machines all wires and coils and springs, the gaunt form of the pendulum myographs, and certain well-worn tables and copper troughs, which for the moment had no use.

He knew that this drug with others, diversely compounded and applied, produced in animals an abnormal intensification of the senses; that it increased – nay, as it were, magnified a thousandfold, the hearing, the sight, the touch – and, he was almost sure, the senses of taste and smell. But of the extent of the increase he could form no exact estimate.

Should he tonight put himself in the position of one able to speak on these points with authority? Or should he go to the Royal Society's meeting and hear that ass Netherby maunder yet once again about the secretion of lymph?

He pulled out his notebook and laid it open on the bench. He went to the locked cupboard, unfastened it with the bright key that hung instead of seal or charm at his watch-chain. He unfolded a paper and laid it on the bench where no one coming in could fail to see it. Then he took out little bottles, three, four, five, polished a graduated glass and dropped into it slow, heavy drops. A larger bottle yielded a medium in which all mingled. He hardly hesitated at all before turning up his sleeve and slipping the tiny needle into his arm. He pressed the end of the syringe. The injection was made.

Its effect, though not immediate, was sudden. He had to close his eyes, staggered indeed and was glad of the stool near him, for the drug coursed through him as a hunt in full cry might sweep over untrodden plains. Then suddenly everything seemed to settle; he was no longer helpless but was once again Professor Boyd Thompson, who had injected a mixture of certain drugs and was experiencing their effect.

His fingers, still holding the glass syringe, sent swift messages to his brain. When he looked down at his fingers, he saw that what they grasped was the smooth, slender tube of clear glass. What he felt that they held was a tremendous cylinder, rough to the touch. He wondered, even at the moment, why, if his sense of touch were indeed magnified to this degree, everything did not appear enormous – his ring, his collar. He examined the new phenomenon with cold care. It seemed that only that was enlarged on which his attention, his mind, was fixed. He kept his hand on the glass syringe, and thought of his ring, got his mind away from the tube, back again in time to feel it small between his fingers, grow, increase, and become big once more.

'So *that's* a success,' he said, and saw himself lay the thing down. It lay just in front of the rack of test tubes, to the eye, just that little glass cylinder. To the touch it was like a water-pipe on a house side, and the test tubes, when he touched them, like the pipes of a great organ.

'Success,' he said again, and mixed the antidote. For he had found the antidote in one of those flashes of intuition, imagination, genius, that light the ways of science as stars light the way of a ship in dark waters. The action of the antidote was enough for one night. He locked the cupboard, and, after all, was glad to listen to the maunderings of Netherby. It had been lonely there, in the atmosphere of complete success.

One by one, day by day, he tested the action of his drugs on his other senses. Without being technical, I had perhaps better explain that the compelling drug was, in each case, one and the same. Its action was directed to this set of nerves or that by means of the other drugs mixed with it. I trust this is clear?

The sense of smell was tested, and its laboratory, with its mingled odours, became abominable to him. Hardly could he stay himself from rushing forth into the outer air to wash his nostrils in the clear coolness of Hampstead Heath. The sense of taste gave him, magnified a thousand times, the flavour of his after-dinner coffee, and other tastes, distasteful almost beyond the bearing point.

But 'Success,' he said, rinsing his mouth at the laboratory sink after the drinking of the antidote, 'all along the line, success.'

Then he tested the action of his discovery on the sense of hearing. And the sound of London came like the roar of a giant, yet when he fixed his attention on the movements of a fly all other sounds ceased, and he heard the sound of the fly's feet on the shelf when it walked. Thus, in turn, he heard the creak of boards expanding in the heat, the movement of the glass stoppers that kept imprisoned in the proper bottles the giants of acid and alkali.

'Success!' he cried aloud, and his voice sounded in his ears like the shout of a monster overcoming primeval forces. 'Success! Success!'

There remained only the eyes, and here, strangely enough, the Professor hesitated, faint with a sudden heart-sickness. Following a intensification there must be reaction. What if the reaction exceeded that from which it reacted, what if the wave of tremendous sight stemmed by the antidote ebbing, left him blind? But the spirit of the explorer in science is the spirit that explores African rivers, and sail amid white bergs to seek the undiscovered Pole.

He held the syringe with a firm hand, made the required puncture, and braced himself for the result. His eyes seemed to swell to great globes, to dwindle to microscopic globules, to swim in a flood of fire, to shrivel high and dry on a beach of hot sand. Then he saw and the glass fell from his hand. For the whole of the stable earth seemed to be suddenly set in movement, even the air grew thick with vast overlapping shapeless shapes. He opined later that these were the microbes and bacilli that cover and fill all things in this world that looks so clean and bright.

Concentrating his vision, he saw in the one day's little dust on the bottles myriads of creatures, crawling and writhing, alive. The proportions of the laboratory seemed but little altered. Its large lines and forms remained practically unchanged. It was the little things that were no longer little, the invisible things that were now invisible no longer. And he felt grateful for the first time in his life for the limits set by Nature to the powers of the human body. He had increased those powers. If he let his eye stray idly about, as one does in the waltz, for example, all was much as it used to be. But the moment he looked steadily at any one thing it became enormous.

He closed his eyes. Success here had gone beyond his wildest dreams. Indeed he could not but feel that success, taking the bit between its teeth, had perhaps gone just the least little bit too far.

And on the next day he decided to examine the drug in all its aspects, to court the intensification of all his senses, which should set him in the position of supreme power over men and things, transform him from a Professor into a demi-god.

The great question was, of course, how the five preparations of his drug would act on or against each other. Would it be intensification, or would they neutralize each other? Like all imaginative scientists, he was working with stuff perilously like the spells of magic, and certain things were not possible to be foretold. Besides, this drug came from a land of mystery and the knowledge of secrets which we call magic. He did not anticipate any increase in the danger of the experiment. Nevertheless he spent some hours in arranging and destroying papers, among others certain pages of the yellow notebook. After dinner he detained his man as, laden with the last tray, he was leaving the room.

'I may as well tell you, Parker,' the Professor said, moved by some impulse he had not expected, 'that you will benefit to some extent by my will. On conditions. If any accident should cut short my life, you will at once communicate with my solicitor, whose name you will now write down.'

The model man, trained by fifteen years of close personal service, drew forth a notebook neat as the Professor's own, wrote in it neatly the address the Professor gave.

'Anything more, sir?' he asked, looking up, pencil in hand.

'No,' said the Professor, 'nothing more. Goodnight, Parker.'

'Goodnight, sir,' said the model man.

The next words the model man opened his lips to speak were breathed into the night tube of the nearest doctor.

'My master, Professor Boyd Thompson; could you come round at once, sir. I'm afraid it's very serious.'

It was half past six when the nearest doctor – Jones was his unimportant name – stooped over the lifeless body of the Professor.

He shook his head as he stood up and looked round the private laboratory on whose floor the body lay.

'His researches are over,' he said. 'Yes, he's dead. Been dead some hours. When did you find him?'

'I went to call my master as usual,' said Parker; 'he rises at six, summer and winter, sir. He was not in his room, and the bed had not been slept in. So I came in here, sir. It is not unusual for my master to work all night when he has been very interested in his experiments, and then he likes his coffee at six.'

'I see,' said Doctor Jones. 'Well, you'd better rouse the house and fetch his own doctor. It's heart failure, of course, but I daresay he'd like to sign the certificate himself.'

'Can nothing be done?' said Parker, much affected.

'Nothing,' said Dr Jones. 'It's the common lot. You'll have to look out for another situation.'

'Yes, sir,' said Parker; 'he told me only last night what I was to do in case of anything happening to him. I wonder if he had any idea?'

'Some premonition, perhaps,' the doctor corrected.

The funeral was a very quiet one. So the late Professor Boyd Thompson had decreed in his will. He had arranged all details. The body was to be clothed in flannel, placed in an open coffin covered only with a linen sheet, and laid in the family mausoleum, a moss-grown building in the midst of a little park which surrounded Boyd Grange, the birthplace of the Boyd Thompsons. A little property in Sussex it was. The Professor sometimes went there for weekends. He had left this property to Lucilla, with a last love-letter, in which he begged her to give his body the hospitality of the death-house, now hers with the rest of the estate. To Parker he left an annuity of two hundred pounds, on the condition that he should visit and enter the mausoleum once in every twenty-four hours for fourteen days after the funeral.

To this end the late Professor's solicitor decided that Parker had better reside at Boyd Grange for the said fortnight, and Parker, whose nerves seemed to be shaken, petitioned for company. This made easy the arrangement which the solicitor desired to make – of a witness to the carrying out by Parker of the provisions of the dead man's will. The solicitor's clerk was quite good company, and arm in arm with him Parker paid his first visit to the mausoleum. The little building stands in a glade of evergreen oaks. The trees are old and thick, and the narrow door is deep in shadow even on the sunniest day. Parker went to the mausoleum, peered through its square grating, but he did not go in. Instead, he listened, and his ears were full of silence.

'He's dead, right enough,' he said, with a doubtful glance at his companion.

'You ought to go in, oughtn't you?' said the solicitor's clerk;

'Go in yourself if you like, Mr Pollack,' said Parker, suddenly angry; 'anyone who likes can go in, but it won't be me. If he was alive, it 'ud be different. I'd have done anything for him. But I ain't going in among all them dead and mouldering Thompsons. See? If we both say I did, it'll be just the same as me doing it.'

'So it will,' said the solicitor's clerk; 'but where do I come in?'

Parker explained to him where he came in, to their mutual consent.

'Right you are,' said the clerk; 'on those terms I'm fly. And if we both say you did it, we needn't come to the beastly place again,' he added, shivering and glancing over his shoulder at the door with the grating.

'No more we need,' said Parker.

Behind the bars of the narrow door lay deeper shadows than those of the ilexes outside. And in the blackest of the shadow lay a man whose every sense was intensified as though by a magic potion. For when the Professor swallowed the five variants of his great discovery, each acted as he had expected it to act. But the union of the five vehicles conveying the drug to the nerves, which served his five senses, had paralysed every muscle. His hearing, taste, touch, scent, and sight were intensified a thousandfold – as they had been in the individual experiments – but the man who felt all this exaggerated increase of sensation was powerless as a cat under kurali. He could not raise a finger, stir an eyelash. More, he could not breathe, nor did his body advise him of any need of breathing. And he had lain thus immobile and felt his body slowly grow cold, had heard in thunder the voices of Parker and the doctor, had felt the enormous hands of those who made his death-toilet, had smelt intolerably the camphor and lavender that they laid round him in the narrow, black bed; had tasted the mingled flavours of the drug and its five mediums; and, in an ecstasy of magnified sensation, had made the lonely train journey which coffins make, and known himself carried into the mausoleum and left there alone. And every sense was intensified, even his sense of time, so that it seemed to him that he had lain there for many years. And the effect of the drugs showed no sign of any diminution or reaction. Why had he not left directions for the injection of the antidote? It was one of those slips which wreck campaigns, cause the discovery of hidden crimes. It was a slip, and he had made it. He had thought of death, but in all the results he had anticipated death's semblance had found no place. Well, he had made his bed, and he must lie on it. This narrow bed, whose scent of clean oak and French polish was distinct among the musty, intolerable odours of the charnel house.

It was perhaps twenty hours that he had lain there, powerless, immobile, listening to the sounds of unexplained movements about him, when he felt with joy, almost like delirium, a faint quivering in the eyelids.

They had closed his eyes, and till now, they had remained closed. Now, with an effort as of one who lifts a grave-stone, he raised his eyelids. They closed again quickly, for the roof of the vault, at which he gazed earnestly, was alive with monsters; spiders, earwigs, crawling beetles, and flies, far too small to have been perceived by normal eyes, spread giant forms over him. He closed his eyes and shuddered. It felt like a shudder, but no one who had stood beside him could have noted any movement.

It was then that Parker came – and went.

Professor Boyd Thompson heard Parker's words, and lay listening to the thunder of Parker's retreating feet. He tried to move – to call out. But he could not. He lay there helpless, and somehow he thought of the dark end of the laboratory, where the assistant before leaving had turned out the electric lights.

He had nothing but his thoughts. He thought how he would lie there, and die there. The place was sequestered; no one passed that way. Parker had failed him, and the end was not hard to picture. He might recover all his faculties, might be able to get up, able to scream, to shout, to tear at the bars. The bars were strong, and Parker would not come again. Well, he would try to face with a decent bravery whatever had to be faced.

Time, measureless, spread round. It seemed as though someone had stopped all the clocks in the world, as though he were not in time but in eternity. Only by the waxing and waning light he knew of the night and the day.

His brain was weary with the effort to move, to speak, to cry out. He lay, informed with something like despair – or fortitude. And then Parker came again. And this time a key grated in the lock. The Professor noted with rapture that it sounded no louder than a key should sound, turned in a lock that was rusty. Nor was the voice other than he had been used to hear it, when he was man alive and Parker's master. And –

'You can go in, of course, if you wish it, miss,' said Parker disapprovingly; 'but it's not what I should advise myself. For me it's different,' he added, on a sudden instinct of self-preservation; 'I've got to go in. Every day for a fortnight,' he added, pitying himself.

'I will go in, thank you,' said a voice. 'Yes, give me the candle, please. And you need not wait. I will lock the door when I come out.' Thus the voice spoke. And the voice was Lucilla's.

In all his life the Professor had never feared death or its trappings. Neither its physical repulsiveness, nor the supernatural terrors which cling about it, had he either understood or tolerated. But now, in one little instant, he did understand.

He heard Lucilla come in. A light held near him shone warm and red through his closed eyelids. And he knew that he had only to unclose those eyelids to see her face bending over him. And he could unclose them. Yet he would not. He lay there, still and straight in his coffin, and life swept through him in waves of returning power. Yet he lay like death. For he said, or something in him said:

'She believes me dead. If I open my eyes it will be like a dead man looking at her. If I move it will be a dead man moving under her eyes. People have gone mad for less. Lie still, lie still,' he told himself; 'take any risks yourself. There must be none for her.'

She had taken the candle away, set it down somewhere at a distance, and now she was kneeling beside him and her hand was under his head. He knew he could raise his arm and clasp her – and Parker would come back perhaps, when she did not return to the house, come back to find a man in grave-clothes, clasping a mad woman. He lay still. Then her kisses and tears fell on his face, and she murmured broken words of love and longing. But he lay still. At any cost he must lie still. Even at the cost of his own sanity, his own life. And the warmth of her hand under his head, her face against his, her kisses, her tears, set his blood flowing evenly and strongly. Her other arm lay on his breast, softly pressing over his heart. He would not move. He would be strong. If he were to be saved, it must be by some other way, not this.

268

Suddenly tears and kisses ceased; her every breath seemed to have stopped with these. She had drawn away from him. She spoke. Her voice came from above him. She was standing up.

'Arthur!' she said. 'Arthur!' Then he opened his eyes, the narrowest chink. But he could not see her. Only he knew she was moving towards the door. There had been a new quality in her tone, a thrill of fear, or hope was it? or at least of uncertainty? Should he move; should he speak? He dared not. He knew too well the fear that the normal human being has of death and the grave, the fear transcending love, transcending reason. Her voice was further away now. She was by the door. She was leaving him. If he let her go, it was an end of hope for him. If he did not let her go, an end, perhaps, of reason, for her. No.

'Arthur,' she said, 'I don't believe ... I believe you can hear me. I'm going to get a doctor. If you *can* speak, speak to me.'

Her speaking ended, cut off short as a cord is cut by a knife. He did not speak. He lay in conscious, forced rigidity.

'Speak if you can,' she implored, 'just one word!'

Then he said, very faintly, very distinctly, in a voice that seemed to come from a great way off, 'Lucilla!'

And at the word she screamed aloud pitifully, and leaped for the entrance; and he heard the rustle of her crape in the narrow door. Then he opened his eyes wide, and raised himself on his elbow. Very weak he was, and trembling exceedingly. To his ears her scream held the note of madness. Vainly he had refrained. Selfishly he had yielded. The cold band of a mortal faintness clutched at his heart.

'I don't want to live now,' he told himself, and fell back in the straight bed.

Her arms were round him.

'I'm going to get help,' she said, her lips to his ear; 'brandy and things. Only I came back. I didn't want you to think I was frightened. Oh, my dear! Thank God, thank God!' He felt her kisses even through the swooning mist that swirled about him. Had she really fled in terror? He never knew. He knew that she had come back to him.

That is the real, true, and authentic narrative of the events which caused Professor Boyd Thompson to abandon a brilliant career, to promise anything that Lucilla might demand, and to devote himself entirely to a gentlemanly and unprofitable farming, and to his wife. From the point of view of the scientific world it is a sad ending to much promise, but at any rate there are two happy people hand in hand at the story's ending.

There is no doubt that for several years Professor Boyd Thompson had had enough of science, and, by a natural revulsion, flung himself into the full tide of commonplace sentiment. But genius, like youth, cannot be denied. And I, for one, am doubtful whether the Professor's renunciation of research will be a lasting one. Already I have heard whispers of a laboratory which is being built on the house, beyond the billiard-room.

But I am inclined to believe the rumours which assert that, for the future, his research will take the form of extending paths already well trodden; that he will refrain from experiments with unknown drugs, and those dreadful researches which tend to merge the chemist and biologist in the alchemist and the magician. And he certainly does not intend to experiment further on the nerves of any living thing, even his own. The Professor had already done enough work to make the reputation of half-a-dozen ordinary scientists. He may be pardoned if he rests on his laurels, entwining them, to some extent, with roses.

The bottle containing the drug from the South Seas was knocked down on the day of his death and swept up in bits by the laboratory boy. It is a curious fact that the Professor has wholly forgotten the formulae of his experiment, which so nearly was his last. This is a great satisfaction to his wife, and possibly to the Professor. But of this I cannot be sure; the scientific spirit survives much.

To the unscientific reader the strangest part of this story will perhaps be the fact that Parker is still with his old master, a wonderful example of the perfect butler. Professor Boyd Thompson was able to forgive Parker because he understood him. And he learned to understand Parker in those moments of agony, when his keen intellect and his awakened heart taught him, through his love for Lucilla, the depth of that gulf of fear which lies between the quick and the dead.

I may be betraying my scruples by including this story in a book called the "Best" horror stories of Edith Nesbit. The tale certainly has its weaknesses. Namely, it suffers from the same sappy, maudlin sentimentality that plagues "From the Dead," "The Haunted Inheritance," "The Power of Darkness," and the unprintable "The Letter in Brown Ink" (wherein a girl imprisoned by a madwoman writes an SOS letter in her own blood and is rescued by young man whom she later marries). Nonetheless, "The Five Senses" has its merits. Animal cruelty, saccharine romance, and womanly devotion aside, it is an intriguing continuation of the themes of *Frankenstein* and *Dr Jekyll and Mr Hyde.* The scientist whose intemperate experiments bleed into his personal life, the eccentric aim of his research, and the fantastical results of his mixed success remind me Fitz-James O'Brien's proto-sci-fi masterwork, "The Diamond Lens" (wherein an amateur microscopist kills his roommate to obtain a rare diamond needed to create the world's most powerful lens, with which he uncovers an atomic paradise and falls in love with a microscopic maiden living in a drop of water). In fact, Nesbit is an underrated writer of science fiction. This story, "The Third Drug," "The Pavilion," "The Haunted House," and other tales of hers straddle the border between fantasy, horror, and sci-fi, and might be aptly termed weird or speculative fiction. Despite its domestic subplot, the story provides an interesting look at a unique line of maniacal research and is a telling commentary on Nesbit's opinions of the patriarchal scientific establishment and men in general.

INITIALLY, science fiction was not a regular genre in Nesbit's resume, but she began to indulge in it increasingly as she aged. There are about half a dozen short stories in her oeuvre that could be termed sci-fi, and while "The Pavilion" treads the ground between that genre and conventional horror story, E. F. Bleiler – the dean of horror anthologists – considered it one of two science fiction stories worth recording in his gargantuan compendium, *Science Fiction: the Early Years.* Although I would consider "The Third Drug" among Nesbit's best sci-fi stories, "The Pavilion" is remarkable for its Wellsian weirdness. In fact, devotees of the genre will instantly recognize Wells' hand in this story about a vampiric plant (his "The Flowering of the Strange Orchid" – alongside Conan Doyle's "The American's Tale," Blackwood's "The Willows," and Frank Aubrey's *The Devil Tree of El Dorado* make up the most influential of the carnivorous herb genre's early entries). There is also a very discernable relationship here with M. R. James' chilling masterpiece, "The Ash Tree." As with "The Power of Darkness," Nesbit returns to a favored plot: two gallant suitors dueling over the possession of a woman's heart, but with insidious intentions. In "The Power of Darkness," the trap-setter fell prey to his own designs, and while I will not spoil the plot for this one, I imagine that – while writing both of them – Nesbit may have had this moral wisdom echoing in the back of her head: *"If you set a trap for others, you will get caught in it yourself. If you roll a boulder down on others, it will crush you instead."*

The Pavilion
{1915}

THERE was never a moment's doubt in her own mind. So she said afterwards. And everyone agreed that she had concealed her feelings with true womanly discretion. Her friend and confidante, Amelia Davenant, was at any rate completely deceived. Amelia was one of those feature less blondes who seem born to be overlooked. She adored her beautiful friend, and never, from first to last, could see any fault in her, except, perhaps, on the evening when the real things of the story happened. And even in this matter she owned at the time that it was only that her darling Ernestine did not understand.

Ernestine was a prettyish girl with the airs, so irresistible and misleading, of a beauty; most people said that she was beautiful, and

273

she certainly managed, with extraordinary success, to produce the illusion of beauty. Quite a number of plainish girls achieve that effect nowadays. The freedom of modern dress and coiffure and the increasing confidence in herself which the modern girl experiences aid her in fostering the illusion; but in the 'sixties, when everyone wore much the same sort of bonnet, when your choice in coiffure was limited to bandeaux or ringlets, and the crinoline was your only wear, something very like genius was needed to deceive the world in the matter of your personal charms. Ernestine had that genius; hers was the smiling, ringletted, dark-haired, dark-eyed, sparkling type.

Amelia had the blond bandeau and the appealing blue eyes, rather too small and rather too dull; her hands and ears were beautiful, and she kept them out of sight as much as possible. It was she who, at the age of fourteen, composed the remarkable poem beginning:

I know that I am ugly: did I make

The face that is the laugh and jest of all?

And went on, after disclaiming any personal responsibility for the face, to entreat the kind earth to "cover it away from mocking eyes," and to "let the daisies blossom where it lies."

Amelia did not want to die, and her face was not the laugh and jest, or indeed the special interest, of anyone. All that was poetic lisence. Amelia had read perhaps a little too much poetry of the type of *"Quand je suis morte, mes amies, plantez un saule au cimetiere"*; but really life was a very good thing to Amelia, especially when she had a new dress and someone paid her a compliment. But she went on writing verses extolling the advantages of the Tomb, and grovelling metrically at the feet of One who was Another's. Until that summer when she was nineteen and went to stay with Ernestine at Doricourt. Then her muse took flight, scared, perhaps, by the possibility, suddenly and' threateningly presented, of being asked to inspire verse about the real things of life.

At any rate, Amelia ceased to write poetry about the time when she and Ernestine and Ernestine's aunt went on a visit to Doricourt, where Frederick Doricourt lived with his aunt. It was not one of those hurried motor fed excursions which we have now and call week ends, but a long, leisurely visit, when all the friends of the static aunt called on the dynamic aunt, who returned the calls with much ceremony, a big barouche, and a pair of fat horses. There were croquet parties and archery parties and little dances, all pleasant informal gaieties arranged without ceremony among people who lived within driving distance of each other and knew each other's tastes and incomes and family history as well as they knew their own. The habit of importing huge droves of strangers from distant counties for brief harrying raids did not then obtain. There was instead a wide and constant circle of pleasant people with an unflagging stream of gaiety, mild indeed, but delightful to unjaded palates.

And at Doricourt life was delightful even on the days when there was no party. It was perhaps more delightful to Ernestine than to her friend, but even so, the one least pleased was Ernestine's aunt.

" I do think," she said to the other aunt whose name was Julia— " I dare say it is not so to you, being accustomed to Mr. Frederick, of course from his childhood, but I always find gentlemen in the house so unsettling. Especially young gentlemen. And when there are young ladies also. One is always on the qui vive for excitement."

"Of course," said Aunt Julia, with the air of a woman of the world; "living as you and dear Ernestine do, with only females in the house"

"We hang up an old coat and hat of my brother's on the hat stand in the hall," Aunt Emmeline protested.

"... The presence of gentlemen in the house must be a little unsettling. For myself, I am inured to it. Frederick has so many friends. Mr. Thesiger perhaps the greatest. I believe him to be a most worthy young man, but peculiar." She leaned forward across her bright-tinted Berlin woolwork and spoke impressively, the needle with its trailing red poised in air. "You know, I hope you will not think it indelicate of me to mention such a thing —-but dear Frederick —your dear Ernestine would have been in every way so suitable."

"Would have been?" Aunt Emmeline's tortoiseshell shuttle ceased its swift movement among the white loops and knots of her tatting.

"Well, my dear," said the other aunt, a little shortly, "you surely must have noticed... "

"You don't mean to suggest that Amelia I thought Mr. Thesiger and Amelia..."

"Amelia! I really must say! No, I was alluding to Mr. Thesiger's attentions to dear Ernestine. Most marked. In dear Frederick's place I should have found some excuse for shortening Mr. Thesiger's visit. But of course I cannot interfere. Gentlemen must manage these things for themselves. I only hope that there will be none of that trifling with the most holy affections of others which... "

The less voluble aunt cut in hotly with, "Ernestine's incapable of anything so un ladylike."

"Just what I was saying," the other rejoined blandly, got up, and drew the blind a little lower, for the afternoon sun was glowing on the rosy wreaths of the drawing room carpet.

Outside in the sunshine Frederick was doing his best to arrange his own affairs. He had managed to place himself beside Miss Ernestine Meutys on the stone steps of the pavilion, but then Eugene Thesiger lay along the lower step at her feet, a good position for looking up into her eyes. Amelia was beside him, but then it never seemed to matter whom Amelia was beside.

They were talking about the pavilion on whose steps they sat, and Amelia, who often asked uninteresting questions, had wondered how old it was. It was Frederick's pavilion after all, and he felt this when his friend took the words out of his mouth and used them on his own account, even though he did give the" answer the form of an appeal.

"The foundations are Tudor, aren't they?" he said. "Wasn't it an observatory or laboratory or something of that sort in Fat Henry's time?"

"Yes," said Frederick; "there was some story about a wizard or an alchemist or something, and it was burned down, and then they rebuilt it in its present style."

"The Italian style, isn't it?" said Thesiger; "but you can hardly see what it is now, for the creeper."

"Virginia creeper, isn't it?" Amelia asked, and Frederick said, "Yes, Virginia creeper." Thesiger said it looked more like a South American plant, and Ernestine said Virginia was in South America, and that was why. "I know, because of the war," she said modestly, and nobody smiled or answered. There were manners in those days.

"There's a ghost story about it, surely?" Thesiger began again, looking up at the dark closed doors of the pavilion.

"Not that I ever heard of," said the pavilion's owner. "I think the country people invented the tale because there have always been so many rabbits and weasels and things found dead near it. And once a dog, my uncle's favourite spaniel. But, of course, that's simply because they get entangled in the Virginia creeper — you see how fine and big it is —and can't get out, and die as they do in traps. But the villagers prefer to think it's ghosts."

"I thought there was a real ghost story," Thesiger persisted.

Ernestine said, "A ghost story. How delicious! Do tell it, Mr. Doricourt. This is just the place for a ghost story. Out of doors and the sun shining, so that we can't really be frightened."

Doricourt protested again that he knew no story.

276

"That's because you never read, dear boy," said Eugene Thesiger. "That library of yours — there's a delightful book —did you never notice it?— brown tree-calf with your arms on it; the head of the house writes the history of the house as far as he knows it. There's a lot in that book. It began in Tudor times—1515, to be exact."

'Queen Elizabeth's time." Ernestine thought that made it so much more interesting. "And was the ghost story in that?"

"It isn't exactly a ghost story," said Thesiger. "It's only that the pavilion seems to be an unlucky place to sleep in."

"Haunted?" Frederick asked, and added that he must look up that book.

"Not haunted exactly. Only several people who have slept the night there went on sleeping."

"Dead, he means," said Ernestine, and it was left for Amelia to ask: "Does the book tell anything particular about how the people died, what killed them, or anything?" "There are suggestions," said Thesiger;" but there, it is a gloomy subject. I don't know why I started it. Should we have time for a game of croquet before tea, Doricourt? "

"I wish *you'd* read the book and tell me the stories," Ernestine said to Frederick, apart, over the croquet balls.

"I will," he answered, fervently; " you've only to tell me what you want."

"Or perhaps Mr. Thesiger will tell us another time—in the twilight. Since people like twilight for ghosts. Will you, Mr. Thesiger? "She spoke over her blue muslin shoulder.

Frederick certainly meant to look up the book, but he delayed till after supper, when he went alone to the library, found the brown book, and took it to the circle of light made by the colza lamp.

"I can skim through it in half an hour," he said, and wound up the lamp and lighted his second cigar. Then he opened the shutters and windows, so that the room should not smell of smoke in the morning. Those were the days of consideration for the ladies who had not yet learned that a cigarette is not exclusively a male accessory like a beard or a bass voice.

But when, his preparations completed, he opened the book, he was compelled to say "Pshaw!" Nothing short of this could relieve his feelings. (You know the expression I mean, though of course it isn't pronounced as it's spelt, any more than Featherstonehaugh or St Maur are.)

"Pshaw!" said Frederick, fluttering the pages. His remark was justified. The earlier part of the book was written in the beautiful script of the early sixteenth century, that looks so plain and is so impossible to read, and the later pages, though the hand writing was clear and Italian enough, left Frederick helpless, for the language was Latin, and Frederick's Latin was limited to the particular passages he had " been through " at his private school. He recognized a -word here and there — *mors*, for instance, and *pallidas* and *sanguinis* and *pavor* and *arcanum*, just as you or I might; but to read the complicated stuff and make sense of it! Frederick replaced the book on the shelf, closed the shutters, and turned out the lamp. He thought he would ask Thesiger to translate the thing, but then again he thought he wouldn't. So he went to bed wishing that he had happened to remember more of the Latin so painfully beaten into the best years of his boyhood.

And the story of the pavilion was, after all, told by Thesiger. There was a little dance at Doricourt next evening, a carpet dance they called it. The furniture was pushed back against the walls, and the tightly-stretched Axminster carpet was not so bad to dance on as you might suppose. And even in those far-off days there were conservatories.

It was on the steps of the conservatory, not the steps leading from the dancing-room, but the steps leading to the garden, that the story was told. The four young people were sitting together, the girls' crinolined flounces spreading round them like huge pale roses, the young men correct in their high shouldered coats and white cravats. Ernes tine had been very kind to both the men, a little too kind perhaps — who can tell? At any rate, there was in their eyes exactly that light which you may imagine in the eyes of rival stags in the mating season. It was Ernestine who asked Frederick for the story, and Thesiger who, at Amelia's suggestion, told it.

"It's quite a number of stories," he said, "and yet it's really all the same story. The first man to sleep in the pavilion slept there ten years after it was built. He was a friend of the alchemist or astrologer who built it. He was found dead in the morning. There seemed to-have been a struggle. His arms bore the marks of cords. No; they never found any cords. He died from loss of blood. There were curious wounds. That was all the rude leeches of the day could report to the bereaved survivors of the deceased."

"How funny you are, Mr. Thesiger!" said Ernestine, with that celebrated soft, low laugh of hers.

"And the next?" asked Amelia. "

"The next was sixty years later. It was a visitor that time, too. And he was found dead, just the same marks, and the doctors said the same thing. And so it went on. There have been eight deaths altogether —

278

unexplained deaths. Nobody has slept in it now for over a hundred years. People seem to have a prejudice against the place as a sleeping apartment. I can't think why."

"Isn't he simply killing?" Ernestine asked Amelia, who said: "And doesn't anyone know how it happened?" No one answered till Ernestine repeated the question in the form of "I suppose it was just accident?"

"It was a curiously recurrent accident," said Thesiger, and Frederick, who throughout the conversation had said the right things at the right moment, remarked that it did not do to believe all these old legends. Most old families had them, he believed. Frederick had inherited Doricourt from an unknown great uncle of whom in life he had not so much as heard, but he was very strong on the family tradition. "I don't attach any importance to these tales myself."

"Of course not. All the same," said Thesiger, deliberately, "you wouldn't care to "pass a night in that pavilion."

"No more would you," was all Frederick found on his lips.

"I admit that I shouldn't enjoy it," said Eugene;" but I'll bet you a hundred you don't do it."

"Done," said Frederick.

"Oh, Mr. Doricourt!" breathed Ernestine, a little shocked at betting "before ladies."

"Don't!" said Amelia, to whom, of course, no one paid any attention; "don't do it!"

You know how, in the midst of flower and leafage, a snake sometimes will suddenly, surprisingly rear a head that threatens? So, amid friendly talk and laughter, a sudden fierce antagonism sometimes looks out and vanishes again, surprising most of all the antagonists. This antagonism spoke in the tones of both men, and after Amelia had said "Don't!" there was a curiously breathless little silence. Ernestine broke it. "Oh," she said, " I do wonder which of you will win! I should like them both to win, wouldn't you, Amelia? Only I suppose that's not always possible, is it? "

Both gentlemen assured her that in the case of bets it was very rarely possible.

"Then I wish you wouldn't," said Ernes tine. "You could both pass the night there, couldn't you, and be company for each other? I don't think betting for such large sums is quite the thing, do you, Amelia?"

Amelia said no, she didn't, but Eugene had already begun to say:
— " Let the bet be off, then, if Miss Meutys doesn't like it. That suggestion is invaluable. But the thing itself needn't be off. Look here,

279

Doricourt. I'll stay in the pavilion from one to three and you from three to five. Then honour will be satisfied. How will that do?"

The snake had disappeared.

"Agreed," said Frederick," and we can compare impressions afterwards. That will be quite interesting."

Then someone came and asked where they had all got to, and they went in and danced some more dances. Ernestine danced twice with Frederick and drank iced sherry and water, and they said good night and lighted their bedroom candles at the table in "the hall.

"I do hope they won't," Amelia said, as the girls sat brushing their hair at the two large white muslin - frilled dressing-tables in "the room they shared.

"Won't what?" said Ernestine, vigorous with the brush.

"Sleep in that hateful pavilion. I wish you'd ask them not to, Ernestine. They'd mind, if you asked them."

"Of course I will if you like, dear," said Ernestine, cordially. She was always the soul of good-nature. "But I don't think you ought to believe in ghost stories, not really."

"Why not?"

"Oh, because of the Bible and going to church and all that," said Ernestine. "Do you really think Rowland's Macassar has made any difference to my hair?"

"What was that?" said Amelia,

"That" was a sound coming from the little dressing-room. There was no light in that room. Amelia went into the little room, though Ernestine said, "Oh, don't! How can you? It might be a ghost or a rat or something," and as she went she whispered, Hush! "

The window of the little room was open and she leaned out of it. The stone sill was cold to her elbows through her print dressing jacket.

Ernestine went on brushing her hair. Amelia heard a movement below the window and listened. "To-night will do," someone said.

"It's too late," said someone else.

"If you're afraid it will always be too late or too early," said someone. And it was Thesiger.

"You know I'm not afraid," the other one, who was Doricourt, answered hotly.

"An hour for each of us will satisfy honour," said Thesiger, carelessly. "The girls will expect it. I couldn't sleep. Let's do it now and get it over. Let's see. Oh, hang it! "

A faint click had sounded.

"Dropped my watch. I forgot the chain was loose. It's all right, though; glass not broken even. Well, are you game? "

"Oh, yes, if you insist. Shall I go first, or you? "

"I will," said Thesiger. "That's only fair, because I suggested it. I'll stay till half-past one or a quarter to two, and then you come on. See? "

"Oh, all right. I think it's silly, though," said Frederick.

Then the voices ceased. Amelia went back to "the other girl.

"They're going to do it to-night."

"Are they, dear?" Ernestine was as placid as ever. "Do what?"

"Sleep in that horrible pavilion."

"How do you know?"

Amelia explained how she knew.

"Whatever can we do?" she added.

"Well, dear, suppose we go to bed?" suggested Ernestine, helpfully. "We shall hear all about it in the morning."

"But suppose anything happens?"

"What could happen?"

"Oh, anything!" said Amelia. "Oh, I do wish they wouldn't! I shall go down and ask them not to."

"Amelia!" The other girl was at last aroused. "You couldn't! I shouldn't let you dream of doing anything so unladylike. What would the gentlemen think of you? "

The question silenced Amelia, but she began to "put on her so lately discarded bodice.

"I won't go if you think I oughtn't," she said.

"Forward and fast, auntie would call it," said the other. "I am almost sure she would."

"But I'll keep dressed. I shan't disturb you. I'll sit in the dressing-room. I can't go to sleep while he's running into this awful danger."

"Which he?" Ernestine's voice was very sharp. "And there isn't any danger."

"Yes, there is," said Amelia, sullenly," and I mean them. Both of them."

Ernestine said her prayers and got into bed. She had put her hair in curl-papers, which became her like a wreath of white roses.

"I don't think auntie will be pleased," she said," when she hears that you sat up all night watching young gentlemen. Good night, dear! "

"Good night, darling," said Amelia. "I know you don't understand. It's all right."

She sat in the dark by the dressing-room window. There was no sound to break the stillness, except the little cracklings of twigs and rustlings of leaves as birds or little night wandering beasts moved in the shadows of the garden, and the sudden creakings that furniture makes if you sit alone with it and listen in the night's silence.

Amelia sat on and listened, listened. The pavilion showed in broken streaks of pale grey against the wood that seemed to be clinging to it in dark patches. But that, she reminded herself, was only the creeper. She sat there for a very long time, not knowing how long a time it was. For anxiety is a poor chronometer, and the first ten minutes had seemed an hour. She had no watch. Ernes tine had, and slept with it under her pillow. There was nothing to measure time's flight by, and she sat there rigid, straining her ears for a foot-fall on the grass, straining her eyes to see a figure come out of the dark pavilion and cross the dew-grey grass towards the house. And she heard nothing, saw nothing.

Slowly, imperceptibly, the grey of the dewy grass lightened, lightened; the grey of the sleeping trees took on faint dreams of colour. The sky turned faint above the trees, the moon perhaps was coming out. The pavilion grew more clearly visible. It seemed to Amelia that something moved among the leaves that surrounded it, and she looked to see him come out. But he did not come.

"I wish the moon would really shine," she told herself. And suddenly she knew that the sky was clear and that this growing light was not the moon's dead cold silver, but the growing light of dawn. She went quickly into the other room, put her hand under the pillow of Ernestine, and "drew out the little watch with the diamond "E" on it.

"A quarter to three," she said, aloud. Ernestine moved and grunted. There was no hesitation about Amelia now. Without another thought for the ladylike and the really suitable, she lighted her candle and went quickly down the stairs, still dark, paused a moment in the hall, and so out through the front door into the grey of the new day. She passed along the terrace. The feet of Frederick protruded from the open French window of the smoking-room. She set down her candle on the terrace it burned clearly enough in that clear air— went up to Frederick as he slept, his head between his shoulders and his hands loosely hanging, and shook him.

"Wake up!" she said. "Wake up! Something's happened! It's a quarter to three and he's not come back."

"Who's not what?" Frederick asked, sleepily. "

"Mr. Thesiger. The pavilion."

"Thesiger? — The — *You*, Miss Davenant? I beg your pardon. I must have dropped off."

He got up unsteadily, gazing dully at this white apparition still in evening dress with pale lair now no longer wreathed.

"What is it?" he said; "is anybody ill?" Briefly and very urgently Amelia told him what it was, imploring him to go at once and see what had happened. If he had been fully awake, her voice and her eyes would have told him many things.

"He said he'd come back," he said. Hadn't I better wait? You go back to bed, Miss Davenant. If he doesn't come in half an hour"

"If you don't go this minute," said Amelia, tensely, "I shall.

"Oh, well, if you insist," Frederick said. "He has simply fallen asleep as I did. Dear Miss Davenant, return to your room, I beg. In the morning, when we are all laughing at this false alarm, you will be glad to remember that Mr. Thesiger does not know of your anxiety."

"I hate you," said Amelia, gently;" and I am going to see what has happened. Come or not, as you like."

She caught up the silver candlestick, and he followed its steady gleam down the terrace steps and across the grey dewy grass.

Half-way she paused, lifted the hand that had been hidden among her muslin flounces, and held it out to him with a big Indian dagger in it.

"I got it out of the hall," she said. "If there's any real danger— anything living, I mean. I thought —but I know I couldn't use it. Will you take it? "

He took it, laughing kindly.

"How romantic you are!" he said, admiringly, and looked at her standing there in the mingled gold and grey of dawn and candle-light. It was as though he had never seen her before.

They reached the steps of the pavilion and stumbled up them. The door was closed, but not locked. And Amelia noticed that the trails of creeper had not been disturbed; they grew across the doorway as thick as a man's finger, some of them.

"He must have got in by one of the windows," Frederick said. "Your dagger comes in handy, Miss Davenant." He slashed at the wet, sticky green stuff and put his shoulder to the door. It yielded at a touch and they went in.

The one candle lighted the pavilion hardly at all, and the dusky light that oozed in through the door and windows helped very little. And the silence was thick and heavy.

"Thesiger!" said Frederick, clearing his throat. "Thesiger! Halloa ! Where are you? "

Thesiger did not say where he was. And then they saw.

There were low stone seats to the windows, and between the windows low stone benches ran. On one of these something dark, something dark and in places white, confused the outline of the carved stone.

"Thesiger!" said Frederick again, in the tone a man uses to a room that he is almost sure is empty. "Thesiger!"

But Amelia was bending over the bench. She was holding the candle crookedly, so that it flared and guttered.

"Is he there?" Frederick asked, following her; "is that him? Is he asleep? "

"Take the candle," said Amelia, and he took it obediently. Amelia was touching what lay on the bench. Suddenly she screamed. Just one scream, not very loud. But Frederick remembers just how it sounded. Sometimes he hears it in dreams and wakes moaning, though he is an old man now, and his old wife says, " What is it, dear ? " and he says, " Nothing, my Ernestine, nothing."

Directly she had screamed she said, "He's dead," and fell on her knees by the bench. Frederick saw that she held something in her" arms.

"Perhaps he isn't," she said. "Fetch someone from the house— brandy —send for a doctor. Oh, go, go, go! "

"I can't leave you here," said Frederick. "Suppose he revives?"

"He will not revive," said Amelia, dully; "go, go, go! Do as I tell you. Go! If you don't go," she added, suddenly and amazingly, "I believe I shall kill you. It's all your doing."

The astounding sharp injustice of this stung Frederick into action.

"I believe he's only fainted or something," he said. "When I've roused the house and everyone has witnessed your emotion you will regret... "

She sprang to her feet and caught the knife from him and raised it, awkwardly, clumsily, but with keen threatening, not to be mistaken or disregarded. Frederick went.

When Frederick came back with the groom and the gardener—he hadn't thought it well to disturb the ladies—the pavilion was filled lull of white revealing daylight. On the bench lay a dead man, and kneeling by him a living woman on whose warm breast his cold and heavy head lay pillowed. The dead man's hands were full of green crushed leaves, and thick twining tendrils were about his wrists and throat. A wave of

285

green seemed to have swept from the open window to the bench where he lay.

The groom and the gardener and the dead man's friend looked and looked.

"Looks like as if he'd got himself entangled in the creeper and lost 'is 'ead," said the groom, scratching his own.

"How'd the creeper get in, though? That's what I says." It was the gardener who said it.

"Through the window," said Doricourt, moistening his lips with his tongue.

"The window was shut, though, when I come by at five last night," said the gardener, stubbornly. "'Ow did it get all that way since five?"

They looked at each other voicing, silently, impossible things.

The woman never spoke. She sat there in the white ring of her crinolined dress like a broken white rose. But her arms were round Thesiger, and she would not move them.

When the doctor came he sent for Ernestine, who came flushed and sleepy-eyed and very frightened and shocked.

"You're upset, dear," she said to her friend," and no wonder. How brave of you to come out with Mr. Doricourt to see what had happened! But you can't do anything now, dear. Come in and I'll tell them to get you some tea."

Amelia laughed, looked down at the face on her shoulder, laid the head back on the bench among the drooping green of the creeper, stooped over it, kissed it, and said to it quite quietly and gently, " Good-bye, dear; good bye ! " took Ernestine's arm, and went away with her.

The doctor made an examination and gave a death-certificate. "Heart-failure " was his original and brilliant diagnosis. The certificate said nothing, and Frederick said nothing of the creeper that was wound about the dead man's neck, nor of the little white wounds, like little bloodless lips half-open, that they found about the dead man's neck.

"An imaginative or uneducated person," said the doctor, "might suppose that the creeper had something to do with his death. But we mustn't encourage superstition. I will assist my man to prepare the body for its last sleep. Then we need not have any chattering women."

"Can you read Latin?" Frederick asked. The doctor could. And, later, did.

It was the Latin of that brown book with the Doricourt arms on it that Frederick wanted read. And when he and the doctor had been together with the book between them for three hours, they closed it and looked at each other with shy and doubtful eyes.

"It can't be true," said Frederick.

"If it is," said the more cautious doctor, you don't want it talked about. I should destroy that book if I were you. And I should cut down the creeper and burn it and dig up the roots. It is quite evident, from what you tell me, that your friend believed that this creeper was a man-eater ; that it fed, just before its flowering time, as the book tells us, at dawn ; and that he fully meant that the thing, when it crawled into the pavilion seeking its prey, should find you and not him. It would have been so, I understand, if his watch had not stopped at one o'clock."

"He dropped it, you know," said Doricourt, like a man in a dream.

"All the cases in this book are the same," said the doctor ; "the strangling, the white wounds. I have heard of such plants; I never believed." He shuddered. "Had your friend any spite against you? Any reason for wanting to get you out of the way?"

Frederick thought of Ernestine, of Thesiger's eyes on Ernestine, of her smile at him over her blue muslin shoulder.

"No," he said, "none. None whatever. It must have been accident. I am sure he did not know. He could not read Latin." He lied, being, after all, a gentleman; and Ernestine's name being sacred.

"The creeper seems to have been brought here and planted in Henry the Eighth's time. And then the thing began. It seems to have been at its flowering season that it needed the — that, in short, it was dangerous. The little animals and birds found dead near the pavilion. But to move itself all that way, across the floor! The thing must have been almost conscient," he said, with a sincere shudder. " One would think," he corrected himself at once, " that it knew what it was doing, if such a thing were not plainly contrary to the laws of Nature."

"Yes," said Frederick, "one would. I think if I can't do anything more I'll go and rest. Somehow all this has given me a turn. Poor Thesiger! "

His last thought before he went to sleep was one of pity.

"Poor Thesiger," he said; "how violent and wicked! And what an escape for me! I must never tell Ernestine. And all the time there was Amelia. Ernestine would never have done that for me!" And on a little pang of regret for the impossible he fell asleep.

Amelia went on living. She was not the sort that dies even of such a thing as happened to her on that night, when for the first and last lime she held her love in her arms and knew him for the murderer he was. It was only the other day that she died, a very old woman.

Ernestine, who, beloved and surrounded by children and grandchildren, survived her, spoke her epitaph. "Poor Amelia," she said; "nobody ever looked the same side of the road where she was. There was an indiscretion when she was young. Oh, nothing disgraceful, of course. She was a lady. But people talked. It was the sort of thing that stamps a girl, you know."

BLEILER begins his entry on "The Pavilion" by noting: "Sensational subject matter, but told in the restrained, indirect manner of a British house-party crime story." He is right to start with a warning: the tale suffers from Nesbit's long-standing weakness – sentimental romance. The fawning, simpering subplot is very difficult to chew, although it does nicely inject sexual tension into the story which would otherwise have been a bland episode of *Scooby Doo* (albeit with a rather darker ending). Like her similarly-themed "The Haunted House," "The Pavilion" draws strength from the expectations of Gothic conventions: we anticipate a fatal specter, but we don't *quite* anticipate a vampiric vine (although my notes in the beginning certainly may have given the secret away – my apologies), and we tensely await the happy conclusion that this little romance seems to promise. But we are disappointed. It truly appears to telegraph a Gothic farce – like "The Haunted Inheritance," where the ghosts were fake and the star-crossed lovers are united – and upon my first read I wondered if it was all a coy sham to force dear little Amelia to betray her love in a fervent display of protective adoration: she rushes to the pavilion, throws herself in, and is surprised to see Thesiger reading a book quietly, but now her flustered worry has revealed the nature of her dear little affections, and the two realize that they are meant to be together. But Amelia doesn't find Thesiger reading. He has been drained to death by his own diabolical trap, and all the characters involved lose their innocence in the fallout of his homicidal treachery.

II.

There is one more element here that is tremendously interesting: Nesbit's autobiographical investment in the hapless, loveless character, Amelia. Upstaged by the sexy, blonde Ernestine, overwhelmed by romantic notions, drawn to toxic men, but ignored by men of all degrees of character (since *all* men apparently favor the vapid and

288

coquettish Ernestines over the sentimental and sincere Amelias), in the end, Amelia dies old, alone, and unloved – just as she so often imagined it. "The Pavilion" was written a year after Nesbit's fanatically adulterous husband had died, leaving her alone. For decades she had suffered quietly through his affairs, cohabitated with his lovers, and raised his children by them. Despite his blaring commitment to socialism, Hubert Bland was a revolting opponent of women's rights and an unrepentant misogynist, famously saying: "Woman's *métier* in the world - I mean, of course, civilized woman, the woman in the world as it is - is to inspire romantic passion... Romantic passion is inspired by women who wear corsets. In other words, by the women who pretend to be what they not quite are." We can hardly wonder that such a man – one who bedded his mistresses across the room from his wife – would leave his neglected and emotionally abused widow feeling like something of an Amelia. In 1914 she was widowed, with nothing left to thank her for her loyalty but a cold bed and a lifetime of bitter regrets. Two years after "The Pavilion" was published – with its surprisingly grim ending and the melancholy demise of her literary double – Nesbit remarried to a man whom she loved, who loved her in return, and so it was that at least her story ended happily.

WE conclude our look at Nesbit with a piece of cake draped in frosting, as it were. A purely decadent bit of Hallowe'en-ish fun. Equal parts vampire tale, ghost story, science fiction, mad scientist story, Gothic farce, Sherlock Holmes mystery, and haunted house story, this tale is probably most often anthologized as a vampire tale, but it fits no simple keyhole: like the protagonist whose DNA is home to African, Chinese, Native American, Celtic, and English genetic material, this story is literary hybrid. As you might already suspect, given the details of the previous sentence, this tale – even from the pen of socialist, Left-wing Nesbit – will warrant some trigger warnings to the 21st century reader, and it is hardly what one could term a *literary* horror story, but it is rather the sort of story that young readers relish in late October: here is the decrepit, Gothic manor house, here the suspicious, leering amateur scientist; here are legends of mysterious deaths, and even the degenerate assistant (the "Igor," if you will). Nesbit has her share of masterpieces, but we close with some Hallowe'en cake – with extra pumpkin-flavored frosting.

The Haunted House
{1913}

IT was by the merest accident that Desmond ever went to the Haunted House. He had been away from England for six years, and the nine months' leave taught him how easily one drops out of one's place.

He had taken rooms at the Greyhound before he found that there was no reason why he should stay in Elmstead rather than in any other of London's dismal outposts. He wrote to all the friends whose addresses he could remember, and settled himself to await their answers.

He wanted someone to talk to, and there was no one. Meantime he lounged on the horsehair sofa with the advertisements, and his pleasant grey eyes followed line after line with intolerable boredom. Then, suddenly, "Halloa!" he said, and sat up. This is what he read:

A HAUNTED HOUSE. *Advertiser is anxious to have phenomena investigated. Any properly accredited investigator will be given full facilities. Address, by letter only, Wildon Prior, 237 Museum Street, London.*

"That's rum!" he said. Wildon Prior had been the best wicket-keeper in his club. It wasn't a common name. Anyway, it was worth trying, so he sent off a telegram.

WILDON PRIOR, 237 MUSEUM STREET, LONDON. MAY I COME TO YOU FOR A DAY OR TWO AND SEE THE GHOST   - WILLIAM DESMOND

On returning the next day from a stroll there was an orange envelope on the wide Pembroke table in his parlour.

DELIGHTED - EXPECT YOU TODAY, BOOK TO CRITTENDEN FROM CHARING CROSS. WIRE TRAIN   - WILDON PRIOR, ORMEHURST RECTORY, KENT.

"So that's all right," said Desmond, and went off to pack his bag and ask in the bar for a timetable. "Good old Wildon; it will be ripping, seeing him again."

A curious little omnibus, rather like a bathing-machine, was waiting outside Crittenden Station, and its driver, a swarthy, blunt-faced little man, with liquid eyes, said, "You a friend of Mr Prior, sir?" shut him up in the bathing-machine, and banged the door on him. It was a very long drive, and less pleasant than it would have been in an open carriage.

The last part of the journey was through a wood; then came a churchyard and a church, and the bathing-machine turned in at a gate under heavy trees and drew up in front of a white house with bare, gaunt windows.

"Cheerful place, upon my soul!" Desmond told himself, as he tumbled out of the back of the bathing-machine.

The driver set his bag on the discoloured doorstep and drove off. Desmond pulled a rusty chain, and a big-throated bell jangled above his head.

Nobody came to the door, and he rang again. Still nobody came, but he heard a window thrown open above the porch. He stepped back on to the gravel and looked up.

A young man with rough hair and pale eyes was looking out. Not Wildon, nothing like Wildon. He did not speak, but he seemed to be making signs; and the signs seemed to mean, "Go away!"

"I came to see Mr Prior," said Desmond. Instantly and softly the window closed.

"Is it a lunatic asylum I've come to by chance?" Desmond asked himself, and pulled again at the rusty chain.

Steps sounded inside the house, the sound of boots on stone. Bolts were shot back, the door opened, and Desmond, rather hot and a little annoyed, found himself looking into a pair of very dark, friendly eyes, and a very pleasant voice said: "Mr Desmond, I presume? Do come in and let me apologize."

The speaker shook him warmly by the hand, and he found himself following down a flagged passage a man of more than mature age, well dressed, handsome, with an air of competence and alertness which we associate with what is called "a man of the world". He opened a door and led the way into a shabby, bookish, leathery room.

"Do sit down, Mr Desmond."

This must be the uncle, I suppose, Desmond thought, as he fitted himself into the shabby, perfect curves of the armchair. "How's Wildon?" he asked, aloud. "All right, I hope?"

The other looked at him. "I beg your pardon," he said, doubtfully.

"I was asking how Wildon is?"

"I am quite well, I thank you," said the other man, with some formality.

"I beg your pardon" - it was now Desmond's turn to say it - "I did not realize that your name might be Wildon, too. I meant Wildon Prior."

"I am Wildon Prior," said the other, "and you, I presume, are the expert from the Psychical Society?"

"Good Lord, no!" said Desmond. "I'm Wildon Prior's friend, and, of course, there must be two Wildon Priors."

"You sent the telegram? You are Mr Desmond? The Psychical Society were to send an expert, and I thought"

"I see," said Desmond; "and I thought you were Wildon Prior, an old friend of mine - a young man," he said, and half rose.

"Now, don't," said Wildon Prior. "No doubt it is my nephew who is your friend. Did he know you were coming? But of course he didn't. I am wandering. But I'm exceedingly glad to see you. You will stay, will you not? If you can endure to be the guest of an old man. And I will write to Will tonight and ask him to join us."

"That's most awfully good of you," Desmond assured him. "I shall be glad to stay. I was awfully pleased when I saw Wildon's name in the paper, because— "

And out came the tale of Elmstead, its loneliness and disappointment.

Mr Prior listened with the kindest interest. "And you have not found your friends? How sad! But they will write to you. Of course, you left your address?"

"I didn't, by Jove!" said Desmond. "But I can write. Can I catch the post?"

"Easily," the elder man assured him. "Write your letters now. My man shall take them to the post, and then we will have dinner, and I will tell you about the ghost."

Desmond wrote his letters quickly, Mr Prior just then reappearing.

"Now I'll take you to your room," he said, gathering the letters in long, white hands. "You'll like a rest. Dinner at eight."

The bedchamber, like the parlour, had a pleasant air of worn luxury and accustomed comfort.

"I hope you will be comfortable," the host said, with courteous solicitude. And Desmond was quite sure that he would.

Three covers were laid, the swarthy man who had driven Desmond from the station stood behind the host's chair, and a figure came towards Desmond and his host from the shadows beyond the yellow circles of the silver-sticked candles.

"My assistant, Mr Verney," said the host, and Desmond surrendered his hand to the limp, damp touch of the man who had seemed to say to him, from the window of the porch, "Go away!" Was Mr Prior perhaps a doctor who received "paying guests", persons who were, in Desmond's phrase, "a bit balmy"? But he had said "assistant".

"I thought," said Desmond, hastily, "you would be a clergyman. The Rectory, you know - I thought Wildon, my friend Wildon, was staying with an uncle who was a clergyman."

"Oh no," said Mr Prior. "I rent the Rectory. The rector thinks it is damp. The church is disused, too. It is not considered safe, and they can't afford to restore it. Claret to Mr Desmond, Lopez." And the swarthy, blunt-faced man filled his glass.

"I find this place very convenient for my experiments. I dabble a little in chemistry, Mr Desmond, and Verney here assists me."

Verney murmured something that sounded like "only too proud", and subsided.

"We all have our hobbies, and chemistry is mine," Mr Prior went on. "Fortunately, I have a little income which enables me to indulge it. Wildon, my nephew, you know, laughs at me, and calls it the science of smells. But it's absorbing, very absorbing."

After dinner Verney faded away, and Desmond and his host stretched their feet to what Mr Prior called a "handful of fire", for the evening had grown chill.

"And now," Desmond said, "won't you tell me the ghost story?"

The other glanced round the room.

"There isn't really a ghost story at all. It's only that - well, it's never happened to me personally, but it happened to Verney, poor lad, and he's never been quite his own self since."

Desmond flattered himself on his insight.

"Is mine the haunted room?" he asked.

"It doesn't come to any particular room," said the other, slowly, "nor to any particular person."

"Anyone may happen to see it?"

"No one sees it. It isn't the kind of ghost that's seen or heard."

"I'm afraid I'm rather stupid, but I don't understand," said Desmond, roundly. "How can it be a ghost, if you neither hear it nor see it?"

"I did not say it was a ghost," Mr Prior corrected. "I only say that there is something about this house which is not ordinary. Several of my assistants have had to leave; the thing got on their nerves."

"What became of the assistants?" asked Desmond.

"Oh, they left, you know; they left," Prior answered, vaguely. "One couldn't expect them to sacrifice their health. I sometimes think - village gossip is a deadly thing, Mr Desmond - that perhaps they were prepared to be frightened; that they fancy things. I hope that Psychical Society's expert won't be a neurotic. But even without being a neurotic one might - but you don't believe in ghosts, Mr Desmond. Your Anglo-Saxon common sense forbids it."

"I'm afraid I'm not exactly Anglo-Saxon," said Desmond. "On my father's side I'm pure Celt; though I know I don't do credit to the race."

"And on your mother's side?" Mr Prior asked, with extraordinary eagerness; an eagerness so sudden and disproportioned to the question that Desmond stared. A faint touch of resentment as suddenly stirred in him, the first spark of antagonism to his host.

"Oh," he said lightly, "I think I must have Chinese blood, I get on so well with the natives in Shanghai, and they tell me I owe my nose to a Red Indian great-grandmother."

"No Negro blood, I suppose?" the host asked, with almost discourteous insistence.

"Oh, I wouldn't say that," Desmond answered. He meant to say it laughing, but he didn't. "My hair, you know - it's a very stiff curl it's got, and my mother's people were in the West Indies a few generations ago. You're interested in distinctions of race, I take it?"

"Not at all, not at all," Mr Prior surprisingly assured him; "but, of course, any details of your family are necessarily interesting to me. I feel," he added, with another of his winning smiles, "that you and I are already friends."

Desmond could not have reasoningly defended the faint quality of dislike that had begun to tinge his first pleasant sense of being welcomed and wished for as a guest.

"You're very kind," he said; "it's jolly of you to take in a stranger like this."

Mr Prior smiled, handed him the cigar-box, mixed whisky and soda, and began to talk about the history of the house.

"The foundations are almost certainly thirteenth century. It was a priory, you know. There's a curious tale, by the way, about the man Henry gave it to when he smashed up the monasteries. There was a curse; there seems always to have been a curse"

The gentle, pleasant, high-bred voice went on. Desmond thought he was listening, but presently he roused himself and dragged his attention back to the words that were being spoken.

"—that made the fifth death There is one every hundred years, and always in the same mysterious way."

Then he found himself on his feet, incredibly sleepy, and heard himself say: "These old stories are tremendously interesting. Thank you very much. I hope you won't think me very uncivil, but I think I'd rather like to turn in; I feel a bit tired, somehow."

"But of course, my dear chap."

Mr Prior saw Desmond to his room.

"Got everything you want? Right. Lock the door if you should feel nervous. Of course, a lock can't keep ghosts out, but I always feel as if it could," and with another of those pleasant, friendly laughs he was gone.

William Desmond went to bed a strong young man, sleepy indeed beyond his experience of sleepiness, but well and comfortable. He awoke faint and trembling, lying deep in the billows of the feather bed; and lukewarm waves of exhaustion swept through him. Where was he? What had happened? His brain, dizzy and weak at first, refused him any answer. When he remembered, the abrupt spasm of repulsion which he had felt so suddenly and unreasonably the night before came back to him in a hot, breathless flush. He had been drugged, he had been poisoned!

"I must get out of this," he told himself, and blundered out of bed towards the silken bell-pull that he had noticed the night before hanging near the door.

As he pulled it, the bed and the wardrobe and the room rose up round him and fell on him, and he fainted.

When he next knew anything someone was putting brandy to his lips. He saw Prior, the kindest concern in his face. The assistant, pale and watery-eyed. The swarthy manservant, stolid, silent, and expressionless. He heard Verney say to Prior: "You see it was too much - I told you-"

"Hush," said Prior, "he's coming to."

Four days later Desmond, lying on a wicker chair on the lawn, was a little disinclined for exertion, but no longer ill. Nourishing foods and drinks, beef-tea, stimulants, and constant care - these had brought him back to something like his normal state. He wondered at the vague suspicions, vaguely remembered, of that first night; they had all been proved absurd by the unwavering care and kindness of everyone in the Haunted House.

"But what caused it?" he asked his host, for the fiftieth time. "What made me make such a fool of myself?" And this time Mr Prior did not put him off, as he had always done before by begging him to wait till he was stronger.

"I am afraid, you know," he said, "that the ghost really did come to you. I am inclined to revise my opinion of the ghost."

"But why didn't it come again?"

"I have been with you every night, you know," his host reminded him. And, indeed, the sufferer had never been left alone since the ringing of his bell on that terrible first morning.

"And now," Mr Prior went on, "if you will not think me inhospitable, I think you will be better away from here. You ought to go the seaside."

"There haven't been any letters for me, I suppose?" Desmond said, a little wistfully.

"Not one. I suppose you gave the right address? Ormehurst Rectory, Crittenden, Kent?"

"I don't think I put Crittenden," said Desmond. "I copied the address from your telegram." He pulled the pink paper from his pocket.

"Ah, that would account," said the other.

"You've been most awfully kind all through," said Desmond, abruptly.

"Nonsense, my boy," said the elder man, benevolently. "I only wish Willie had been able to come. He's never written, the rascal! Nothing but the telegram to say he could not come and was writing."

"I suppose he's having a jolly time somewhere," said Desmond, enviously; "but look here - do tell me about the ghost, if there's anything to tell. I'm almost quite well now, and I should like to know what it was that made a fool of me like that."

"Well" - Mr Prior looked round him at the gold and red of dahlias and sunflowers, gay in the September sunshine - "here, and now, I don't know that it could do any harm. You remember that story of the man who got this place from Henry VIII and the curse? That man's wife is buried in a vault under the church. Well, there were legends, and I confess I was curious to see her tomb. There are iron gates to the vault. Locked, they were. I opened them with an old key - and I couldn't get them to shut again."

"Yes?" Desmond said.

"You think I might have sent for a locksmith; but the fact is, there is a small crypt to the church, and I have used that crypt as a supplementary laboratory. If I had called anyone in to see to the lock they would have gossiped. I should have been turned out of my laboratory - perhaps out of my house."

"I see."

"Now the curious thing is," Mr Prior went on, lowering his voice, "that it is only since that grating was opened that this house has been what they call 'haunted'. It is since then that all the things have happened."

"What things?"

"People staying here, suddenly ill - just as you were. And the attacks always seem to indicate loss of blood. And—", he hesitated a moment. "That wound in your throat. I told you you had hurt yourself falling when you rang the bell. But that was not true. What is true is that you had on your throat just the same little white wound that all the others have had. I wish" - he frowned - "that I could get that vault gate shut again. The key won't turn."

"I wonder if I could do anything?" Desmond asked, secretly convinced that he had hurt his throat in falling, and that his host's story was, as he put it, "all moonshine". Still, to put a lock right was but a slight return for all the care and kindness. "I'm an engineer, you know," he added, awkwardly, and rose. "Probably a little oil. Let's have a look at this same lock."

He followed Mr Prior through the house to the church. A bright, smooth old key turned readily, and they passed into the building, musty and damp, where ivy crawled through the broken windows, and the blue sky seemed to be laid close against the holes in the roof. Another key clicked in the lock of a low door beside what had once been the Lady Chapel, a thick oak door grated back, and Mr Prior stopped a moment to light a candle that waited in its rough iron candlestick on a ledge of the stonework. Then down narrow stairs, chipped a little at the edges and soft with dust. The crypt was Norman, very simply beautiful. At the end of it was a recess, masked with a grating of rusty ironwork.

"They used to think," said Mr Prior, "that iron kept off witchcraft. This is the lock," he went on, holding the candle against the gate, which was ajar.

They went through the gate, because the lock was on the other side. Desmond worked a minute or two with the oil and feather that he had brought. Then with a little wrench the key turned and re-turned.

"I think that's all right," he said, looking up, kneeling on one knee, with the key still in the lock and his hand on it.

"May I try it?"

Mr Prior took Desmond's place, turned the key, pulled it out, and stood up. Then the key and the candlestick fell rattling on the stone floor, and the old man sprang upon Desmond.

"Now I've got you," he growled, in the darkness, and Desmond says that his spring and his clutch and his voice were like the spring and the clutch and the growl of a strong savage beast.

Desmond's little strength snapped like a twig at his first bracing of it to resistance. The old man held him as a vice holds. He had got a rope from somewhere. He was tying Desmond's arms.

Desmond hates to know that there in the dark he screamed like a caught hare. Then he remembered that he was a man, and shouted, "Help! Here! Help!"

But a hand was on his mouth, and now a handkerchief was being knotted at the back of his head. He was on the floor, leaning against something. Prior's hands had left him.

"Now," said Prior's voice, a little breathless, and the match he struck showed Desmond the stone shelves with long things on them - coffins he supposed. "Now, I'm sorry I had to do it, but science before friendship, my dear Desmond," he went on, quite courteous and friendly. "I will explain to you, and you will see that a man of honour could not act otherwise. Of course, you having no friends who know

300

where you are is most convenient. I saw that from the first. Now I'll explain. I didn't expect you to understand by instinct. But no matter. I am, I say it without vanity, the greatest discoverer since Newton. I know how to modify men's natures. I can make men what I choose. It's all done by transfusion of blood. Lopez - you know, my man Lopez - I've pumped the blood of dogs into his veins, and he's my slave - like a dog. Verney, he's my slave, too - part dog's blood and partly the blood of people who've come from time to time to investigate the ghost, and partly my own, because I wanted him to be clever enough to help me. And there's a bigger thing behind all this. You'll understand me when I say" - here he became very technical indeed, and used many words that meant nothing to Desmond, whose thoughts dwelled more and more on his small chance of escape.

To die like a rat in a hole, a rat in a hole! If he could only loosen the handkerchief and shout again!

"Attend, can't you?" said Prior, savagely, and kicked him. "I beg your pardon, my dear chap," he went on suavely, "but this is important. So you see the elixir of life is really the blood. The blood is the life, you know, and my great discovery is that to make a man immortal, and restore his youth, one only needs blood from the veins of a man who unites in himself blood of the four great races - the four colours, black, white, red and yellow. Your blood unites these four. I took as much as I dared from you that night. I was the vampire, you know." He laughed pleasantly. "But your blood didn't act. The drug I had to give you to induce sleep probably destroyed the vital germs. And, besides, there wasn't enough of it. Now there is going to be enough!"

Desmond had been working his head against the thing behind him, easing the knot of the handkerchief down till it slipped from head to neck. Now he got his mouth free, and said, quickly: "That was not true what I said about the Chinamen and that. I was joking. My mother's people were all Devon."

"I don't blame you in the least," said Prior, quietly. "I should lie myself in your place."

And he put back the handkerchief. The candle was now burning clearly from the place where it stood - on a stone coffin. Desmond could see that the long things on the shelves were coffins, not all of stone. He wondered what this madman would do with his body when everything was over. The little wound in his throat had broken out again. He could feel the slow trickle of warmth on his neck. He wondered whether he would faint. It felt like it.

"I wish I'd brought you here the first day - it was Verney's doing, my tinkering about with pints and half-pints. Sheer waste - sheer wanton waste!"

Prior stopped and stood looking at him.

Desmond, despairingly conscious of growing physical weakness, caught himself in a real wonder as to whether this might not be a dream - a horrible, insane dream - and he could not wholly dismiss the wonder, because incredible things seemed to be adding themselves to the real horrors of the situation, just as they do in dreams. There seemed to be something stirring in the place - something that wasn't Prior. No - nor Prior's shadow, either. That was black and sprawled big across the arched roof. This was white, and very small and thin. But it stirred, it grew - now it was no longer just a line of white, but a long, narrow, white wedge and it showed between the coffin on the shelf opposite him and that coffin's lid.

And still Prior stood very still looking down on his prey. All emotion but a dull wonder was now dead in Desmond's weakened senses. In dreams if one called out, one awoke - but he could not call out. Perhaps if one moved But before he could bring his enfeebled will to the decision of movement - something else moved. The black lid of the coffin opposite rose slowly - and then suddenly fell, clattering and echoing, and from the coffin rose a form, horribly white and shrouded, and fell on Prior and rolled with him on the floor of the vault in a silent, whirling struggle. The last thing Desmond heard before he fainted in good earnest was the scream Prior uttered as he turned at the crash and saw the white-shrouded body leaping towards him.

"It's all right," he heard next. And Verney was bending over him with brandy. "You're quite safe. He's tied up and locked in the laboratory. No. That's all right, too." For Desmond's eyes had turned towards the lidless coffin. "That was only me. It was the only way I could think of, to save you. Can you walk now? Let me help you, so. I've opened the grating. Come."

Desmond blinked in the sunlight he had never thought to see again. Here he was, back in his wicker chair. He looked at the sundial on the house. The whole thing had taken less than fifty minutes.

"Tell me," said he. And Verney told him in short sentences with pauses between.

"I tried to warn you," he said, "you remember, in the window. I really believed in his experiments at first - and - he'd found out something about me - and not told. It was when I was very young. God knows I've paid for it. And when you came I'd only just found out what

302

really had happened to the other chaps. That beast Lopez let it out when he was drunk. Inhuman brute! And I had a row with Prior that first night, and he promised me he wouldn't touch you. And then he did."

"You might have told me."

"You were in a nice state to be told anything, weren't you? He promised me he'd send you off as soon as you were well enough. And he had been good to me. But when I heard him begin about the grating and the key I knew - so I just got a sheet and"

"But why didn't you come out before?"

"I didn't dare. He could have tackled me easily if he had known what he was tackling. He kept moving about. It had to be done suddenly. I counted on just that moment of weakness when he really thought a dead body had come to life to defend you. Now I'm going to harness the horse and drive you to the police station at Crittenden. And they'll send and lock him up. Everyone knew he was as mad as a hatter, but somebody had to be nearly killed before anyone would lock him up. The law's like that, you know."

"But you - the police - won't they"

"It's quite safe," said Verney, dully. "Nobody knows but the old man, and now nobody will believe anything he says. No, he never posted your letters, of course, and he never wrote to your friend, and he put off the Psychical man. No, I can't find Lopez; he must know that something's up. He's bolted."

But he had not. They found him, stubbornly dumb, but moaning a little, crouched against the locked grating of the vault when they came, a prudent half-dozen of them, to take the old man away from the Haunted House. The master was dumb as the man. He would not speak. He has never spoken since.

ALTHOUGH, as I previously mentioned, "The Haunted House" suffers from melodramatics, racial insensitivity, hack science, and a weak plot, it has something of the Sherlock Holmes atmosphere to it: a craven nonconformist – unfortunately empowered by the brain of a genius – removes himself from society to a remote country manor where he whets an appetite for criminal sin. He lures a young, pleasant-eyed man into his web of decadence, nearly vanquishing him before a rescue is made at the last moment. Here, too we see the supernatural ruse (cf. *The Hound of the Baskervilles*, "The Devil's Foot," "The Sussex Vampire"), the insidious criminal genius (cf. Professor Moriarty, Dr. Grimesby Roylott, Charles Augustus Milverton, Colonel Moran), a deserted, vulnerable manor house (cf. *Baskervilles*, "The Copper Beeches," "The Solitary Cyclist," "The Greek Interpreter," "The Engineer's Thumb"), and, alas, some racially-charged stereotypes (cf. "The Yellow Face," "The Three Gables," *The Sign of the Four*, etc., etc.). It has a *particularly* strong relation to three of Sir Arthur Conan Doyle's stories: *The Hound of the Baskervilles*, where a legendary curse about a family ghost is used to explain away foul play, "The Adventure of the Engineer's Thumb," where a young engineer is lured to a country house to fix machinery for a criminal operation and barely escapes death, and "The Climbing Man," where science fiction flirts with mystery in the case of a mad professor engaged to a young woman who transfuses himself with gorilla blood as a form of Edwardian Viagra, but then adopts unwanted ape-like qualities. While "The Haunted House" is nowhere nearly as well written or plotted out as a typical Sherlock Holmes story, it does deliver action, adventure, and atmosphere. It is a truly unconventional vampire story, and its greatest strength – like that of "Number 17" and "The Haunted Inheritance" – lies in its defiance of Gothic tropes and horror conventions. No masterpiece of horror, it could nonetheless never be accused of conformity.

—FURTHER READING—
Critical, Literary, and Biographical Works

Briggs, Julia. *A Woman of Passion: The Life of E. Nesbit*. New Amsterdam Books, 1991.

Fitzsimons, Eleanor. *The Life and Loves of E. Nesbit: Victorian Iconoclast*. Overlook Press, 2018.

Margree, Victoria. "The Feminist Orientation in Edith Nesbit's Gothic Short Fiction." *Women's Writing*, vol. 21, no. 4, 2014, pp. 425–443.

Moore, Doris Langley. *E. Nesbit: A Biography*. Ernest Benn, 1967.

Nesbit, E., and Hugh Lamb. *In the Dark: Tales of Terror*. HarperCollins, 2017.

Nesbit, Edith. *The Power of Darkness: Tales of Horror*. Wordsworth Editions Ltd, 2006.

— ABOUT THE EDITOR AND ILLUSTRATOR —

MICHAEL GRANT KELLERMEYER (b. 1987) is a former English professor and current bibliographer, illustrator, editor, critic, blogger, and author based in Fort Wayne, Indiana. He earned his Bachelor of Arts in English from Anderson University (2010) and his Master of Arts in Literature from Ball State University (2012). He taught college writing and literature in Indiana for nine years at, variously, Ball State University, Ivy Tech Community College, and the Indiana Institute of Technology. He retired from higher education in 2019 to publish and write full time.

Michael founded Oldstyle Tales Press (www.oldstyletales.com) in the spring of 2013 after noticing that it was difficult to find literary criticism or commentary on short horror fiction. Its first title, *The Best Victorian Ghost Stories*, was published in September 2013, followed shortly by editions of *Frankenstein* and Edgar Allan Poe. Today it has 37 titles in print.

Each book in the "annotated and illustrated" collection includes a critical introduction, opening contexts and closing analyses for short stories, and footnotes for selected stories. Michael leans heavily toward the historical, psychoanalytical, Jungian, archetypal, and structuralist traditions of criticism.

Michael also creates the illustrations using a technique called negative drawing: pencil sketches are done in negative (the pencil marks represent bright areas, and the blank paper dark areas), then scanned, the color is inverted, and then edited to enhance the contrast. His artistic influences are Edward Gorey, Barry Moser, Gustave Dore, Arthur Rackham, and N. C. Wyeth.

In his free time, Michael plays violin, watches old movies, and spends time walking in nature, or swinging on his front porch with his wife Kierstin and daughter Charlotte. Michael finds joy in straight razors and sandalwood shaving cream, briarwood pipes, and air-dried sheets. He loves listening to Classical music, jazz standards, sea shanties, watching the films of Vincent Price, Alfred Hitchcock, and Stanley Kubrick, and nursing Hendricks gin tonics, stovetop coffee, and mint tea.